Praise for the runaway *New York Times* bestseller

REAL

"I have a new book crush and his name is Remington Tate."

—*Martini Times*

"Unlike anything I've ever read before. Remy and Brooke's love story is one that has to be experienced because until you do, you just won't get it . . . one roller-coaster ride that you'll never forget!"

—*Books over Boys*

"Sweet, scary, unfulfilling, fulfilling, smexy, heartbreaking, crazy, intense, beautiful, oh did I mention hot?! Kudos are in order for Ms. Evans for taking writing to a whole new level. She makes you FEEL every single word you read."

—*Reality Bites*

"I loved this book. As in, I couldn't stop talking about it."

—*Dear Author*

"Wow—Katy Evans is one to watch."

—*Wicked Little Pixie*

"Remy was complex and his story broke my heart . . . made me cry! This author had me gripped and on the edge of my seat through the whole story. . . . Without a doubt I absolutely fell in total LOVE with Remy."

—Totally Booked

"Remy is the king of the alpha-males."

—Romance Addiction

"Some books are special. . . . What a rare gift for an author to be able to actually wrap your arms around your readers and hold them. Katy Evans does just that."

—SubClub Books

REAL

katy evans

G

Gallery Books

New York   London   Toronto   Sydney   New Delhi

G

Gallery Books
A Division of Simon & Schuster, Inc.
1230 Avenue of the Americas
New York, NY 10020

First Gallery Books trade paperback edition September 2013

GALLERY BOOKS and colophon are registered trademarks
of Simon & Schuster, Inc.

The Simon & Schuster Speakers Bureau can bring authors to your live event. For more information or to book an event contact the Simon & Schuster Speakers Bureau at 1-866-248-3049 or visit our website at www.simonspeakers.com.

Designed by Davina Mock-Maniscalco

Manufactured in the United States of America

10 9 8 7 6 5 4 3 2 1

Library of Congress Cataloging-in-Publication Data is available

ISBN 978-1-4767-5559-5
ISBN 978-1-4767-5543-4 (ebook)

to life, love, and music

CONTENTS

REAL PLAYLIST   ix

ONE "I'm Remington."   1

TWO Unexpected   20

THREE To Atlanta   36

FOUR Running   52

FIVE Dancing to the Music   77

SIX Miami Is Not So Hot   92

SEVEN Come Away with Me   118

EIGHT Austin   150

NINE An Adventure   157

TEN A Visitor   197

ELEVEN Secret Meeting   219

TWELVE Pictures of You   251

THIRTEEN Seattle Is Rainier Than Ever   275

FOURTEEN Epilogue   301

CONTENTS

Dear Readers   305

Acknowledgments   307

About   309

REAL PLAYLIST

These are some of the songs I listened to while writing *Real*. The first two are so meaningful, you might enjoy listening to these particular two songs while Brooke and Remington do. ☺

"IRIS" by Goo Goo Dolls

"I LOVE YOU" by Avril Lavigne

"THAT'S WHEN I KNEW" by Alicia Keys

"LOVE BITES" by Def Leppard

"HIGH ON YOU" by Survivor

"LOVE SONG" by Sara Bareilles

"IN YOUR EYES" by Peter Gabriel

"KISS ME" by Ed Sheeran

"COME AWAY WITH ME" by Norah Jones

"ALL I WANNA DO IS MAKE LOVE TO YOU" by Heart

"ANY WAY YOU WANT IT" by Journey

"PULL ME DOWN" by Mikky Ekko

"LOVE YOU LIKE A LOVE SONG" by Selena Gomez

"MY LIFE WOULD SUCK WITHOUT YOU" by Kelly Clarkson

"FLAWS AND ALL" by Beyoncé

"THE FIGHTER" by Gym Class Heroes

ONE

"I'M REMINGTON."

Brooke

Melanie has been shouting in my ear for the past half hour and my nerves are so frazzled by what we're witnessing, I can barely even hear anything. Only my heart. Beating like crazy in my head as the two fighters in the underground boxing ring lunge at each other, both men equal in height and weight, both extremely muscled as they pound each other's faces in.

Every time one of them lands a punch, cheers and claps burst across the room, which is crowded with at least three hundred spectators, all of them thirsting for blood. The worst part of it all is that I can *hear* the god-awful sound of bone cracking against flesh, and the hairs on my arms prick in utter fear. Any minute now I expect one of them to fall and never, ever, get up again.

"Brooke!" Melanie, my best friend, squeals and hugs me. "You look ready to puke, you are *so* not cut out for this!"

I'm seriously going to kill her.

As soon as I take my eyes off these men and make sure they're both breathing when they finish this round, I'm going to murder my best friend. And then myself for agreeing to come here in the first place.

But my poor, dear Melanie has been internet-stalking her new man-crush, and as soon as she found out the object of her nightly fantasies was in the city participating in these "private" and very "dangerous" underground club fighting games, she begged me to come with her and watch him. It's just hard to say no to Melanie. She's effusive and insistent, and now she's jumping around in glee.

"He's next," she hisses, not caring who won or lost this last round, or if they even survived. Which apparently, thank god, they both did. "Get ready for some serious piece of eye candy, Brookey!"

The public falls silent, and the announcer calls, "Ladies and gentlemen, and noooww . . . the moment you've all been waiting for, the man you're all here to see. The baddest of the bad, I give you the one, the *only*, Remington 'Riptide' Tate!"

A shiver runs along my spine as the crowd goes crazy over the name alone, especially the women, and their eager shouts tumble one atop the other.

"Remy! I love you, Remy!"

"I'll suck your cock for you, Remy!"

"REMY, POUND ME, REMY!"

"Remington I want your Riptide!"

All heads turn as a figure in a hooded red robe trots toward the ring. The fighters tonight apparently don't wear boxing gloves but tape, and I see his fingers flex and fist at his sides, his taped hands enormous and his knuckles tanned, his fingers long.

Across the ring from me, a woman waves a poster reading REMY'S #1 BITCH proudly in the air, and she's screaming the same thing at the top of her lungs in his direction—I guess in case he doesn't know how to read, or misses the neon pink letters, or the glitter.

I'm so astounded, realizing my crazy best friend isn't the only female in Seattle who's apparently lost her head for this guy, when I feel her squeezing my arm. "I dare you to look at him and tell me you wouldn't do anything for that man."

"I wouldn't do anything for that man," I instantly repeat, just to win.

"You're not looking!" she squeals. "Look at him. *Look.*"

She grabs my face and swings my gaze in the direction of the ring, but I start laughing instead. Melanie loves men. Loves to sleep with them, stalk them, drool about them, and yet, when she catches them, she can never really hold on to them. I, on the other hand, am not interested in getting involved with anyone.

I'm still at that awkward *no, thanks* phase when I get any attention. I guess I haven't felt that good about myself in a while. Plus my romantic little sister, Nora, has had enough boyfriends, and drama, for *both* of us.

I stare up at the ring as the guy whips off the red satin robe with the word RIPTIDE on the back, and the spectators stand screaming and cheering as he slowly turns to acknowledge them all. His face is suddenly before me, illuminated by the lights, and I just stare like an idiot from my place. My god.

My.

God.

Dimples.

Dark scruffy jaw.

Boyish smile. Man's body.

Man's body.

Killer tan.

A shiver shoots down my spine as I helplessly drink in the entire package everyone else seems to be gaping at.

He has black hair, standing up sexily as if women have just had their fingers there. Cheekbones as strong as his jaw and forehead. Lips that are red-kissed and swollen, and, as a souvenir from his walk to the ring, there's lipstick on his jaw. I look down his long, lean body and something hot and wild settles in my core.

He's mesmerizingly perfect and incredibly hard. Everything, from his beautifully slim hips and narrow waist to his broad shoulders, is solid. And that six-pack. No. It's an eight-pack. The sexy V of his obliques dips into his satin, navy blue shorts, which gently hug his powerful legs, thick with muscle. I can see his quads, traps, pecs, and biceps, all gloriously tight and cut. Celtic tattoos circle both of his arms, exactly where his bulging biceps and the rigid square deltoids of his shoulders meet.

"Remy! *Remy!*" Mel shouts hysterically at my side, hands cupped to her mouth. *"You're so fucking hot, Remy!"*

His head angles to the sound, one dimple showing with a sexy smile as he faces us. A frisson of nervous energy passes through me, not because he's extremely gorgeous from this perfect view— because he is, he definitely is, goodness, he *really* is—but mostly because he's looking straight at me.

One eyebrow cocks, and there's a glimmer of amusement in his entrancing blue eyes. Also something . . . warm in his gaze. Like he thinks I'm the one who shouted. Oh, shit.

He winks at me, and I'm stunned as his smile slowly fades, morphing into one that's unbearably intimate.

My blood simmers.

My sex clenches tight, and I hate that he seems to know that.

I can see he thinks he's the ultimate creation, and he seems to believe every woman here is his Eve, created from his rib cage for him to enjoy. I'm both aroused and infuriated, and this is the most confusing feeling I've ever felt in my life.

His lips curl, and he turns when his opponent is announced with the words "Kirk Dirkwood, 'the Hammer,' here for all of you tonight!"

"You little slut, Mel!" I cry when I recover, shoving her playfully. "Why did you have to scream like that? He thinks I'm the nutcase now."

"Omigod! He did not just *wink* at you," Melanie says, visibly stunned.

Oh my god, he had. Hadn't he? He *did*.

I'm just as astounded as I relive the wink in my head, and I'm totally going to torture Melanie because she deserves it, the little tramp.

"He did," I finally admit, scowling at her. "We telepathically communicated, and he says he wants to take me home to be the mother of his sexy babies."

"Like *you* would have sex with someone like him. You and your OCD!" she says, laughing her head off as Remington's opponent takes off his robe. The man is all beefy muscle, but not an ounce of him can visually compete with the pure male deliciousness of that "Riptide."

Remington flexes his arms at his sides, stretches his fingers out and forms fists, then bounces on the balls of his feet, his calves flexing. He's a large, muscular man but surprisingly light on his feet.

Hammer throws the first punch. Remington evades it with a smart duck, and he comes back up with a full swing that connects and knocks Hammer's face to the side. I inwardly flinch at the power in his punch; my body clenches at the sight of his muscles contracting and tensing, working and releasing, with each blow he delivers.

The crowd watches, enraptured, as the fight continues, those awful cracking sounds filling me with goose bumps. But there's something else bothering me. The fact that beads of perspiration pop on my brow, in my cleavage. As the fight progresses, my nipples strain, ever more puckered and tight, against my top, pushing anxiously against the silk of the fabric. Somehow watching Remington Tate pound a man they call "Hammer" makes me squirm in my clothes in a way I don't like, much less ever expected.

The way he swings, moves, *growls* . . .

Suddenly, a chorus begins: *"REMY . . . REMY . . . REMY."*

I turn and see Melanie jumping up and down and saying, "Omigod, hit him, Remy! Just knock him dead, you sexy beast!" She screams when his opponent falls to the ground with a loud thump.

My panties are soaked, and my pulse has gone haywire. I've never condoned violence. This isn't me, and I blink in stupefaction at the sensations whipping through my system. Lust, pure, white-hot lust, flutters through my nerve endings.

The ringmaster lifts Remington's arm in victory, and as soon as he straightens from the knockout blow he just delivered, his gaze swings in my direction and crashes into me. Piercing blue eyes meet mine, and something knots and pulls inside my tummy. His sweaty chest rises and falls in a deep pant, and a drop of blood rests at the corner of his lips. Through it all, his eyes are glued to me.

Heat spreads under my skin, and the flames lick me all over. I will never admit this to Melanie, not even to myself out loud, but I don't think I've ever seen such a hot man in my life. The way he stares at me is hot. The way he stands there, with his hand held in the air, his muscles dripping sweat, with that air of authority Mel told me about in the cab—it's just *hot*.

There's no apology in his stare. In the way he ignores everyone who shouts his name and stares at me with a look that's so sexual I almost feel taken right here. An awful awareness of the exact way *I* look to him sweeps over me.

My long, straight hair, the color of mahogany, falls to my shoulders. My button-up white shirt is sleeveless, but it goes up my throat in a lacy mock-neck, and the hem is tucked nicely into a pair of high-waisted, but perfectly presentable, black pants. A small set of gold hoop earrings nicely complements my honeyed, whiskey eyes. Despite my conservative choice of clothes, I feel completely naked.

My legs wobble, and I'm left with the distinct impression this man wants to pound me next. With his cock.

Please, god, I did *not* just think that; Melanie would. Another tightening in my womb distresses me.

"REMY! REMY! REMY! REMY!" people chant, the sound growing in intensity.

"You want more Remy?" the man with the microphone asks the crowd, and the noise builds around us. "All right then, people! Let's bring out a worthier opponent for Remington 'Riptide' Tate tonight!"

Another man steps into the ring, and I can't bear it anymore. My system is on overload. This is probably why it's not a good idea to forego sex for so many years. I'm so worked up that I can barely talk right or even make my legs move as I turn to tell Mel I'm going to the restroom.

A voice blares loudly through the speakers as I charge down the wide path between the stands. "And now, to challenge our reigning champion, ladies and gentlemen, is Parker 'the Terror' Drake!"

The crowd comes alive, and suddenly, I hear an unmistakably hard *slam*.

Resisting the urge to look back at what's causing the commotion, I round the corner and head straight for the bathroom hall as the speakers flare up again. "Holy cow, that was fast! We have a KO! Yes, ladies and gentlemen! A KO! And in record time, our victor once again, I give you, Riptide! Riptide—who's now jumping out of the ring and— *Where the hell are you going?"*

The crowd goes crazy, calling all the way to the lobby, *"Rip-tide! Riptide!"* and then they fall completely quiet, as though something unscripted has just happened.

I'm wondering about the eerie silence when pounding foot-steps echo at my back. A warm hand engulfs mine, and the touch frissons through me as I'm spun around with surprising force.

"What the . . ." I gasp in confusion, and then stare into a sweaty male chest, and up into glowing blue eyes. My senses reel out of control. He's so close the scent of him tears through me like a shot of adrenaline.

"Your name," he growls, panting, his eyes wild on mine.

"Uh, Brooke."

"Brooke what?" he snaps out, his nostrils flaring.

His animal magnetism is so powerful I think he just took my voice. He's in my personal space, all over it, absorbing it, absorb-ing me, taking my oxygen, and I can't understand the way my heart is beating, the way I stand here, shivering with heat, my entire body focused on the exact spot his hand is wrapped around me.

With trembling effort, I pry my hand free and glance fear-fully at Mel, who comes up behind him, wide-eyed. "It's Brooke Dumas," she says, and then she happily shoots out my cell phone number. To my chagrin.

His lips curl and he meets my gaze. "Brooke Dumas." He just fucked my name right in front of me. And right in front of Mel.

And as I feel his tongue twist roughly around those two words, his voice sinfully dark, like things you crave to eat but re-ally shouldn't, desire swells between my legs. His eyes are hot and almost proprietary when he looks at me. I've never been stared at like this before.

He steps forward, and his damp hand slides to the nape of my neck. My pulse skitters as he lowers his dark head to set a small, dry kiss on my lips. It feels like he's marking me. Like he's preparing me for something monumental that could both change and ruin my life.

"Brooke," he growls softly, meaningfully, against my lips, as he draws back with a smile. "I'm Remington."

❤ ❤ ❤

I STILL FEEL his hands on the ride home. I feel his lips on mine. The softness of his kiss. God, I can't even breathe right, and I'm as coiled up as a cobra in a corner of the backseat of a taxi, staring blindly out the window at the passing city lights, desperate to vent from the sensations spinning inside my body. Unfortunately, I have no one to vent with other than Mel.

"That was so intense," Mel says breathlessly at my side.

I shake my head. "What the hell just happened, Mel? The guy just kissed me in public! Do you realize there were people with their phones trained on us?"

"Brooke, he's just so hot. Everyone wants a picture of *that*. Even *my* insides are buzzing from the way he went after you and I'm not even the one he kissed. I've never seen a man go after a woman like that. Holy shit, it's like porn with the romance."

"Shut up, Mel," I groan. "There's a reason why he's banned from his sport, you're the one who told me! Clearly he's dangerous or crazy or *both*."

My body is wound up with arousal. His eyes, I can feel them on me, so raw and hungry. I feel instantly dirty. My nape tickles where he touched it with his sweaty palm. I rub it but it won't stop pricking, won't calm my body, won't calm *me*.

"Okay, seriously, you need to get out more. Remington Tate may have a bad rap, but he's sexier than sin, Brooke. Yes, he was banned for poor conduct because he's a naughty, wicked boy.

Look, who knows what shit went on in his personal life? All I know is it was god-awful and made a couple of headlines, and now nobody even cares. He's the favorite in the Underground League, and all kinds of fight clubs adore him. They're packed with girls when he's on."

A part of me can't even believe the way the guy stared at me, honed in on me, from a crowd of screaming women, he just looked at *me,* and it winds me up even more when I think about it. He looked at me with crazy hot eyes, and I don't want crazy hot eyes. I don't want him, or any man, period. What I want is a job. I've just finished my internship at a middle school academy, and I've been interviewed by the best sports rehab company in the city. But it's been two weeks and no call—I'm at the point where I'm starting to get into the mental funk where you feel *no one* will *ever* call.

I'm beyond frustrated.

"Melanie, look at me," I demand. "Do I look like a whore to you?"

"No, sweetie. You were easily the classiest lady out there."

"If I wore a suit to this sort of event, it would be precisely to prevent slime like him from noticing me."

"Maybe you should start dressing more like a slut and blend in?" She smirks, and I instantly scowl.

"I hate you. I'm never coming with you to this type of thing ever again."

"You don't hate me. Come get a hug." I lean into her embrace and hug her lightly before remembering her betrayal.

"How could you give him my number? What do we even know about this man, Mel? Do you want me to end up murdered in some dark alley and my body parts tossed into some trash can?"

"That's *never* going to happen to someone who's taken as many self-defense classes as you."

I sigh and shake my head at her, but she grins an adorable grin at me. I can never really stay angry for long.

"Come on, Brooke. You're supposed to be reinventing yourself," Mel whispers, perfectly reading me. "New and improved Brooke has to have sex now and then. You used to like it when you competed."

The image of a naked Remington pops into my head, and it is so disturbingly hot that I squirm in my seat and glance angrily out the window, shaking my head more emphatically this time. What angers me most are the feelings the mere thought of him rouses in me. I feel . . . fevered.

No, I'm not against having sex *at all,* but relationships are complicated, and I don't have the emotional equipment right now to deal with any of it. I'm still a little broken from my fall and trying to find my way into a new career. There's an awful video of me on YouTube titled *Dumas, Her Life Is Over!* that was taped by some amateur during my first Olympic tryouts and has had quite a bit of traffic—like all videos of humiliated people do. The exact moment that my life shattered around me was perfectly immortalized in video and can now be played and replayed, over and over, so the world can watch for their enjoyment. It shows the very second my quads knot up and I stumble, and the instant that my ACL—the anterior cruciate ligament—just tears and my knee gives way.

It lasts for over four minutes, this charming little video. In fact, my anonymous paparazzi stalker kept the camera solely on me and on no one else. You can hear her voice, "Shit, her life is over," in the background. Which obviously inspired the title.

So there I am, in this real-life homemade movie, hopping in miserable pain off the track, crying my heart out. Crying not because of the pain in my knee, but from the pain of my own failure. And I just want the world to swallow me and I want to die because I know, know, know right this second, that all my training has been for nothing. But instead of the earth opening up and sucking me right in, I get filmed.

The slew of comments under the video are still fresh in my mind. Some people wished me well in other endeavors and said it was a shame. But others laughed and joked about it, like I had somehow begged for this to happen.

These same comments have plagued me with doubts day and night for years as I replay both days and wonder what went wrong. And I say "both" because I tore my ACL not only once, but a second time when, refusing to believe "my life was over," I stubbornly went for tryouts again. Neither of those times do I even *know* what I did wrong, but clearly it is now physically impossible for me to compete again.

So now I'm just trying very hard to go on with my life like I never dreamed of competing in the Olympics in the first place. And the last thing I need is a man taking up time I could dedicate to building a future in the new profession I've chosen.

My sister, Nora, is the romantic, the most passionate one. Even though she's barely twenty-one and three years younger than me, she's the one living out in the world, sending me postcards from different places, telling Mom and Dad and me of all the "lovers" she meets on the road.

Me? I was the one who spent her entire young years training her heart out, my one and only dream being a gold medal. But my body gave up long before my soul wanted it to, and I never even made it to a worldwide competition.

When you need to accept the fact that your body sometimes can't do what you want it to, it hurts almost worse than the physical pain of being injured. This is why I love sports rehab. I might still be depressed and angry if I had not received the help I needed. This is why I want to try to help some young athletes make it, even if I didn't. And why I want to get a job so I can feel, maybe, at last successful in *something*.

But strangely, as I lie awake at night, it's not my sister I think about, or my new career, or even the awful day the Olympics became unreachable for me.

The only thing on my mind tonight is the blue-eyed devil who put his lips on mine.

❤ ❤ ❤

THE NEXT MORNING, Melanie and I go for a run in the shaded park in our neighborhood, like we do every weekday, rain or shine. Each of us wears an armband with our iPod inside, but today, it seems we're listening to nothing but each other.

"You made Twitter, you whore. That was supposed to be me." She's clicking through her cell phone, and I scowl, trying to peer at what she's reading.

"Then you should've given him *your* cell instead of mine."

"He call yet?"

"'City hall at eleven. Leave the crazy best friend home,' was all he said."

"Ha-ha, real funny," she says, grabbing my phone, handing me hers, and pressing my pass code to get into my messages.

I narrow my eyes because the devious little cat knows all my passwords, and I probably couldn't hold a secret from her even if I wanted to. I pray she doesn't see my Google history, or she'll know I'd been stalking him at 3 a.m. I honestly don't even *want* to get into the fact that I've been punching his name into the Google search bar more times than I can count. Thankfully, Mel just checks my missed calls, and of course, there's no call from him.

Judging from the articles I read last night, Remington Tate is a party god, a sex god, and basically, a *god*. And a troublemaker, to boot. At this exact point in time, he's probably hungover and drunk, littered with sated naked ladies in his bed and thinking, "Brooke *who*?"

Melanie snatches her phone back, clears her throat, and reads the Twitter feed. "Okay, there are several new comments you should hear. 'Unprecedented! Did you all see Riptide kissing a spectator? Holy crap, what a rush! I heard a brawl ensued when he tried to go after her and shoved a man! Fighting out of the ring is illegal and RIP might not be allowed to fight for the rest of the season—or for eternity. Yeah, that's why he got kicked out of pro! Well, I'm not going if Rip isn't fighting.' These are multiple commentators," Melanie explains as she lowers her phone and grins. "I love that they call him RIP. So his opponents rest in peace, get it? Anyway, *if* he's fighting, he's got just this Saturday before the fight moves to the next city. Are we going or are we going?"

"That's what he wanted to know when he called."

"Brooke! Has he or hasn't he called?"

"What do you think, Mel? He's got how many Twitter followers? A million?"

"He's actually got two point three mil."

"Well there's your damned answer." Now I'm just angry, and I don't even know why.

"But I was *sure* he had a real big craving for Hooky with Brookey last night."

"Someone's already taken care of that by now, Mel. That's the way these guys work."

"We still need to go Saturday," Melanie decrees with an angry scowl that makes her pretty face almost comical. She's just not the type to ever be angry at anyone. "And *you* need to wear something that will make his eyes bug out and make him regret not calling you. You guys could've had a rocking one-night stand, and I mean *rocking*."

"Miss Dumas?"

We're heading back to my apartment and I peer through the morning sunlight at a tall, fortyish woman with a short blonde bob standing on the steps of my building. Her smile is warm and almost confused as she holds out an envelope with my name written on it. "Remington Tate wanted me to personally deliver these to you."

Hearing the name from her lips makes my heart stumble, and suddenly, it's racing harder than it did during my morning run. My hand trembles as I open the envelope and take out a huge blue and yellow pass. It's a backstage pass to the Underground with tickets for Saturday clipped to it. They're front row center seats, and there are four of them. My insides do funny things when I notice the pass has my name written on it in manly, messy letters I suspect to be *his*.

I seriously can't breathe.

"Wow," I whisper, stunned. A little bubble of excitement builds rapidly in my chest, and I almost feel like I need to run an extra couple miles just to pop it.

The woman's smile widens. "Shall I tell him you said yes?"

"Yes." The word leaps out of me before I can even think about it. Before I can even further contemplate all the headlines about him I read yesterday, most of them highlighting the words "bad boy," "drunk," "bar fight," and "prostitutes."

Because it's just a fight, right?

I'm not saying yes to anything else.

Right?

I stare in disbelief at the tickets again, and Melanie gapes at my profile as the woman climbs into the back of a black Escalade. As the car roars away, she playfully hits my shoulder. "You whore. You want him, don't you? This was supposed to be *my* fantasy, you idjut!"

I laugh as I hand her three tickets, my brain spinning with the fact that he actually made some sort of contact today. "I guess we are going, after all. Help me round up the gang, will you?"

Melanie grabs my shoulders and whispers in my ear as she steers me up the steps to my building. "Tell me that didn't just make you feel a little tingle."

"That didn't make me feel a little tingle," I automatically say, and before I slide into my apartment, I add, "It made me feel a *big* one."

Melanie squeals and demands to come in to select my outfit for Saturday, and I tell her that when I want to look like a whore, I'll let her know. Eventually, Mel gives up on my closet, saying there's nothing even remotely sexy in it and she needs to get to work, so she leaves me alone the rest of the day. But the little tingle doesn't go as easy. I feel it when I'm getting showered and dressed, and even when I'm checking my e-mails for more job openings.

I can't explain why I'm so nervous at the thought of seeing him again.

I think I like him, and I dislike that I do.

I think I want him, and I hate that I do.

I think he truly is the perfect material for a one-night stand, and I can't believe I'm starting to wonder about that too.

❤ ❤ ❤

NATURALLY, LIKE ANY female with working cyclical hormones, by Saturday I'm at a total different point in my monthly cycle, and I've regretted more than a dozen times having said I'd go to the fight. I console myself with the fact that the gang, at least, is excited.

Melanie summoned Pandora and Kyle to come with us.

Pandora works with Melanie at the interior design firm. She's the resident, cutting-edge goth with whom every man wants to decorate his bachelor pad. Kyle is still studying to be a dentist, and he's my apartment neighbor, longtime friend, and a friend of Mel's since middle school. He's the brother we never had, and he's so sweet and shy with other women that he actually had to go pay some professional to take his virginity at twenty-one.

"I'm so glad you're driving us, Kyle," Melanie says as she rides in the back with me.

"I swear that's all you guys want me for," he says, but he's laughing, clearly stoked about the fight.

The crowd in the Underground tonight is at least double what it was the other night, and we wait about twenty minutes to climb into the elevator that lowers us into the arena.

While Melanie and the others go find our seats, I slip the backstage pass around my neck and tell her, "I'm going to slip some of my business cards somewhere some of the fighters can see it."

I'd have to be crazy to let this opportunity go to waste. These athletes are major, major muscle and organ destructors, one lethal weapon fighting against the other, and if there's ever a chance to do some temporary rehab work, I've just figured it's here.

As I wait in line to be allowed into the restricted-access part, the scent of beer and sweat permeates the air. I spot Kyle waving from our seats at the very center to the right of the ring, and I'm stunned at how close the fighters are going to be. Kyle would be able to touch the raised ring floor if he just took one step and extended out his arm.

You can actually watch the fight from the far end of the arena without having to pay a dime except perhaps a tip to the bouncer, but the seated tickets run from fifty dollars to five hundred, and the ones Remington Tate sent us are definitely the expensive ones.

Being that I've been jobless for two weeks since my graduation and I'm stretching the savings for my previous small endorsement deals many years ago, I'd have *never* afforded them otherwise. My friends, who are all recent grads, couldn't have afforded them either. After getting out of college, they had to accept practically *any* job they could get in this shitty job market.

Crammed among people, I finally get to flash my backstage pass with a happy little smile, and I'm allowed down a long hall with several open rooms along one side.

Each room holds benches and rows of lockers, and I spot several fighters at different corners of the room, conversing with their teams. In the third room I peer into, he's there, and a bolt of nervousness rushes through me.

He's perfectly relaxed and seated, hunched over, on a long red bench, watching as a man with a shiny bald head bandages one of his hands. His other hand is already bandaged, everything covered with cream-colored tape, except for his knuckles. His face is pensive and strikingly boyish, and it makes me wonder how old he is. He raises his dark head, as if sensing me; when our eyes meet, a flash of something strange and powerful sparks in his eyes, and it zips through my body like lightning. I stifle my reaction and see that his coach is busy telling him something.

Remington can't take his eyes off me. His hand is still outstretched, but seems forgotten as his coach continues taping him up and issuing instructions.

"Well, well, well . . ."

I turn to the voice to my right, and a sliver of dread opens up in my midsection. An enormous fighter stands only a foot away, scrutinizing me with eyes that are pure intimidation, like I'm all dessert and he has the perfect spoon to use.

I see Remington grab the tape from his coach and throw it aside before standing and slowly winding his way to my side.

As he positions himself behind me and slightly to my right, an awareness of his body close to mine seeps into my every pore.

His soft voice by my ear makes me tremble as he faces my admirer. "Just walk off," he tells the other man.

The man I recognize as Hammer is no longer looking at me. Instead, he looks above my head and slightly to the side. I think that, next to Remington, he doesn't look all that big after all.

"She yours?" he asks with narrowed beady eyes.

My thighs go watery when the answering voice slides across the shell of my ear, both velvet and chillingly hard. "I can guarantee you, she's not *yours*."

The Hammer leaves, and for the longest time, Remington stands there, a tower of brawn almost touching me, his body warmth enveloping me.

I dip my head and murmur, "Thank you," and quickly leave, and I want to die because I swear to god he just ducked his head to smell me.

TWO

UNEXPECTED

He's about to come on, and his name is already tearing through the microphone as the crowd goes wild. "Once again, ladies and gentlemen, Riptide!"

I still haven't recovered from seeing him up close, and my bloodstream already carries all kinds of strange, bubbly, hot little things. The instant he comes trotting down the wide hall between the stands, in that shiny red hooded robe, my pulse jumps, my tummy clenches, and I have the awful desperate urge to flee back to my home.

The guy is just too much. Too much male. Too much masculinity and pure raw beast. Put together, he's just like sex on a stick and every female around me is shouting at the top of her lungs how much she wants to *lick*.

Remington climbs into the ring and goes to his corner. He yanks off his robe, exposing all those flexing muscles, and hands it to a young blond man who seems to be aiding his bald coach.

"And now, I give you the Hammer!"

Hammer proceeds to join him in the ring, and Remington

smiles lazily to himself. His gaze slides directly to mine—and I realize that *of course* he knows exactly, exactly, where I'm sitting tonight. Still smiling that I'm-all-that smile, he jabs one finger in the air toward Hammer, and then points at me as if saying, "This one's for you."

My stomach drops.

"Shit, he's killing me. Why the hell does he do that? He's so fucking alpha I can't stand him!"

"Melanie, get a grip!" I say, then sit back weakly in my chair, because he's killing me too. I don't know what he wants from me, but I'm tied up in knots because I never expected that I would also want something very sexual and very personal from *him*.

The toe-curling memory of standing close to him only minutes ago sweeps through me, but the bell rings and snaps me out of it. The fighters go toe to toe, and Remy feints to one side while Hammer swings stupidly, following the mock move. And once his side seems open, Remington comes at him from the left, jabbing him in the ribs.

They bounce apart, and Remington acts cocky, feinting and pissing Hammer off. He turns to me, points at Hammer and then at me again before ramming him so hard that the guy rebounds on the net behind him, falls to his knees, and shakes his head before standing up again. My sex muscles clench every time Remington hits his opponent, and my heart grips every time an opponent returns a blow.

During the night, he goes through several fighters in just this way. Each time he's declared victor, he stares at me with that smug smile, as though he wants me to know he's the dominant man here. My entire body shakes as I watch his body move, and I'm unable to stop fantasizing. I imagine his hips rolling over me, his body inside mine, those big hands touching me, flesh to flesh. During the last few rounds, he wears an intent look on his face, and his chest heaves with exertion and glistens with sweat.

Suddenly, I've never wanted anything so much in my life.

I want to go crazy. Bungee. Sprint again. Date. All those dates I never had, because I was training for something that never happened. Thrill rides I didn't take for fear of breaking a bone that eventually broke anyway. Staying sober. Keeping my grades up so I could do track. Remington Tate is everything I've never, ever done, and I have a condom tucked in my bag and suddenly I know exactly why I put it there. This guy is a fighter. I want to touch his beautiful chest and I want to kiss those lips. I want to have those hands on me. When I feel those hands on me, I'm probably going to come the second he thrusts inside me.

This is the most intense foreplay I've ever felt, and suddenly I want it to be more than play. I want it to *happen*. Tonight.

When he wins for the tenth and final time, I feel his eyes on me again, and I can only stare back at him, willing him to know I want him. He smiles at me, all sweaty and cocky with blue eyes glinting and dimples showing. Grabbing a cord hanging over the ring, he easily swings his body over it and lands gracefully in the aisle before me.

Melanie freezes at my side as his beautifully sculpted and gleaming tan body approaches.

There is no doubt about his destination.

Holding my breath until I feel like my lungs are going to burst, I stand on wobbly legs because I really don't know what else to do. The crowd roars and women behind me shout.

"Kiss his heart out, woman!"

"You don't deserve him, you bitch!"

"You go, girl!"

He flashes his dimples at me, and I keep waiting for his hands as he leans over. I can almost feel the way those hands felt on me last time, big, strange, and a little bit wonderful as they practically engulfed my face. I'm already dying. Dying with want. With reck-lessness. With anticipation.

Instead, he bends his dark head to whisper against my temple, and the only thing of his body touching mine is his breath, bath-ing my skin with heat as his gruff voice rumbles in my ear, "Sit tight. I'll send someone over for you."

He smiles and backs off as the crowd keeps screaming, and he climbs up into the ring, leaving me blinking after him. It takes the woman next to me about a full minute of shaking and hyper-ventilating to get out, "Omigod, omigod, omigodgodgodgod, his elbow brushed me, his elbow *brushed* me!"

"RIPTIDE, PEOPLE!" the announcer screams.

My knees go soft, and I drop to my seat, weightless as whipped cream, clasping my hands together to keep them from shaking. My brain is so melted I can't even think past the point where he swung down from the ring and whispered close to my ear, in that terribly sexy voice of his. Just remembering makes my toes curl. Melanie is speechlessly gaping, and Pandora and Kyle stare at me like I'm some holy being who just brought a wild animal to his knees.

"What the hell did he say?" Kyle mouths.

"Jesus, Mary, and Joseph," Melanie says, squealing and hug-ging me. "Brooke, that guy is *hot* for you."

The woman beside me touches my shoulder with a trembling hand. "Do you *know* him?"

I shake my head, not even sure how to answer. All I know is that from yesterday to now, there hasn't been a second when I haven't thought about him. All I know is that I hate and love the way he makes me feel, and the way he looks at me fills me with wanting.

"Miss Dumas," a voice says, and I snap my head up to the two men in black standing between me and the ring. Both are tall and slim; one is blond and the other has curly brown hair. "I'm Pete, Mr. Tate's PA," Brown Curls says. "And that's Riley. He's the coach's second. If you'll follow us, please, Mr. Tate wants a word with you in his hotel room."

At first, I can't even register who Mr. Tate is. Then understanding dawns, and a red-hot bolt of lightning streaks through me. He wants *you* in his hotel room. Do you want *him*? Do you want to do *this*? A part of me is already doing him ten ways until Sunday in my mind, while another part of me won't move from this stupid chair.

"Your friends can come with us," the blond man adds in an easy voice, and he signals to the stunned trio.

I'm relieved. I think. Sheesh, I don't even know what I feel.

"Brooke, come on, it's Remington Tate!" Melanie hauls me up by force and urges me to follow the men, and my mind starts racing at full speed, because I don't know what I'm going to do when I see him. My heart is pumping adrenaline like crazy as we're led out of the Underground, to the hotel across the street, then up the elevator to the "P."

A spike of nervousness ripples through me as the elevator pings at the top floor, and I feel exactly the way I used to when I competed. It's been a roller-coaster ride just imagining this man's body inside mine, and I'm suddenly close to the peak where it could be a reality. My stomach clenches from the thought of how exhilarating the downhill could be. *One-night stand, here I come. . . .*

"Please tell me you're not going to do this guy," Kyle tells me, his face scrunched in worry as the doors roll open. "This is not you, Brooke. You're far more responsible than this."

Am I?

Am I really?

Because tonight I feel *crazy.* Crazy with lust and adrenaline and two sexy dimples.

"I'm just going to talk to him," I tell my friend, but even I'm not sure what my intentions are.

We follow the two men into the first part of the enormous

suite. "Your friends can wait here," Riley says, motioning to the gigantic black granite bar. "Please help yourselves to a drink."

As my friends flock to the shiny new bottles of alcohol, an unmistakable squeal escapes Melanie, and Pete motions me to follow him. We cross the suite and go into the master bedroom, and I spot him sitting at the bench at the foot of the bed. His hair is wet, and he holds a gel pack to his jaw. The visual of such a primal male nursing a wound after he repeatedly broke man after man with his fists is somehow fabulously sexy to me.

Two Asian women kneel on the bed behind him, each of them rubbing a shoulder. A white towel is draped around his hips, and rivulets of water still cling to his skin. Three empty bottles of Gatorade have been tossed on the floor, and he has another in his hand. He slaps the gel pack on the table and downs the last of the Gatorade. Blue as his eyes, the liquid drains in one swig; then he tosses the bottle aside.

I'm mesmerized as his ripped muscles clench and relax under the women's fingers. I know massage is normal after intense exercise, but what I don't know, and can't understand, is why watching him get one affects me like it does.

I know the human form. I revere it. It was my church for six years, when I decided a new career for me was in order, when I realized I wouldn't be sprinting again. And now, my fingers itch at my sides with wanting to probe his body, push and release, get deep into every muscle.

"Did you enjoy the fight?" He watches me with a little cocky smile, his eyes glimmering, like he knows I loved it.

It's a love-and-hate thing for me, to watch him box. But I just can't compliment him after hearing five hundred people scream how good he is, so I just shrug. "You make it interesting."

"Is that all?"

"Yes."

He seems irritated as he abruptly jerks his shoulders to halt the massage therapists. He stands and rolls those square shoulders, then cracks his neck to one side, then the other. "Leave me."

The two women offer me a smile and head out, and the instant I'm alone with him, my breath goes.

The enormity of being here, in his hotel room, isn't lost on me, and suddenly I'm anxious. His tanned, long-fingered hands rest idle by his sides, and a rush of wanting runs through me as I imagine them running over my skin.

My body pulses, and with an effort I lift my eyes up to his face and notice he's staring at me in silence. He cracks his knuckles with one hand over them, then does the same with the other set. He looks agitated, as though he hasn't expended enough energy pounding half a dozen men to the ground. Like he could easily go a couple more rounds.

"The man you're with," he says, flexing his fingers open at his sides as though to get some blood flow, his eyes watching me. "Is he your boyfriend?"

Honestly, I don't know what I expected coming here, but it may have gone something along the lines of being led straight to his bed. I'm so confused and more than a little anxious. What does he want from me? What do *I* want from *him*?

"No, he's just a friend," I reply.

His eyes flick to my ring finger and back up. "No husband?"

A strange little buzz courses in my veins, straight to my head, and I think I'm light-headed from the scent of the massage oil they rubbed on him. "No husband, not at all."

He studies me for a long moment, but he doesn't look overcome with lust like I'm personally, shamefully, feeling. He's merely assessing me with a half smile in place, and he appears genuinely intent on what I'm saying. "You interned at a private school rehabbing their young athletes?"

"Wha—what? *You* looked *me* up?"

"Actually, *we* did," the two familiar voices of the men who brought me over say, and as they reenter the room, Pete carries a manila folder and passes it to Riley.

"Miss Dumas." Once again, Pete, with the curly hair and soft brown eyes, speaks to me. "I'm sure you're wondering why you're here, so we'll just cut to it. We're leaving town in two days, and I'm afraid there's no time to do things differently. Mr. Tate wants to hire you."

I stare for a moment, dumbfounded, and frankly, confused as hell.

"What is it, exactly, that you think I do?" A frown settles on my face. "I'm not an escort."

Both Pete and Riley burst out laughing, but Remington is alarmingly silent, slowly settling back down on the bench seat.

"You're on to us, Miss Dumas. Yes, I admit when we're traveling, we find it convenient to keep one or several *special friends* of Mr. Tate's to, shall we say, accommodate his needs either before or after a fight," Pete laughingly explains.

My left eyebrow shoots up. Really, though, I'm perfectly aware of how these things work with athletes.

I used to compete and know that, either after sports or before them, sex is a natural and even healthy way of relieving stress and aiding performance. I lost my virginity at the same Olympic tryouts where my knee was shot to hell, and I lost it to a male sprinter who was almost as nervous about competing as I was. But the way these guys speak about Mr. Tate's "needs," so casually, feels suddenly so personal, my cheeks burn with embarrassment.

"A man like Remington has very particular requirements, as you might guess, Miss Dumas," Riley, the blond-haired man who looks like a surfer, continues. "But, he's been very specific in the fact that he's no longer interested in the friends we have secured for him during our trip. He wants to focus on what's important, and instead, he wants you to work for him."

My insides clench as I glance at Riley, then Pete, and then Remington, whose jaw seems even squarer than I remember, like it's made of the most gorgeous, most priceless piece of granite the world has ever seen.

There's no way for me to know what he's thinking, but although he's not smiling anymore, his eyes remain alight with mischief.

His face is swelling slightly on the left side, and my nurturing instincts make me want to take the gel pack and put it on his jaw again. Hell, in my mind, I've already put salve on the red scar in the middle of his lower lip. I'm so overcome with these thoughts that I realize I can't trust myself with someone as powerfully attractive as him. I am still, *still*, wired just knowing we're in the same room.

Pete flips through the folder. "You interned at the Military Academy of Seattle in sports rehab for their middle graders, and we see you graduated only two weeks ago. We're prepared to hire your services, which will cover the duration of the eight cities we have left to tour and Mr. Tate's continued conditioning for future competitions. We will be very generous with your salary. I don't feel I need to tell you it's very prestigious to tend to such a followed athlete and would be impressive on any résumé. It might even allow you to be a free agent if, in the future, you decide to leave us," Pete says.

I find myself blinking several times.

I've been anxiously applying for jobs, with no callbacks as of now. The school where I interned offered to have me return when classes resume in August, so at least I have that option. It is, however, months away, and the restlessness of having a degree and not doing anything with it is eating at me.

Suddenly I realize everyone's eyes are on me, and I'm especially aware of Remington's eyes.

On me.

The thought of working for him after I've been already having sex with him in my head makes me more than a little queasy.

"I'll have to think about it. I'm not really looking for something away from Seattle." I glance at Remington hesitantly, then at the other two men. "Now if that's all you wanted to say to me, I'd better get going. I'll leave my card on your bar." I swing around, but Remington's commanding voice stops me.

"Answer me now," he snaps out.

"What?"

When I turn back, he tilts his head and holds my gaze, and the glimmer in his eyes is no longer playful. "I've offered you a job, and I want an answer."

Silence descends. We stare at each other, this blue-eyed devil and I, and these exchanged stares are complicated. I can't decide if his is just a stare or more. Something that feels like a living, breathing thing inside me, and it flares when I look into his eyes, and see the way he looks back at me with heartbreaking intensity.

All right, then. Screw the stupid lust. I need this so much more.

"I'll work with you for the three months you have left to tour if you include room, board, and my transportation, guarantee me references for my next job application, and let me promote the fact that I've worked with you to my future clients."

When he merely stares, I swing around, supposing he'll want to think about it. His voice halts me again.

"All right." He nods meaningfully, and my mind reels in disbelief.

He's hired me?

I took him on as my first job?

Slowly, pressing the towel to his waist to keep it from unraveling, Remington rises and looks at his men. "But I want it on paper she's not leaving until the tour is over."

Muscles bulging in a way I try hard not to notice, he tucks his towel into place and starts coming over, and once again, he looks feline and predatory in his approach, his self-assured smile making him even *doubly* so. It is a smile that tells me he knows he unsettles me. And boy, does he unsettle me. I'm watching over six feet of pure brawn walk over in oil-slicked glistening skin and flaunting an eight-pack, which I know is physically actually impossible, but how can I deny it when it's there? *God*.

My heart kicks when he engulfs my small hand in his massive one and bends his head to look straight at me. He whispers, while he squeezes me in his powerful grip and his touch shoots like an electric shock through me, "We have a deal, Brooke."

I think I just fainted.

He steps back, and his smile blazes through me, charged with a thousand megawatts, and then he turns to his men. "Get it on paper by tomorrow, and see her safely home."

MELANIE JUMPS FROM the bar the instant she spots me, her eyes wide with curiosity. I think I just caught her shoving a miniature bottle of rum into her clutch bag. "What? Was that a quickie? I thought the man would have more stamina than that," she says in pure annoyance on my behalf.

"Dude, he just knocked out ten other men the size of goddamned grizzly bears. Of course he's shot," Kyle says, the only one of the three without a drink in his hand.

"Guys, relax. I didn't *do* him." I shake my head and almost laugh at the forlorn expression on Mel's face. "But I *did* take a job for the summer."

"Whaaat?"

I can't even begin to relate the details to my friends before both of Remington's men flank me. "Ready, Miss Dumas?"

"Brooke, please." I feel ridiculous at being called "Miss Dumas." My friends will probably not stop ribbing me about it later. "Really, I've got this. There's no need to follow me anywhere."

Riley tosses his blond head, his smile crooked. "Trust me, neither Pete nor I will sleep tonight if we're not sure you're home safe."

"Well, hello there, I don't think we've been properly introduced," Mel says, voice soft, eyes sparkling on Riley with pupils dilated and everything. Then she goes on to charmingly work on Pete. "And who are *you*?"

Groaning, I quickly make the introductions, then grab each of the girls by the arms as we head out to the elevators and then to Kyle's car, my heart still kicking fiercely into my rib cage.

They're all gushing over the whole "experience" except Kyle, who's scowling as he climbs behind the wheel. "That was one weird-ass interview. In a fucking hotel room?" he protests.

"Tell me about it." My woman's pride is pricked because somewhere down the line I'd convinced myself the guy wanted to sleep with me. Instead, he offers me a job? Not bad, but totally unexpected, that's for sure.

I think I've got my sensors out of whack, and he's probably the one to blame too.

"I feel so important seeing that they're tailing us," Mel informs us minutes later, and she swiftly lifts her phone and takes a pic.

"What are you doing?" Yes, I just asked her, but I'm not even sure that I want to know.

"I'm tweeting about it."

"Remind me never to go out with you again," I groan, but I'm so restless, I can't stand myself. Blue eyes. Dimples. Shoulders a yard wide. Slick, glistening bronzed skin. But no sex . . . definitely no sex with *him* now.

"What do you think the deal with those guys is?" Mel wants to know.

"I don't know. Riley, the blond you want to do, is the coach's second, and Pete is his personal assistant, I think."

"I want to do *both,* actually. Pete is cute, with that good-boy kind of look, but he needs more meat on his bones. And Riley looks easy-breezy. They're definitely both warm, verging on hottish. How *old* do you think they are? Thirtyish?"

I shrug.

"Remington is twenty-six," she says. "I think they're a tad older. Remy's definitely younger. How do you think they met?"

"*You're* the one with all the tidbits, so what are you looking at me for? I don't spend all day stalking people on Google." Only him. Shit.

"Brooke, tell us about your new job," Kyle breaks in from the driver's seat. "You're not seriously considering leaving with a guy with his reputation?"

It takes a moment for me to answer, because I'm still dumbstruck that I have a job, even if it's only temporary.

I'd always been told I was born to run when I was younger, and when I got broken, there were many days—not days, *months*—when I felt like I amounted to nothing. Sports rehab healed me in ways I might not have healed otherwise, and now the more that I think about it, the more I would love to help a man as aggressive as Remington, whose brutally pounded body for sure needs some serious TLC.

"I am, Kyle. In fact, if all goes well and their contract terms aren't crazy, I leave Sunday. I promise you I can take care of myself: ask my self-defense class teacher. I've kicked his ass several times.

I'll be traveling, which will be fun, and I might have a chance to become a free rehab agent if I get good references. And if that happens, I won't even have to endure any more job interviews."

"This guy can take down an elephant, Brooke. Didn't you see him? Pandora sure as hell saw him."

"Dude, there was nothing to see *but* him. That guy could take down a freaking elephant *train*," Pandora says from up front. She's been busy sucking on her e-cigarette and blowing vapor into the air, since this is the first week of her having "quit" real cigarettes.

"I wonder what the guys behind us would do if we stop at the Jack in the Box's drive-through, place a big order, and say they're paying," Melanie says.

"Melanie," I say warningly. "How many have you had?" I notice she has a small bottle of vodka in her hand and I immediately deduce she really did steal from Remington's bar. I grab it, put the cap back on, and shove it into my bag. "I'm going to be working with these guys for three months, so behave, please."

"Just to see what they do, girl, come on," Pandora pleads.

Laughing, Kyle makes a right into the drive-through and begins ordering one of everything. I grab my purse containing the lone condom and my credit card. "You dick," I say, throwing the condom at him. "You guys are infantile. Stop at the damned window. You're going to eat all that you ordered."

When Kyle stops at the McDonald's drive-through next, I'm seriously fuming. I make him pay for the order, and then I step out of the car and go over to the Escalade. I hand two Happy Meals with two apple pies through the driver's window. "Here. Sorry about that. I told you it was unnecessary to follow me. I seem to be riding around with children. But I'll get home safe, please just go back to the hotel."

"Can't," Pete says from behind the wheel as Riley digs into the fries.

"These are the best damned fries," he mutters.

"Yeah, thanks, Miss Dumas," Pete adds, his expression genuinely nice as he looks at me in amusement.

"Brooke. Please." I glance at my friends as they sit in the car with the hazard lights on and their faces turned in this direction, and I sigh. "So do you always follow his instructions to the letter?"

"To a T." Pete gets out of the car, walks over to Kyle's Altima and opens the back door for me. The inside of the car falls silent until I'm safely tucked inside and we're finally heading home.

"I think it's hot that he wants you home safe."

"Melanie, right now you think McDonald's is hot, and you barfed when you saw *Super Size Me* and have banned it ever since. Your breath smells like vodka and Quarter Pounder."

"Well, Brooke, if you had a drink with me, you wouldn't be *able* to smell me. No more excuses. No more 'I have competition tomorrow.' You should get drunk and go give Remington all the babies he wants."

"He wants twins but I already said I want to wait until the Vegas wedding." I hand her a little vitamin B and C complex chewing tablet. "Here, suck on this. I know it's not what you want, but it'll get that alcohol out of your system sooner."

"Thanks, doctor. I'm going to miss you. But it's high time not only Nora got all the fun—it sucks that your little sister has a better sex life than you when you're so much prettier, Brookey. Please, pleeeeze promise to text me every day."

Smiling, I bring her close and wish she wasn't drunk so I could actually talk to her. I have no idea what I've done, but I'm excited. All I know for sure is I'm not backing out of this agreement. My mom and dad will be ecstatic to see I'm giving my life some momentum in a new direction, and I'll be only too glad that when I make my Sunday morning call to them, the answer to their greeting, which is always "Any job offers?" will finally be *yes*.

All right, so it's only for three months, but it will do wonders for my career. Plus, it feels good to be wanted in a professional sense, after all the preparation.

"I will, Mel. Every day," I tell her, as I listen to her busily sucking on the tablet.

"When he kisses you, you need to text me that very second."

"Mel, he *hired* me as a specialist. There will be *no* kissing, it's all professional here."

"Fuck professional!" she protests.

"Stay professional, Brooke," Kyle says warningly. "Otherwise I'm stopping over and having words with him."

"I'm glad you said 'words,' Kyle, because that's all a man like you can actually get away with when facing Remington Tate," Pandora tells him before she bursts out laughing.

I smile, because the image of Kyle standing up to Remy really is funny. An image of the latter flashes in my mind, and I see him as I just saw him, looking at me unapologetically, as sexy as sex itself, and I wonder how it's going to feel when I have to put my hands on him.

My job is extremely tactile. There's no way of helping my clients without having some sort of contact. I've rehabbed my students, nursing injuries like I nursed my knee, but I've never touched a man that I actually *want* like this one. Whenever he trains, he'll need stretching after, and that is right up my alley. Now, my sole purpose will be making sure Remington Tate keeps fighting like a champion.

Suddenly, I can't wait to be back on a team, even if I'm on a different side of the action.

THREE

TO ATLANTA

The private jet is enormous, and Pete signals for me to board before he does. He picked me up at my place less than an hour ago, and he looks sharp in a *Men in Black* suit. I head up the stairs and realize you can actually fit standing up inside the plane, like in a larger airliner. No commercial plane I've ever been in has had a fraction of the luxury this one does. Suede, leather, mahogany, gold trimmings, and state-of-the-art screens adorn the interior. It's all extravagance in this big, amazing, rich man's toy.

The seats are arranged in sections that resemble small living rooms, and in this first section there are four plush ivory leather seats, each bigger than a first-class seat. They contain a smiling Riley, who stands to greet me, as well as the other two members of Remington's staff—his personal trainer, Lupe, a fortyish, bald man who looks like Daddy Warbucks from the movie *Annie*, and the chef and nutritionist, Diane, who I recognize as the woman who came to my apartment.

"Nice to meet you, Miss Dumas," Coach Lupe says, with a kind of scowl on his face I somehow figure is his natural expression.

I shake his hand. "Likewise, sir."

"Oh, bah. Call me Coach. Everyone else does."

"Well, hello again," Diane says, her grip smooth and gentle. "I'm Diane Werner, the chef slash nutritionist slash ticket-delivery girl."

I laugh. "It's so nice to meet you, Diane."

The air between them is actually very open and real, and a twinge of excitement flits through me at the thought of belonging to a team again. Truly, what would make me enormously happy and satisfied as a professional is that if from now on, when Remington Tate fights in a ring, he flows like a ribbon with the strength of a dozen oxen, and I just love knowing I'm working with other specialized people whose goals and energy are on par.

"Brooke." Pete gestures toward to the back of the plane, and down the long carpeted aisle, passing another section of four more seats and a large TV screen and an enormous wood-paneled bar, is a bench that looks remarkably like a sofa. And there, in the middle of it, with his dark head bent as he listens to his headphones, is Remington Tate, six-foot-plus tower of testosterone.

An unexpected heat shoots directly into my bloodstream at the first sight of him in daylight. He wears a black T-shirt that clings to his muscles, and low-slung worn denim, and his ridiculously ripped body wears it all with centerfold perfection as he lounges on the spacious taupe leather bench.

My heart gives a wild kick, because he looks just as impossibly sexy as ever, and I really wish I didn't automatically notice. I guess you just can't hide something as blatantly sexual as him.

"He wants you back there," Pete tells me. And I can't help noticing he almost sounds apologetic.

Swallowing the moisture in my mouth, I make my way uneasily down the plane aisle when he looks up, his eyes catching mine. I think I see them flare, but fail to read anything in his expression as he intently watches me approach.

His stare makes me so nervous I feel the tingle once again, right in my center.

He's the strongest man I've *ever* seen, in my entire life, and I'm familiar enough with the subject to know that wired into my genes and DNA is a natural desire for healthy offspring, and with it comes a desperate urge to just full-out *mate* with whoever they deem the prime male of my species. I have never in my life met a man before who sparks up my crazy mating instincts like him. My sexuality burns with his nearness. It's unreal. This reaction. This *attraction*. I'd never believe it if Melanie was explaining it to me and I wasn't feeling it like a bubbling cauldron under my skin.

How am I going to get rid of this?

Lips curling slightly, as though amused at himself over a private joke, he pulls off his headphones when I stop an arm's length from him. The rock music trails into the silence, and he abruptly clicks off the iPod. He signals to his right and I take a seat, fiercely trying to block his effect on me.

Bigger than life, like that of a movie star seen in the flesh, his charisma is staggering. He has an aura of pure raw strength, and every inch of him is lean and muscled, which gives off the impression of his being a man, but with a charming playfulness in his expression that makes him look young and vibrant.

It strikes me that we're the youngest people in the plane, and I feel even younger than I am as I sit next to him, like I've just become a teenager again. His lips curl, and honestly I have never, ever, met a more self-assured man, lounging back almost sensually in his seat, his eyes missing nothing.

"You've met the rest of the staff?" he inquires.

"Yes." I smile.

He stares at me, his dimples showing, his eyes assessing. The sunlight hits his face at just the right angle to illuminate the flecks in his eyes, his lashes so black and thick, framing those blue pools that just suck me right in.

I want to start this new relationship off professionally, since that is the only way I can see it working, so I loosely fasten the seat belt around my waist and get to business.

"Did you hire me for a particular sports injury or more to help with prevention?" I query.

"Prevention." His voice is rough and invites a surge of goose bumps on my arms, and I notice, by the skewed way his big body is turned toward me, that he doesn't deem it necessary to wear a seat belt on his plane.

Nodding, I let my eyes drift to his powerful chest and arms, then I realize I might be staring too blatantly.

"How are your shoulders? Your elbows? Do you want me to work on anything for Atlanta? Pete tells me it's a several-hour flight."

Without answering me, Remington merely stretches out his hand to me, and it's enormous, with recent scars on each of his knuckles. I stare at it until I realize he's offering it to me, so I take it in both of mine. A buzz of awareness feathers from his hand and deeply into me. His eyes darken when I start rubbing his palm with both my thumbs, searching for knots and tightness. The skin-to-skin contact is staggeringly powerful, and I rush to fill in the silence that suddenly feels like deadweight around us.

"I'm not used to such big hands. My students' hands are usually easier to rub down."

His dimples are nowhere in sight. Somehow I'm not sure he hears me. He seems especially engrossed in watching my fingers on him. "You're doing fine," he says, his voice low.

I become entranced by the planes and dips of his palms, every one of his dozens of calluses. "How many hours do you condition a day?" I ask, softly, as the jet takes off so smoothly I barely realize we're airborne.

He's still watching my fingers, his eyes at half-mast. "We do eight. Four and four."

"I'd love to stretch you when you're done training. Is that what your specialists also do for you?" I ask.

He nods, still not looking at me. Then his eyes flick upward.

"And you? Who pats your injury down?" He signals to my knee brace, visible beneath my knee-length skirt, which rose slightly when I sat.

"No one anymore. I'm done with rehab." The idea of this man seeing my embarrassing video makes me queasy. "You Googled me too? Or did your guys tell you?"

He pulls his hand free from mine and signals down. "Let's have a look at it."

"There's nothing to see." But when he continues staring at my leg through those dark lashes, I bend and lift my leg a couple of inches to show him my brace. He seizes it with one hand and opens the Velcro with the other to peer down at my skin; then he strokes his thumbs across the scar on my kneecap.

There's something wholly different about him touching me.

His bare hand is on my knee, and I can feel his calluses on my skin. I. Can't. *Breathe*. He probes a little, and I bite my lower lip and exhale what little air remains in my lungs.

"It still hurts?"

I nod, but still can only really think about his large, dry hand. Touching my knee. "I've been running without a brace, and I know I shouldn't yet. I just don't think I've ever really recovered."

"How long ago was this?"

"Six years ago." I hesitate, then add, "And two . . . the second time it happened."

"Ahh, a double injury. So it's sensitive?"

"Very." I shrug. "I guess I'm glad that by my second, I'd already started my master's for rehab. Otherwise I don't know what I would have done."

"It hurts not to compete anymore?"

He looks at me with complete openness and interest, and I don't know why I'm even answering. I haven't talked about this openly with anyone. It hurts in every part of me. My heart, my pride, my very soul. "Yes. It does. You'd understand, right?" I ask, quietly, as he lowers my leg back down.

He holds my gaze as his thumb lightly strokes across my knee, then we both glance at his hand, as though equally stunned to realize how easy it was for him to leave it there while we had an entire conversation—and for me to allow it. He lets go and we say nothing.

I put back my Velcro but underneath the brace, I feel like he's just doused my skin with gasoline, and it will burst up in flames any second he touches me again.

Shit.

This is so not good, I don't even know what to do. My relationships with the clients I've had have always been informal. They call me by my name, and I call them by theirs. We do a lot of work and have a lot of contact, but they never touch me. Only I touch them.

"Do this one." He puts his far hand out to me in a fist as he speaks, and I'm kind of grateful for the opportunity to get seriously accustomed to touching this man for work purposes.

Shifting to my side, I take his hand in both of mine and spread it open with my fingers. He leans back on the seat and stretches his free arm, the one closest to me, all along the seat behind me. Hyperawareness of that outstretched arm sizzles through me even if he isn't touching me, and once again, I'm awed and strangely compelled by his palm, how rough, firm, and callused it is.

I don't know why he seats himself on a bench instead of a single seat, but suddenly his thigh is too close, his legs spread wide, taking up two seats and leaving me with one, and I can feel and smell every inch of him.

Our other four flight companions laugh up front and his eyes flick up there, then back to me. I'm entirely aware of his gaze as I press into his palm with my thumbs, pushing hard into the tissue until I feel the little knot I found fade away. I keep probing and searching for more but can't find any, so I move to his wrist.

He has the broadest, sturdiest wrist I've ever seen, and his forearm is powerfully built and corded with thick veins that run up his arm. I hold his hand as I twirl his wrist, and I'm lost in the movement of his joint, perfectly mobile. I probe his forearm then his bicep, which hardens and clenches for me. I close my eyes and work deep within the muscle. All of a sudden, the arm behind me folds, and his hand curls around my neck. He leans in and whispers, "Look at me."

I open my eyes to see his eyes are sparkling, and he looks perfectly amused. I think he knows I'm getting a little worked up. I want to drop his arm and squirm, but I don't want it to be too obvious, so I lower it carefully and smile back. "What?"

"Nothing," he replies, revealing his dimples. "I'm very impressed. You're very thorough, Brooke."

"I am. And wait until I get to your shoulders and back. I might have to stand on you."

He cocks one dark eyebrow and looks supremely entertained. "How much can you possibly weigh?"

I wink. "I look slim, but I'm still a little muscular."

He scoffs, then tilts his head curiously as he reaches out to my arm and grasps my small bicep between two fingers. Thankfully, it stays firm when he clenches.

"Hmm," he says, his eyes dancing with mirth.

"What? What does 'hmm' mean?" I prod.

He brazenly grabs my hand and wraps my fingers around his gut-wrenchingly sexy bicep muscle. He doesn't even flex, but his smooth, taut skin and total firmness under my fingers leave me breathless. He's such a . . . *boy.* Showing me his bicep. I notice he's watching me, and his blue eyes shine with playful intensity. I bite my lower lip in response.

Since my job requires I touch him, a lot, it would feel a little odd for me to withdraw my hand. So instead, I give a little squeeze with my fingers. It's like palpating an enormous rock with absolutely *no* give to it. At all.

"Hmm," I say with my best poker face, trying to mask the emotions inside. I'm undone. Completely undone. Every sexual organ in me is awake and aching. My genetically induced mating instincts are at full attention, roaring to life.

He laughs and runs his hand up the length of my bare arm again. He dips his fingertips under the sleeve of my button-down shirt and slides them right over my triceps muscle at the back of my arm. His eyes glint devilishly because he knows he's totally got me. This is one of the worst parts for a woman, a place where body fat can be measured with a mere pinch.

There's not a single place on his body I could get even a pinch of fat from. He probably consumes twelve thousand calories a day to maintain his lean muscle mass, which is around what that famous Olympic swimmer Michael Phelps consumes when actively training. His caloric intake is easily something like five times what I eat to maintain my weight, but I can't really do the math right now. His fingers are still there, under my sleeve, touching my skin. He's got this playful smile on his face, his eyes dancing in mischief, and yet the atmosphere has shifted so that I feel like not only are *we* incredibly aware of our bodies, but the other people on the plane are, as well.

"Hmm," he says, softly, and finally gives a little pinch. We both laugh.

I clear my throat and straighten, unable to stand any more touching. I feel dangerously giddy and am definitely not happy about it. So I extract my iPod and headphones from a small travel bag I'm carrying and set them on my lap. He stares down at them, then snatches my iPod and connects his headphones and starts going through my music, handing me his. I search through his selection and absolutely loathe all his songs. He's into *pure* rock, and I drop my headphones and grab my iPod back.

"Who can relax to that?"

"Who wants to relax?"

"I do."

"Here." He hands me his iPod back. "I've got to have some easy listening for you. Listen to one of mine and I will listen to one of yours."

He's selecting a song for me from his own apparatus, so I look for one I like in mine, and I settle on a girl-power song called "Love Song," by Sara Bareilles, which is basically this girl telling the guy that he's not getting a love song from her. I play it for him.

My love for girl-power songs is almost legendary. Old and new. It's all my friends and I hear. Even Kyle sings them.

So then I put on my headphones to see which one he selected for me, and something happens to my body when I hear the first words of the song, *And I'd give up forever to touch you* . . . from the Goo Goo Dolls' "Iris."

> *And I'd give up forever to touch you . . .*
> *'Cause I know that you feel me somehow . . .*
> *You're the closest to heaven that I've ever been and*
> *I don't want to go home right now . . .*

I duck my head to keep him from noticing that I'm blushing and almost have to force myself not to pause it because it feels unbearably intimate.

To listen to this song.

That he strangely selected for me to listen to.

But I don't dare pause it. Even when he leans forward to catch my expression. His knee brushes mine, and the point of contact blazes through me as the song keeps spilling into my ear.

I think I'm not even breathing, I don't even know if I can.

He's also listening to my song, and his eyes are so close to mine when I peer up at him, I can count each one of his spiky dark lashes. I swear his irises are bluer than the Caribbean Sea.

His lips twitch with humor, and he shakes his head with what I think is a chuckle. A chuckle I obviously can't hear because I'm listening to the end of "Iris," which I first heard in the movie *City of Angels* and which also made me cry, like, for days. A guy gives up, literally, forever to be with the girl he falls in love with, and then something tragic happens—like in a Nicholas Sparks movie.

When silence follows the end, I slowly take my headphones off and return his iPod. "I wouldn't have guessed you had slow songs in there," I murmur, fully engaged in a new conversation with my own iPod, as he returns it.

His voice is low and intimate. "I have twenty thousand songs—everything is here."

"No!" I say in automatic disbelief as I turn and verify, and it's true. Mel thinks she's the shit because she has ten thousand, and I'm going to have to inform her she is certainly *not*.

And now, what I just can't get over is that, from twenty thousand songs, he played *that* one for me?

"Did you like it?" His eyes pierce me, and I know he can see my blush, I can't help that.

I nod.

My iPod feels warmer than usual as I nervously start to play with it, and I refuse to think it's from his hand. But it's from his big, scarred, tanned, beautiful manly hand. Cheeks flaring even hotter, I try to sink into my own musical world.

Occasionally, during the flight, he passes me his headphones and iPod and makes me listen to a song, and I look for one for him. I don't know what's up with me, but when he smiles at me with that lazy smile that shows both dimples, listening to all the girl-power songs I hand him over, like "I Will Survive" from Gloria Gaynor, I want to melt, especially when at the same time, the devil grins in mischief and seems to decide to pick on me as he plays "Love Bites" by Def Leppard for me.

I die as the powerful sound of his Dr. Dre beats spill into my ears, pushing the low, masculine vocals so deep inside my body, every sexy word seems to pulse shamelessly in my sex. The words are so raw and carnal, they make me think about him and me, touching and kissing and loving . . . and I hate that for a fraction of an instant, I even believe that's exactly what he wanted me to think.

❤ ❤ ❤

WE'RE IN ATLANTA and I'm rooming with Diane, who I learned is divorced and thirty-nine, and who I love because she keeps her toothbrush, toothpaste, and all her girly necessities as neatly tucked away as I do. She's a *great* roommate, sunny and positive every moment of the day, and I love that we get to talk about healthy cooking during the evenings, when we each hit our own queen-size bed. She told me about the tour stops while we chatted after lights-out, and I was excited to find out that the last fight is in New York, a city I've always wanted to visit.

Diane shops for the best local, freshest ingredients every

morning, and she feeds Remington only top organic food, every single day, on schedule every three to four hours—which is why his workouts seem to be spaced in sections of either 3-2-3, or 4-4 with heavier meals in the case of the latter. The man eats for three fully grown, hungry lions. A lot of protein. A lot of vegetables. And in the half-hour window after his workouts, so many carbs that even *I* get carb-high just thinking about those delicious sweet potatoes and pastas he wolfs down.

She spices all his meals with organic herbs like thyme, basil, rosemary, a little dash of garlic or cayenne pepper, and some kick-ass combinations that I've been jotting down for when I get back home.

Tomorrow Remington has his first fight out of two in Atlanta, and this afternoon I find myself hanging out at the sidelines of his privately rented gym, waiting to stretch him once he's finished. It's our third evening here, and I've already realized that Remington Tate trains like a madman.

A.

Mad.

Man.

Today in particular, he seems unstoppable.

"Any reason why he's still going strong at this hour today?" Pete asks Coach Lupe.

"Hey, Tate! Stop showing off in front of Brooke!" Coach yells, and we hear a laugh from across the gym, where Remington is killing—heartlessly *murdering*—a speed bag.

"I can't wear him out," Lupe says as he turns back to us. He drags a hand down his bald head as he checks some sort of timer he has draped around his neck. His usual scowl deepens in intensity. "We're going on nine hours today and he's still got juice. But don't even look at me, Pete. We *both* knew this was going to happen since he—"

Both their heads swing toward me, as if they can't speak until

I make myself scarce, and I raise my eyebrows. "What? Do you want me to leave?"

Lupe shakes his head and goes back to Remington, who's still on the speedball; it is flying in the wind like a bat flapping everywhere. His arms swing with perfect precision, each thrust hitting the ball dead center as it swings back. The sound it makes is rhythmic and comes faster than every second, *thadumthadumthadumpthadump* . . .

"Nine hours a day really is excessive, don't you think? Even seven a day is crazy," I tell Pete from the sidelines. Today we've gone way past his 4-4 training times, and I'm stunned that the man still keeps going.

Even when I trained for the Olympics, I didn't hit it quite that hard. Remington's training schedule leaves me agog. Today he's done hanging abs, where he hangs from his feet and swings his body up to his knees, as fast as he can, perfectly working those washboard abs like it's nothing. He does pull-ups, push-ups, mountain climbers, planks. He jumps rope with only one foot, then switches to the other, then he crosses the rope, swings, twists, and turns, all while I barely even get to *see* the rope, he makes it fly so fast as it rhythmically slaps the ground. After that, he shadowboxes or hits the ring with a sparring partner, and if his sparring partner wears out before he does, like he did today, Remy goes back to the heavy bags or the speedball, and ends up *soaked.*

"He likes wearing himself out," Pete explains to me as we keep watching him. "If he can still give a punch late in the day, he bites Coach's head off that he didn't ride him hard enough."

It takes one more hour for him to slow down, and by the time Coach whistles for me, I'm the one who's dead tired, from the visual stimulation of watching Remington Tate work out. Every move he makes is so aggressively primal it feels *sexual* to me.

Even though he's wearing sweatpants and an easy T-shirt, there's no way you can miss the clench of the muscles of his upper body through the damp cotton fabric, and the way his sweatpants hang low on his narrow hips make my breasts feel so heavy and painful I swear to god I can't imagine how it will feel when I'm lactating one day.

Stifling a hot little shiver, I make my legs move and head over to the floor mats, where Remington is standing, waiting for me, already shirtless. Rivulets of sweat run down his torso, and I know he's perfectly warm and that his muscles have been trained to exhaustion. There's no more muscle glycogen in storage, his glucose will be low, and he'll be so hot he'll be like a warmed pretzel when I maneuver him. The mere prospect of it makes me equally hot. It's a dream of mine, to dedicate my life to this, but it's such a tactile job that with this man, it's a big challenge. Not only because his muscles are so strong compared to my own, but because I can barely make contact with his bronzed skin without feeling buzzed. Every pore in my body jumps to attention and hones in on whichever part of my body is touching his. I really hate this loss of control in myself.

Now I watch his muscles bulge as he towels himself off and haphazardly drags the towel across his damp hair, leaving it even more sexy and spiky. I'm wearing tennis shoes and a tight running gear outfit to make myself move easily over him, and those striking blue eyes sweep over me as I approach.

He's panting, unsmiling; then he drops on a bench while I go around and come up to him from behind.

He groans when I wrap my fingers around his shoulders and start digging deep. Sparks of excitement strike me low in my tummy when I make contact, but I try quelling all my reactions and focus on loosening his neck, his triceps, his biceps. I push into his pectorals, his core, trying not to respond like a woman to every clench of his muscles under my fingers, the amazing firmness of his skin beneath my touch.

We work on every joint, pulling everything loose, my moves occasionally making him make a low, purring sound. My sex muscles clench and I try to relax them, but every time he groans, they grip and clench tighter.

I hate it when they do that too.

It seems that the art of relaxing this man seems to wind *me* up to the tenth power.

But at least I'm not jobless anymore.

Breathing slow and deep, I spend extra time as I rub his deltoids, the roundest, squarest part of the shoulder. I stretch and roll them, and then I follow to the supraspinatus, a small muscle of the rotator cuff, and also the most easily injured of the four muscles surrounding that cuff.

He's still panting when I'm done. Except now, so am I.

Coach whistles. "All right, hit the showers. See you at six a.m. tomorrow and ready to fight. Now go *eat*. A whole goddamned cow."

Remington pulls me up from where we'd worked on his back on the floor, his blue eyes sparkling as he clenches my fingers a second longer than I expected. "No standing on me yet?"

It takes me a moment to remember our conversation from the plane, and I smirk. "Not yet. But don't worry. If you keep working out like this, we'll get there before you know it."

He laughs, and drapes a towel around his neck as he heads to the showers.

❤ ❤ ❤

HOURS LATER, I'VE figured that he must have fallen dead asleep after the exertion he put himself through. I, on the other hand, lie awake, sleepless. I've already squeezed my triceps three times since our arrival and have determined I'm not fat, and even then, I still wonder what *hmm* means.

Ever since I stopped competing, I've gained body fat and am now at a healthy eighteen percent. I'm curvier than I ever used to be, with a little extra lift in my butt, and nice padding to my breasts. But I have never been more aware of my body and all its inner and outer parts than when I interact with this one man. I just don't even know if I can ever get used to it. Can ever make him stop doing this to me. Can ever let myself "own" the fact that—yes, this man drives my body out of control.

I think about the plane and his hands on my triceps and his blue eyes on my face and the way his gaze rakes me when I walk over to stretch him. I think of the way he's teased me and amused himself with me these past three days, and I just don't understand why all that makes me squirm inside and feel sharp little chills everywhere.

My adrenals are going to be shot if this keeps up.

I try to think of something else, but my legs are restless under the sheets, and the need to go out and run eats at me. I wish I could sprint my heart out, feel those endorphins instead of these odd little pings in my nerves that gnaw me raw, this strange need that blooms up inside me when I see Remington Tate. Even when I denied it to Melanie, I was *so* sure he'd wanted me that first night in Seattle, I just don't know what happened that I got hired instead.

But it's what I wanted, isn't it? A job.

Except that the price to pay for my new job is a little bit of sexual torture. Big deal. I'll just block him out better tomorrow. With that new resolution, I grab my iPod from the nightstand and turn on my music and force myself to listen to any songs except the ones he's played to me.

FOUR

RUNNING

"Remy! Call out Remy already! REMINGTOOOOON!"

The group of women on the seats behind me are screaming their throats off.

So you can understand how it is really, really hard to *block out* the man when everyone around me is clamoring for him, especially when my body is alive with adrenaline for the fight that's about to start.

It's a deliciously familiar feeling, actually, the one that simmers in me as I sit among the spectators at the Atlanta Underground, waiting for Remington to come out to the ring. I feel like I'm the one competing, and my body is perfectly ready. My blood rushes hot and liquid inside me, my adrenals pump me full of the right hormones, and my mind seems as clear as newly scrubbed crystal. My legs are motionless under my seat, and so are my hands, but this is merely a ruse. The stillness of preparation. Where outwardly all is calm, inwardly there's a fire roaring. This is the one minute where everything goes quiet and gathers inward, so that when it's time to explode outward, it will be with concentrated precision that your energy unleashes in a perfectly planned burst.

Even now, I remember my perfect crouching position at the starting blocks, the way all my senses seemed to hone in on the one sound of the starting shot, when everything—and I mean everything—zaps awake on that sound, and you go from a standstill to running your heart out in a fraction of a second.

Now it seems that all I'm waiting to listen to is *his* name being announced, and when I finally hear "REMINGTON TATE, RIIIIPTIDE!" there's a new rush sweeping through me, and yet there's nowhere for me to run, there's no relief to what's coursing in my body, only this incredibly powerful ache being fed by the very same hormones my body keeps outputting, which I have no way of stopping.

I rise from my seat as the entire roomful of people do, but that's all I can do as I watch him take the ring in the way only he knows how to do. The crowd gets instantly high on him, and I'm light-headed too. There he is, a woman's living, breathing fantasy, doing his slow, cocky turn, spiky black hair, darkly tanned chest, dimpled smile—*killer* smile—all in the package of Remington Tate. He's perfection itself, and a new surge of excitement sweeps through me as I do what the rest of the crowd does and take him in, so blatantly on display in those low-riding boxing shorts and so strikingly sexy that he becomes the center of my attention.

The center. Of my. World.

"And now, the famed and acclaimed Owen Wilkes, 'the Irish Grasshopper'!"

While his feisty red-haired opponent takes the ring, Remington's blue gaze sweeps the crowd until he spots me. Our eyes lock, and I'm instantly breathless. His dimples come out to form such a perfect smile, it runs all the way through me, electrifying my nerve endings.

I'm still smiling like a dope when the bell rings, and I don't mean to hold my breath while I'm watching, but I do. Remington looks almost like a bored Rottweiler as his opponent, "the Grasshopper," seems to jump all over the ring and around him like a baby kangaroo.

He knocks him out quickly, and because he keeps winning, Remington fights a line of new opponents, one after the other. From what Pete has told me, only the last eight finalists in each city will compete in the next designated city, and it will all come down to a big fight at the end of the tour, in New York, where only the top two men will engage in a long sixteen-round fight, rather than a handful of three-round fights.

Now Remington takes on a man who looks more like a wrestler than a boxer. His abs are flabby and bulky, and he's about double as wide as Remington. Something fierce and primitive grips my core, and I'm on my feet with a silent "no!" the instant the man they'd called "the Butcher" rams a hit into Remy's rib cage. Remy's slammed so hard I can hear the breath tear out of him.

My insides seize in dread even when he recovers easily, and my heart doesn't stop pounding in my chest. I bite my lip as I watch him land a set of perfect punches on Butcher's core. He moves so fluidly, every part of his body flexible and strong, sometimes I forget he's fighting against someone else merely because of the way he hypnotizes me with his moves.

I love watching those powerful legs, with thick muscles, and how they balance him and move with both strength and agility. I love each flex of his quads, his shoulders, his biceps, the way the vine tattoo that circles his arms only emphasizes how finely formed his shoulders and biceps are between them.

"Boo! Boo-hooo!" the crowd starts shouting, and it's all after Remy sustained another hit in his upper torso. I wince when Butcher follows with a straight punch to Remy's lips. His head swings, and I see drops of blood splatter at his feet, and hear my-self say "no" again, softly. He straightens once more and regains his position, licking the blood up from a cut part of his lip. But I don't understand why he's letting down his guard.

It seems like he's not covering, and even Coach and Riley are scowling in puzzlement from the corner of the ring as they watch the fight continue, Remington landing his punches always excel-lently, but strangely allowing Butcher too much access into his upper thoracic region. I'm confused and anxious for it to finish, and all I know is that every punch the awful man slams into Rem-ington I can actually *feel* inside me like a cut in the gut.

When Butcher slams his side once more and Remy drops to one knee, I want to die.

"No!" The scream is torn out of me.

And when the woman beside me hears me, she cups the sides of her mouth and shouts, "Get up, Remy! Get UP! Beat the crap out of him!"

A ragged breath of relief leaves me when he jumps back up and wipes blood from his lips, but his eyes flick in my direction, and he takes another punch that swings him back to bounce against the cord.

My nerves are tattered in such a way that I need to duck my head and stop watching for just a minute. There is, literally, a ball of fire in my throat, and I can't even swallow my saliva. There's just something about watching *him* take a pounding that makes me feel as helpless as I did when I tore my knee and could no longer do anything about it. This passivity is just not me. I'm being eaten with the sheer need either to go up there and hit that fucking fat man too, or just flee here. Fight or flight.

But instead I just *sit* there, and it's awful.

Suddenly, his usual chorus begins: *"REMY . . . REMY . . . REMY."*

And something happens when I'm not looking, for chaos breaks loose in the Underground, and the people start screaming, *"Yeah! REMY, REMY, REMY!"*

The announcer's voice bursts through the speaker. "Our victor, ladies and gentlemen! RIPTIDE! Ripppppptiiiiide! Yes, you hungry ladies out there, scream your hearts out for the baddest bad boy this ring has ever seen! Ripppppppptiiiiide!"

I start, and my head shoots back up in surprise as my eyes fly back to the ring. Fat Man is being removed with aid from the ring medics, and I'm struck by the fact that Remington seems to have broken his ribs.

But my guy is no longer in the ring.

And he might have a broken rib too.

My god, what in the hell just happened?

As quickly as I can get through the crowd, I head backstage, my heart still bonkers and my body still aching for an outlet. I find Lupe heatedly arguing with Riley about how "the bastard is playing with fire," and when they both notice me, Coach turns away from me and Riley jabs a finger that signals "upstairs"; then he flips out the key to Remy's suite from his back jeans pocket to me. I take it and head to the hotel, which is thankfully just around the corner.

❤ ❤ ❤

I FIND REMINGTON sitting in the bench at the foot of his bed, his spiky dark hair as beautifully rumpled as always, his breath still slightly uneven, and a wave of relief washes through me when he raises his head and his lazy smile, the one that shows only one dimple, appears.

"Like the fight?" he asks, his voice rough with dehydration.

I can't say no, but I can't really say yes; I just don't know why it's such a complicated experience for me. So I say, "You broke the last one's ribs."

One sleek black eyebrow sweeps upward; then he drains the last of a Gatorade and sends the bottle spinning empty across the floor. "Are you worried about him, or me?"

"Him, because he's the one who won't be able to stand tomorrow." I meant that tongue-in-cheek, but although he grunts, he doesn't smile.

We're alone.

And suddenly every pore in my body becomes aware of this.

My hands feel slightly unsteady and I seize some salve and kneel between his legs to put it on the cut part of his lips. It's not bleeding anymore, but it cracked right on the fleshy middle of his lower lip. Time fades away as I press my finger in there, his eyes hooded as he watches me.

"You," I whisper. "I worry about you."

A sudden awareness of the exact rhythm of his breath overcomes me. I'm so close I think I just inhaled the same air he exhaled, and without warning his scent is inside me. He smells so good, salty and clean as an ocean, and I'm helpless to stop my reaction to him. My brain is spinning inside my cranium. I imagine bending my head to his damp neck and running my tongue over each and every drop of sweat I see on his skin.

Scowling at my own thoughts, I cover up the salve tin but remain on my knees, debating if I just start on his legs now that I'm down here.

"I messed up my right shoulder, Brooke."

My roughly spoken name stirs the top of my head, and the way he says it affects me, but I cover up with a sigh of mock dreariness. "With a bulldozer like you, I knew it was too much to hope that you'd survive this night with just a cut lip."

"Are you going to come fix it?"

"Of course. Someone has to." On my feet, I head over to kneel on the end of his bed and grab his shoulders. I'm no longer surprised at the way every cell in my body hones in on the feeling of this man's body connected, through my hands, with mine. I just close my eyes and allow myself to enjoy it for a moment as I try to loosen him up, but the tension in his body is more unrelenting than ever. I prod deeper into his right shoulder and whisper, "That ugly bastard landed a pretty hard one here. He landed *a lot* of hard ones. Does it hurt?"

"No."

I think I heard a hint of amusement in his voice, but I'm not sure. My focus drifts to his muscle, complaining and pushing back into my fingers, and I know for a fact it hurts. It must. "I'll rub you down with arnica, and we'll do cold therapy."

He sits perfectly still as he lets me work some oil into his skin, and when I peek at his dark profile, I notice his eyes are tightly shut. "Does it hurt?" I murmur.

"No."

"You always say no, but I can tell this time it does."

"There are other parts of me that are hurting more."

"What the hell?" The outer door to the suite slams shut, and Pete storms into the master bedroom, as angry as I've ever seen this gentle man look. His choirboy features seem sharper and not so angelic today, and even his curls look more pronounced.

"What. The. *Hell?*" he repeats.

Remington's body becomes a wall of brick under my touch.

"Coach's in a snit," Riley adds as he follows Pete inside. "What we all want to know is: why the fuck are you letting your ass get kicked?"

With even the easy-breezy Riley scowling today, a strange tumultuous vibe grabs hold of the room, and my hands instantly stop moving on the back of Remington's shoulders.

"Yes or no, you let him get in on purpose?" Riley shoots him a sinister glare.

Remington doesn't answer. But his torso is fully erect now, and every muscle seems engaged.

"Do you need to get laid?" Pete demands, signaling at him. "*Do* you?"

My insides clench, and I know I don't really want to stay here and listen to these guys make sexual arrangements for Remington, so I mumble—mainly to myself, since nobody is paying any attention to me anyway—something about going to help Diane in the kitchen; then I head out of the room.

As I go down the hall, I hear Pete again. "Dude, you can't let them do this to you just so you get her hands all over you. Look, we can arrange some girls. Whatever it is you're doing, you can't play these damned games like a normal person. You're just torturing yourself, Rem. This is a dangerous thing you're doing with her."

I've slowed down almost to a halt, and I think my lungs just turned to rocks. Are these guys talking about *me*?

"You bet all your money on yourself this year, remember *that* episode?" Pete adds. "Now you need to defeat Scorpion at the final *no matter what*. And this includes her, dude."

The timbre of Remington's voice is lower than the others, but somehow, that soft growl is infinitely more threatening. "Scorpion's a fucking dead man, so just back off."

"You pay us to prevent this shit, Remy," Pete counters.

But that only makes Remington lower his voice even more. "I've got it. Under. Control."

The silence that follows the deadly whisper snaps me into movement, and I head to the kitchen to find Diane retrieving a small organic turkey from the oven. The scent of rosemary and lemons makes my mouth water, but it does nothing for my pounding heart.

"What are those guys yelling about?" Diane asks as she arranges her presentation, scowling sweetly at her baby turkey when it refuses to look pretty on the plate she chose.

"Remy got hit tonight," I say. Because that's what it had been about. Hadn't it?

Diane shakes her head and clucks to herself. "I swear that man has the reddest self-destruct button I've ever seen. . . ."

She trails off when the door swings open behind me, and a large hand clamps around my elbow and spins me around.

"Do you want to run with me?"

Remington's icy blue eyes blaze fiercely into me, and I can feel his frustration all the way to where I'm standing. It circles around him like a black whirlwind, and suddenly he seems on edge and more than a little threatening.

"You need to eat, Remy," Diane says chidingly from the corner.

Smirking, he grabs a gallon of organic milk on the counter and starts downing it until it's almost all in his stomach. Then he slams the container down and wipes his lips with the back of his arm, saying, "Thanks for dinner." He then slants an eyebrow and waits for me to answer. "Brooke?" he prods.

A shiver runs through me.

I don't like that my name on his lips hits all the right notes. Like a romance movie.

Scowling at my reaction, I glance at his chest and wonder whether anything except putting him in a tub of ice is a good idea. But somehow I feel testing his limits even more today is not an option. "How do you feel?" I ask, and narrowly study him.

"I feel like running." His eyes peer intently into mine. "Do *you*?"

The request makes me hesitate. It's just that no one except runners truly knows that running with someone can be a very big deal.

A very. Big. Deal.

Especially when you're used to working out alone. Like Remington. And, aside from Melanie, I never run with anyone either. My running is my *me* time. Thinking time. Centering time. But I nod. I think he really needs it, and I've been needing this for hours. "Let me grab my sneakers and put on my brace."

Ten minutes later, we're running down the nearest path to our hotel, which is a winding dirt trail dotted with a couple of trees and thankfully well-lit at night. Remington wears his hood and sweatshirt, and he's thrusting in the air in true boxer fashion, while I'm just enjoying the cool breeze against my skin as I try to keep up. I settled upon wearing running shorts and a short-sleeved athletic top with my favorite pair of Asics, while Remington has a pair of kick-ass Reeboks for running, which are different from the high-top sneakers he uses for boxing.

"So what happened to Pete and Riley?"

"Out looking for whores."

"For you?"

He thrusts a fist in the air, then the other. "Maybe. Who cares." We resume running in silence.

I'm truly disappointed I've lost stamina, for half an hour into it, the pace has my lungs straining and I'm seriously sweating despite the cool night breeze. I halt and put my hands on my knees, waving for him to continue. "Go on, I'm just gonna catch my breath, I'm getting a cramp."

He stops with me and bounces on his toes so his body doesn't cool down; then he withdraws an electrolyte gel pack from his sweatshirt's center pocket. He extends it to me, and he gets so close that I get a whiff of him. Of soap and sweat and Remington Tate. My head swims a little. Maybe the cramp I thought I was getting in my ovaries might not be a cramp at all, but just my insides almost convulsing every time his shoulder brushes accidentally against mine.

He eases back and keeps on thrusting the air as he watches me open the gel pack at the corner and slide it onto my tongue.

The blood pumps wildly in my veins, and there's something insanely intimate about the way his blue eyes watch me lick the juice off an electrolyte packet that had belonged to him.

He stops bouncing. Breathing hard. "Any left?" he asks.

I immediately pull it out of my mouth and hand it over, and when he wraps his lips around it in the same fashion I did, my nipples harden like diamonds, and I can hardly remember anything except the fact that he's licking the same thing I just licked. I shudder with the reckless compulsion to run my tongue along the cut on his lip, take that gel pack off his mouth, and press my lips to his, so that the only thing he will be licking will be *me*.

"Are they right? What Pete said? Are you doing it on purpose?"

When he doesn't answer, I remember the "button" Diane mentioned, and my worry doubles.

"Remy, sometimes you break something and you never get it back. You *never* get it back," I emphasize. I glance out at the distant street and passing cars for a moment, afraid of him catching the emotion in my voice. He just has me on edge, and I need to get a grip on myself.

"I'm sorry about your knee," he says, softly; then he slam-dunks the packet into the nearest trash can and jabs right and left, and we start up running again.

"It's not about my knee. It's about you not taking your body for granted. Don't ever let anyone hurt you, don't *ever* allow it, Remy."

He shakes his head, his eyebrows drawn low over his eyes as he steals a glance in my direction. "I'm not, Brooke. I just let them get close enough so I can fuck them over. Little sacrifices in search of the win. It gives them confidence to get a couple of punches in; then it starts getting to their head, that I'm easy—that I'm not like they've heard I am—and when they get drunk on how easy they're pounding Remington Tate, I go in."

"All right. I like that so much better."

We run for over half an hour more, and at five miles, I'm panting like an old dog who's just delivered twelve little puppies or something. My pride is aching and so is my bad knee. "I think I quit. I'm going to be so sore tomorrow, I'd rather hit the sack now than require you to carry me to the hotel, later."

"I wouldn't mind," he says, with a delicious little chuckle, then he cracks his neck to his left side, then his right, and runs back with me.

In the hotel elevator, several other people board with us, and Remington pulls his hoodie down over his hair and ducks his head, his profile shadowed by the material. I notice he does this to keep from being recognized, and it makes me smile in amusement.

A young couple shouts from the lobby for us to "hold the elevator!" and I press the OPEN DOOR button until they hop in. My heart skips when Remington grips my hip and pulls me close to him once they board. And then I'm dying because he ducks his head, keeping it angled toward me, and I can hear the deep inhale he takes. Oh, god, he's scenting me. My sex muscles clench. The need to turn around and bury my nose in his neck and lick the dampness on his skin burns through me.

"You feel any better?" I ask, turning slightly into him.

"Yeah." He ducks his head closer, and my temple is bathed by his warm breath. "You?"

His pheromones are like a drug to me, and my throat feels so thick I only nod at him. His hand clenches on my hip, and my womb clenches with it so much it's painful and I almost whimper.

I hit the shower as soon as I'm in my room, and I make it as cold as I can stand it, my teeth chattering but the rest of my body still wound up in knots, over him. Him. Him.

When I hit the bed, Diane murmurs hello, then continues reading a recipe book, while I just say good night and close my eyes and try to pretend I'm not roasting inside my skin.

But I ache so bad I'm squirming under the sheets, haunted by what I heard Pete tell Remington. Haunted by his full, sexy mouth with its recent cut on his lower lip, wrapped around that electrolyte pack as his tongue squeezed the last of the gel from it. I think about what it would have been like to be that gel pack, and feel his lips sliding over my tongue, gently suckling, and the thought draws a fresh pool of moisture to gather between my thighs.

I'm desperate to give myself some relief from the continual, exhausting hormonal rampage of being exposed to him. Like with radiation, there's something I should be able to take to protect myself, but I just can't figure it out. His face, his scent; it makes me crazy. He's my client, but he's also . . . like a friend. And I just need to touch him. I know I can't kiss him full on that sexy mouth, but I can at least *stretch* him.

He must be warm from our run, and fatigued after his fight, and I crave the contact of his skin like a drug addict. Before I know what I'm doing, I slip into a velour pantsuit, head for his suite, and knock on his door.

I don't know what I'm going to say. I don't know anything except I will probably not be sleeping one wink until I see him and at least offer to ice his upper thoracic injuries, or just rub him down with an anti-inflammatory, or . . . I *don't know.*

Why did he ask me to run with him?

Why did Pete think he was getting purposely injured so I would touch him?

Did he *want* my touch so bad?

Riley swings the door open, and past his shoulders, I spot a woman in see-through lingerie dancing sexily in the middle of the living room coffee table, and hear another female voice in the background speaking. ". . . birdie told us you wanted to play with us, Remy. . . ."

"Yeah?" Riley asks me, and I just stare like an idiot, my stomach sinking because, of course, these are the whores that . . . I duck my head and frantically think of something to say. "Did I leave my pho—oh shit, I got it." I glance at my cell phone in my hand and roll my eyes, like I'm so stupid.

Which I am.

Shit, I really, really *am*.

"Never mind. Good night, Riley."

I hear Remington's deep voice. "Who is it?"

And I run to my room and shut the door, feeling numb inside. This time when I slip back into bed, I'm pretty sure every inch of arousal has fled my system, but I still can't sleep. Because now the woman Remington is kissing in my mind so hungrily with that full, beautiful mouth of his, the woman who gets to lick that scarred cut on his lip that I got to put salve on, is unfortunately not me.

REMY IS SPARRING today the way Coach thinks he should have fought *yesterday*.

He's knocked out two of his sparring partners, though, and now Coach is pissed once more.

"These are sparring partners, Tate. If you'd only stop knocking them down and just have fun and work on your moves, you'd still have someone to train with today. Now we've run out and you have no one to spar with anymore."

"Then stop giving me little pussies, Coach." He spits off the ring. "Send Riley up here."

"Ha. Not even if he were suicidal. I need him conscious tomorrow."

"Hey, I know how to spar," I tell Riley from where we watch at one outside corner of the ring.

His blond head swings to mine, and he suddenly looks impressed. "You did not just offer to go up with this guy?"

"Sure I did. I got moves he hasn't ever seen," I boast, but frankly, I just want the opportunity to kick the shit out of Remington for being such a womanizing shithead who makes me fantasize day and night. And for licking the electrolyte packet after *I* did. What a flirting dickwad.

"All right, Rem, I've got a little something for you," Riley calls, clapping to get his attention. "I know for sure he's not going to knock out this one, Coach," he calls out to Lupe at the other corner; then he signals laughingly at me.

Remington sees me and tosses his headgear on the floor as he watches me hop into the ring in my tight little black one-piece tracksuit. His eyes rake me, like they always do. He's such a man, he can't help checking me out every time I walk toward him. But as I approach, his eyes glint in amusement, and slowly, his smile appears, and it just pricks my irritation.

He's been moody today, from what I—and his fallen sparring partners—can tell. But my own grumpiness rates about a solid ten too. Not even coffee lifted my spirits this morning, and yet I know *this* will. Even if I lose, I just want to freaking spar with someone.

"Don't smile like that. I can knock you down with my feet," I warn him.

"It's not kickboxing. Or are you going to bite too?"

I swing out my leg high in the air in a precise kickboxing move, which he deflects, very gently, and cocks a brow.

I try another one, and he deflects, and then I notice he's standing in the center of the ring while I'm basically circling him. I know I don't stand a chance in terms of strength, but my plan is to dizzy him and then try to knock him down a peg. Riley calls what I'm going to do "weaving." Which is just turning and twisting around your opponent so he misses. So I weave a little, and he's clearly very entertained by me, so I try a test punch. He easily catches it in his full fist, then lowers my arm.

"No," he chides softly, and curls his hand around mine to teach me how to fist my fingers correctly. "When you punch, you need to align your two lower arm bones—your ulna and radius—on par with your wrist. Your wrist can't be slack, so hold it perfectly straight. Now start with your arm folded to your face, tighten your knuckles, and as you punch out, twist your arm so that your ulna, radius, and *wrist* feel like one piece of bone when you hit. Try it."

I try it, and he nods. "Now use your other arm to guard."

I keep one arm folded to cover my face, and then attack again, and again, noticing he's just covering, not counterattacking.

Already the adrenaline pumps heady in my body, and I don't know if it's the mock fighting, or having those blue eyes so fixed on me, but I feel electrically charged suddenly. "Show me a move I don't know," I say breathlessly, liking this more than I anticipated.

He reaches out for both my arms and folds them up to guard my face with my fists. "All right, let's do a one-two punch. Always cover your face with your hands, and your torso with your arms, even when you're punching. Swing first with your left." He pulls my arm toward his jaw. "Then shift your balance on your legs so you can follow with a power punch with your right. You need good footwork here. Rip the strength from the punch from down here"—he pushes a finger into my core, then drags his hand all the way up my bare arm to my fist—"and send that power all the way to your knuckles."

He makes a mock double blow that is fluid and perfect and makes little beads of sweat pop along my cleavage, and then I try it. Hitting left, squatting, shifting, and hitting harder with the right.

His eyes spark delightedly. "Try it again. Hit me at a different spot on your second punch." He gets in position, his hands open to catch my blows.

Following orders, I use the first arm to deliver a quick punch to his left hand, which easily catches my blow; then I power-punch the other hand with my right. My punches are delightfully accurate, but I think I need to put more strength into them.

"Double punch on your left," he says, and moves his hand up to catch my blows.

"On your right," he says, and on my first hit, I strike his open hand with my fist—poof. Then I decide to surprise him and land my right power punch in his abs, which contract automatically as I hit and send surprising pain shooting up my knuckles. But even *he* looks surprised I got that last one in.

"I'm so good," I taunt him as I ease back, bouncing on my toes like he does, and playfully sticking out my tongue.

He totally misses that, for he's watching my breasts bounce. "Real good," he says, getting back in position. His eyes have darkened in a way that makes my insides roil with heat, and I decide this moment he's distracted with my girls is better than any.

I swing out like I learned in self-defense. Legs are the strongest part of a woman's body, and certainly an ex-sprinter's. My aim is to strike his Achilles tendon with the ball of my foot, and knock both his big body and his ego to the ground.

But he moves the instant I swing, and I hit his tennis shoe instead. Pain screams up my ankle. He quickly catches me by the arm and straightens me up, his eyebrows jerking into a frown. "What was that about?"

I scowl. "You were supposed to fall."

He just looks at me, his face blank for a moment. "You're kidding me, right?"

"I've toppled men much heavier than you!"

"A fucking tree topples sooner than Remy, Brooke," Riley shouts.

"Well, I can see *that*," I grumble, and cup my mouth to yell, "Thanks for the heads-up, Riley."

Cursing under his breath, Remy holds my arm as he leads me, hopping, to the corner, where he drops down on a chair and, since there's only one, hauls me down on top of him so he can test my ankle. "You fucked your ankle, didn't you?" he asks, and it's the first time I ever actually hear him sound so . . . annoyed at me. And the very first I sit here, pretty as you please, on his freaking *lap*. I'm dying just a little.

"I just seemed to *wrongly* send all my weight to my ankle," I grudgingly admit.

"Why'd you hit me? Are you pissed at me?"

I scowl. "Why would I be?"

His eyes peer intrusively into mine, and he looks frighteningly solemn and definitely annoyed. "You tell me."

Ducking my head, I stare down at my ankle and refuse to spill my guts out to anyone but Melanie.

"Hey, can we get some water over here?" he calls out, a sharp note of frustration in his words. Riley brings over a Gatorade and a plain bottle of water and sets them both on the ring floor at my feet.

"We're wrapping up," he tells us, and then, sounding concerned, asks me, "You all right, B?"

"Dandy. Call me tomorrow please. I can't wait to get back in the ring with this dude."

Riley laughs, but Remington doesn't spare him a glance.

His chest is soaked with sweat and his dark head is ducked low as he inspects my ankle, his thumbs pressing around the bone. "That hurt, Brooke?"

I think he's worried. The sudden gentleness with which he speaks to me makes my throat ache, and I don't know why. Like when you fall, and it doesn't hurt, but you cry because you feel humiliated. But I've already fallen worse in front of the world, and I wish I hadn't cried back then just as fiercely as I now wish not to break down in front of the strongest man in the world.

Scowling instead, I reach to try to inspect my ankle, but he doesn't move his hand away, and suddenly several of our fingers surround my ankle, and *all* I can feel are his thumbs on my skin.

"You weigh a ton," I complain, like it's his fault I'm an idiot. "If you weighed a little less I'd have toppled you. I even toppled my instructor."

He glances up, scowling. "What can I say?"

"You're sorry? For my pride's sake?"

He shakes his head, clearly still annoyed, and I smile sardonically and reach down for the Gatorade, unscrewing the top.

His eyes drop to my lips as I take a sip and I can feel, suddenly, something big and hard beneath my bottom. As the cool liquid runs down my throat, it makes me realize the entire rest of my body is feverishly hot and getting hotter.

"Can I get some?" His voice is strangely husky as he signals to my drink.

When I nod, he grabs the bottle in one big hand and tilts it up to his mouth, and my hormones discharge all at once at the sight of his lips pressing against the rim.

Right over the spot mine have just been.

His throat works as he swallows; then he lowers the bottle, his lips now moist, and when he hands the Gatorade back to me, our fingers brush. Lightning shoots up my veins. And I'm entranced by the way his pupils have darkened, and the way he's staring at my eyes without any laughter in his own. When I automatically try to cover my nervousness by taking another swallow, he watches me way too intently, unsmiling, his lips beautifully pink. The cut on his lip's still healing. The one I want to lick. A ribbon of longing unfurls deep inside me. And it hurts. I'm on his lap, and I realize one powerful arm is around my waist, and I've never been so close. Close enough to touch him, kiss him, wrap all my body around him. I'm suddenly dying and flying. I just can't pretend this is no big deal anymore. I want him. I *want* him so badly I can't think straight. It *is* a deal. A big deal.

I've never felt like this.

I know it's crazy, and that it's never going to happen, that it can never happen, but I just can't help it. He's like my Olympics, something that I'm never going to have, but which I crave with my entire being. And I absolutely loathe the thought that his arms were around one, possibly two, women less than twenty-four hours ago, when I wanted it to be me.

Agitated all over again at the memory, I try standing, carefully, and he takes my Gatorade and sets it aside as he grabs two towels from a basket and wraps one around his neck, then drapes the other around mine, all the time holding me up by the waist. "I'll help you up so you can ice that."

He lowers me from the ring like I weigh no more than a cloud, and then I have to lean on him, my arm around his narrow waist as we walk out.

"It's fine," I keep saying.

"Stop arguing," he says.

In the elevator, he keeps me close to his side and his head ducked to me, and I can feel his breath near my temple. I'm painfully aware of how big he is, compared to me, and of his five fingers splayed around my waist, and of the exact moment he shifts his nose and lowers it to the back of my ear. It tickles when he exhales, and he's so close, his lips would brush the back of my ear if he speaks. I hear his deep inhale all of a sudden, and my sex organs throb so fiercely, I ache to turn around and bury my nose in his skin and suck all the air I can into my lungs. But of course I don't do this.

He walks me to my room, and my body is in such a state my brain can't even come up with a topic of conversation to get rid of the tense silence that accompanies us.

"Hey, man, ready for the fight?" A uniformed hotel staff member, who seems to be a fan, asks from across the hall.

Remington gives a thumbs-up with a dimpled smile before turning to me, pressing his jaw into the hair at the back of my ear. "Key," he says in a guttural whisper that elicits goose bumps. He swipes it and brings me inside.

Diane isn't here, and I know she's probably making his super-luxe dinner right now. He sets me down on the edge of the second queen bed, which I guess he figures is mine because Diane has a picture of her two kids facing the first bed, and he grabs the ice bucket. "I'll get you ice."

"That's fine, Remy, I'll do it later—"

The door closes before I can finish, and I exhale as I bend to palpate my ankle to assess the damage I caused.

He leaves the lock out so he doesn't have to knock, and I stiffen when he returns and slams the door shut. He runs the water in the bathroom, and then he's back, looking enormous and commanding inside my hotel room as he plops the bucket on the carpet.

He kneels at my feet, and at the sight of his powerful body and dark head bending down to tend to me, a rush of wanting ripples through me with such force, I stare down at the ice and want to dip my head in the bucket.

He yanks off my tennis shoe and then my sock; then he holds my leg gently by the calf as he eases my foot inside. "When we get this fixed I'm going to show you how to knock me down," he whispers. When I can't answer and am completely undone by his touch, he glances up, and his eyes are both tender and intimate. "Cold?"

Though the rest of me is anything *but*, my toes start freezing as the water envelops them. "Yeah."

As he sinks my foot deeper, my entire body tenses from the frigidness, and he pauses midway down. "More water?"

I shake my head and ram my foot down the rest of the way, thinking, *No pain no gain.* My lungs seize up as my body absorbs the cold. "Oh, shit."

He notices my grimace and yanks my foot out; then he shocks me, flattening my icy-cold feet against his stomach to warm me. His abs clench under my toes, and his eyes hold mine in a grip so powerful, I'm drowning.

Voltage surges through me. His warm, big, callused hand is curved around my instep, holding my foot to his stomach so firmly it almost feels like he wants me there. I wish my hands were my feet, feeling those washboard abs under my fingers. Every dent perfectly presses against the arch of my foot and my toes, and the numbness has left me completely.

"I didn't know you gave pedicures, Remy," I say, and I can't understand why I sound so breathless.

"It's a fetish of mine."

He shoots me a lazy smile that clearly tells me he's all bullshit; then he reaches into the bucket with his free hand and pulls out a single ice cube. He sets it lightly on my ankle and drags it over the tender flesh, carefully watching what he does. My reaction is swift and violent, seizing my entire body with a complete and total awareness of him.

My heartbeat suddenly roars in my head. God, this man is more tactile than I am. Then, as if to confirm my thoughts, the hand holding my foot to his stomach shifts slightly, and he rubs his thumb along my arch while continuing to drag the cool ice cube across my skin. A tingling begins at the center of my stomach, and I'm afraid that within minutes it will take over my body.

My voice trembles like the rest of me. "Do you do manicures too?"

He glances up at me again, and my heart turns over from the effect his blue eyes have on me.

"Let me do your feet, first, then I'll do the rest of you."

My stomach clenches when he finishes that phrase with another smile, this one quite slow. Every muscle in my sex starts to ripple as the ice slowly continues to stoke a gently growing fire through my insides.

I'm entranced as he watches the ice move over my creamy white skin, the silence charged with electricity. Helplessly I drag my foot slightly over his stomach, feeling the ridges of his abs under me. He looks up, and the piercing intensity in his eyes draws me right in until I'm breathless and drowning.

"Feel better?" he murmurs, raising his dark brows, and I can't believe how his voice affects me, how his touch affects me, his scent, how another human can have such power over me. I can't let it.

I.

Can't.

Let it.

I remind myself that when you want a man, you're in control of what you give him. In control of what you let him take. But I can't block out the images of him and me together. Of *me* tearing *his* clothes off, and of *him* crushing *me* against *himself.* Images of his lips on mine, of us falling recklessly into bed together, throb through me. He makes me feel eighteen. Virginal and wanton. Just thinking about boys . . . except he only makes me think of one boy. And he's very male. Very manly. But a little bit playful, like a boy.

A big, bad boy who had fun with his little whores on his coffee table last night . . .

The sudden, brutal reminder cools me down like a dip in the frigid waters of Alaska. "It feels perfect now. Thank you," I say, my voice cool as the melting ice as I try wiggling my foot free from his grip.

I'm about to successfully pull free when the door opens with an unlocking noise, and Diane enters. "There you are. I must feed you now so you can recharge for tomorrow!"

Staring at me as though confused about the change in me, Remington frowns slightly as he tosses the thawing ice in the ice bucket and sets my foot back on the carpet as he stands. "I *am* sorry about your ankle," he says to me softly as he straightens, his expression confused and almost vulnerable. "Don't worry if you can't make it to the fight."

"No. It wasn't your fault. I'll be fine," I rush out.

"I'll ask Pete to get you some crutches."

"I'll be fine. Serves me right for messing with trees."

He stops at the entry then glances back at me on the edge of the bed, his face unreadable.

"Good luck, Remy," I say.

He stares at me, then at Diane, then rakes a hand through his hair, and leaves, looking somehow . . . agitated.

Diane stares at me in complete puzzlement. "Did I come at a bad time?"

"No." I shake my head. "You came just in time before I made a total fool of myself."

Not that trying to knock a man like him off his feet had been a very smart move to begin with.

FIVE

DANCING TO THE MUSIC

Pete wants me out of backstage. And so do Coach and Riley.

"He needs to zone out. Go take your seat, you're distract-ing the hell out of him," Pete tells me, and although he's the one I consider most gentle among the men in the team, he really sounds frustrated today. Maybe because it's birthday number thirty-two for him and he'd rather be anywhere else. "Here. Take this ticket and go meet the girls next to you. They're nice people, and they're here with us. We're all partying later."

Minutes later, I discover the girls both look like Miss Uni-verse contenders and like the kind of women who walk around in bikinis at precisely these sorts of events. But their smiles as I head toward them are genuine, and I can't help but notice how both their gazes rake approvingly over my little black skirt and short-sleeved glittery top.

"Hi. I'm Friday, this is Debbie," the redhead who'd only re-cently been dancing atop Remington's coffee table says, signaling to the blonde as Debbie.

"Hi. I'm Brooke."

"Oh! You're the girl that went to the suite the other night," Friday says.

"I didn't go anywhere," I say, all huffy over the fact that they knew that I had. So Riley did tell them it was *me* at the door? How embarrassing.

Friday bends over and whispers in my ear, "I think Remy wants to fuck you."

Feeling the wind knocked out of me, I adjust myself in my seat and then the other girl, Debbie, leans to me as well. "Remy *really* wants to fuck you. He got so hard when you came to the room and spoke to Riley. I felt it when I was on his lap and he just heard your voice and wham. He was up full force."

"TMI! Seriously!" I cry, shaking my head with a nervous laugh. I'm completely red now, struggling with a thousand and one emotions all at once.

"I even offered him to take care of it," Debbie adds, "but he was like, 'Just drop it, I'm fine,' and got away, telling us to do his friends, and then he went to his room and locked himself in. Pete wants to make sure that doesn't happen again tonight."

I stare down at my lap and an overwhelming feeling of possessiveness I never knew I could even experience flits through me. "Why does he have to get laid every night?" I ask them, unable to hide my annoyance.

"Are you kidding? He's Remy. He's like, used to getting a lot of it. Daily."

Scoffing, I wave my hand and turn to stare at the empty ring, not really wanting to think how much of "it" Remington is used to getting, but a visual of his beautiful body entwined with anyone else's makes my stomach grip so uncomfortably, if I had eaten anything recently, I'd be in danger of losing it.

Ten minutes later, I hear his name ripping through the speakers: "And noooow, ladies and gentlemen, say helloww to the one, the ONLY, Remington Tate, RIPPPPPTIIIIIIDE!"

A stream of sensations shoots through my body as he comes trotting out, and I instantly feel liquid heat gushing into my panties. God, I hate how many times during the day I look at him and want to make him mine. I want to touch him, to know him.

He climbs into the ring, with that shiny robe that contrasts completely with his utter manliness, and the instant he bares himself to the crowd, everyone screams. Just like my heart does as I take him in like I need my fix. His dark hair is perfectly recklessly up today, those tanned muscles flexing as he extends his arms and does his little turn. And here I am, my breath caught between my lungs and my lips as he turns around and scans the crowd. As soon as he spots me, his eyes come alive, as alive as I feel when he smiles at me. He holds my gaze while those dimples flash, and I swear he stares at me in a way that makes me feel that I am the only woman here. Every time he's in the ring, he's completely in character. And his eyes just . . . take me. I know it's not true. I know I'm seeing only what I want to see.

But for a little second, I just want to sit in this stupid chair and believe there is this sort of magic between two people and I can be this prized someone to this sexy, raw, primitive man who's so strong, mysterious, and playful to me, he *compels* me like nothing in my life ever has.

I can't stop thinking that he didn't have sex with the girls Pete and Riley brought him, and that's all I can think of as I watch him take on his first opponent, delighting not only me, but hundreds of other women with the power and grace of his perfectly trained body.

Breathless, I watch him take his second, and his third, and I feel such a rush of pride for him every time the word "victor" is attached to his name. He works so hard, trains so hard, and I now know boxing terms and can see exactly what he does. I see his one-two punches. His jabs. His hooks. And suddenly he blocks a right-handed power punch with his left arm, then steps inside and buries a left hook to his opponent's ribs and follows that with a right cross to the jaw that knocks the man out completely. His opponent tries to get up and slumps back down, bloodied and exhausted.

The public roars as his name takes over the entire room.

"*RRRRRRIIIIIIPTIIIIIIDE!*"

My god. He fights like a true champion, and he *deserves* to be the champion at the end of it all. Heart knocking wildly inside me, I watch as the ringmaster heads over to raise his arm, and I wait in a strange mix of anxiety and anticipation for the moment he's declared the winner, for I know that in this instant his gaze will swing to mine, like it has at every single fight since my first.

"Our victor, ladies and gentlemen. Riptiiiide!!"

By the time those electric blue eyes seek me out in the stands, my heart throbs fiercely in my temples, and my insides bubble with emotion when he spots me. He stares straight into my eyes, and his eyes are only mine, and his smile is only mine, and for this fraction of an instant, nothing else matters but us.

Tonight I really miss Melanie. Melanie, who would have been shouting at him at my side, and telling him everything I would like to say but am too much a coward to say out loud. But in my mind I hear her and I wish she'd come visit so I could scream to him like she does, and tell Remington Tate he's so fucking hot I can't stand it.

❤ ❤ ❤

I CLIMB INTO a black Lincoln with a hotel chauffeur over an hour later, and both Riley and Pete get into a separate car with Friday and Debbie. I don't know who arranged this in such a way, but I'm told to wait in the car, which I do until suddenly Remington slides into the backseat next to me. My chest grips in nerves and excitement because he's showered after the fight, and changed into drool-worthy black denim and a black button-down shirt with the cuffs rolled up to his elbows, and the scent of his soap instantly makes my lungs feel achy.

The backseat is spacious, but somehow as we wind into traffic, I realize Remington is sitting close to me. Too close. I can feel the back of his hand against the back of my hand. I should probably move my hand, but I don't. Instead I gaze out the window at the nighttime lights dotted across the city as we approach the club, but I'm not seriously seeing anything. My body is honed in on the part where our bodies touch.

Why is he touching me?

I think he's watching me, measuring my reaction, when he moves his thumb and traces it along the top of mine.

I want to shiver. To close my eyes. Just absorb him. I can't forget what the girls told me, and the little candle of hope they lit up for me is now blazing like a torch inside of me. I need to know. If he wants me. Does he want me?

He looks so impossibly handsome my insides flutter with renewed intensity.

"Did you like the fight?" he asks me, his voice low and rough as he studies my profile in the shadows of the car, his eyes glowing intently.

He always asks me this question after an event in the Underground. As if my opinion is important to him.

"No. I didn't like it," I say as I face him; then I grin when he scowls. "You were amazing! I *loved* it!"

He laughs, the sound rich and male; then he startles me when he grabs my hand in his warm grip and lifts it. My breath freezes when he slowly brushes his lips across my knuckles, and I can feel the plump softness of his mouth down to the delicious scar on his lower lip, which is now almost completely healed. A little buzz travels through my bloodstream as his eyes hold me trapped the entire time he grazes me. The way he stares through those heavy dark lashes makes my nipples throb.

"Good." His murmur is hot and damp against my skin, and when he lowers my hand back to the seat and slowly untangles his fingers from mine, I have to bring it back to my lap and hold it with its partner, just because it suddenly feels too empty.

The club they chose tonight is packed and bursting outside with lines of people, but the second Remington steps out of the car, he hauls me up to the bouncer, who immediately allows us inside, where Riley waits for us just outside of a private room in the back.

"Pete's getting a lap dance," Riley tells Remington. "You don't mind treating him to one as a birthday present?"

Through the open door, we watch a woman in a glittering silver bikini approach Pete, who sits on a couch near the end, smiling as he watches her. I'm so uncomfortable I think I just squirmed, for suddenly Riley looks at me, his eyebrows shooting up to his hairline.

"You shy about this, Brooke?" he asks in amusement.

My heart stops when I realize Remington is looking at me too. He peers intently into my eyes; then his gaze flicks to my mouth, then back into my eyes. His hand suddenly envelops mine and he whispers, "Do you want to watch?"

I shake my head no, and he leads me back out to the bar and dance floor area. There's an unreal amount of noise, and the entire dance floor throbs with music and the fiery warmth of dancing bodies.

"Oh, I love this song!" I cry as I spot Debbie jumping in the middle of the stage, and she catches sight of me and comes to haul me onto the dance floor.

"Remy!" Friday crushes him into the throng at the same time that Debbie squeals and pulls me tight to her body; then she grabs my hips and starts grinding in some sexy girl move. I laugh and turn around, my arms in the air while Usher's "Scream" fills the room with music, and then I spot Remington only feet away, towering among the crowd.

He's not dancing.

In fact, he's not even moving.

He's watching me, his smile in place, eyes glinting, and suddenly he grabs me and slams me against his body, ducking to my neck. He brushes my hair to the side and presses his body into my spine, breathing me in so hard—I can *feel* his deep inhale. My stomach clenches in response, and I feel his mouth part at the curve between my neck and collarbone. He grazes my skin with his teeth, and then his tongue comes out to lick me.

My body electrifies. Reaching up and behind me, I grab his head and pin it down as I follow his hips, people dancing around us, the heat building in the room. His hands catch my hips, squeezing as he pulls me harder against his front, and my buttocks feel how hard he is. He wants me to feel how much he wants me. His tongue trails up my neck to the back of my ear. A shiver runs through me as he splays a hand on my stomach and turns me to face him.

Our eyes meet. Hold. The music throbs within me, desire for him knotting and twisting in my core, and I wrap my arms around him and push my body up to his, tilting my head up for his mouth.

I need to know his taste. The feel of him. He didn't sleep with those whores. His erection that day had been mine. He hasn't looked at another woman the entire night. Not during the fight, not here. He hasn't had eyes for anyone but *me*.

And I have eyes for no one, nothing, but this jaw-droppingly gorgeous man before me, who plays me songs and runs and spars with me and puts ice on my injury. Blue eyes glazed with lust, dark eyelashes looking heavy as he stares into my eyes, at my mouth, he grabs my face in one hand, ear to ear, and breathes me in again, his eyes drifting shut as he nuzzles my face with his. "Do you know what you're asking for?" he asks in a hoarse rasp, breathing harsh and fast. "Do you, Brooke?"

I can't reply, and he grabs my ass and hauls me to him, putting his mouth almost, almost, on mine. He's driving me insane. Insane. I want to have him. I want to let myself have him. I slide my fingers up his chest, into his hair, so silky under my fingers.

"Yes." My heart pounds in my ears as I push up on tiptoe, drawing his head down, when someone bumps into me from behind. I stumble forward. Remington catches me with one arm and pins me protectively to his side.

"If it isn't Riptide and his new pussy."

My head swings around and I realize whoever shoved me, it was not by accident. Four men flock around us, and they're all enormous. One of them has an icky black scorpion tattooed on his right cheekbone, and he's even larger than the others.

Remington glances at them like they're as significant as a bunch of flies; then he puts an arm around me and takes me off of the dance floor.

"What's your girlfriend's name? Whose name does she call out when you fuck her, huh?"

Remy remains wordless, but his fingers have clenched into an angry fist at the back of my top as he pushes me toward the bar. The men march behind us, but Remington continues to ignore them. He turns me away and blocks my view of them with the wall of his chest. "Go back with Riley and ask him to take you to the hotel," he whispers.

Alarm bells clang inside my head as I realize this is provocation was designed simply to get Remington in trouble. I've been with the team enough to know that an altercation outside of the ring can land Remy in jail and out of competition. "You can't get in a fight, Remy," I warn, when suddenly the beefiest of the four men speaks, raising his voice enough to be heard perfectly above the music.

"We're talking to you, douche-nozzle."

"I heard you, asshole, I just don't give a fuck what you have to say," Remy shoots back.

The giant's friend tries to land a punch, but Remington quickly ducks and shoves him back so hard he stumbles and falls. Suddenly I realize the tactic. The friends of the scorpion guy are going to attack Remy so that he has no choice but respond and kick the shit out of them, thereby getting himself kicked off the tour and possibly tossed in jail. Meanwhile, the guy with the tattoo will have done "nothing." *What a loser scumbag!*

Remy is getting full-blown angry at my side, grabbing one of them by the shirt and hissing, "Take a hike or I'll cut your fucking balls off and then feed them to your mother!" He shoves the man back, then grabs the other two and shoves them at the same time, one with each arm. He looks so pissed that I'm getting really concerned. Veins pop up his hands, arms, neck, and when the first man recovers and approaches him from behind, Remington's elbow flies out behind him and perfectly slams into the poor man's face. "Sorry, dude, my bad," he apologizes, and the man curses under his breath and covers his bloodied nose.

Meanwhile, I see the guy with the scorpion tattoo is happily watching with a grin.

Oh, no, you don't, dipshit!

The fight-or-flight response is full force in my body now. My brain buzzes as the blood shoots hot and urgent through my system. I already feel it feeding my muscles, my heart pumping wildly. I run to the bar, reach over, grab two bottles, and come back to swing them at two of the assholes' heads. They crash down evenly as glass shoots everywhere.

I know there's another bottle on the bar that has the third guy's name written all over it, but when I quickly turn to go grab it, a huge hand clamps around my wrist and spins me around, where I find Remington staring down at me with a face that is progressively getting scarlet. He grabs me by the waist and tosses me up on his back like a potato sack, then stalks through the crowd to Pete.

"Remington," I complain, slamming his back with my fists as I squirm. My hormones skyrocket when I realize one of his hands is on my ass. I hear him whisper something to Pete, and then we blur past the bouncers until, finally, the blood in my head goes back in the correct direction when he shoves me inside our car. Adrenaline pumps through me. I've never been in a fight. It feels amazing. *Amazing.*

Our hotel chauffeur slides behind the wheel and tears into the city traffic, and I notice Remington is breathing hard and fast.

Like I am.

Our gazes meet in the shadows across the car, and his eyes are eerily dark, his face etched with red-hot fury. "What *in the hell* did you think you were doing?" he explodes.

His hands are fists over his thighs, and for a moment I think he's going to slam them into the back of the bench seat. The look in his eyes is fiercely raw and strange. Almost animal. Kind of . . . possessive. And it causes a strange little thrill to rocket up inside me.

I'd been ready to kiss him. My hands are clenched in my lap as I try to keep them still.

But god, I'm so wound up, I'm thoughtless with need as I

look at him. Thoughtless and broken inside from the painful longing of wanting to be with him. His fingers are restless and I just want to grab his hand and make it curl around my breasts and beg him to touch me.

"I just saved your ass and it felt amazing," I say, and a new rush of adrenaline courses through me at the reminder.

Remy seems to be hanging on by a thread as he rubs his face and sets his elbows on his knees, kneeling forward, rubbing the back of his head with hands that I now notice are fiercely trembling. He's not breathing right either. "For the love of fucking god, don't ever, *ever*, do that again. EVER. If one of them sets a hand on you, I'll fucking kill them, and I won't give a rat's fuck who *watches* me!"

A shudder of excitement shoots through me as he leans back and looks at me with a lust that is mind-blowing. He catches my wrist and squeezes so tight, I gasp, and he glances down and releases me. "I mean it. Don't fucking *ever* do that again."

"Of course I'll do it again. I won't let you get into trouble."

"Jesus, are you for real?" As fiercely agitated as I've ever seen him, he rubs his face and then stares bleakly out the window, his body trembling angrily. "You're a stick of dynamite, do you know that?"

I shrug, and then nod a little, feeling as jacked up as he is.

Neither of us is breathing right.

And we're still not breathing right when we pull into our hotel driveway.

We cross the lobby like we're both in a rush then board the elevator. We're riding alone, but he's standing on the opposite side of me.

He's wired. Hyper. His eyes looking at everything except me. He cracks his knuckles, then his neck.

"It's okay," I say, touching his shoulder gently, and he stiffens as if I'd zapped him, glancing at my hand on his shoulder. I step back to my corner, and we stare into each other's eyes. The air between us almost rumbles, like thunder. He seems to want to both jump me and get away from me, all at once. He flexes his hands at his sides and softens his voice as we head down the hall to our rooms, but it still sounds gruff with emotion. "I'm sorry you had to see those assholes," he murmurs. He's visibly trying to calm himself as he rakes a hand through his spiky hair. "I'm going to fucking break all Scorpion's bones and pull his goddamned eyes out when I get a chance."

My eyes widen when I realize that guy is the one he needs to beat, and I nod to appease him, because I think he's really thirsting to do violence to them, but also because I'm so wound up I just don't know what I'll do alone in my room. I don't know where to put my hands, my thoughts, all this rush inside me going round and round and heading nowhere. "Can I come to your room until the guys get back?" I ask.

He hesitates, then nods, and I follow him to his door. We settle down on the living room couch, and he turns on the TV to the first channel that appears. "Do you want something to drink?"

"No," I say. "I never drink the day before flying or I'll get doubly dehydrated."

He nods and brings two water bottles from the bar.

He plops down next to me.

His thigh ends up so close, I can feel his quad muscle. My heart still pounds like crazy. I remember the way we danced, and my skin flushes hot again.

"Why did you get in trouble when you were pro?" I ask him.

"A fight like the one you just prevented."

He stares at the screen, his jaw working, and I stare helplessly at the play of light and shadows across his face, mesmerized.

He stretches his right arm on the couch behind me with deceptive calm, but I can feel the tension emanating from his body, and suddenly I feel my heart speed up in exhilarating anticipation. Strange noises from the TV filter into my mind, and then I realize the couple on TV are kissing. My stomach clenches. I've never seen this movie before, but as the background music flares up, I know a scorching sex scene looms ahead.

A flash of torment passes through his gaze as he grabs the remote and shuts the TV off. Tossing the control aside, he lowers his hand to my nape, curving his fingers gently around the back of my neck. His hand feels warm and incredibly strong, four fingers going to one side of my neck, his thumb to the other; then he circles his thumb gently over my skin as he turns to me.

That his touch can arouse me to the extent it does makes me feel drunk and high and impossibly trembly.

"Why'd you do that for me?" His voice is unbearably intimate as he gazes at me in the shadows.

"Because."

We're both staring as intently as we've ever stared, and I'm hyperaware of every point of contact of our bodies. His thigh against mine. His hand under the fall of my hair, gently squeezing. "Why? Somebody tell you I can't take care of myself?"

"No."

He eyes my lips, then my eyes, then he slowly closes his eyes and sets his forehead on mine, and all I can do is breathe him in like a junkie, my insides intoxicated with just a whiff. Nothing in my life has ever smelled so good to me as him. Him recently showered. Him sweaty. Just him.

His own deep inhalation reaches my ears, and I find myself touching his mouth with a lone fingertip. His lips are so plump and firm, but at the same time smooth and silky. I feel a quick, damp flick as his tongue flashes out to lick me, and a shudder shoots through my spine. He groans and pulls my whole finger into his mouth and closes his eyes as he sucks it.

"Remington . . ." I breathe.

"Honey, I'm home!"

We spring apart at the sound of a slamming door and Pete's sarcastic voice.

"Just wanted to make sure you guys got here okay. Wow, Rem, Scorpion sure seems to have a hard-on to get your ass back in jail—for *some* reason I can't fathom."

The lights flare on, and Remington drops my finger as if it's a loaded gun and rises and goes to the window, and he's breathing hard, audibly hard. As hard as I am.

I'm instantly on my feet. "I'd better go."

Pete takes in the scene with an impassive face, and he doesn't say anything as I rush across the room to leave. "I'll just wait for you here, Rem," Pete says calmly.

Remy doesn't respond but follows me to my room.

I feel his body warmth on my back as I slide my key into the slot. I hear him breathing behind me, still a little unevenly, against my hair. I want him, but I can now see past my open door to the first of the queen beds, where Diane's feet stick out.

My nipples are two hard points pushing into my bra, my panties soaked from all night of desperately wanting him. I want him so bad I feel a knot of need and frustration doubling in size in my throat—because I can't have him. How will things change if we do anything? It just can't work. It can't *be.* I'm his employee and this is only temporary and a one-night stand with him is no longer an option. Is it? I like him too much. Oh, god. I like him. Too. Much.

"Good night," I whisper, forcing myself to look at his handsome face.

The violent tenderness in his eyes seeps into every pore of my body, and he grabs me and plants a kiss on my lips, quick and dry, but it bursts open a wealth of longing inside me, like it did the first night he kissed me in Seattle, and he whispers, "You look beautiful." He runs his thumb with desperation along my jaw and tilts my chin up, kissing my lips, dry and quick again. "So damn beautiful I couldn't take my eyes off you all evening."

Then he's gone, and I'm once again in my room, hearing him call me beautiful, I'm so *beautiful,* and I'm shaking as if I'm naked and alone in the middle of a hurricane.

All but ignoring Diane, I get ready for bed, cover myself with all the blankets, and put my fist against my lips as though that can lock his kiss in them, and an eternity later, I hate that I'm still awake, and that I'm still trembling.

And I just don't know what I'm going to do, but I want to make him mine more than I've ever wanted anything.

Even the Olympics.

SIX

MIAMI IS NOT SO HOT

We're flying to Miami today.

The front section of the plane is talking about Scorpion and the "off-ring fight" that almost ensued last night. I sit in the rear with Remy, and, as seems to be becoming usual, we've just brought out our headphones. He has his iPod in his hand and is already searching his songs, and I'm searching mine, not sure if what I'm choosing will be listened to by me or by him.

In the car on our way over, he extended his arm and whispered, "Fix my wrist for me."

He has the thickest, most dense wrist I've ever seen, and as soon as I started moving it, I just knew it was an excuse to get me to touch him, for it felt perfectly mobile, and my pussy clenched when I realized his ploy.

Does he want my touch as badly as I want his?

"Put a song on for me," he whispers now. Amazing, how one look from him can flip my heart over.

I nod, but I'm wavering between a couple of choices. He's searching around too, and I see him hesitate as well.

Neither of us is smiling anymore. Neither of us has smiled since yesterday. When we almost did something crazy and . . . wonderful.

I'm still looking for a song when he hands me his iPod and I plug my headphones in to listen. Survivor's "High on You" Starts up, and it flashes me back to his first fight as I pay attention to what the lyrics say.

They play in my ear, sounding fun, upbeat, and joyful, reminding me how I stood watching him fight, and later, how the crowd crushed around us and how his hand touched mine, and how we both felt electrified. . . .

I'm feeling so equally mischievous and frustrated, I just want to see what he'll do if I do something crazy, so I pull up a really fun older song I recently heard revived in an episode of *Glee* called "Any Way You Want It," by Journey, and I pass it over to him.

He starts listening with a smile, and when he realizes the chorus is basically saying he can get "it" any way he'd like, he lifts his eyes to mine. There's a question inside those eyes, and his gaze jumps restlessly between my eyes and lips, eyes and lips, until it falls and sticks on my lips. I lick them, and I notice his eyes seem weighted.

"Rem," Pete calls from up front.

"He's got headphones on, he can't hear you," I respond, my song having already ended.

"Jesus, stop turning him on, Brooke. Especially if you're not going to . . ."

A laugh escapes me, and Remy, oblivious to what Pete just said, seems deeply absorbed with me and the music. I don't know what his stare means, but he dips his head closer. "Play me another one," he commands roughly, his somber blue eyes staring intently.

I hesitate for a moment, but inside, I'm bubbling with lust

and mischief, so I go all out with another oldie that seems fitting, and play, "All I Wanna Do Is Make Love to You," by Heart.

The moment the chorus begins, I notice that his pupils are wildly dilated. My breath catches, and I realize by playing that song, I am basically begging the man to make love to me, to say that he will. . . .

Anxiety about the ravenous look on his face makes me slide back on the couch as he leans forward. His gaze holds mine even as he dips his dark head lower, his stare so hot it galvanizes me.

He slides his hand around my waist and brings me a little closer to him; then he angles his head and presses his lips into my ear. I think he just kissed my ear. My nerve endings sing when he grabs his iPod and puts on music for me. He plays "Iris" again, watching me as every beat steals my breath again, and the lyrics make me want to weep.

Flooded with longing, I cling to his gaze and listen; his eyes are as ardent and consuming as the words I'm hearing. When the song ends, he removes my headphones and pulls off his, his breath ragged and uneven as he leans into me and kisses my ear again.

"Do you want me?" he asks in a guttural voice that sends the hairs on my body up in alert.

I nod fiercely against his head, and his hands clench around my hips. He ducks into my neck and inhales me. A shudder bursts through me, and I'm awash with the sudden certainty that tonight, tonight after the first Miami fight, Remington is going to make love to me.

The rest of the flight he keeps his arm around my shoulders and pins me to his strong side, and he keeps toying sexually with my ear, the only place where the others can't really see what he's doing to me. He tugs my earlobe with his teeth, licks the shell of my ear, and has forgotten all about playing music for me. I shudder wantonly, wet and squirming as I keep glancing at his jeans, which burst with the fullness of his erection. The volume straining the denim is so staggering that my hands itch. My tongue wants to taste him, lick him. My pussy clenches in desperate desire.

We arrive at the five-star hotel, and the heady combo of anticipation and arousal I've been struggling with shoots through the roof when I realize Remy has booked me into the two-bedroom presidential suite with him. As the keys are handed out, everyone else seems to notice this too.

"I sincerely hope you know what you're getting into," Pete says in a concerned whisper, his brow scrunched worriedly at the corners.

Diane's eyes are almost tear-filled when she tugs me aside at the lobby. "Oh, Brooke, please reconsider rooming with me again?"

Riley comes over and looks at me with all openness, patting my shoulder like I'm going to war. "He's trying the hardest I've ever seen him try, all for you, B."

Their attitudes don't really confound me. I know they're worried this will end badly. I'm Remington's employee, and only a temporary one at that—and he has a bad reputation with tons of evidence behind it. He obviously has a little bit of a temper and can prove too hot to handle. But even though he's so strong, I know instinctively that he'd never hurt me, and he's never done anything to demonstrate otherwise. The rest doesn't matter right now. It just doesn't matter to me at all. I want him. With a force I haven't felt in years. And I'm going to go for it.

Maybe I have a red self-destruct button too?

The nerves about what will happen run me raw as we go up to our rooms to ready for the fight, and suddenly I need Melanie so bad I pull my cell phone out of my purse and immediately text her, since it's been a couple of days since I have.

Brooke: How's my BFFFFFFFFFFFF!

Melanie: Miz u! But I forgive u if u tell me you've gotten sexy piece of man-ass already!

Brooke: Oh, sigh

Melanie: What? You HAVE???

Brooke: Mel

Melanie: What?? What?

Brooke: I think I'm falling in love with him

❤ ❤ ❤

REMY TOOK MIAMI like an avalanche.

We're back from his first fight, and I'm still breathless with exhilaration. His opponents barely grazed him in the ring. He was supercharged, his body precise and so powerful he didn't even have to deliver many punches to knock down the other fighters. He swept through every one of them like he was on vacation, and by the end of the evening, people were screaming with delight and even the announcer was out of breath.

"May these poor men rest in peace! My goodness, this man can hit! You go, RIP!!!! Rip their heads off, you bad bastard! Riiiiptide, ladies and gentlemen! Riptiiiiiide!"

Even Riley was so excited from where he watched at the corner that he climbed on Coach's back and pumped his fists in the air, yelling his head off. Meanwhile, Pete seemed to have left his responsible self back in Atlanta, for before we left the Underground, he declared, "We should fucking celebrate!"

Before Remington even knew what happened, there was already a crowd heading with us to the hotel in about a dozen different cars. So now we're in the presidential suite with what feels like a thousand strangers, but of course, there can't possibly be so many for real. And actually, Pete says most of these people have previously partied with Remington, so they're only strangers to *me*.

The crowd is so vast, people are even pushing out into the hallway and making so much noise I can't help thinking what a blessing it is the other two enormous presidential suites at the top hotel floor are empty, or else we'd probably be looking for somewhere else to sleep tonight.

I'm disappointed I haven't even been able to see him since he showered and changed. He was flocked by admirers and is being brought to the hotel by a group of old Miami friends, who are letting him drive the Ferrari one of them brought.

Now, as I wind through all the people crammed in what is supposedly my and Remy's suite, I wonder if I should join the merriment and go all out and get drunk, when applause breaks out by the entry, followed by unmistakable cheers only one man I know can cause. He comes into the room carried on the shoulders of four guys. My heart stutters. He's got this big smile on his face, cocky Remy to the tenth power, high on his wins, and the women scream, high on *him*. "Remy! *Remyyyy!*"

"That's right—who's the man?" he shouts, and pounds his fists on his chest. I laugh, completely sucked in, mesmerized and enchanted by him. The aura he emanates makes him blaze like a sun tonight. If right now he said he could fly, I think we'd all believe him. Everyone present seems magnetized by him, helplessly gravitating to where he is. He spots me, and his smile softens and his eyes light with a strange, hungry, and somehow glowing look. "Brooke."

He hops down to his feet and beckons me forward, and the crowd parts to let me pass. He smiles at me, and his dancing blue eyes hold mine as he slowly walks forward and meets me halfway. He lifts me in his powerful arms and swings me around, and then he kisses me.

The instant he takes my lips, fireworks shoot off in my body.

All the pent-up desire of days and weeks adds up to this one moment when everything that I am, and everything that I want, is narrowed down to this. To *me,* pulling Remington Tate's dark head closer to mine as I open my mouth and let him give me anything and everything he wants to.

His kiss spins my stomach into a wild swirl. He holds me tightly by the hips and deftly moves his lips as he rubs his tongue to mine. A rumble vibrates deep in his core as he gathers me closer and forces me to feel his erection, all while he angles his head and tongue-fucks my mouth like there's no tomorrow.

People *whoot* loudly nearby, and when they tell him to *"go fuck that pussy!"* Remy tears free. He breathes harshly through his nose as he drags his mouth to my ear, where he whispers, hot and gruff, "You're mine tonight."

A fevered moan escapes me. He cups my face in those big hands that make me feel fragile and tiny, and he hungrily recaptures my mouth. He takes it slowly this time, as if I'm precious and valuable. "Tonight you're mine."

He looks into my face again, his eyes seething with desire. I think I just nodded in agreement, but I'm too shaky to know for sure. A sweltering fever runs unleashed through me. My legs won't stop trembling as every one of my cells screams in lust because I want him now. I want him *now.*

"Remy, I want you, take *me*!" a woman shouts, but he ignores her, ignores everything. But me.

His eyes dark and intent, he scrapes the sides of my face with the pads of his big, callused thumbs, then spreads his fingers wide over my scalp as he kisses me again, our mouths hot and wet as they blend, thirsty and anxious. I grip the soft gray material of the T-shirt he wears in my fists, dying with sensation. I don't even care who's watching, am oblivious to the crude things they're whistling. I hadn't realized how much I wanted this, *needed* this, until these shivers ripple through me and I'm in flux under his insistent sexy mouth, the look in his eyes that makes me feel like I'm the only woman alive to him.

"Take her to your room, Tate!" someone yells. But he seems engrossed only in me, and I in him.

Holding me protectively in his strong arms, he brushes my hair back as his lips buzz along the bare curve between my neck and collar, his fingers sliding up my neck as he once again, like a chant, nuzzles my ear and tells me, "Mine. Tonight."

"So are you." I'm cupping his jaw and searching his darkened gaze when, suddenly, he's plucked away by four men who swiftly swing him up in the air once more.

"Remy, Remy . . ." they chant, bouncing him in unison. Laughter fills me, and bubbles of happiness pop inside my chest. I'm happy for me. For him. For this night.

Nearby, Pete and Riley watch the scene with faces so bleak and pinched, it feels like they're burying a cadaver tonight.

"Have fun, guys!" I say laughingly as I approach. Very possibly both my grandfathers party better than these two. But they just shake their heads and keep looking positively glum.

"He's getting speedy," Pete mutters, mostly to Riley.

"I know, man. Shit."

"Yeah." Pete scratches his curls. "Did I actually instigate this whole party?"

"Prepare for crash landing," is all Riley returns, and then he heads down the hall, tossing his head from side to side.

Confusion hits me. "What's wrong?" I ask Pete.

"Nothing. Yet." He glances at his watch, then at Remy as he's carried back to the bar. "But anything goes off in a way he doesn't like, then we're going to be in trouble. Big. Trouble."

Glancing around, I see there are only smiles and laughter while crazy rock music from Remy's iPod bursts from the suite speakers. I truly don't know what these two are worrying about. Everyone is having fun, and Remington works as hard as anyone I've ever known. He deserves to let loose. Yes, he's a little hyper, but to me it's obvious that he's got a rush from the fight and it's been added to the same thing that has been having us both, Remington and me, feeling coiled like hungry cobras, for *weeks*.

All day today, when we came up to settle our suitcases in our suite, when we went down to lunch with the team, when he prepared before the fight—every instant of these moments—our eyes were wildly searching each other, and as soon as they locked, the sparks leapt between us in arcs so powerful the need to be with him cut me like whiplashes. Even at the fight, when he turned to look at me before it began, his blue eyes simmered with a fierce appetite to have me. I know that he feels the same hunger I do now as I wait in fevered anticipation of this evening. My body hums in arousal, and after such an amazing fight, I know Remington is buzzing like crazy. He's all jacked up. Stoked and primed.

His energy is so powerful tonight it actually pulls at every cell and atom in my body, bathing me in pure female awareness of his hot masculinity.

Now I watch as he pours some tequila shots behind the bar, and a striking blonde at his side squeezes lemon juice on her cleavage and adds a dab of salt. When she jams a shot glass right between her tightly squeezed tits, she tugs on Remy's wrist and signals for him to come get it. Jealousy clenches all my inner muscles, only loosening when Remy grabs the nearest man around and pushes his face into her boobs, laughing, loud and manly.

Then he grabs the two shots he'd poured and starts to come back to me.

His eyes lock on mine, and they go dark and wild. As dark and wild as the fluttering in my insides. He seems to want to party with no one but me, and that knowledge hits me square in the knees. Between my thighs, I've grown sensitive, wet, and swollen.

He carries a saltshaker and lemons in one of his palms. "Come here," he says, gruff but soft as he sets the shot glasses on a console by the entry. He sucks the lime wedge between his lips and bends his head to pass it to me. I open my mouth and the lime juice spills into my mouth from his; then he draws the fruit away and sticks his tongue in with mine. He groans—we both do—as we linger and kiss, licking each other until he groans once more and steps back to hand me the shot glass.

I've never gotten really drunk before, and suddenly I'm just glad it's with him. Reckless joy courses through my veins. I feel wicked and impulsive, doing everything I've never done. Taking the glass between my fingers, I toss back the liquid and feel it burn a path down my throat, and when he hands me the lime again, I'm absolutely crazy with excitement.

Repeating the same thing he did, I stick the lime wedge into my mouth, and he ducks and sucks the lime juice from me. A moan escapes me when he tugs the lime away and replaces it with his tongue. Need rips through me, and my arms go around his neck.

The empty shot glasses crash to the ground as he grabs my ass, boosts me up to the console, slides between my legs, and thrusts his tongue into my mouth.

He shoves his hips and hardness against me, the desperation in the move shooting lightning bolts through my body. "You smell so good . . ." he rasps into my ear. His hands clench on my thighs as he rubs his hardness against me. His mouth grazes a path down my temple, to my chin, and his lips my buzz, fast and fevered, over mine. "I want you now. I can't wait to get rid of these people. How do you like it, Brooke? Hard? Fast?"

"Any way you want it," I murmur, intoxicated with the feel of his arms, his mouth, the scrape through our clothes of his sex against my sex. I think my words make him remember the song I played, for he groans and ducks his head to lightly nibble on my lower lip.

"Wait here, little firecracker," he says, and he makes his way back to the bar.

We have a second set of shots, and then he goes off for rounds three and four, and I'm definitely woozy by the fourth. Being relatively new to drinking, I don't think my system is equipped to handle it. My head spins as I watch him go for round five with a dopey smile. Some of the men once again grab him and shoot him up in the air, shouting, "Who's the man? Who's the man?"

"You bet your asses it's me, *motherfuckers*!"

They set him back on his feet at the bar and then start yelling as they push an enormous glass of beer to him, and they shout at him, with triple cadence as their fists bump the granite, "Rem-ing-ton! Rem-ing-ton! Rem-ing-ton!"

"Cool down, guys," Pete says as he approaches, trying to calm things down.

"Who the fuck is this nerd?" one bearded guy says, and Remy grabs him and shoves him up against the wall as easily as if he weighed no more than a premature baby.

"He's my bro, you toad. Show some fucking respect."

"Calm down, dude, I was only asking!"

Remy drops him to the ground and goes back to fix our te-quilas.

I know he's going to come back to me with more shots, but

people keep detaining him, and my stomach is making noises. I can't feel my tongue, and suddenly I'm pretty sure I need to throw up.

Covering my mouth, I rush to the bathroom of the smallest but closest bedroom and ignore the couple making out on the bed as I charge into the bathroom, slam and lock the door, then drop at the side of the toilet, grab my hair, and barely manage to lift the lid as I puke my guts out.

Five minutes later I'm still at it, gasping as I begin to have a private pity party with myself. Right here in the bathroom.

God. My stomach. My poor liver. Poor me. I'm so *frickin'* glad I did track in my teenage years instead of te-kill-ya! I can't even believe Melanie likes to do this. I groan in misery as the nausea comes back up my throat again. I hang my head into the toilet once more and convulse as everything rips out of me.

When I think I'm done, everything is a blur and I'm still dizzy. I wash my mouth and search for my vitamins in the stuff I'd left in this room's bath in case I'd rather not share a bathroom with Remington, which seems like a great plan now that I might be spending all night puking. I grab a red-colored B complex and vitamin C mix and pop one in, and I figure I should start hydrating myself, but I feel too lazy to go get a water bottle, so instead I flush the toilet a third time, close the top, and lean my forehead against it in case I get nauseous again. I grab my phone and text Mel.

> Fel like shiz!@ Drunk as a firkin don%ky! but Im gunna furck Remy if i survve th8 teqila!

Then I think I even doze off.

❤ ❤ ❤

WHEN I COME to, my temples throb, and the noise outside in the main room is deafening. I have the good sense to wash my mouth and calm down the tangles in my hair and wash my hands; then I peer out into the bedroom. The lovers are gone, so I pad out into the living room toward the noise. No. Not noise. The pandemonium.

Blinking, I absorb the scene before me with disbelieving eyes. I don't know what's happened, but something. Definitely. Has. Happened. Feathers from torn pillows are littered everywhere. Glass crunches under my feet as I walk. People are shoving against each other, somehow drunk and panicked as they try to save themselves from something.

Then I see him.

Remington "Riptide" Tate, the sexiest man alive, is tossing anything in his path and yelling at the top of his lungs, "What the fuck did you tell her about me? *Where the fuck is she?*" while Pete is jacketless, and tieless, and desperate to calm him down. Remy flings a crystal decanter into the wall with a fantastic crash, and people scream both in fear and laughter while Riley tries ushering them out through the open suite doors.

My drunkenness instantly fades, or at least it drops down about fifty percent, and I am almost fully sober from the shock. I jump into action and start shoving all the bodies I come into contact with toward the door, "Out, out, *out!*" I scream like a banshee.

Remy hears my voice and whips around and sees me. His eyes flash with something feral as he tosses the lamp he has in his hands and sends it crashing with a big explosion of glass behind him. Then he starts for me.

But Pete grabs him back, pulling desperately at his arm. "See, dude? She signed a *contract*, remember? You don't need to destroy the hotel, man." As Remington stares into my eyes with an expression of pure raw pain, Pete rams something into his neck and his eyelids flutter.

His head slumps forward, and I freeze in complete and total horror. Clouds of confusion impede any rational thought as I try to process the fact that Pete, gentle Pete, just shot something up Remy's jugular.

Riley continues shoving people out of the room as Remy slumps down and Pete struggles to prop him up against the nearest wall. When we manage to get the last person out, Riley drapes one of Remy's arms around his neck and the other goes around Pete. His feet are dragging beneath his body as they start hauling him to the master bedroom, and when I hear his beautifully male voice speak, he sounds not only drunk now, but super drugged, his timbre low and barely intelligible.

"Don't let her see."

"We won't, Rem."

His head hangs forward as if he has no strength to support it. "Just don't let her see."

"Yeah, man, got it."

Icy dread spreads along my insides as I move dazedly, like a sleepwalker, and follow them to the door. I stay at the threshold, torn between going after him and my utter confusion about what's going on and my OCD, which just begs me to start cleaning all this damned mess—and then there are the tequila shots, which still make me feel like a donkey.

"What's wrong with him?" I ask Pete as they both come out. Riley heads out to the living room phone.

"He's fine, just a little low." Pete grabs the doorknob to close the door.

And suddenly I'm concerned out of my ever-loving mind and hold on to Pete's arm like a lifeline. "Don't pull this shit on me. What doesn't he want me to see?"

My voice trembles, but I'm so scared and drunk and sexually frustrated that if he doesn't give me an answer I think I may just go and smash the rest of what Remington left intact.

Pete hesitates, then pries my arm free from the death grip I seem to have on him. "He doesn't want you to see *him*."

I'm stunned speechless, but my need to make sure Remington is all right is so overpowering that I still try to go in. Pete quickly yanks me firmly aside.

"Look, he's been speedy since you got here, and this kind of thing happens after the speedy. All he needs is some physical contact to make him feel good, get him out of that funk, and he'll be fine soon. We knew it was coming; it was just a matter of days. It always begins when he can't be worn out in the ring. And the fact that he's been panting after you like a dog doesn't help, Brooke."

"And who the hell gives you the right to shoot chemicals up his veins, Pete?" I demand, reeling in fury on Remington's behalf.

"*He* does. A thousand trashed hotel rooms, Brooke—I've been with him a decade, and so has Riley. He's the most high-maintenance man you're ever gonna meet!"

Riley walks back to us with a bleak expression. "They're on their way."

"You got two?" Pete asks.

"Three. New ones. See if that will whet his damned stubborn appetite."

When I realize what they're talking about, I immediately want to hit them. "Three new what? *Prostitutes?*"

With a fresh glimmer of concern, Pete pats my shoulder in an appeasing *there-there* mode. "This is standard protocol, all right? These are clean women, and very expensive. He won't care who it is. We shouldn't have let him go so long without working that off, especially with *you* around. Sorry about being graphic, but this is our problem to fix now, and he can't fight like this tomorrow. Hell, it's going to be a miracle if we get him out of bed."

Something bleak and green twists inside me, knotting viciously in my chest. "I don't want those women here," I tell them with deceptive calm.

Maybe I don't have a say in the matter, but I remember Remy's kiss tonight, the gentle cup of his hands. His words. *You're mine tonight. . . .*

The sudden, vivid image of his body entwined with someone else's makes me want to rush to the toilet again and throw up. I'm a little drunk, or maybe already hungover. I don't know. But my heart hurts and my stomach roils at the mere thought of anyone else touching him. And suddenly I *do* need to cover my mouth and rush to the toilet again for real.

I spend the next twenty minutes there, then wash my mouth again, clean everything up, and wind my way back to the living room just in time for the stinking prostitutes to arrive. Riley seems to have gone down to the lobby to bring them up—as no respectable hotel would allow these women access on their own—and when Pete opens the door to let them inside, with their stinking perfumes and glittery ensembles, I gape and feel green and twisted all over again.

They're so beautiful, and I realize with horror I may be the kind of drunk who starts yelling at people and then crying, because I feel like doing both. And when I see Riley pull out his wallet to hand them several packets of *condoms*, I'm sure I can feel steam coming out of my ears. I'm so furious I charge forward and halt the women only two steps into the living room, all three of them stopping when they see my messed-up hair and my angry glare.

"We don't need your services anymore, ladies. I'm sorry for your time; here's cash for your expenses coming over."

Grabbing all the money in Riley's wallet, who is also the jerk who had the gall to *call* them, I shove the women out into the hall and slam the door in their faces. Then I spin around, a scowl biting into my face.

"That's the last time you call some tramps when he's like this," I say, sticking a finger out threateningly, my heart pounding in pure rage and protectiveness. "I realize I'm in no condition to make decisions here, but neither is *he*. He doesn't *want* them!" I cry.

The men, both of them completely sober and always quite sharp in their "bodyguard-looking" suits and ties, though Pete lost a little form tonight, just stare at me in utter confusion, making me feel like I've gone mad.

Well?

Have I?

I'm not sure. But my chest aches for the man in the master bedroom and my breasts heave from my fast breaths as I fight to stand my ground. I *know* what these guys are thinking. I know they want to know why the hell I won't let those women in. They think *I* want to fuck Remington, and that I think he truly wants *me*. And maybe I do. I desperately *do*. I not only want to fuck him, I may possibly have gone all out and developed deep, complicated feelings for him.

But the thought of anyone touching him makes me want to breathe fire. I don't care that he's not mine. I care that Pete just shot something up his veins, his beautiful body is on standby and his brain is powered down. If I can stop this nightmare from happening, I will, and I just *did*.

"I'm not drunk now," I state to the men when they only keep staring at me.

Both of them sigh. "I'm going to bed in case he starts up again when it wears off," Riley says, and stalks to the door.

"Don't go in there," Pete warns to me, gesturing toward the master bedroom. "Sleep in the other room. He's possibly not going to remember anything you say right now, and if what we gave him wears off too soon, he can get more difficult than you can imagine."

"Fine," I lie, and go to other room to get into my sleep shirt. But I just can't leave it at that, and when the door shuts after Pete, I know Remy and I are alone.

Wending my way through the minefield of glass everywhere and shoving aside the compulsion to clean up, I go into the master bedroom. My pulse is a frantic drum pounding at my temples as I take in the scene. The drapes are partly open, and I feel a rush of possessiveness and protectiveness surge through me as I spot his shadowed form on the bed, briefly illuminated by the city lights. I tell myself I just want to make sure he's okay. But I'm so wired and worried, I'm afraid seeing him won't be enough and I'm going to need to search for a pulse or something.

Easing quietly inside, I trap my breath in my throat and soundlessly close the door behind me.

Silently I remove my shoes, then approach him with light steps. My eyes adjust to the shadows. He's facedown on the bed, and when he groans, my heart goes crazy with pain. The sheets rustle and the mattress squeaks as he shifts, and I'm so crazy about this man, I just want to eat him up with a spoon and do a whole lot of other things I've never wanted to do with anyone else.

The bugs flutter all over my stomach as I remember him telling Pete and Riley not to let me see. Does he worry about what I think of him? I really want to tell him he's still "all *that*" to me. I want to tell him a lot of nice things. How well he fought. That I think he's the hottest thing I've ever seen. That he's had me walking on cloud nine all night just with his kisses. I know that I too needed to hear this when my world came crashing down, my body broke and my spirit caved in, and Mel held my hand and told me I was still her number one. I want Remy to know I would also proudly hold up a poster that says I'm his number one fan. But I just can't talk through this ball of emotion in my throat. I'm so worried to see him like this it's eating me. And my liver isn't coping so well, so I'm experiencing about a thousand emotions I don't even know how to deal with right now. I think I just want to caress and cuddle him, but I'm afraid he'll kick me out if he knows I'm here.

Nervous as I lean over, I set a hand on his big bare shoulder. His warmth seeps from his smooth skin and into me as I bend to the shell of his ear and softly buzz my lips along his earlobe, like he did to me in the plane.

The scent of his shampoo and the natural smell he emanates that drives me mad with lust seeps into me, and I can't help but slide my fingers down his back, over the round curve of his buttocks.

He's so beautiful, my body weeps with longing to know his.

Lightly, full of regret for our lost night, I touch up the curve of his back and shiver at the contact of his warm skin, silken and smooth, sliding under my fingers. My pussy grips with pure longing, and a selfish part of me desperately wants him to open his eyes, see me, and pull me into his arms until we're both out of breath and exhausted from what's been building.

But another part of me dreads that he will send me away.

There's such a high probability that he will. I don't even know why I'm still here, when I was so clearly warned to stay away. Maybe I'm weaker than Remy is. Maybe I'm crazier. I just want to be next to him tonight. He's sedated, big and helpless right now, and I just know he would never hurt me.

As quietly as possible, I edge to the side of the bed and spread my body out next to his. Suddenly he groans softly and rolls over fully to his back, and I hold my breath as the complete expanse of his beautiful muscled body is exposed to me.

My breath just goes.

His nakedness in the moonlight makes me wet in the mouth, and between my legs, legs that feel like cotton now. I can see every muscle in his body, see where each adjoins the next, and how his skin is perfectly tight over every inch. I could delineate each muscle with a pencil. He's so perfectly virile, I'm blazing hot and drenched, and I'm just desperate to feel his lips under mine, his tongue grazing mine.

I want him to wake up so I can tell him that I want him, in my mouth, inside me. I want to strip off my clothes and glue every inch of my skin to his golden body. I want to bend down and touch and kiss him right *there,* where he's just as big and hard as the rest of him. Right there, where he's so much . . . man.

Briefly, I allow my eyes to caress him, the length of his muscled legs, his narrow hips, his beautiful cock, so thick and long and velvety . . . up the sexiest star tattoo I've ever seen and then up higher over his washboard abs, his hard chest, his thick, powerful neck, and to his gut-wrenchingly handsome face.

His eyes are closed, his lashes two dark moons against his high cheekbones, his jaw perfectly square, even at rest. I stroke a finger across the scratchy stubble there.

"You're so beautiful, Remy."

He groans and turns his face into the touch, and I wrap my arm around his waist and cover us up, listening to his breathing, his big chest rising and falling as I press my body to his for warmth.

I must have eventually fallen deeply asleep. By the time his cell phone alarm goes off at 5 a.m. neither of us hears it, and it's 10 a.m. when Riley wakes us up, clapping and laughing to get our lazy asses out of bed because Rem could use a trip to the gym today.

Riley actually seems delighted that I appear to have "slept" with Remy. He was probably eager for Remy to work off whatever "it" was, either with those prostitutes or with me.

Because he leaves quickly, Riley totally misses the way we both jump to a sitting position after his little wake-up call. Remington looks anything but groggy the instant he notices me across the opposite side of the bed. I think my hair is tousled and I must look every inch as trampled as I feel, but I can't help noting his beautiful body is fully naked and the most amazing thing I've ever seen by daylight.

We take each other in for several heartbeats.

Heartbeats where every kiss he gave me last night swells in my memory and on the flesh of my lips.

The sunlight streams into the room, and the bed is undone, and we're both in it, and our eyes are wildly going up and down.

A desperate urge to jump his sexy bones rushes through me, and I notice the primitive alertness that settles in his eyes as he quietly rakes me, top to bottom, as my body shakes in lust inside an old Disney World T-shirt courtesy of one of Melanie's yearly "stay young" trips.

His eyes look so dark this morning I swear to god there's not a fleck of blue in that hot-deviled gaze anymore.

❤ ❤ ❤

BEFORE REMY COULD even ask what I was doing in his bed, I had hopped to my feet and briskly left to change, insanely aware of his eyes tracking my movements across the room.

But he never came after me.

"It's normal, when this happens." Pete shrugs at the gym, when Remy doesn't appear after two hours. "You might want to do something with your day, Brooke. There's no point in you not enjoying yourself and getting a little sun."

Really, after a night of drinks, the word "sun" is not as welcoming as it is usually to me, but I nod and walk a little of Miami, trying to soak up the amazingly vibrant cultural mix of Latinos and others, but I just don't have the energy for it.

I've never been hungover in my life.

It's definitely an experience I don't *ever* want to repeat.

I find that no matter how much water I drink I'm still parched. I'm also nauseous and foggy-headed, weak and unwell, and I can barely open my eyes wide enough to see where I'm going.

But I still make an effort, and decide to call my parents as I head down the shops at Midtown Miami.

"Where are you now?" my mother demands. "Your father wants to know if you're going to that famous restaurant, What's-It-Called, the one where the movie stars go?"

"Mother, I'm *working*," I tell her. "This isn't a vacation to me. And if you *told* me the actual name of What's-It-Called, I might have a clue about what you're talking about."

"Oh, never mind! But we got a new postcard from Nora! She's in Australia, and she sends all her love. You should see the beach in the picture, goodness! Now *that's* paradise. I wonder if she's seen any real alligators. Or is it crocodiles that live there? Crocodiles or alligators?"

"Crocodiles, Mom. And I think there are some here in Florida, as well. Hey, I don't want to run out of battery; I'll call you next weekend, all right? I just wanted to check up on you."

After quick goodbyes, I hang up, because it was seriously not a good idea to call my parents today. They're great and I love them, but they're my *parents*.

They're nosy and opinionated and they naturally get on my nerves. I especially resent the fact that their dreams for my worldwide stardom shattered the day that my knee tore, and I know that they don't truly believe that I will ever be able to live a "full" life now.

It would be so much easier to deal with them if Nora would do more than just send a monthly postcard too.

Heading back to the hotel, I spot Diane at the gift shop, and she encourages me to share a quick lunch.

"Pete tells me our guy isn't doing well today," she says, her tone both questioning and sad.

I pick at my salad and keep hydrating with natural fruit juice, merely because my temples have been throbbing all day. I just know my liver is not used to the kind of abuse it received yesterday. I've always treated my body kindly. Today it's just angry at me for alcohol overload, bad food choices, and unfulfilled lust.

"Does it happen frequently?" I ask, looking up from my lettuce with vinaigrette to her.

She nods.

"I see," I say weakly, and set my fork down. "Is it because he doesn't handle alcohol well or is it some sort of anger issue?"

"I'd say it's an anger issue but I don't know for sure." Lifting her iced tea, Diane leans back and shrugs. "I'm the one who knows the least about it. All I know is Remy is a handful." She nods meaningfully and sips through the straw. "A *handful*. Which is why I really, truly want you to reconsider before you . . . well, of course, unless you already . . . ?"

"Nothing happened, Diane." I rub my forehead and ask for the check.

We sign off and she invites me over to her room to check recipes, but instead I go to the suite, which I notice Pete or Riley kept closed with a DO NOT DISTURB sign hanging from the doorknob. I head inside anyway and quietly start cleaning up the worst of the mess.

It takes hours to get the room into a semblance of order, and once I've got all the glass in piles near the door, I call housekeeping and request a dozen plastic bags to haul it all out. Once that's done, I jump in the shower.

I'm still sleeping in the presidential suite, no matter that Diane offered to have me room with her tonight. I just . . . can't go anywhere else. I *wanted* to sleep with Remy, and now that we're sharing a room for the first time, I'm not moving out and leaving him alone here.

Especially if he's unwell.

But at night, the suite feels so deathly quiet, my heart won't settle as I stare wide awake in my own bed, thinking of him, of everything that's happened. I want to ask Pete and Riley about what's wrong, and on the other hand, I want *Remington* to tell me.

I don't know how much time passes, but eventually the bedroom door opens while I'm still staring bleakly at the wall. I'm groggy, but I sit up and see his silhouette. He must have taken a bath. A pair of pajama bottoms drapes low on his narrow hips. His tan torso glistens, and his hair is all wet and spiky, not a strand falling on his proud forehead.

My heart shudders. I think the sedative has worn off, since he stands perfectly upright, with only one hand braced lightly on the door frame, maybe for support. I straighten up higher on my arms.

"Are you all right?" I ask, my voice concerned and cottony.

His voice is gruff and craggy. "I want to sleep with you. Just sleep."

My stomach turns.

He waits for me to reply, but I can't. I want to cry and I don't know why, but I attribute it to being hungover and dangerously close to falling in love with a man I don't even know.

He comes over, lifts me, and carries me down the hall, back to the master room, to the wide, unmade king bed.

He sets me down, and when he slides under the covers and

gathers me close so that my face is on his chest and his nose is buried in the top of my head, I don't understand the overwhelming sensations I feel, but this . . . him . . . being in this bed with *him* . . . makes me feel way too good. Too safe. Too happy.

I desperately want him to tell me what's wrong. What happened? Can't he control himself? Why did Pete and Riley react like this? Does Remy have a problem with violence and unresolved anger issues? Who the fuck *hurt* him? I think of why he was kicked out of boxing, how angry he'd been with Scorpion at the club, how dangerously close to sabotaging his career again. But I don't think he wants to talk right now. He seems lazy and gentle, and the darkness, the silence, feels so holy, I don't want to break it.

Instead, I lie next to him while every pore in my body screams for us to physically connect. I try not to want it, because I know that this is not the moment. I don't know what kind of sedative he was given, or how long it lasts, but I know that later he might not even remember that he's here with *me*. Even *I* might not remember. I'm so tired and hungover I don't trust my thoughts at this point.

"Just sleep, okay?" I whisper at his throat, even though I swear I ache for this man somewhere beyond my body, beyond even my heart.

"Just sleep." He pulls me closer to him, and I can feel his erection between us, fiercely hard and pulsing with life, making me shiver inside. "And this," he murmurs.

He cups my jaw and puts his lips on mine with such gentleness that all my cells seem to fuse with his. I moan and part my lips, sliding my hands into his hair, feeling a little crazy as I push my breasts up to his chest. Suddenly I want his hands on me, I want his tongue all over me. When he brushes it, slick and hot, against mine, I feel like I vanquished the impossible. Trembling, I clutch his face, kissing him harder.

He slows me down with his tongue, his fingers twined in my

hair, guiding my head to the slow, drugging rhythm of his mouth. God, I want him to touch me in all the parts where he can fit. Everywhere. Anywhere. I'm so swollen and ready, I thrum, and he's so hard between our abdomens, I know how much he wants me too. But he said just "sleep" . . . and "this" . . . and now I don't want "this" to stop.

He kisses me so slowly and so deeply that I run out of breath. He only unlatches my mouth to allow me to catch my breath, and then he brushes his tongue back against mine, stroking my lips, the roof of my mouth, and my teeth. He suckles, sucks, turns, twists. I fall in love with his kiss so fast, that soon I don't know where my hands are, where I'm lying.

My entire body is consumed by the way he fucks my mouth until my lips are raw and swollen and it hurts to kiss him back even though my frenzied body demands more. When I'm sure I've tasted blood from either his lips or mine or both, I draw back to breathe and pant, noticing his cut has reopened. He's the one bleeding from kissing me. I moan softly and lick him gently, and he groans with his eyes closed. He sifts his fingers down my hair and pushes my face to the crook of his neck, cuddling me, his chest rising hard and fast under mine.

The sheets are somewhere at our feet but he's so hot and warm that I press as tight as I can to his body and fall asleep.

When I stir during the night, I'm awakened by the odd, novel sensation of a powerfully built arm tightening around me and settling me back against the spot I've warmed against him. My extremities tingle when I peek up at his shadowed face and take in the fact I'm in bed with him. He's sleeping, or at least he appears to be. Then he turns his head, his eyelids parting, and when he sees me, he kisses my lips again, licking them softly before he draws back to press his nose into my hair, tucking me back into him.

SEVEN

COME AWAY WITH ME

We're flying to Denver now.

Pete and Riley ride up front with Diane and Lupe, and I'm in the back of the plane with Remington. He's got his beats on, but I don't, since I'm trying to listen to Pete and Riley's heated conversation. Remy hasn't trained in four days, even after we slept in the same bed together. I had changed and waited downstairs that morning, but Remy never appeared. He didn't come out of his room any of the following days either.

Except for me.

There's something going on between us, and I'm afraid to give it a name. For the past three evenings, he's come to get me from my room and carry me back to his, and on the last one, I even stayed the full day until it was time to get to the airport.

At night we kiss each other like it's all we've been waiting for during the day, which in my case is the complete truth. Melanie texted after my drunken message about having sex with Remy. She wanted to know if I'll be popping out little Remys soon, but I just don't know what we're doing. The way he kisses me feels like

I'm his crack and he gets high on me. As soon as we hit the bed, his mouth fuses with mine and doesn't let go. His arms hold me pinned to his body as if I ground him. I feel like his anchor, and he feels as powerful and exciting as a free fall.

"His points can't keep him in first place forever," Riley mutters now, and there's no mistaking the impending doom in his voice. "He's already down to second, verging on third for missing that second Miami fight. He can't lose a single night, and he definitely can't miss another fight."

Unlatching my seat belt, I make my way to them with a frown. "What's wrong?" I remain standing in the aisle and prop a shoulder on the back of Diane's seat.

"Remy can't miss any more fights. It's all about points, so if we're going for first, then he can't miss any more fights and he *certainly* can't afford to lose."

"He's not eating," Diane says ruefully.

"He's not training," Coach adds bitterly.

"And his eyes are still black."

I scowl at that last from Pete, and realize, that yes . . . for the past days, Remy's eyes have looked really dark. But we also haven't slept. We're just kissing like maniacs all night and our bodies are haywire, and we've been ordering room service because I can't seem to get him to agree to allow anyone from his team to come into the suite. I stare at their bleak faces, and Riley shakes his head.

"If he goes out with those devil black eyes to fight and one little part of him disagrees with what the referee says, he might take the fucking asshole out."

I scowl. "Don't be ridiculous. He knows the rules. And he's not a machine to go twenty-four/seven. Let him recover. He trains even Sundays; he's dangerously close to being overtrained. Every athlete needs downtime."

"Remy is not every athlete; if he doesn't train, he gets speedy," Pete tells me.

I roll my eyes, sick of the term already. "Anything *not* drive him speedy?"

"Actually, yes. Peace and quiet. But he's not turning into a monk anytime soon, is he?"

Seriously, I don't see what's so wrong about him taking time out. Some of my athlete friends get completely depressed and crash after competition. What comes up so high has to come down, and neurotransmitters sometimes get a little wacky. "Look, your body can only be pushed so far, especially the way *he* pushes. So he missed a fight? Big deal. His strength will likely improve with a couple days' rest and he'll kick ass in Denver."

They fail to respond and study me in silence, and I know they're wondering what the hell is going on between us since Remington is acting really possessive of me, glaring at Pete whenever he talks to me and even at Riley when he offered to help with my suitcase today. Grabbing it out of his hand, Remy asked him if he had nothing else to do other than stare at me.

Yes, they seem desperate to know what's going on between Remington and me. But since even *I* don't know, I guess we'll all remain wondering.

Sighing at the silence, I turn to go back, and when I do, awareness shoots through me as I spot him watching me.

There's something very male in his eyes as he watches me return. It's a dark, possessive look, and it triggers a little ripple to slide along my nerve endings. I'm flashed back to the four nights we spent in the presidential suite, where we locked out the world. I feel like Beauty and the Beast, except I willingly locked myself in with my beast so he could kiss me senseless, and *he's* the beautiful creature who tortures me with wanting him.

I'm close to shuddering as I remember. Remy's hand sliding up my throat. His eyes half-closed as he looks down at me. Our ragged breathing. His mouth hot and damp and shamelessly kissing me. He only kisses my mouth, my throat, and my ears. He licks and tastes, and triggers all kinds of sensations in my body.

I remember moaning. Remember the way he smiles against my lips at the drawn-out sound, and the way he turns very serious and intense as he comes back to taste me and suck my lower lip before biting and suckling the skin at my throat. I remember his body pressing against mine and my pussy throbbing with the nearness of his erection. Our tongues. Hot and desperate, flicking and probing. I want him so much it's all I can think about. I think I begged him last night, "Please . . ." but I was so drugged with lust I'm not even sure. What I do know is that he stops sometimes, when his breath is crazy fast, and takes a cold shower.

But then he comes back, wearing drawstring pants or tight sexy boxers, and once again envelops my body with the sheer size and protective shield of himself, only to bend that dark head to mine and continue the torture. He fucks my ear with slow, deep flicks of his tongue. He does the same to my mouth. Laps at and tastes my throat. My collarbone. He gets me so hot, my teeth chatter from the way the air feels so cold on my flesh. Arousal drips down my thighs. My nipples become hard as diamonds. He works me into a lather, to the point where a mere movement of his mouth makes me moan from deep inside, like I've just been penetrated.

He's taking it so slowly with me I feel like a teenager and a virgin, though I certainly am neither. But I feel claimed, and bonded to him like animals do. I feel like I've been already caught and trapped and he's merely priming me, leaving me to simmer in my juices, anxiously waiting for the moment when he takes his first bite.

I seriously can't stand it and am wet even *now.*

We don't talk much when we bond in his bedroom. I sense I'm sort of in his man-cave these days, and I understand it's his territory. Yesterday, he didn't even let me come out, and kept me pinned down in his bed, a helpless slave to his kisses.

When we need to stop, sometimes we listen to music, turn on the TV, or eat. But most of all, we kiss. I sometimes hear nothing but the slick sounds of him on me, and our fast breaths, tearing one after the other. The night before last, I was so primed by the time he came to fetch me from my room, I almost jumped into his arms. By the time we sank into his bed, my hands were already in his hair, my tongue desperately pushing into his warm, delicious mouth, and he responded with an animal growl and a powerful kiss so feverish I felt each of his pulls on my tongue ping quick bolts of pleasure to my sensitized little clit. It swells and throbs when we kiss, and I get delirious remembering it. Now just the tiniest look from him swells me up. When he glances at my lips. When he tucks a loose strand of hair behind my ear. I know we're sending our adrenals to hell, doing this. Keeping up the output of this lust is just not healthy, but I can't stop him. In fact, I want more. I want him to stop because we're suffering and I want him to go on until I lie dead in his arms, burnt to ashes from my want of him.

I want him. Every hour, minute, and second.

I wanted him that first night, even though I tried to brainwash myself and pretend I didn't. And now I want him like I want to breathe, to eat, to live a happy life, to see my sister again, to be satisfied in a career. I want him like I want to live my present without any fear whatsoever of what may, or may not, happen tomorrow.

I'm not even afraid that he will hurt me. I *know* this will hurt.

When I go back home, when this has to stop, it's going to hurt. Nothing lasts forever and I know it better than anyone.

But fear has never been a friend of mine.

When I decided to compete in track, it wasn't with a fear that I would lose, or that I would break my knee and have wasted a decade of my life training for nothing. You go after something because you want it bad enough to expend every one of your efforts to get it and will even risk some losses in its pursuit. Now, all the efforts in my body seem to hone in on the soul-consuming physical need for closeness to this man. Sometimes when I stretch him out, the need to feel him embedded deep inside me where he makes it *hurt* is so overwhelming that I just don't even know what to do with it and I need to stop.

Even now, I realize I've settled down as close as I can without sitting on top of him, all the length of my pink jean–clad thigh pressing against his jean-clad thigh, and he smiles the dimpled smile that curls my toes, because I think he likes me to be close to him too. He takes off his headphones and then ducks his head to me, as if silently asking me to tell him what's going on.

"They're worried about you."

He turns to hold my look. "Me or my money?"

His quiet question feels as intimate to me as what he whispered to me when he kissed me in his room last night, when he whispered *kiss me back* and called me *pretty* and kept telling me I *smell so good*.

"You. And your money," I tell him.

Those dimples come again but only briefly, appearing as if two angels just squeezed his lean cheeks. "I'm going to win. I always do."

I smile, and when his gaze drops to my smile, an awareness of my mouth seizes me.

My lips feel swollen and red today, raw from his. His eyes darken even more as he studies them, and a shiver rushes through me. I try to stifle it at the same time I fight not to stare back at his own beautiful mouth, which *does* look deliciously, gut-wrenchingly pinker and thicker from my kisses today.

"Do you want to run today? To get ready for tomorrow?" I ask him, and it's taking all my effort to focus on anything but the fire raging inside me.

He shakes his head.

"You're tired?" I prod.

He nods with sad eyes, his voice low, but not apologetic. "So fucking tired I could barely pull myself out of bed."

I nod in understanding, because I feel a little of that too. I didn't want to get up. Especially with this enormous muscled man in the same bed, where I just wanted to torture myself all over again with my wanting him.

I lean back, feel his shoulder against mine on the backrest, and I want to curl up like I did last night after we couldn't keep up the kissing and caught a couple of hours of sleep. I think he senses I'm tired too, and he shifts slightly so I can rest my head on him.

He passes me a song.

I'm too lazy to pass him any of mine, so I just listen. Norah Jones's smoky, beautiful "Come Away with Me" begins playing, sensually proposing that I do exactly as the title suggests.

The tone is so sexy and reminds me so badly of our nights together, our stolen moments kissing, that it gives me a fever. Suddenly he leans over to try to listen through my earphones, and when I get a closer whiff of his clean male scent, my muscles throb painfully tight. I instantly grab my music and select a modern song that's been playing on the radio lately about a boxer who's strong and fights incredibly hard. I wanted to play "Iris" for him. I wanted to play something to beg him to make love to me. But his team is worried, and I know that whatever we're doing at night isn't conducive to good athletic performance. No matter how much I crave those moments and crave what they're leading to, I can't sabotage him like this. He's too important.

I watch his profile as he listens. His expression is unreadable at first. When he finally raises his head, his gaze is dark and troubled. "You play me a song about a fighter?"

I nod.

He tosses my iPod aside with a scowl. Then he reaches around and grabs my hips. He drags me onto his lap, and my breath goes when I feel how much, how unmistakably, he wants me.

"Give me another one," he demands.

The primal look in his eyes makes me shudder.

I shake my head. "We can't keep doing what we're doing, Remy. You need your sleep," I whisper.

"Give me another song, Brooke."

He sounds so stubborn that I want to scowl, but it actually . . . excites me. He wants my songs as badly as he wants my kisses, and it makes me high. All right then. If he wants it, then we need to go all the way tonight and make love, not just jack ourselves up. So I find "Iris" and hand him my iPod. I straighten and watch his profile as he listens. He is unreadable once more, but when he raises his head this time, his eyes are torpedoes of heat. His erection is fierce under my lap, and I feel his heart pulsing rhythmically there. In his hardness.

"Ditto," he says.

"To what?"

His eyes flick up to the other passengers before grabbing my hair and drawing my head down so he can lick my lips side to side with his tongue. "To every lyric."

I shudder and pull back. "Remy . . . I've never had an affair before. I just won't share you. You can't be with anyone else while you're with me."

He strokes a thumb across my damp lower lip, his gaze intense. "We won't be having an affair."

I stare dumbly, certain I just heard an organ in my chest crack open.

His hands clamp around me, and he crushes me to his body as he slides his nose along the shell of my ear. "When I take you, you'll be mine," he says, a soft promise in my ear. He slides his thumb along my jaw, then gently kisses my earlobe. "You need to be certain." His eyes are so hot that I'm on fire with the lust in them, and the word "mine" makes the empty place between my legs swell with longing. "I want you to know me first, and then, I want you to let me know if you still want me to take you."

The word "take" is also having an effect. I'm just a big mass of quaking need. "But I already know I want you," I protest.

He looks at my lips with fierce intensity, then into my eyes, his stare so pained and tormented I'm stunned with the darkness I see. He strokes a hand down my bare arm, waking up all the little hairs there. "Brooke, I need you to know who I am. What I am."

"You've had tons of women without this requisite," I plead.

His big hands engulf my bottom as he hauls me closer again, his eyes brimming with need, gobbling up my features and drowning me in their depths.

"This is my requisite with *you*."

A flash of wild need rips through me as I realize what he's telling me.

He won't take me yet.

Even when it's all I think about. All I want.

Today, it's daylight, and I'm still living in the last bed I was in, with him, with his mouth devouring mine.

He wants me to know him, and I *want* to know him, but if I

know him and like him just a little bit more than I already do, our emotional connection will be too strong for me to ever go back to the way I was *before* him.

He's powerful physically, but emotionally, he demolishes me. I can't take much more of this. And neither should *he*.

Feeling an odd heaviness in my chest, I lean into his ear and whisper, "We still can't keep this up, Remy. Not when your championship is on the line. So you either come get me tonight to make love to me, or you leave me alone so we can both rest."

I expect this threat to elicit more of a reaction. He's a man. This is an open invitation to uncomplicated sex, just what men want. I'm making it easy for him, basically accepting him "as is," no more questions asked. He will either work it out in bed with me and be able to train tomorrow, or he'll have a restful night of sleep without me.

He studies my face with eyes that I notice are definitely, definitely, not blue today. "All right," he says, with a smile I'm not quite sure reaches his eyes.

He sets me down at his side, grabs his iPod, clicks his own music, and doesn't give me another song.

So now I guess I won't be sleeping with him either.

Wow.

I think I just broke my own heart.

❤ ❤ ❤

WE'RE IN LOS Angeles now, and the weather here is so blessed by the gods, I just want to be outside all day. Diane and I are roommates again, and we love having breakfast on our little balcony.

In fact, ever since we went to chilly Denver almost a week ago, ever since my idiotic make-love-to-me-or-die ultimatum to Remy, we've been back to sharing quarters. Although *I* was totally forlorn to realize I was no longer *his* roommate to be deliciously taken at night, Diane was so excited when we got to our room, she actually leapt over and hugged me. "You should room with me more often, you!"

Turns out Remington booked us a presidential suite like his, and we each had our own room, with a shared living room and dining area. I still didn't know if I wanted to sigh, or laugh, or cry, that's how wound up he's got me.

That evening we arrived, I remember his body in my hands, his sweaty bare skin under my fingers, and it was all I could do to keep my pulse under control as I rolled and rubbed the firm, lean nape of his neck. I edged closer to whisper in the back of his ear, "Mind telling me why Diane and I are in a suite, Remy?"

He let me turn his neck to one side, then the other, my fingers lightly resting on his scratchy jaw with a sexy day's worth of whiskers, and he never answered. "You can't do this, Remington," I added.

But he turned his head slowly, and he touched my lips so that every part of my body remembered having his lips on them. "Stop me. I dare you," he said, then grabbed his towel and walked away.

I just don't understand him.

I miss having Melanie to talk to.

I wish I could talk to Nora too. My little sister is always in crush, in lust, or in love with a boy, and I'm sure she would know why in the world an insanely sexy man who's single and healthy and clearly physically *responds* to you does not seize the opportunity to have sex with you.

If I were a little less confident, I'd be experiencing all kinds of complexes right now.

Although, I am beginning to wonder if my body is no longer attractive with the extra little fat I've gained in the past years. Maybe my hair needs a new cut other than the plain length I wear it. I might wear bangs. Or add some highlights?

"Stop staring at yourself—you look amazing in anything you wear," Diane tells me this morning when she catches me checking out my butt in the full-length mirror at the entry of our room.

I laugh, but it's not funny.

Remy booked Diane and me in a presidential suite again in LA.

I don't want a suite. But what I *want*, he won't give to me.

I'd never let anyone get to me like this.

I used to feel pretty, and whether or not a man agreed with me was beside the point. I *liked* myself and that was enough.

Now I find myself feeling a little sad during the day, and Diane often finds me staring at a stupid wall, helplessly wondering what Remington thinks of me.

This is our third night in LA, and he's still in second place point-wise, but he's been fighting like a champion. He's worked out the best I've ever seen him, and all this ever since his eyes became electric blue again in Denver.

He trains like an *animal*. Hours and hours with Coach, and then he still seems as fresh as sunshine when he comes to ask me to run with him in the evenings. The energy in his muscles explodes like dynamite with every move he makes, and I can almost *see* his ATP—the adenosine triphosphate in charge of transporting chemical energy throughout our cells—recycling so quickly in his body that it's like it doesn't even take him the usual eight seconds for turnover. I have *never* seen him so focused. So strong. Or so magnificent.

Every part of me notices.

Every.

To my despair.

Pete and Riley are stoked. "Brooke!" Pete calls as I enter the Underground in the afternoon. Here in LA, the fighting ring is situated in the basement of one of the city's most frequented nightclubs, and they're expecting a full house of over a thousand. "Get over here, we need you." Pete waves me into the locker room.

The whole sexy package of Remington Tate is seated in a bench at the far end while Coach wraps his right hand with tape.

I'll never get used to the feeling I get when I look at him.

Nor the one I get when he's about to fight.

I feel wound up like a spring and tighter than a triple knot.

He's got his Dr. Dre Beats on; I think he listens to music to get in the fighting mode and zone everything out.

"Come on over, Brooke, loosen up the man."

Riley and Coach greet me with twin nods, and I notice the instant that Remington spots me, he hooks his thumbs into his headphone cords and yanks them down to drape around his neck. The look we exchange is, in fact, so intent, we don't smile at each other. The answering smile I'd given to Riley and Coach vanishes from my face as the heavy metal song Remy had been listening to trails into the room.

Quietly, I lean over to pause his iPod; then I go behind him and seize his shoulders, methodically working my thumbs into his muscles.

There are a couple of knots I worked off his posterior deltoids and trapezius muscles yesterday. They've been stubborn and keep returning, so once again, I work on both. He groans the instant my bare skin touches his. God. The low, purr-like sound is like foreplay to me. It steals into every feminine part in my body, especially those that have been run ragged with need. My cheeks start burning as Coach, Pete, and Riley watch us.

I drop my face so they can't see my blush and resist the urge to draw my hands back.

"Deeper." Remington's rough command reaches me, and my womb clenches helplessly as I go deeper. A large knot bites into my thumb, so I bring my other thumb to press alongside it. Remy lets his head hang forward and draws in a deep breath, and when the knot disintegrates under the pressure, his groan vibrates deep inside my core.

"Good luck," I whisper into his ear, drawing back, my fingers tingling from the contact we'd just made.

He looks at me when he stands, unsmiling as his stare holds mine in a grip so intense, my mind goes blank from everything but the blue in his eyes and the black in his pupils and the length of his dark lashes.

He extends his arms out as Riley slips on his black boxing gloves, a requisite for today, and then he taps them together. An alert from the door tells them "Riptide" is up soon, and he nods.

He rams his arms into his red satin robe and then trots out toward the wide hall that leads to the ring, and an entire farm full of animals awaken in my stomach, not just butterflies. Dragging in a deep breath, I wait a moment to recover before I slowly make my way outside to take my seat with the spectators.

The noise is deafening. Pete told me this morning that his fans are freaking out because Remy's not leading the championship, and there seems to have been some serious demand for tickets tonight. As the last sixteen contenders unite, this is the first night Remington will fight Scorpion up until the final. Scorpion is in first place now, and my nerves are killing me.

"Hey," Pete says, nudging me gently forward as he walks up behind me. "Get the hell up there. The man will be looking for you."

Somehow I manage the impossible and both laugh and scowl. "He will *not*!"

His eyebrows shoot upward in apparent disbelief. "He fights his best when you watch him—even Coach agrees. His testosterone jacks up like crazy in his lab work when he's in contact with you. Come on."

Hating the thrill that shoots like lightning through my veins, I quickly scuffle toward the ring and for my seat as I hear Scorpion introduced.

"Benny, 'the Black Scooooooorpion'!"

And there he is again—the odious man who goaded Remington at the club. I loathe him with such force, I instantly glare at everyone who cheers for him. I'm a couple of steps from reaching my seat, where I'm completely prepared to hold on to my pants—for this night is going to be brutal—when I see, across the ring and between Remy's powerfully built legs, a familiar face among the crowd.

The face is oval shaped and creamy skinned, and it carries a pair of hazel eyes. Eyes similar, in color, to mine. Eyes that, last I knew, belonged to Nora.

My twenty-one-year-old sister.

Nora.

Nora, who only recently sent a postcard from Australia. Nora, whose hair has been dyed blood red, instead of its normal soft brown. Nora, who has a big, black, ugly tattoo of a scorpion on her left cheekbone. Nora, who looks lost and sick and the complete opposite of the lively girl I knew. For a moment, I'm standing in the middle of this wide hall, staring at her while telling myself, over and over, that this cannot *possibly* be Nora.

She looks bad.

She looks really, really bad.

Like the life has been sucked out of her and all that remains are fake red hair, skin, and bones.

She spots me, and my stomach sinks to my toes when I realize, without the shadow of a doubt, that it's her. Recognition flares in her eyes, and her hand flies up to her mouth to cover it.

"Nora," I gasp, and without thinking twice, I charge after her, shoving people aside as the bell for the fight chimes.

The multitude in the room erupts in cheers and screams, and

my heart trots frantically inside my chest when Nora twists around and shoves through a throng of people in a sudden startling effort to get away from me. She's blending through the crowd, into the darkness, and I'm frantic as I scream, "Nora? Wait. Nora!"

I can't believe she's running away. From me. I can't believe that all the traces of youth vanished from her once vibrant face.

My sister.

Who I shared a bedroom with until I moved out of our parents' house.

Who used to watch every version of *Pride and Prejudice* with me.

The big, beefy man who'd been standing to her right grabs me and yanks me aside as I try to pass. "Stay the fuck away from her," he snarls.

Paralyzed in a mix of surprise and fear, I forget all my self-defense moves except the groin one. I shift my weight and jerk my knee up. "Let go of me."

He doubles over but doesn't release me. Instead his hands clench convulsively on my arms. "You little bitch, you leave Scorpion's property alone," he hisses, and I think the wet splatter that just hit my cheek was his spit.

"She's not his property!" Fiercely, I struggle to pry free as I simultaneously rub my cheek on the sleeve of my blouse.

A fresh wave of booing and shouting erupts full force across the room as the announcer yells through the speakers, "The victor, Scorpion! Scooooooorpiooooooon! Remington Tate has been disqualified from this round! *Dis-qualified!*"

All hell breaks loose, and suddenly something grabs the hands manacling my arms and with an easy thrust, sets me free. Then I'm yanked back and a pair of tanned, muscled arms crush me against a familiarly large bare chest. Every inch of my body recognizes him, and I sag in relief.

Until I remember Nora.

Gasping, I struggle with renewed force. "No. No! Remy, let me go, I need to follow her." Fighting futilely to be released, I try twisting in his grip. "Let go, Remy, let go, *please*."

But as the angry crowd flocks around us, he clenches me tighter to him and ducks to my ear. "Not now, little firecracker." His voice is low and calm, but the warning instantly makes me stop squirming. Using one arm, he tucks me into his side and shoves forward, his big body bulldozing through the multitude.

A multitude who shout insults in my face.

They claw me as we pass. "Bitch. It's your fault, you stupid bitch!"

My eyes widen in horror as I absorb the murderous faces of Remington's fans, and I'm so startled I curl myself into his arms and let him usher me out without a single complaint. Pete, Riley, and Coach wait for us out by the car.

"Fucking shit!" Coach starts as soon as the door slams shut behind us and the limo pulls into traffic.

"You're down to third. Third. Possibly fourth," Pete glumly informs him, handing him the T-shirt and sweatpants he usually wears after a match.

"You had this one down, Rem. You were training so fucking well you would have had his ass on a stick, man."

"I've got it, Coach, just relax." Remington briskly shoves himself into his casual clothes without removing his boxing shorts; then he immediately pins me down to his side as if he thinks I'm going to fling myself out of the car.

He rubs his hand down my scratched arm as he calmly faces the three angry men before us, but I'm so agitated I squirm free and slide to the window, where I stare at all the faces spilling out of the club in search of Nora.

Added to my disappointment of having completely *ruined*

Remy's fight is an incredible sense of guilt for my sister. How could I not have seen my sister was in trouble? How could I have bought the bullshit she's been feeding us, through postcards, for an entire year?

"You're in the worst placement you've been in years, man, your concentration is shit!"

"Pete, I've fucking got it—I'm not screwing this up."

"I think Brooke should stay in the hotel next fight," Riley mutters.

Remington's laugh drips pure sarcasm. "Brooke comes with *me,*" he snaps back.

"Rem . . ." Pete tries to reason.

When we reach the hotel, we're all in the same elevator, and I'm agitated as I watch the numbers climb slower than ever. I don't know what I'll do about Nora, but I know I have to do something. The doors roll open on my floor, and I hear Pete address Remington while I get out, and Remy's annoyed voice snapping close behind me, "Pete, we're talking about this later, just cool your nuts, all three of you."

"Get back here, Rem, we need to talk to you!"

"Talk to the wall!"

Desperate to get away, I storm into my suite but hear him immediately behind me. "You all right?"

He shuts the door, and the sudden visual of him in a pair of low-hanging sweatpants and a soft T-shirt that hugs all his muscles, and that beautiful tanned face full of concern, his spiky black hair deliciously messed-up, it makes my heart lurch and my legs want to run to him so I can feel the strength of his arms around me again.

I desperately want those arms to hold me right now, while my mind is spinning in all directions, reeling from what just happened. But I know I don't deserve these arms to hold me in the first place. It's obvious that he fucked up because of *me*; as if it's not enough that I've been lately feeling woefully inadequate and unworthy of him, I now have to live with the fact that he's dropped to third or fourth on *my* account. God.

He looks so strong and powerful as he stands before me, all sweaty, corded arm veins pumping with his strong, healthy blood, I desperately wish he could tell me that my sister is going to be all right. But he doesn't even *know* my sister, and now that I've gotten him disqualified, he's the last man in the world I should be begging support from.

I drag in a breath and my hand shakes as I signal at the door past his shoulders. "Go talk to them, Remy."

I've noticed that his voice sometimes sounds terser when he speaks to me more than with anyone else, but this time it's even *more* thick and textured than usual. "I want to talk to you first."

He stays, but neither us says anything. I'm busily trying to formulate an apology for fucking up his fight, and at the same time am reluctant to accept the blame when I *didn't ask him to come after me!*

He paces restlessly from the door, dragging all five fingers of his hand across his hair, down to the back of his neck. He drops it with a sigh. "Brooke, I can't fight and keep an eye out for you."

"Remy, I had it *covered*," I insist.

"My fucking ass, you had it covered!"

His tone makes me jerk in surprise, and I can't help but notice the fists he's just formed at his sides and the sudden width of his alarmingly challenging stance. The cloud of fury hovering above his head only serves to bring mine out with a vengeance, and I jump into defense mode. "Why is everyone looking at me like it's my fault? You're supposed to be fighting *Scorpion*!"

His eyebrows snap over his eyes. "And you're supposed to be in your goddamned seat on the front fucking row to my left!"

"What difference does it make? You've been fighting for years without having me in the audience! What does it even matter where I'm at?" Suddenly this is so *not* about Nora that I don't even know where this is coming from, but it's ripping off my chest like an open wound. "I'm not even a fling, Remington! I'm your *employee*. And in less than two months, I won't even be that, I'll be *nothing* to you. Nothing."

Suddenly he looks completely vexed and aggravated, and he clenches his hands until his knuckles go white. "Who is that girl you were chasing?" he demands, his face a mask of distress.

I drop my voice to a whisper, suddenly loathing my own weakness and my emotional outburst. "My sister."

A silence stretches between us as he seems to register, his expression revealing his distaste. "What's your sister doing with Scorpion's goonie?"

"Maybe she's wondering the same about me," I say with a bitter laugh.

He joins in, but I have to say, his laugh is infinitely more bitter than mine. "Don't mistake me for a fuckup like him. I may be fucked up but that guy eats virgins and spits them out like vomit."

Unsettled even more at that, I start pacing, remembering her face, so sad and lifeless. My stomach roils at the prospect of her being god-knows-what to a sick man like that. I stop and close my eyes and hang my head. "Oh, god. She looked awful. *Awful.*"

There's a silence, and then I hear the doorknob click open. Remy's voice contains a new timbre, low and troubled, as if some powerful emotion had touched him. "You're not nothing. To me."

The door shuts after him, and I feel an instant squeezing hurt as his words register. I'm in so much turmoil, suddenly I want to beg him to come back and hold me. No. I want to beg him to come back and make love to me.

But I don't, and only stare at the spot he'd just occupied. I'm so shaken it takes me a moment to register his words, and their meaning, and then link them to the very real possibility of him going out in *search* of the man he believes has my sister.

Spurred to action by the thought, I storm out of my room and knock rapidly on door. "Where is he?" I ask a grim-eyed Riley when he answers.

"We were about to come ask you the same question."

"Is he going to get in a fight?" I ask in alarm.

"Seriously, Brooke, we personally think you're a great girl, but you've got the guy more wound up than—"

"Save it, Riley! I think he may have gone to look for Scorpion. Where can I find him?"

"Son of a bitch. We're barely out of one and he's heading directly for another. Goddammit!"

There's no time to wait for them to formulate a plan. Instead, I run to the elevators and after him, realizing how stupid it was for me to bring Remy into this thing with my sister in the first place.

Scorpion and Remington obviously have been at each other's throats for a while, and the last thing I need is to give cause for Remy to go fight him outside of the ring. I'm going to have to find a way to rescue Nora from that awful insect *myself*.

Outside, the hotel is littered with an immense crowd of people, including photographers. Flashes burst all around me as I exit through the revolving glass doors.

"That's her. Her fault he was disqualified tonight!"

I see something flying toward me and duck, but it's too late. There's a hard impact on my head, followed by another loud crack as something slaps into my stomach. A sulfur-like smell reaches me.

Eggs? Great.

Just *wonderful*.

Ducking when another egg flies in my direction, I cover my

head and give the crowd my back as I hurry to the valet. "The strong guy I just came into the hotel with! Where did he go?"

The valet is a youngish boy whose widened eyes seem to eat up his face when he looks past my head at something. "He's about ten steps behind you."

Another egg crashes into my shoulder as I pivot around, and Remy looks like an avenging angel storming toward me. His eyes blaze in anger as I realize that his fans are calling me a bitch and a whore, and he swiftly turns and blocks another egg, which I hear crack against his back.

He grabs me and scoops me up like I weigh nothing, then he raises his voice as he swings around, angry and commanding. "It's because of this woman I'm still fighting!"

A sudden silence falls across the crowd, and Remington's hard, enraged voice continues telling them, "Next time I'm in the ring, I'm going to fucking *win* for her, and I want all of you who hurt her tonight to bring her a red rose as an apology and tell her it's from me!"

The resulting silence doesn't last a second longer.

Screams erupt. Cheers. Claps. And I think what's generating most of the commotion is my heart: a winged thing fluttering against my rib cage in complete confusion and disbelief at what just happened.

He takes me back into the hotel and carries me across the lobby, his square shoulders and arms hunched into my body, somehow guarding me. Suddenly, I'm so stunned by this evening I start to laugh. It's a nervous kind of laughter, but it's laughter all the same, as he presses the elevator button repeatedly.

"And they say Justin Bieber's fans are crazy," I say, gasping for air from the shock.

His voice is asperous as he brushes away the eggshells from my top. "I apologize on their behalf. I disappointed them today."

My laughter fades when I realize that his rapid, angry breath trembles the loose hair at the top of my head. It's warm and scented of something minty like mouthwash, and it does me in. Like everything else about him.

Struggling not to shake, I clutch my hands around his firm, wide neck as we board the elevator, grateful when the couple watching us like we're horny, drunk, young adults decide not to get on with us. I just don't want him to let me go yet. I'm selfish and needy like that. I think what convinced them to wait for the next one was Remy's murderous expression when he snapped "You coming?" at them, like they were the ones who threw eggs at us, as he held the door open with one arm and cradled me to his chest with the other, "You coming?"

They had both instantly stepped back and mumbled, "No."

Now we're riding alone, and I can't stop myself from pressing my nose to his neck. "Thank you."

He clutches me tighter and I feel so safe here, I think I want this to be my new home. I think if I'd known this man the day I broke my knee, and he'd held me like this, my knee wouldn't have even mattered. Only the fact that his arms were around me would have.

Pete and Riley are still in his penthouse when he slides the key into the slot and carries me inside. "What the fuck is going on, Rem?" Pete demands.

"Just get the hell out, guys." Rem holds the door open for them with one arm, and me still aloft in the other. "I do what I want, you hear me?" he snaps at them.

Both men stare at me for a moment, and they both look as startled as I feel. "We hear you, Rem," Riley meekly answers as he shuffles out after Pete.

"Then don't fucking forget it."

Remington slams the door and bolts it after them so that nobody, not even those with a key, can come in, and he carries me into the bath of the master bedroom. I admit I'm not ready to let go, and when I wind my fingers tighter at his nape, he gets the message and keeps an arm around me as he maneuvers to turn the shower knob.

The water starts falling, and he kicks off his shoes, takes off mine, and then steps into the stall with me in his arms.

"Let's get this shit off you." He runs his big hands over my wet hair, and I end up sliding down the length of him to my feet. The water feels incredible on my skin, and when he peels off my dress and lifts it over my head, I feel his soapy hands rubbing everywhere, even over my underwear. I bite my lip and try to block off his touch, but it filters inside me. It's all I can feel, or know, or think of.

I no longer worry that Pete and Riley hate me, that I'm fucking up Remy's fight. That his fans hate me. That my sister doesn't want to see me. That I miss Mel. That I can't sprint anymore. That I will soon be out of a job.

It's all about this man, my body remaining utterly still as I find myself waiting in breathless anticipation just to see what he will do. Where his hands will slide to next. What part of my hot flesh will feel his wet fingers on it next.

Methodically he touches me, and though I'm breathless from the contact, he's not in the least bit affected. He spreads my arms up and slides soap into my armpits, between my legs, my neck; then he whips his T-shirt off and scrapes himself quickly. His powerful shoulders bulge, and the sight of his nipples excites me.

"I can't believe your groupies called me a whore," I say, trying not to think about the fact that I'm almost naked in the shower. And he's in only the drawstring sweatpants and is now fully shirtless, every muscle of his torso glistening wet.

He quickly lathers his hair. "You're going to survive."

"Do I have to?"

"Yeah, you do."

He comes to lather my scalp with more shampoo, and his attention, so wanted, is now solely on me and my hair. "They hate me," I say up at him. "I won't be able to go to your fights now without fear of getting lynched."

He grabs the showerhead and angles it directly above me. I close my eyes and let the soap bubbles drip down my face, and when I open my eyes, he's looking straight at me. Rivulets of water slide down his square jaw and cling to his eyelashes as he brushes a strand of wet hair away from my forehead, and I become aware of the fast gait of my pulse.

His eyes are brilliant blue, and as they remain resting on mine, they feel a thousand times more brilliant than usual. He's just as wet as I am, and suddenly he holds my face between his hands and stares deeply into me. He's breathing hard. His eyes slide down the length of my nose, to my mouth. He strokes my lips with a fingertip that is thick, blunt, and callused. And I can feel that stroke in every cell of my being. "That's never going to happen," he says in an odd, hot whisper.

Weakness travels up my legs and takes over every ounce of my willpower. I've never craved anyone's gaze like I crave his. Needed anyone's touch like I need his. Or wanted anything as painfully fiercely as I want him.

My throat feels achy as I speak. "You shouldn't have . . . said that about me, Remy. They're going to think you and I . . . that you and I . . ." I shake my head, aware now of how my fingers tingle in the water with the urge to touch his wet spiky hair.

"That you're mine?"

The word "mine" on his lips, spoken as those intent blue eyes look into me, makes my stomach constrict with painful unrequited lust. I laugh.

"What's so funny?" He shoves open the glass door and wraps a towel around his hips, easily letting his wet drawstring pants slap to the floor. He comes back and covers me in a large towel and hauls me to the bed. Setting me down in the center, his voice tinged with a hint of laughter, but his face frowning, he asks, "Is the thought of being mine funny?"

He reaches under my towel and pulls off my panties, and then my bra, then works the towel through my hair and over my body, his bright eyes not glinting anymore. "Is the idea of being mine funny?" He covers both my breasts with the towel and dries me, still watching me. "Is it funny, Brooke?" he insists, peering intently into my eyes.

"No!" The word is just a gasp as desire shoots through my nerve endings. My hips tilt up when he starts drying me between my legs, and I can't help but be totally turned on.

He runs the towel down the length of my legs, and I lick my lips as he bends his head at last, and my bones become liquid with pure red-hot want. He seems especially obsessed with drying my bad knee. The towel almost feels loving as he rubs it over my scar. A burning fever follows the path of the towel as I helplessly watch him.

A drop of water clings to one of the small, brown tips of his nipples, and it takes all my willpower to fight against a deep, soul-shattering need to lean over and suck it into my mouth.

My heart pounds when I reach out, my hand quaking as I touch the top of his head. "Have you ever been anyone's?" I ask, a feathery whisper in the quiet bedroom.

He lifts his head to mine, and I want him so bad I feel consumed, like he's already possessed my soul, and now my soul aches for him to possess my body.

A powerful emotion tightens his features as he reaches out to cradle my cheek in his big hand, and there's an unexpected fierceness in his eyes, in his touch, as he cups me. "No. And you?"

The calluses in his palm rasp on my skin, and I find myself tucking my cheek deeper into them. "I've never wanted to be."

"Neither have I."

The moment is intimate. Heavy with things unsaid. Charged with something without a name, leaping between us. From him to me. Me to him.

He drags his thumb along my jaw like he's memorizing it.

Ripples shoot across my body, rocketing from his thumb straight to my core as he continues caressing my face, all the time watching me with those breathtaking, heartbreaking, beautiful blue eyes as though engrossed. His voice is velvet on my skin. "Until I saw this lovely girl in Seattle, with big gold eyes, and pink, full lips . . . and I wondered if she could understand me . . ."

My chest heaves at his unexpected words, and when he bends his head closer, his gaze almost asking permission, I border on sensory overload, his scent of soap and shampoo and water clinging to my nostrils.

The ache for his touch throbs through me, but instead of reaching for me, he spreads the towel and draws it over my body and gently covers me. His voice is rough with emotion.

"I want to say so many things, Brooke, and I just can't find the words to tell them to you."

He sets his forehead on mine and inhales deeply. Slowly, still breathing me in, he drags his nose along the length of mine.

"You tie me up in knots." He presses my mouth with his. Briefly. Then he withdraws, breathing hard, and looks at me with heavy-lidded eyes. "I want to play you a thousand different songs so you get a clue of what . . . I feel inside me. . . ."

Raw need streaks through my bloodstream, my nerves, my very bones, as he strokes his thumb up my jaw and around the shell of my ear. Shivers run through my body as he slides his index finger across my top lip. He strokes liberally across my bottom one too, and I whimper. There's an ache in my beaded nipples, my wet sex, my heart.

He holds my face between his palms and angles his head, fitting my lips softly to his and drawing my tongue into his mouth, sucking strongly on me.

I moan and grip his shoulders with my nails, locking him to me. "Why won't you take me, Remington?"

He groans and pulls me closer. "Because I want you too much."

His tongue dips hard against mine, and sensations spark up in my nerve endings as he leans his body into mine, his skin damp and hot, the towel falling to my waist and my breasts getting flattened by his diaphragm.

I gasp into his mouth as he pulls me closer and continues his sensual assault with his lips.

"But I want you *so* much, and I'm protected," I pleadingly cajole. "I know you're clean. You get tested all the time and I . . ." I shudder at the feel of his chest muscles against the sensitive tips of nipples, hard and bulging. My hips tilt up by pure instinct, and I'm just a female. Seeking my male. His hardness. His touch. I can't breathe, can't think, want him want him *want him*.

An orgasm is not what I want and I know it. What I want, need, is so much more than that. It's the connection. The exhilarating contact with this human being, a being who compels me like no other. I miss his touch, his kiss. I don't care if he gives me just a little kernel of what he can give; I'm just starving to be fed, and my body has never been this hungry.

"I want you in my bed again. I want to kiss you, hold you," he whispers.

"I can't do this anymore, please just make love with me . . ." I beg.

Pressing into him as he hungrily takes my mouth, I shift my body until one of his legs is wedged between my thighs.

He nibbles and bites my lips, his hands fisting my hair. I'm so desperate I rake my nails down his arms as I rub my sex against his hard thigh. Sensations shoot off. I whimper, feeling the coiled tension in his shoulders, the smooth velvet of his chest as he devours my mouth, until, the continued feel of my sex brushing against the rock-hard quad muscle of his thigh makes my insides clench, and tighten, and I explode.

Shuddering uncontrollably, I feel him stiffen in surprise at my startlingly powerful convulsions. His hands quickly spread on my back and flatten me to him as he lifts his leg higher between my thighs and grinds his muscle into my clit, his ravenous mouth taking all my breaths inside him.

When I'm done, he brushes my hair back and looks positively intimate. His voice. Intimate. Mild with tenderness. "Did that feel even half as good as it looked?" His fingers trail along my cheek in a whisper touch, and there is still not enough air in my lungs for me to scream at him.

I. Hate. Him.

I feel like I just gave him everything and got nothing back, even though *I* was the one who was pleasured. Angrily securing the towel around myself, I glance around the room, at anything but his odious, beautiful, sexy face.

"I assure you that's not happening again," I whisper in complete and total embarrassment.

He kisses my ear, his voice husky. "I'm going to make sure that it *does*."

"Don't count on it. If I wanted to have an orgasm all alone I could have taken care of myself without giving *anyone* a show." With the towel clutched to my chest, I sit up and ask, "Can I borrow a damn shirt?"

Slowly, his lips curl into a dimpled, kind of cocky smile that makes me suspect he likes the idea of me wearing his man stuff, and he heads to his closet while I wait for him to come back, feeling all kinds of slutty and wanton.

His beautiful torso is still a little damp, and I can't stop admiring the way the towel hugs his narrow hips. His body is perfection. His butt defies gravity, it is so perfectly tight, round, and muscular. Every time I see it in any kind of clothes, I drool roughly a small ocean.

I want to see him naked and touch him. And once again tonight, I loathe that I won't be able to sleep from the torment of wanting to feel him inside me. Can I even stay here to sleep? Wanting what he's not ready to give me?

No, I'm not going to sleep with him tonight, only to kiss like teenagers, going only to first base and second and third, without going for it all. . . .

No.

Hell no.

I want him to make love to me. I. *Need*. Him to. Damn him. I hate that he can control himself and hold back while I am completely undone for him.

He hands me a black T-shirt I've seen him wearing before, on our very first flight to Atlanta. "This okay?" he asks, blue eyes all-knowing and deep.

I slip it on, feeling the fabric slide along my skin and feeling it awaken tingles all over my body. He remains standing at the foot of the bed, and his eyes probe me. They're intimate eyes, eyes that have seen me naked and make my pussy ache so deep I feel like squirming. "Come eat something with me," he says, and I follow him out into the suite, not one whit relaxed even after the amazing orgasm he gave me.

"Let's see what Diane left you," I tell him as we study the

contents in the hot drawer of the suite's kitchen. He uncovers the plate and I shoot him a smile. "Eggs. They must've been on sale tonight."

Those dimples again, boyish and sexy as he glances at my mouth and stays there. I don't even think he realizes he's staring so ardently at me. In silence, he extracts two forks from a drawer and comes over. "Come share."

"Oh, no. No more eggs for me tonight. You enjoy."

He sets the forks down and follows me to the door, grabbing my wrist to halt me. "Stay."

The abrupt request shoots a ripple of heat through me, but it's the intensity in his blue eyes that nearly rends me open.

"I'll stay," I say, my voice smooth but firm, "when you make love to me."

We stare; then he sighs and holds the door open for me, putting his body in such a way that I have to brush past him to leave. The contact burns me. His eyes watch me all the way to my room. They burn me as well.

At night, I lie awake, in another master bedroom of another presidential suite, Diane in the other bedroom, and I'm still in flames. I'm in bed with the door open, my ears alert for any noise, in case Remy has an extra key and decides he might come get me.

His T-shirt is large and wonderful on my much smaller frame, and it smells of him. It feels soft against my skin, and here I am, shivering with need, wishing he'd break down and come tell me he's ready for me. I am so ready for him. *Just come make love to me,* I think helplessly.

At 2 a.m. he still hasn't, and I'm still awake.

I can't see how a man who really wants a woman can hold back like this. Remy is disciplined and the strongest man I've known, but I watch the door and remember his touch, the way I came for him, and don't think it's even possible that he could hold back if he wanted me the way I want him. My sex aches like never before. It is so swollen remembering the powerful strokes of his tongue in my mouth and the way his thigh grazed me. My hunger has not only not been appeased, it has tripled and made me rabid. He sparked an unquenchable thirst and I don't feel satisfied, just feel empty and anxious. My entire existence tonight is focused on watching that door.

Does he feel anything for me even remotely as strong as I feel for him?

There's this mean little part of me—the girl who tore her ACL and who failed to accomplish her dream, the girl who doesn't believe I can really have anything wonderful, this little part that makes me wonder if he really wants me at all.

Or if he just wants to play with me.

Then I suddenly wonder if this is the sort of feeling that got my sister Nora in trouble in the first place.

EIGHT

AUSTIN

In Austin, we're staying in a six-bedroom home with a red barn included, a fabulously crafted old-fashioned structure where Remington trains. He's been pushing tractor tires all day. Running up the outside stairs with cement bags atop both his shoulders. Climbing ropes slung from the barn rafters, swinging from them and then running with me around the property. He's training like a beast, and is as moody as a mad gorilla, as well. Although he seems to be especially moody with the *other* members of his team and *I* seem to be the only one who calms him, so Riley and Coach keep begging me to go stretch him when he starts getting upset about something like the fit of his "damned-for-shit gloves nobody can fight with."

It's been torture for me, these frequent stretches. Sliding my hands along his sweaty chest. Austin is hot in July, and he takes off his shirt and the skin-to-skin contact unsettles every little and big part of me, flashing me back to the sensation of being naked in bed with him.

Every night since the egg incident a week ago, I've lain in

bed staring at my door. I know I should touch myself just to find some relief, but what I want from him is so far beyond sex now, I don't even want to put a name to it. Though I know perfectly well what it is.

On our flight here, we exchanged music, and I find I'm always breathless waiting to see what song he will play for me. I tried to keep my selection unromantic for him, and actually got a private thrill when he scowled at all the girl-power songs I handed over.

He, on the other hand, played me the most romantic song I'd ever heard in my growing-up years, which was featured in a chick flick in which a guy plays the song to the love of his life while holding his boom box up near her window. The movie is called *Say Anything*, but the song is called "In Your Eyes" by Peter Gabriel.

I wanted, seriously, to melt into the leather of the plane bench when it started playing, his somber blue eyes intently watching me as I soaked up the lyrics about finding the light in her eyes. . . .

Damn.

Him.

He hasn't touched me since the night we showered together. But the things he said . . . the way he kissed me . . . I want him so bad, sometimes I just want to hit him in the head and haul him into *my* woman's cave, where nobody's opinion matters but mine. And I say we go at it all night long and that's that.

Today I'm inside the house, retrieving some elastic bands from my suitcase, which I might use to stretch him in the end of the afternoon session. This is just a tactic so I don't have to touch him skin to skin anymore, and can spare myself another sleepless night of arousal. I pass by the front door with the band dangling from between my fingers, and I spot Pete there, holding it partly closed as he speaks to someone on the other side.

As I pass through, I see a silver-haired man and a woman through the corner of my eye, and suddenly they call me.

"Young girl! Please, won't you let us talk to him?"

The feminine voice stops me in my tracks, since I'm the only "young girl" in the house, last I heard.

When I step forward, the tall, slender, frail-looking woman rushes to tell me, her face pale and her sullen eyes a dark chocolate, "We didn't know what to do. He felt abandoned but he was too strong and nobody could control him, least of all me."

My brain processes her words in silence, and while it does, I stare at them but remain standing behind Pete.

"Again, I'm really sorry," Pete formally replies. "But even if he weren't busy, there's no way I can get him to see you. But please rest assured I will make contact if that ever changes."

He slams the door shut a little harder than called for, and releases a long, pent-up sigh.

And finally my mind speaks to me. "Are those Remy's parents?" I ask, bewildered and shocked.

Suddenly I realize the man's eyes were an unmistakable blue color, and although white-haired he had incredibly large and healthy bone structure.

Pete nods and rubs his forehead, appearing extremely agitated. "Yeah. They're the folks, all right."

"Why won't Remy see them?"

"Because the bastards locked him up in a psych ward at thirteen and *left him* there until he was old enough to sign himself out."

An awful sensation settles in my gut, and for a moment, the only thing I do is gape. "A psych ward? For *what*? Remy's not crazy," I say, instantly outraged on his behalf as I follow Pete across the living room.

"Don't even look at me. It's one of the most frustrating injustices I've ever had to witness in my life."

Chest wound tight, I ask, "Pete, were you with him when he was kicked out of mainstream boxing?"

He shakes his head in a negative, not breaking his stride. "Remy has a short fuse. You light it, he blows up. His competition wanted him out. Picked on him out of the ring. He bit the bait. Was kicked out. End of story."

"Well, is he still angry about it?"

He opens the terrace doors that lead across the garden and to the barn, and I follow, shielding my eyes from the glare of the sun with my hand.

"He's angry, all right, but not specifically about that," Pete says. "Fighting is all he knows. It's all he's had that he can control in his life. Growing up, it was pure rejection for Rem. It's damn near impossible to get him to open up. Even with those who've been with him so long."

"How do you think his parents knew where we were? I thought this house was meant to keep the press away since the egg incident?"

"Because this is Rem's house," Pete says as I spot the charming red barn looming ahead across the lawns. "After he got out, he made money fighting; then he got this house, trying to prove to the old folks that he could be someone. . . . The folks still didn't want anything to do with him. He kept the place but now only uses it when we're in the city to keep the press from hounding him at the hotels. He has *a lot* of fans in Austin."

I feel shot at from all sides with this information. Pure un-diluted outrage for young Remy fills me to my core, making me sound breathless. "What kind of parents abandon their child like they did, Pete? And why on earth would they look for him *now*?"

Pete sighs. "Why indeed." He shakes his head ruefully; then we spot Remington inside the open barn, hitting a speedball Coach has hung from the rafters. Looking slightly panicked,

Pete instantly snatches me up by the elbow and draws me closer. "Don't let on that you know anything about this, I beg you. He's been in a pissed-off mood ever since he knew we were coming here. His parents drive him totally speedy too, and his temper is for shit these days."

I nod and squeeze his elbow back. "I won't. Thanks for the confidence."

"Hey, B, you might try stretching him, his form's not ideal. Coach thinks it's a lower-back knot," Riley calls out.

Nodding, I walk over, and I hear, rather than see, Remington punching the bag harder and faster with each step I take closer to him. Frankly, I'm surprised that he doesn't stop when I stand right next to him.

"Coach isn't happy with your form and Riley thinks I can help," I say, and as I watch this lean, mesmerizing creature keep slamming the speedball with both rolling fists, a deep, concentrated frown on his face, I can't help but admire what Remington has made of himself despite the rejection he faced when he was younger.

"Remy?" I prod.

He doesn't answer, and instead shifts sideways and thrusts out one fist after the other in a matter of nanoseconds, making that poor bag fly.

"Will you let me stretch you?" I go on.

He tilts his body yet again and gives me all his gorgeous back, and keeps on hitting like mad. I want to touch him, especially after everything Pete told me, so I drop the elastic band at my feet, for now the last thing I want is anything between him and me.

"Are you going to answer me, Remy?" My voice drops as I step closer, reaching out with one arm.

Whack, whack, whack . . .

I touch his back. He stiffens, drops his head, and whips

around, removing his boxing gloves and tossing them aside. "Do you like him?"

His whisper is low, his touch gentle as he reaches out and puts his taped hand right where Pete touched me. "Do you like it when he touches you?"

But his eyes, dear god. They blaze into me. His hand is double the size of Pete's and doing all things to my body.

I stare into him, butterflies exploding in my belly, and whatever it is we're playing, I want it to go on endlessly, but I want it to stop. There's something incredibly animal about the way he acts around me that brings out the deep-rooted instincts from within me as well.

"You have no right to me," I say in breathless anger.

His hand clenches. "You gave me rights when you came on my thigh."

My cheeks burn red at the reminder. "I'm still not yours," I shoot back. "Maybe you're afraid I'm too much of a woman for you?"

"I asked you a question, and I want an answer. Do you fucking like it when other men touch you?" he demands.

"*No*, you jerkwad, I like it when *you* touch me!"

After my lashing outburst, he stares at my mouth as his thumb dips into the crease of my elbow. His tone goes gruff. "How much do you like my touch?"

"More than I want to," I snap back, panting and breathless because of him.

"Do you like it enough to let me feel you in bed tonight?" he asks tersely. My skin tingles, and between my legs, I'm growing incredibly warm. His pupils are completely enlarged with hunger.

"I like it enough to let you make love to me."

"No. Not make love." He tightens his jaw and stares at me with tormented blue eyes. "Just touching. In bed. Tonight. You and me. I want to make you come again." He watches me, a question in his expression. I feel his dark temper roiling underneath the surface in frustration. There's a need in me that wants to appease it . . . but I *can't* follow it.

I want to touch him so bad; I just can't understand why *he* can resist the call and not take me. I can't stand a night in his arms without going all the way.

Pulling free, I harden my voice. "Look, I don't know what you're waiting for, but I won't be your plaything."

He grabs me again and brings me close, ducking his head to me. "You're not a game. But I need to do this my way. *My* way." He buries his face in my neck and scents me, and his tongue flashes out to lick my ear. He groans and jerks my chin up so our eyes meet. "I'm taking it slow for you. Not me."

My knees threaten to fold, but I somehow manage to shake my head in disagreement.

"This is growing old. Let's just stretch you." I go to his back, and he jerks free as if I'd sliced him with a knife.

"Don't fucking bother. Go stretch Pete."

He grabs his towel, swipes it over his front, then goes to punch the speed bag with his bare knuckles.

Marching out with a fierce scowl I tell Riley, "He doesn't want me."

"Like a desert doesn't want rain, girl," he says, rolling his sad surfer-boy eyes.

NINE

AN ADVENTURE

The Underground simmers with energy tonight, and about an hour ago I quit looking for Nora among the crowd, somehow fearing the sight of me has encouraged her to go into hiding. I'm determined to make her come out—I just don't know how I'm going to do it yet. But I'm definitely plotting.

For now, I've let myself be swept into the magic of the fights, and I find myself watching all the contenders more avidly than I ever have before, if only to try to see their fighting strategies in case they final and have to face Remington.

Some fight extremely dirty, and I realize there's *no one* who fights like *he* does. Remy fights like he loves it. He has a blast up in the ring, making himself a lion and his opponents mice he's just playing with. He jumps up and down sometimes, making the crowd participate when he clinches his opponent only to then let go and point at him, as if asking, "Do you all want me to beat this asshole's face in?"

Of course the crowd roars, and I'm all wound up, jacked up, and more, exhilarated just watching him.

When he was announced tonight, the Austin crowd went wild, most everyone present standing and hollering. I watched with a fluttering stomach as he strutted down the pathway and climbed into the ring—the room suddenly coming alive with his presence. Now banners keep waving across the room as he pounds his third opponent of the night, and he's worn the other man down so bad, it will probably end in a couple more minutes.

He's on a roll. He's taken out anything and everything they bring out. I haven't really seen any of his opponents able to get a really good hit on him, his face is intact and so is his guard.

Somehow I feel that he's proving something to this city where he was born. I feel like he's telling his parents with every punch that they were *wrong*. And it makes me privately cheer for him even more. I'm so stunned from what I learned, and I just can't picture Remington being locked up anywhere, helpless and angry. He's a man who is strong and primitive, who knows exactly what he wants, and it enrages me to think anyone hurt him when he was younger and more vulnerable. It makes me feel fiercely protective of him, and makes me wish I'd known him sooner, as if I could have even done something to stop it.

I hear the *slam* of his KO and the screaming that follows, and my heart is already skipping in my chest as the ringmaster grabs Remy's arm and raises it.

"Our victor of the night, Remingtoooooooon Tate, your RIP-TIDE!!"

His arm raised in victory, I hold my breath in anticipation and wait for what follows. What he *always* does next.

He seeks me out with those blue eyes.

My body seizes the instant he swings his gaze to mine. His smile flashes, but it has an edge to it today. He's been fighting with fierce intensity, and his smile is as equally intense, a blast of sex, and suddenly there's nothing innocent or playful about it. He keeps his gaze trained possessively on me as his breaths continue jerking out of his powerful chest and rivulets of sweat slide down his body, and he looks as perfect as he did the first moment I laid eyes on him in Seattle.

I want him more than ever.

I'm so wet, and so desperate with what he makes me feel, I just stare back at him, not returning his smile, my eyes imploring him to finish whatever is going on between us, whatever it is that leaps like currents of electricity between us whenever we're close. I've put it all out there, telling him I want him, and he continues to be as unattainable to me as a comet.

With glinting blue eyes, he points at me now, then at himself, and then at a figure approaching me in the pathway before my seat. The figure is carrying a bright red rose.

She shoves it in my line of vision. "From Remy," the smiling young girl whispers.

Another rose follows, and a different voice proudly states, "From Remy."

A third one falls in my hand. "From Remington."

A fourth. "From Riptide."

"From RT. Sorry those jerks egged you . . ."

"From Remy."

My pulse is somewhere near the moon, while at the same time, my world drops from underneath me. I stare in utter disbelief at the line of people forming before me, easily several dozen, all of them handing me red roses from *him*. Rem watches, with that dimpled smile that fairly tells me that I belong to him, and my heart aches so much I want to rip it out of my chest and throw it somewhere. Word of what he did in Los Angeles must have gone out through Twitter or I don't know how—all I know is my arms are full of roses, and they're all from *him*.

From a man who fights like crazy, arouses me like no other, is the sexiest thing I've ever seen. From the man who plays me sexy music, gives me his T-shirt to sleep in, protects me as fiercely as a lion, and yet won't take me when I'm naked and trembling in his arms.

And suddenly I can't stand it anymore.

I don't even glance at him when we ride back to the house. His gaze is glued to my profile, every cell in my body aware of it. I know he wants to know if I'm grateful for my roses, but my insides are so wound up, I'm simmering. All my desire for him has not been appeased, and it has morphed into the sort of anger that will probably give me a disease and kill me.

I'm shaking with it. With need. With pain. With fury.

How dare he.

Make me want him like this.

Offer me the job of my dreams, and then become the center of my very existence, until I'm ready to risk everything for him. Even my job. My family. My friends. The city where I grew up.

How dare he touch me in the shower, and kiss me like he wants to eat me for every meal until he dies! How dare he be my living, breathing fantasy come to goddamned life only to tease and torture me until I can't stand it. I used to feel so damned free and happy that I didn't have any romantic dramas. I used to hear Melanie rant and rave and I'd tell her, "Mel, he's just a man. Chin up and onto the next." And now I'm in knots because of *one* man, and my own advice is worth *shit* because there is *no* other man like him to me.

I no longer even feel free. I'm taken and yet the man who's taken me won't have me. If I weren't so angry and frustrated, I'd throw the biggest damn pity party of my life, second only to the one I threw following the Olympic trial fallout.

"You were awesome, Rem!" Pete tells him in the car, sighing with pure delight. "Man, what a great night."

"Great fight, son," Coach says, sounding the happiest I've ever heard the somber man. "Never broke form. Never dropped guard. Even Brooke felt the love tonight, huh, Brooke?"

Silence follows, and I hold still in my seat and just watch the lights flickering out the window as though I'm not even hearing their conversation. I absolutely *refuse* to gush about my roses or compliment him. Yes, his fans showered me with roses and he fought like a true freaking wonderful champion. . . . My pussy clenches as I remember the powerful blows of his fists, and now I refuse to think more about that either.

"You totally killed it," Riley says.

I notice Remington doesn't respond to their compliments. His gaze now feels like a scorching brand on my profile and his energy is becoming as tumultuous as mine. He must have wanted a different reaction to his gesture. He must have wanted me to be all gushy and tell him, "Oh my stars, you're so amazing!" But I won't. Because I hate what he does to me. I hate that I want him like this, I hate that I feel so volatile I want to tear his eyes out and then go cry about it. I want to fling all these roses in his lap and tell him to fuck *them* now because I don't even want him to fuck *me* anymore!

So when the roses are set with water in one of the ice buckets in my room and my anger has festered into gargantuan proportions, I storm down the hall and find Pete in the living room outside the master bedroom.

"Remington?" I demand.

"Showering." He points to a door, and I charge forward through it, slamming and locking it behind me.

I spot him across the room, standing on the threshold of the bathroom.

He's fully naked, dripping wet, fresh out of the shower with a towel in his hand, and instantly he jumps erect.

His stunned gaze fixes on me, and the towel falls at his feet.

I've never had this view of him in the nude, and to see his physical perfection and the most beautiful cock I've ever seen, perfectly working, only enrages me further. The blood rushes like burning lava in my veins as I charge forward and slam my fists repeatedly into his chest, as hard as I can without breaking my own bones. "Why haven't you touched me? Why don't you fucking take me? Am I *too fat*? Too *plain*? Do you just delight in fucking torturing me senseless or are you just plain damn *mean*? For your information, I've wanted to have *sex* with you since the day I went into your stupid hotel room and got *hired* instead!"

He grabs my wrists and angrily yanks me forward, pinning my arms down. "Why'd you want to have sex with me? To have a fucking adventure? What was I supposed to be? Your one-night-fucking-stand? I'm every woman's adventure, damn you, and I don't want to be *yours*. I want to be your fucking REAL. You get that? If I fuck you, I want you to belong to me. To be mine. I want you to give yourself to *me*—not Riptide!"

"I won't ever be yours if you don't take me. Take me! You son of a bitch, can't you see how much I want you?"

"You don't know me," he strains out through gritted teeth, his face anxious as he clenches my wrists at my sides. "You don't know the first thing about me."

"Then tell me! You think I'll leave if you tell me whatever it is you don't want me to know?"

"I don't think it, I know it." He grabs my face in one open hand and squeezes both my cheeks, his eyes violently blue and almost frantic. "You'll leave me the second it gets too steep, and you'll leave me with nothing—when I want you like I've never wanted anything in my life. You're all I think about, dream about. I get high and low and it's all about you now, it's not even about me anymore. I can't sleep, can't think, can't concentrate worth shit anymore and it's all because I want to be the fucking 'one' for you, and as soon as you realize what I am, all I'll be is a fucking mistake!"

"How can you be a mistake? Have you seen you? Have you seen what you do to me? You had me at hello, you fucking asshole! You make me want you until it hurts and then you won't do shit!"

"Because I'm fucking *bipolar!* Manic. Violent. Depressive. I'm a fucking ticking time bomb, and if one of my staff messes up when I get another episode, the next person I hurt can be *you.* I was trying to break this to you as slowly as possible so I could at least stand a chance. This shit has taken everything from me. *Everything.* My career. My family. My fucking friends. If it takes this chance with you, I don't fucking even know what I'm going to do, but the depression will hit me so deep, I'll probably end up killing myself!"

My eyes sting as the words float like awful whiplashes in my head. Every shocking word stuns me to my bones. He curses and releases me, and I take a step back and watch him angrily step into a pair of drawstring pants.

Helplessly, I watch him grab a T-shirt from the closet, and my heart has completely stopped beating in my chest. The word "bipolar" is not really one I'm familiar with. I've never met anyone who's been bipolar, but suddenly I go back through these weeks, and I get a little hint of what it is. I do. I get it. Remy both loves and hates himself. He loves and hates his life. One second it's all good, the next it's all bad. He's hot, then he's cold. Maybe he's never been accepted, not even by himself, and maybe everyone drops him cold the second it gets . . . steep.

A thousand emotions roil in my chest, and I can barely contain them all in my body.

His chest heaves as he watches me across the room now, his eyes brilliantly blue as he clenches his hands at his sides and waits for me to speak, the T-shirt still in his grip, dangling at his side.

Suddenly all I know is that this man has assumed godlike proportions in my mind, but now I realize he's also human and imperfect, and with every aching, quaking inch of my body, I want him all the more. So much I want to drown if he denies me tonight.

Dragging in a fortifying breath, I feel my hands tremble as I slowly open the buttons of my top, sifting them one by one through my fingers. The rustle makes his eyes drop to my chest and his eyes flash in pain. His stare devours me so fiercely I feel the bite of his eyes in my heart.

"I'm take as-is. I'm not medicating. It makes me feel dead and I intend to live my life alive," he warns in a rough, angry whisper.

I nod in understanding. I refused to take antidepressants when I supposedly, clinically, needed them after my fall. I believe it is your choice how you live with your sickness, and sometimes the remedy is worse than the disease. He's a man who eats right, and any chemical can unbalance him even further. He controls his environment and what he can, and I can see how he strives for the keys to good health—exercise, good sleep, and good food intake—to keep him as stable as possible.

I'm no one to tell him what to do. But does he even realize how important he is? Where he's gotten to, all on his own? Does he see what a great team he's built? I can see how Coach, Diane, Pete, and Riley love him even when they quarrel. I wanted to belong to this team, but now I just want to belong to this man.

And I want him to belong to me.

"Take your clothes off, Remy."

Flicking my last button, I part my shirt through the middle, and the T-shirt he's still holding in his balled grip falls to the floor as his fingers spasmodically open.

His eyes rake me, his voice an angry pained rasp. "You have no idea what you're asking for."

"I'm asking for you."

"I won't let you fucking leave me."

My throat closes up with emotion, making the words hard to pronounce. "Maybe I won't want to."

Pained desperation flashes in his eyes. "Give me a goddamned guarantee. I won't let you fucking leave me, and you're going to want to try. I'm going to be difficult and I'm going to be an ass, and sooner or later, you're going to have fucking *enough* of me."

Shaking my head, I toss my top to the floor, then push my skirt down my hips and step out of it. Trembling down to my soul, I stand in only my plain cotton bra and panties, my breasts rising and falling. "I'll never have enough of you, never."

At first, my words seem to have no effect on him.

And I think I'm slowly dying.

Then a low, hungry sound rips up his throat.

My breath stalls in my throat.

He stands watching me, motionless in those loose pants, his legs braced in a fighting stance, his eyes bursting with need. His broad shoulders jerk with his breaths, and he curls his fingers into fists at his sides. The deep roughness of his voice scrapes my flesh. "Come here then."

The command comes so unexpectedly my legs quake. All my systems rush to work together, but at the same time, I can't *move*.

I feel like a bunch of organs struggling to come into one. Rapid heart. Sweating skin. Tremors in my nerve endings. Complete uselessness of my lungs.

All of my body wants the same thing but it seems too wound up to unite.

When I at last come together with a ragged breath, I feel so alive and yet so unraveled, even my toes tingle when we—me and this heart and these bones and this skin—finally manage to take the first step.

A fierce nervousness eats me raw, all the way to my destination.

Remington's breathing escalates. His powerful chest rises even faster as I approach. Step by nerve-wracking step, I feel my pulse throb in my temples as the heat of his stare creeps into me. Between my legs, I burn for him. My nipples throb. The hard tips push painfully against the cotton of my bra. Each pore in my body wants to beg him to suck them. To touch me. To love me.

Stopping a foot away, I can barely breathe as the smell of his soap envelops my lungs, drugging all my senses. His arms come out, and he tangles ten angry fingers in my hair as he yanks my head back in his fists and buries his nose in my neck, growling softly. His deep inhale reaches me, and a shudder runs through my body as I do the same, absorbing every color and flavor of his strong male scent into my body. His tongue flashes out to lick a wet path up my neck as an arm coils around my waist, and he crushes me to his body, whispering, "Mine."

Lust and love burst through me. "Yes, yes, yes, Remington, *yes.*"

Tangling my fingers up in his hair, I eagerly push my breasts to his chest and anxiously rub my pained nipples against his diaphragm, my arms violently locking his head to me as he continues scenting me with deep, somehow desperate inhales. My body jolts with pleasure.

He grabs my face with his callused hands and drags his tongue from my neck, along my jaw, breathing roughly as he heads for my mouth. He licks the seam of my lips. Dampening me. Priming me.

His tongue probes at the seam; then he adds his lips and uses them to open me. He nibbles my lower lip to tease it apart from the top. A soft whimper feathers out of me and he muffles the sound when he dives in to taste me, wet and hot and hungry. My response is fast and wild, and our tongues collide in a heated frenzy of wetness and panting.

My pliant body melts into his hard one until his strong arm, coiled around my small waist, is all that holds me upright. I don't know if I'm bad for him, or him for me. All I know is that this is as inevitable as an incoming tsunami, and I'm just bracing for the swim of my life.

We taste and suckle each other, and I'm so thirsty he could feed me his kiss all night and I'd still be dying in the desert. He grips my hair tighter in one fist and keeps me in place as though he fears I'll pull away from his delicious mouth, and I'm so afraid this is a dream that my fingers tighten reflexively in his wet hair because if there's a fire in this hotel, if an army of crazy fans comes storming inside, or if Scorpion himself comes into this bedroom, I am still not letting Remington Tate break away from me.

The wet heat of his mouth unravels me, makes me so high I moan and suck lightly on his thick tongue, loving how Remington groans with me and pushes it deeper, giving me more.

He grows restless. Among the slick kissing sounds echoing in the room, his drawstring pants rustle as he shoves them down his legs, his arm muscles bulging as they clench against me. The linen fabric pools at our feet, and then he rams his thumbs into the front opening of my bra and yanks at opposite sides until it jerks loose. My breasts bounce free, and I've never felt so full as when he cups them in one big hand and lifts them higher to suck. He laves my nipples with his tongue, first one and then the other, and he brings up the other hand to engulf both gentle curves as he runs his calluses across my straining nipples. I moan gratefully when he sticks his tongue back in my mouth, because I'm just so hungry I can't stop shuddering.

The slick kissing sounds echo around us once more. He

squeezes one breast and shoves a hand between my legs, cupping me under my panties. He rubs me with the heel of his palm, and then rubs his longest finger along the moist folds of my entrance. Tremors of anticipation ripple in my womb.

He tears his mouth free, sets his forehead on mine, and watches as his hand moves sinuously under my white cotton panties. We're so breathless I don't expect his voice, guttural and rough as it explodes on my face, his forehead still resting on mine as he watches his hand caress my wetness: "Tell me this is for me."

My arms clench around his strong neck as he teases the very tip of his finger inside, and a mind-blowing pleasure bolts through me. "It's for you." Gasping, I kiss his hard temple, his jaw. A sound of protest leaves me when he withdraws his hand; then he grabs the edges of my panties and tears them off in a single breath.

Excitement runs through me. He grabs me by the waist and flips us around, slamming me back against the wall. My legs fly around him as he cups my ass in his hands, and the next second I feel him—there, at my entry. His hardness meets all the exterior part of my slick opening, and he grabs my wrists and pins my arms up above my head, locking them in one hand.

"Are you mine?" he asks gruffly, as his hand returns between my thighs and briefly enters me.

I gasp. Undone. Delirious. "I'm yours."

His expression is tense, ravenous, so hot as he shoves his finger deep into my channel. "Do you want me inside you?"

My need clogs my windpipe as pleasure shoots down my legs. "I want you everywhere. All over me. Inside me."

His hand trembles with restraint as he withdraws it, and, once again, he settles his erection between my legs. He doesn't enter, but he allows me to feel what he will give me. Our gazes cling desperately as we rub. We rock our hips together. We pant. We want. And I can't take my eyes off him.

He's even more beautiful than when he fights and is cocky and angry. More beautiful than when he trains and is sweaty and tired. More so than when he's smiling and playful. Even more than when he's thoughtful and relaxed being rubbed down with oil. He's more beautiful than anything I've ever seen—his face taut and raw with need, his eyes dark and half-open, his nostrils flaring, his mouth parted to breathe, his neck corded with veins, his tan deeper and darker as his overpowering arousal rushes color through his skin.

He holds my arms imprisoned as he caresses me with his hardness. Tempting me. Promising me. All I can do is whimper in a silent plea for him to take me. My sex ripples. My blood storms through my body. I'm being claimed by the man I love, and I am ready.

I.

Am.

Ready.

Darkened blue eyes watch me for a heart-stopping moment. One second I'm empty, the next he's in me. He fills me slowly and carefully, like I'm his prized treasure and he doesn't want to break me—as if he thinks no one else will receive him as snugly, and willingly, and lovingly as me. He's wide and hard, all man, impaling me. He shudders and groans as my sex muscles grip his pulsing length, and he's so big. A new whimper comes, almost painful as I squirm, wanting more, wanting less. Deciding my need for more is beyond anything, I drop down even farther and throw my head back, a weak sound escaping me as my body adjusts.

Gently he grabs both my breasts in his callused hands and pushes his tongue into my mouth until I swallow my own scream and drink everything his tongue gives me. He's pulsing fiercely in my channel, holding himself fully seated inside. My body trembles in delirium when he drops his head and runs his tongue over my jaw, along my chin, down my neck. When he suckles a nipple into his hot mouth, my insides grip as my orgasm starts building, and I shudder in fevered heat and thrust my hips wantonly against his.

"Remy," I beg as my arms tighten around his neck. I clench my thighs around him, tilting my pelvis. The move shoots excruciating pleasure through my body as his hardness drags inside me. My eyes roll into the back of my head.

I'm not going to last. He's too big, feels too good, I need him too much.

"Remy . . ." I moan, out of my mind, rocking my hips. "Please, please . . . *move*."

He groans as though he's afraid he won't last either. But he tries to please me, and withdraws, and then thrusts back in. We're both undone, and a similar desperate sound of pleasure tears from our throats. He repeats the motion of his hips and drops his forehead to mine with a growl of restraint, and then he starts kissing me like his life depends on it.

"Brooke," he rasps into my mouth. His hands clench on my hips as he pulls out and plunges back in, deep enough to bury every inch in me. He immediately goes off. The warmth of his incredibly violent convulsions and the powerful jerks of his cock shuddering inside me take me. Tremors crash through my body. My systems stall and restart as a bunch of stars fall through the back of my eyelids.

I clutch his muscled body as it clenches and twists against mine, licking his neck as his muscular body strains and finally relaxes. He growls in quiet satisfaction into my temple.

We continue panting and gently rocking our hips even as the orgasms stop, and Remington vibrates against me with so much need, he doesn't even let me catch my breath.

He grabs me by the ass, my legs still locked around his lean hips, and carries me to the bed. He's still inside me, still hard.

He sets me down and props a pillow under my head, and then he starts moving inside me, so slowly I mew and rake my nails down his back, watching him brace up on his shoulders, loving his perfect arms, his perfect thick throat, his face undone with pleasure as he starts fucking me fast and hard, like an animal. My nipples throb just looking into his lust-darkened eyes.

He brings his head to mine and feeds his tongue past my lips until I swallow my own gasps. "You wanted me." His breaths come fast, his eyes wild. "Here I am."

He fucks his cock into me ten times, fast and hard, making me yelp in delight over his claiming, and when my muscles seize up and my body prepares for another earth-shattering orgasm, he lets me come, keeping the frantic pace. Then, growling and prolonging his own orgasm, he pulls out to rub himself over my skin.

Quaking, my throat rumbles with a moan as he drags the slickened head of his cock along my inner thigh while one of his hands caresses a throbbing breast tip. I've always liked the fullness of my B cups, but they feel small and fragile in his big, callused hands.

He groans, though, like he really likes to squeeze them, and twirls his tongue up my neck. "I've wanted to touch you for so long, little firecracker."

Pleasure shoots across my nerve endings as he pinches and tweaks. His teeth graze the skin under my jawline, exposed when I arch up to his body.

His muscles surround me, hard and strong, clenching and flexing, his cock gut-wrenchingly hard and sexy, rubbing all over my body and smearing his semen on me. I'm so delirious, I want to have this man inside my sex and my mouth, and in my hands, all at once.

He suddenly plunges back into my sheath, harder and deeper, his fingers digging into my hips, and I'm still so wet and swollen, I meet his every thrust, desperately moaning his name. *"Remington."*

This isn't about foreplay. It's about claiming and taking, about relieving this throbbing, painful physical ache that is so powerful it makes my soul hurt. But I'm singing inside now. I can't even believe the way he smells, the way he feels. Better than all my fantasies.

And I realize while I'm gasping *please, oh god, you're so hard, you feel so good*, he has his own chant, telling me *so sweet and wet* as he licks every part of me he can. I love that he rubbed his scent on me, that he licks me everywhere, that I get to feel his teeth, his calluses, his skin, the bite of his blunt fingertips on my flesh.

Wild sounds tear out of me, ragged like my breaths. There's no way for me to trap these raw, lustful noises. The deeper ones Remington makes make me crazy. He surges back to watch my breasts bounce as he fucks me fiercely hard, and his eyes glow like a predator's as his hips slam against mine. He's primal, animal, taking me; and he's mine.

My teeth knock as my body grips every inch of his thrusting cock. My fingers dig into his drool-worthy buttocks as I draw him in deeper, twisting under his weight until I snap. I release a cry when his warmth spills inside me, and he follows with a low moan, clenching my hips as he slows the pace until we're a mass of tired muscles and bones, sweat slicked and entangled on the bed.

I feel delicious afterward. Loose and warm, and very, very wanted.

Sighing, I grab one heavy male arm and drape it around my shoulders so I can snuggle in the nook against his chest, and then I kiss his nearest nipple. He has the sexiest, smallest, brownest, most perfectly pointed man-nipples I've ever seen, without a single hair anywhere on his chest. Just kissing it makes my sex clench again, even when it's completely sore.

He grabs my languid body and positions me right above his body as he lies flat on his back, like he's my bed and my legs run down the length of his, my body facedown as he faces the ceiling. We're abs to abs, belly button to belly button. He nuzzles his nose across my temple as he slowly caresses my ass. "You smell of me."

"Hmmm," I say.

He clenches one ass cheek in his hand and buzzes his nose against my temple. "What does 'hmmm' mean?"

I smile in the darkness. "You said it first."

"It means I want to eat you. Your little biceps. Your little triceps." He kisses me on the mouth and drags his tongue over my lips. "Now you."

Seizing his hand, I squeeze it in between our bodies so that he can feel everything that he smeared me with all across my abdomen. "It means I'm going French this week and not showering so I can smell you on me."

He groans and shifts us so that my side hits the bed, and then he reaches between my legs to where I'm drenched in what he just gave me. His eyes glow in the shadows as he slides the soft liquid semen dripping down my thigh in a path leading back into my swollen entry, as if he doesn't want to come out of my body.

"Sticky?" he asks in a gruff murmur, bending his head and licking my shoulder as he pushes his semen back inside with one finger. "Do you want to wash me off you?"

The thought of him pushing his semen back inside me makes me so hot, I grip his head and come closer to him. "No. I want you to give me more."

He brings his damp fingers to my face and pushes his middle finger into my lips, as though asking me to taste. "I wanted you since the first night I saw you." His voice comes out gruff as he watches me suck his finger into my mouth.

His taste does crazy things to me and my sex ripples with the need to feel him inside me again. "So did I." I'm breathless and straining for a decent breath as I lick every drop.

He shoves a second damp finger into my mouth, and his salty ocean taste invigorates me. My eyes drift shut as I drag my tongue all down the length of his fingers. I'm so eager I think I moan. "Do you like my taste?" he thickly murmurs.

"Hmm. That's all I want from now on." Mischievously I take a little bite of his fingertips, and suddenly, I can feel his erection coming back up against me. Something I said . . .

"I'll always want my Remy fix after dinner," I continue, and I'm the one getting super thrilled when he continues thickening. "And maybe before breakfast. And after lunch. And at teatime."

He groans, then drags himself between my parted legs and bends his head downward to taste *me*. His tongue flashes into me. My eyes flutter closed as my spine arches, the heat of his mouth shattering me. He grabs my buttocks in his hands and squeezes my flesh as his wet tongue slides across my clit over and over again.

"I . . . want to . . . come . . . on every part of your body . . ." he murmurs into me, his eyes closed as he surges up and shoves his erection against the outer slit of my entry.

I'm on fire with want. I need him inside me again, in my mouth, in my sex, in all my being. I grip the back of his head and rock my hips restlessly in a silent plea as I push my tongue into his mouth. "Come wherever you want, inside me, outside me, in my hand, in my mouth."

When I grab his hardness in my fist, he instantly goes off, hot and liquid, spilling on my wrist. The convulsions are as powerful as he is, and my sex creams up hotly when I watch. He's so magnificent and raw that suddenly I roll him onto his back and jump down on his erection, taking him in me with a whimper of surprise over his size again. He barks out in pleasure and throws his head back, gripping my hips and pulling me up, then lowering me again as he rams back up and his hardness keeps jerking inside me. Eventually, and before I know it, a scream of ecstasy tears through me as I convulse with him, feeling his warmth burst deep inside me again.

I'm totally limp and near comatose when I fall back on him.

"The night they sedated you . . ." I ask him, hours later, as I buzz the tip of my nose against his nipple again, still breathless over a long petting session. We can't get enough. We're like teenagers. Making up for weeks and weeks of wanting. "That was an episode?"

The pillow rustles as he nods, and I slide my hand over his speed-bump abs and rub him gently as I peer up at him, unsure whether he wants to do this right now. "Can we even talk about it?"

My touch seems to make him close his eyes, his voice velvety smooth as he cups the back of my head in one big hand, and he presses me down against his neck, cuddling me to him. "You can talk to Pete about it."

I'm sticky with our desire and I like it, run my hands over him and know that he's sticky too. The thought of taking a bath with him, washing "him" off, and then getting sticky all over again makes me want to moan. "Why don't *you* talk to me about it, Remington?" I ask softly.

He sits up and twists his feet off the bed; then he drags his hands down his face. "Because a lot of episodes I don't remember what I do." He pushes to his feet and moves away from the bed.

Shit. I made him pace now.

"All right, I'll talk to Pete about it, but come back to bed," I say, quickly relenting when I notice the tension in his stance.

He stares out the window, his body perfect. So perfect. Legs braced apart, arms crossed, his muscles perfectly fed, formed, and taut. "I remember you." His voice roughens. "In my last episode. The tequila shots. The way you looked. The little top you were wearing. The nights you slept in my bed."

To think he notices what I wear does something tingly to me. I'm almost sure when he turns around I'll be a pool of lava on the bed, already waiting for him to come fuck me.

He seemed so happy that day, with the shots—his energy was like that of a sun.

And then it flipped into night so quickly.

"I wanted us to happen so bad," I painfully admit.

He turns. "You think I didn't? I've wanted us to happen since . . ." He comes back to bed and drags me to him, kissing my lips fiercely. "Every second I want us to happen."

I touch his jaw. "Have you ever hurt someone?"

Grief flicks into his eyes again, and he looks haunted, dropping his arm from me. "I hurt everything I touch. I destroy things! That's the only thing I'm good at. I've found whores in my bed I can't remember bringing back with me, and I've tossed them naked out of my hotel room, pissed like hell because I don't remember what I did. I've stolen shit, vandalized shit, woken up in places I don't even remember getting to . . ." He drags in a breath and sighs. "Look, since Pete and Riley alternate days off, there's always someone to knock me out for a day or two when I get out of hand. I hit a low, and then I'm back. Nobody gets hurt."

"But you. Nobody gets hurt but *you*," I whisper sadly, and I reach out and snatch his closest hand within mine merely because I'm afraid he'll get out of bed, and I don't want him to. It feels like it took me a lifetime to get him here with me in the first place.

"Remy, do they have to knock you out like that?" I lace my fingers through his as I ask the question.

"Yes," he says, emphatic. "Especially if I want . . . this. . . ." He signals to me, and to him, with his free hand, and clenches me with the other. "I want this. Very badly." He nuzzles my nose with his. "I'm trying not to fuck it up, all right?"

"All right."

He kisses the back of the hand that is holding his, his eyes sparkling once more. "All right."

❤ ❤ ❤

MY INTERNAL CLOCK just won't let me sleep past 6 a.m., even after a night such as the one I spent with him. Tickles of delight rush across my skin as I remember all the ways we made love to each other last night. My gaze lands on him, and the immense proprietary sensation that overcomes me is so powerful, it's all I can do not to attach myself permanently to his big body of sin.

Quietly and with a dopey smile that won't leave my face, I slip out of bed, knowing Riley and Pete won't let him oversleep much, and definitely not beyond 10 a.m.

Pete is already in the kitchen, pouring himself some coffee, and since there are a thousand things I want to ask him, I join him. Curling my legs under my body on a chair in the small breakfast table, I watch him view the morning paper as I take a few sips of my coffee; then I clear my raspy throat and say, "He told me."

For a moment, the only emotion on Pete's face is shock, but then it changes to dubiousness. "He told you what?"

"You know what." I set my coffee down and arch an eyebrow.

Pete lowers the paper, not smiling. "He never tells anyone."

His words make me frown. "Don't look so alarmed. He told *you* once. Didn't he?"

"He didn't tell me, Brooke, I was his *nurse*. At the ward. At least for his last year."

My mind spins in confusion as I try to envision Pete in scrubs and taking care of my big bad fighter in some hospital. I just didn't see this one coming. At all. The image is so incongruent I have trouble holding it in my head. "You were with him at the ward?" Okay, I know I sound stupid, but that's all I seem to be able to ask.

Pete's lips clench tightly as he nods. "It pissed me off." He scowls darkly at his coffee, then shakes his head. "He's a good dude. A little reckless—but it's not his fault! He *never* picked on anyone. He was as closed off as a damned wall, that kid. He just ran like hell out in the yard and did his pull-ups on a tree outside, all day wearing his headphones and blocking everything out. They had him all drugged ever since one time he got speedy and told everyone they should escape. They all followed, and there was a big mess, and from then on, no one would even give him a chance to get speedy again; they just kept shooting shit up his veins and sparing themselves the trouble."

"My god." The shock, horror, and anger I feel sweep over me like a sickness, and I can barely swallow the sip of coffee I have in my mouth.

"Remy's not crazy, Brooke," Pete emphasizes, "but they treated him like he was. Even his parents. All he had in terms of comfort were some damn headphones. Which is why the guy rarely expresses himself. He just can't. He's been too closed off for years."

With a heart that's just melting for him, I realize that since the beginning, Remy has opened up to me through music, which is something that seems familiar and comforting to him, and suddenly, vividly, I want to hear each one of the songs he's played me all over again.

My eyes sting a little, and I lower my head so Pete doesn't see that I'm touched beyond words. Remy is a quiet man. He's a physical man and yields to his physical instincts, but I don't think he even knows how to verbalize his emotions very well.

I wonder if I'm a little closed off like Remy too?

In my life, I've frequently counted on Melanie to say things that I want to but feel too shy or embarrassed to admit out in the open. I never even told anyone after my ACL tore that it fucking *sucked.*

Remy's so different from me, and yet we're so alike I swear I can understand this man in my *soul.*

Suddenly I have to fight the impulse to get on my feet, go back to bed, and curl up with him.

"Was the night at the hotel . . . when you shot him up with something . . . what was that?"

"An episode. It's not really another personality like people think. Well, it *is,* in part, but it's more like a mood. It's an alternate gene expression, conflicting with his previous one. Typically, some external trigger will shut down a gene expression and another becomes activated, which shifts his mood dramatically." Pete meets my gaze with his warm, worried brown eyes, his features twisting in pain. "He suffers greatly, Brooke. Not only because it's confusing for him, but because he doesn't remember what he does when he goes manic."

I'm flashed back to all those nights he came for me in my room, with those darkened eyes, and kissed me senseless until morning. "But he told me he remembered some things?" I say hopefully.

"Sometimes he does, but sometimes he doesn't. The point is, he can't trust himself to know for sure what he will do when he goes black."

Which is why he's been trying to be so careful with me . . .

My insides go mushy all over.

"So who told Riley, then?"

"*I* told Riley. I had to hire an extra so I could take a day off now and then. Otherwise I'd come back and Rem would've gotten himself in shitloads of trouble. Coach also knows about it, of course, and Diane suspects something is up, but she doesn't know the actual diagnosis. She just thinks he's moody."

Sighing at that, Pete pours himself some more coffee. "I helped him sign out of the ward the moment he could. I'd just quit, and he told me he wanted to go see his parents, and he'd pay me if I gave him a lift, so I agreed." Anger slashes across Pete's face as he returns to his seat. "But the parents wanted nothing to do with him. They were scared at the mere sight of him. Shit, you should've seen the drama. The mother started crying, the father told Rem they wanted to live in peace, and Rem just stood there. I could see him struggling for words. I don't know if he wanted to beg them for a chance or not, but he didn't say anything. They all but slammed the door in his face. So we left, and Remy started fighting for money. He was good, so he got into pro boxing and hired me full-time as his assistant. He got a house in Austin and took another shot with the folks, and when at last they seemed to be pleased with his growing fame, they invited him to dinner. But it was the weekend the competition provoked him, and they hired some asshole to follow him out of a match. Remy has a short fuse even when he's in a *normal* mood."

My coffee has grown cold, so I also go and fix myself a new one as I process all of this. Pete continues as he watches me sit down.

"So he got kicked out, it was all over the news, and the parents never showed up at the restaurant." He sighs while I sit there, both of us sad and hurting for Remy; then he adds, "It doesn't sound like much, what he told you, Brooke. But living with it can get difficult."

His eyes bore into the top of my head, and I know he's gauging me. I can feel the question in his eyes almost as if he'd spoken it. He's worried about me leaving Remington. And I don't know what guarantee I can give anyone, especially when I have no idea what to expect from his bipolarness. But I know I want to stay. I really do.

"He tried to go to college too," Pete offers. "But he couldn't finish a degree, was always getting into fights. With any provocation, the guy's instinct is to *charge*, and he kept introducing his knuckles to anyone at school he thought deserved it."

"Was that where he met Riley?"

"Not on the other side of his knuckles, no." He laughs, his eyes sparkling for a moment. "Rem actually stood up for Riley. Riley wasn't the charming young man you see now when he was in college." He winks playfully. "He was like me. Both geeks, I tell you. Neither of us was all that cool. But Rem saved Riley's ass once, and Riley followed him like a dog right afterward, asking him for a couple of pointers to defend himself. That's how I met Riley, when they sparred." He grins. "But hell, Brooke, even with the moves, he was still geek material. But Remy was the coolest bad boy ever. Everyone wanted a piece of him, especially the women. He'd get them all over him, all day, and even the guys would follow, especially when he was getting high. Excesses abound when he's in his beginning black days. Alcohol, women, adrenaline, adventure.

"He was actually under intense scrutiny all those years at the psych ward because of the eye-color change," he adds. "It's not uncommon for BPs to have it, but it's rare. Two conflicting gene expressions, varying when one is triggered and the other is shut down. We have cocky, confident Remy, and black Remy. Black

Remy still has a good heart, but he's not reasonable. He's not mean and certainly not evil. But he's unpredictable and violent, and tends to destroy things, even himself. He flies high and then crashes low. This time you saw his low, it wasn't nearly as bad as his other lows. Somehow Riley and I felt maybe it was because you kept him interested. He seemed to want to see you and kept coming out at least for that."

"Pete, how can I help him?" I ask helplessly, pushing my coffee aside and giving him my full attention. "Please tell me how to help him, I get sick thinking of you using that stupid shit you shoot up his veins again."

He sighs and tugs on his perfect black tie, loosening it a little. "I just don't know with you, Brooke, but I know you're a game changer. He's never gone after someone the way he went after you, but even then, I'm sorry, but I can't stop using the sedative—and he doesn't want me to. Remy . . . his whole life is waiting for the other shoe to drop. You have to understand what it's like, that his normal side sometimes doesn't remember what the black one does. There have been instances when police come knocking on his door, telling him he just broke into a liquor store and robbed it, and he'd be, 'No fucking way—I've been in bed all night,' and they go, 'Sir, the liquor is still in your car.'"

"Seriously?" I blink at that.

He nods somberly. "He fears he's going to get black, then wake up blue and you will be gone. Because he did something to hurt you."

I think of how important my contract of three months working for him had seemed. And remember the night he went crazy, yelling at Pete and Riley where the fuck was I, and what had they told me about him?

Somehow the realization makes me feel warm and claimed once more.

"Everything *bad* happens to Remington when he's *black*," Pete adds with a clatter of his empty coffee cup. "He wakes up and finds he was kicked out of boxing. Last time he bet all his money and woke up to find that if he loses this season, he'll end up with very little to stand on. Riley and I try to get him under control, but he's a handful. He's too strong and too damn stubborn. And now there's you. I don't know if you're good for him, or the worst kind of Achilles' heel there is. But it's not our choice, is it? Remington wants you."

Pete's words roll inside my head as I stare off at the peach-colored walls. It's taking me time to absorb all of this information. I don't know what it is to love someone like this. My life in Seattle awaits—Melanie . . . my parents. I've got at least one more month, and I want to spend every second I can with him. I just love him more with every bit that I learn. He's complicated and complex, a labyrinth I want to lose myself in. He's my fighter, and I really want to fight to be with him.

But I just don't know what I'm going to have to fight against. If it's some fear in me . . . some fear in him . . . or that black side of him.

"I want him badly too," I tell Pete, patting his shoulder. "So much I might shoot some shit up your veins if you keep shooting him up with that, you know?"

He laughs.

And I carry my empty cup to the sink, wash it, then fiddle around with some breakfast items, and send a text to Melanie telling her:

The earth moved. Yes! It was that freakingfuckingtastic OMG!!!!!!!!!!!!

And finally, just before 10 a.m. and before Riley comes to molest us, I go back to bed and lock myself in with Remy. Setting a tall glass I mixed up for him on the nightstand, I lean over his naked form and murmur, while my heart and my sex organs swell up with his nearness, "Get up, you sexy piece of man-ass."

Then I grab Remy's sexy ass and squeeze those rocks and clench my teeth because I want to bite them, he's so frickin' juicy and hot.

"I'm not Diane, but this used to be the breakfast of champions before the champion tore her ACL and shot her knee to hell. Now you get her services in bed, consisting of all sugary treats for this"—I squeeze his biceps—"and these"—I slide my hand over his abs—"and this." I tap his lovely head and his mesmerizing maze of a brain.

Suddenly I realize that if it weren't for that double accident, I wouldn't be here. With this man. And it's the first time I realize I might not only be glad, but grateful, that the universe redirected me in my path.

His sexy voice is muffled by the pillow. "Why are you bringing me breakfast in bed?"

I slap his bum, and his flesh doesn't move one whit. "Because you look like my every fantasy and feeding you gets all my juices going. It's a female thing. Come on, drink."

He sits up, squinting those baby blues, and grabs the glass. It's a protein shake made of dates. I'm wild about dates: they taste like caramel and I can eat about two dozen in a sitting when I get my period and get that unstoppable hunger.

"That's so fucking good," he says, then tips the glass back for more.

I grin and watch him drink the rest, feeling warm all over. I love how well he eats, really clean. His body likes him for it, and so does his skin. I've never seen Remy eat junk food. Even when he's pigging out on room service, it's vegetables and fish or meat for him. I don't think he likes treats. It shows discipline and responsibility with his body, and I admire it. His fighting is aggressive to his cells and demanding of his ATP, which is the source of energy the cells produce, and I love that he feeds himself correctly right after. He's an athlete in heart, mind, and body, and it's incredibly hot to me.

My phone pings while he downs the last of the drink, and the message is actually Melanie's answer to my text. Figuring she must be running this morning without me, I set it aside to answer later. "It's Melanie, my friend. She's excited that there's been some action between tua and mua." I grin.

He laughs, the sound rich and awesome; then he sobers, his eyes so tender on my face my insides go mushy. "You miss her?"

I nod and want to tell him that she knows Nora also, and that she's like my shrink, but suddenly he bounds out of the room, so I start gathering my athletic gear. In a couple of minutes, he returns with a piece of hotel stationery.

"Tell her to present herself at the Southwest counter, with the code on this paper. There's a ticket under her name so she can meet us in Chicago. I'll take care of her room."

"No!" I say in pure thrilled disbelief.

His answering two dimples go straight to curl my toes.

"Remy, I . . ."

I don't know what I want to say, but actually I do.

I want this man to know that I am absolutely wild about him, and I'm not going to quit as soon as it gets steep. But I'm too afraid of being the only one to say something so . . . lasting.

If I say the "L" word to him, what will it mean for my future? I want him concentrated. I want my fighter to win. And I want him to say the "L" word to me not because he heard it first, but because deep in his inner complicated emotional world, he's certain that he feels this for me.

"Why are you doing this?" I ask instead.

One dark eyebrow quirks upward as he comes over with his two dimples. "Why do you think?" He kisses my ear and whispers, into my hair, "Because your ass looks great in those tight pants you wear. It's a guy thing."

A laugh escapes me, and his dimples deepen. He tugs me closer and scents me, and I bury my face in his neck, smelling it; then we need to part with a sound that's a mutual groan. I go to my old room to get changed, and on my way there I text Mel.

> Brooke: My man is so wild about me he just got tickets to fly my BFF over to meet me in Chicago. Just please don't offer anything sexual in gratitude because a) I will have to kill you and b) that's what I'M going to do but c) there's always Pete and Riley around.
>
> Melanie: OMG OMG OMG! You're serious? I'm going to go work the boss so I can go!
>
> Brooke: Work her hard! I'm dying to see u!!

The thought of seeing Melanie makes me grin and my insides bubble during the day. I urgently need to talk to her or I'm going to explode with what I'm feeling.

THAT DAY, AS Remy works out, I get busy on my phone and make a few discreet calls to the hotels in town. Nora isn't checked in at any of them, but I know she's with that Scorpion man. He's so gross I can't even fathom why my romantic little sister would get involved with him. He's not even a sexy badass like Remington. But I'm formulating a plan, and Melanie is going to be the one to help me bring it about perfectly without setting off a single one of Remington's protective instincts.

The thought makes me glance at him, and he's easily jumping rope, making those slapping sounds as the rope flies all over him in twisting, turning, one-foot-then-the-other moves. My loins heat up as I remember the feel of him, the many times we've made love. I'd wanted to know what it feels like to have him inside me. Now I do. And I feel like I'm being possessed by everything male and powerful in the world.

Later, when I stretch him, and my hands roam so freely over his warmed muscles, I feel like he's been made for me. Mine to touch. Mine. Mine. Mine. Scorching heat rages through me as his slick torso clenches under my fingers. His chest is heaving, and he's tired, and he needs to go eat, and all I can think of is jumping him when I get him back in bed with me.

As I go around the bench to work on his back, he snatches me in one arm and draws me onto his lap, burying his nose in my hair. "Hmmmm," he softly growls in my ear.

My nipples instantly perk up. Now that I know that "hmm," to Remington, means he wants to eat me and my traps and my biceps, I can't help the liquid heat flooding between my thighs.

He draws back with glinting male eyes and tucks a strand that came loose from my ponytail behind my ear. "I can smell how hot you are for me," he murmurs with a famished gaze on my mouth.

My breath goes choppy, and I slightly peer past my shoulder. I see that Coach and Riley are busy picking up all the stuff Remy left littered about, like gloves and ropes, so I turn back into him and whisper, "Well, have *you* seen you?" My lips brush the shell of his ear as I slide my hands around his shoulders and run my fingers down his muscled back. "*Have* you seen you? I can barely take my hands off you. Asking me to take my eyes off you is like asking me to deliberately drown—I just can't do it."

His sparkling blue eyes capture mine, and he lifts one hand and grabs my ponytail, working it free of its elastic band. He tosses the ribbon aside, then runs his fingers down my loose hair. "You're mine now. I won't let anyone else have you."

"I know." I sigh dramatically. Like it's a chore.

He smiles tenderly at me, then forces my arms around his sweaty neck. I see the drops of moisture still clinging to his forehead and they just make me want to dry him with my mouth.

"I like me when I see myself through you, Brooke." Gently, he seizes my ankles in his grip and guides my legs around his hips. His eyes glint in pure male contentment when his erection hits the spot between my legs, and he sweeps his head down and takes a nip from my outstretched arms, his teeth nibbling my bicep through the sleeve of my track jacket. "Hmm. And I like you like this even more."

"Remington!" I try prying free but he holds me down on his lap, laughing as I pointedly slide my eyes in the direction of Riley and Coach, who are still cleaning up. "What is this? Free-sex-show day?"

"Take a hike, guys!" he shouts, and within five fast heartbeats, we're alone. With the enormous gym and all the mat area, the weight equipment area, and the boxing ring, just for the two of us. The gyms he uses are always rented entirely for him, and the knowledge that no one will be coming shoots fire through my veins.

Remy slides his hands around my hips and spreads his fingers over my ass as he pins me down on his erection.

My breath stalls as I brazenly bring one of those big male hands upward; then I slowly force his grip around the curve of my breast, the swell covered in a skintight tank under my open track jacket.

He doesn't move for a heart-stopping moment. Then he ducks his dark head and uses his nose to nudge my jacket wider open to one side, and then the other. The sensual way his face nuzzles and reveals me hitches my temperature several degrees. I feel fevered by the time the mounds of both my breasts become fully exposed in my tank. Before easing back, Remy angles his head slightly to lick my chin; then he leans back to watch, engrossed, as his fingers curl tighter around my breast, his eyes at half-mast.

A world of sensation rushes through my bloodstream when he squeezes me with the hand I had put on me.

His thumb scrapes to stroke across the pebbled tip that pushes into my sports bra and top. I gasp. He's breathing hard now. His eyes eclipse as they coast down my flat abdomen in the skintight tank, taking in my toned thighs in my track pants, down to where my pussy is nestled in a tight V of emerald green nylon against his cock.

My inner muscles clench wantonly when those blue eyes settle and focus solely on this part of my body. Where my wet little kitten presses against the large erection swelling prominently in his gray sweatpants.

"I want you naked," he rasps.

"Remy, how can I look them in the eye if they know we're doing that right now? Right here?"

His gaze glints in pure mischief as he slowly eases my open track jacket off my shoulders. "I thought you couldn't take your eyes off *me*."

"I can't."

"So you admit you like my muscles?"

"I love your muscles."

"You like how I use them?"

"Yes." My breath is short and choppy as he grabs me by the hips, lifts me to standing, and pulls down my track pants until I'm in panties and sports bra.

"You like what I do to you with my mouth?" he continues.

"Yes."

This very moment I want to kiss my Under Armour sports bra almost as much as I want to kiss *him*. It has a zipper right in the middle, and it is as easy to get off as a front-clasp bra. When Remy slowly lowers the zipper, I bite my lip and watch his face. Lust filled. Male. Making me tingle all over.

"You like what I do to you with my fingers?" His voice is low and smooth, and I'm completely entranced by the questions he asks me.

"Yes, Remy."

He bares my breasts, and if I glance anywhere but at him, I know I will see myself naked in the tall, mirrored walls that surround us. He has a monopoly on virility, this man, and I don't know what it will do to me to get such a vast view of him from all angles. My sexy muscled Remington, gloriously naked, and multiplied by ten? Oh, god.

"Do you like what I do to you . . . with this . . .?" When he slides his sweatpants off, I'm fainting with the sight of ten Remington's butts in the reflections behind him, his powerful legs from behind, his narrow waist and broad shoulders.

And his cock, standing before me.

I've just died.

"Definitely, yes."

Up on tiptoe, I use his shoulders to propel me upward and crush his mouth with mine, and he sucks on my tongue and yanks my panties down my legs and sets me down on the mats, our naked flesh sliding smoothly against the other's.

"What if someone comes?" I halfheartedly protest.

"No one's coming here but you."

He's splayed me open and drawn my legs and arms out, and now he just looks his fill.

I pant in anticipation, feeling exposed. To him. His piercing blue stare strokes the flesh of my bare pussy lips, and I feel that stare inside me. Where I'm clenching wet and swelling. My clit throbs, and if he only parted my lips, he could see how swollen he makes me.

My heart pounds wildly as I hear the rustling sound of the mats when I brazenly spread my legs apart even more. Need catches thickly in my throat when his face tightens; then he brushes his hand between my legs, his thumb moves lightly across my pussy lips.

His eyelids droop, and his expression softens as his thumb dips into the fissure. My breath stalls, and I catch my lower lip between my teeth.

A shudder sweeps through me as he drags his thumb from my pussy to my belly button, then between my breasts, to stroke the lips of my mouth with the same thumb he just used to caress my sex. He cups the swell of my breast in another hand and thumbs it while he thumbs my mouth too, and I'm no longer breathing. The touches are painfully teasing, and a tremor rushes through me as he finally tightens the flesh of my breast in his palm, pushing my nipple outward as he slowly bends his dark head. He prolongs the moment, making me whimper by the time the tip of his damp tongue slides slickly across the hardened pebble.

My eyes blur. Tremors of fire shoot through me, and I desperately part my mouth to taste the finger he used to caress my pussy, which still hovers against my lips and is scented of me. I need to lick something, need to use my tongue on something, and as he heads to my other breast, he watches me intently and pushes his thumb deep into my mouth as if he knows what I want.

My tongue wraps feverishly around him as he nips the tip of my throbbing nipple. Ecstasy crashes through my body. Gasping, I bite down on his thumb as he uses his lips to nip my breasts equally hard. Pleasure radiates through all my being as he tugs on my nipple with his teeth, and I desperately grab his shoulders and sink my nails into his skin while he slides one hand between my thighs.

"Do you need me to make you come?"

He pushes his thick, long finger deep into me, and my sex squeezes him. My entire body clenches from the exhilarating sensation of his touch inside me.

"Yes, but I want you inside me," I gasp.

"That's where you're going to get me."

He strokes my inner channel, and I close my eyes as I disintegrate under him. My hands slide up his rock-hard torso, and I store the firm, fabulous feeling to memory as my pelvis pushes up to his palm in anxious need.

My nipples ache, and I stretch to rub my breasts against his chest while I trail my fingers along his back. "Make love to me."

He groans and strokes his tongue against mine. "Not yet . . ." he murmurs, and sucks the flesh of my lower lip into his mouth, releasing it to blow air across the tender wet flesh. "Not yet, but soon . . ."

His voice is guttural, but there's a gentleness in it that dissolves my insides so that I can do nothing but pant. He drags himself between my parted legs and buries his head between my thighs, and his tongue flashes across my clit.

My eyes slam shut as I arch to him, the heat of his mouth short-circuiting my senses. He cups my buttocks in his huge hands and locks me to him, his wet tongue sliding in to taste my clit again and again.

"You like that?" he asks, the words muffled.

I nod. Then, realizing he can't see me, I rasp, "Yes," just as he looks up.

He lowers his face to me again, growling deep but gently as he buries his dark head between my legs and teases my clit with his tongue. My knees tremble as my legs try to swing open even wider.

An orgasm keeps building in my core, all my muscles clenching taut, and I claw at the top of his head, grabbing a fistful of damp hair, "No . . . please . . . I want to come with you."

He doesn't listen.

His head is busy moving between my parted thighs. He makes low purr-like sounds between my legs and is so surprisingly ravenous I can feel his teeth. His nails bite into my thighs as he devours me like he's the one deriving pleasure from the act, and I'm so turned on by the way he laps me up that I come.

Convulsions rock me beneath him, and he makes another sound and keeps on going as he adds a finger in me. He lifts his head and watches me climax—and I keep going off like a rocket for him, exploding in a thousand and one pieces. It's always so intense with him. . . . I'm shuddering as he comes up, and he's pulsing against my hip bone as he crushes my mouth.

"Let me," I breathe, and I reach between our bodies, but he clamps my wrist within his big hand.

"Easy," he tells me, struggling to catch his breath, but I ignore him and anxiously grab the top part of his shaft.

Arousal shoots through me again when I feel the silky wetness at its crown. Groaning, he lowers his dark head and licks my earlobe, his breath hot and fast in my ear. I touch him hesitantly, somehow expecting him to stop me, but he doesn't.

I make a sound of pleasure and turn my head to him.

We start kissing.

He takes the kiss to the next level, adding tongue and teeth, which lights up a fire in me. Sensations rush through my body with each damp flick, my fingers clenching in his shaft as my grip slides over him.

My other hand goes to his hair, and I hold his kiss to me. I wind my fingers in the silky sable of his thick, soft hair as I bury my entire being in his taste, in him. His erection vibrates in my hand, and I shake with a new, even fiercer need when I feel his size, his strength, pulsing hot and commandingly.

He's so overwhelmingly sexy that every second I lie here, underneath him, I die a slow death. I want to gobble him up. I love the way he guards me, protects me, the way he looks *back* at me, the way he feels—this is the most aroused, stunning man I've ever held in my hand.

I try to close my fist around him, and though I can't, I sense whatever holds him back, breaks when I try to squeeze him.

He pulls me up to crush my mouth with his, then easily flips me around and hauls me up to a doggy position. "Like this," he commands in my ear, then forces my head around to crush my mouth again until my lips feel swollen because of him.

He tears free and sets his forehead at the back of my head with a hungered groan that resonates in my core. My sex pulses when he inhales me, and he keeps scenting me as he rubs his cock along my bottom.

It feels too good when he pushes in. I cry and turn my head. And then I see his reflection, how he's completely over me. Mounting me. And he's so beautiful it mesmerizes me. He's naked and glistening from his exercise, and all his muscles are engaged as his hips rock, his arms holding his upper body aloft from me. He uses his arms to fuck me, his back, his abs, his thighs, his buttocks. His whole body. I don't even see myself, just a quick glance at how petite I look under him, apricot-white against his tan, my hair no longer in a ponytail falling down the sides of my face and my shoulders, my breasts bouncing, and the look on my face . . . I never even knew I could look so smoky and aroused, my rosy cheeks and my eyes shining like crazy because I'm looking at the only man I've ever truly had feelings for.

He holds me up on my hands and knees and whispers, "Look at me." And urges my head up so I meet his gaze in the mirror.

He wants me to see, and I can barely keep my eyes open. The sight of us making love is excruciatingly addictive. My eyelids flutter shut, and Remington pulls out and drags himself along my fissure, squeezing my ass cheeks around him, then thrusts with a decadent groan into my achingly wet pussy. "Look at me."

I do. When I open my eyes, I see all those packed muscles, his square shoulders, his flat, hard pectorals and his small, brown nipples glistening wetly, and I tremble as I see the muscles of his right hand flex as he slides it down my abdomen and between my legs. His body vibrates against mine, and I'm ready to come when he adds his thumb in heart-stopping circles across my sensitized clit. I bloom open with need. He's beautiful, and he's the most virile thing I've ever seen. And he's mine.

The look of passion on his face is because of me. The lust in his eyes for me. A fierce orgasm coils in my midsection, and I moan feebly, begging him for its release.

He hears me.

He watches me in the mirror like he's never seen anything like me . . . his eyes wild, primal. Possessive.

Every ounce of me throbs in pleasure as he withdraws and halts the crown of his hard cock at my wet entry, the move halting my climax at the tremulous pinnacle, and then he pushes back into my body in a slow, delicious rhythm again.

"*Yeah* . . ." he rasps, his eyes closed as he shoves himself forward. My orgasm tightens and strains inside me. I shudder at the sexy image of him, lost to me, and suddenly he growls and grabs my hair in his fist, turning my head and slamming his mouth to mine.

My pussy is liquid with want. His cock drags inside me, thick and hard, in my sex, in my being. I grip him tighter with my sex muscles and rock my hips back restlessly in silent plea. "Push every inch of you in me . . . I want every inch of you," I beg.

He thrusts deeper with a roar, the move startling a whimper out of me. The pace we set suddenly is feral, rapid. I can see my breasts bouncing as he rams me, my body jerking under the powerful rocking motions of his hips. His biceps clench as he grips my hips and holds me still for him.

He's undone already.

His hips rock on me and I'm a mass of quaking lust with the magnificent sight of him behind me. Eyes closed, muscles bulging, face taut. I push backward and swallow a moan as he spills in me, warm inside my depths. The convulsions are as powerful as he is, and my sex creams up hotly as I watch and instantly follow.

He keeps pumping into my pussy as the tremors seize me, holding his hand between my thighs and caressing my clit with those big callused hands that drive me crazy. I cry his name softly and he groans mine, and when we're sated on the mats, I just know.

I know. For sure. One hundred percent to the tenth power.

I've fallen head over heels, irrevocably in love with him.

TEN

A VISITOR

At the Chicago O'Hare International Airport, Pete and I are seated out by the baggage claim among the bustle of people as we wait for Melanie's flight to arrive.

"Pete, there's something I've been meaning to talk to you about," I tell him as I keep scanning the flight arrival screens above. He looks like my bodyguard in that *Men in Black* suit, following me even when I stand to stretch my legs. I just know it's because Remy told him not to take his eyes off me, and if Melanie were here, I also know she'd be anxious for us to go "pee" just to see what the poor man would do—like with that Whataburger incident. But Pete is such a good guy, I wouldn't dream of putting him in a tight spot with Remy. Except maybe . . . under duress.

Which means, possibly, now.

"So, Pete, do you remember the night Remy ditched the ring because I was following someone? *Of course* you remember."

The obvious disgust in his expression makes me laugh out loud a little.

Then we realize our small seating space has been taken over

by a group of college students, and we walk over to stand by the side of the carousels.

"That girl was my sister, Pete. She's my little sister, who I think has gotten herself involved with the wrong crowd, and I really think I need to step up and help her. No. I don't think it. I know it," I emphasize. When Pete pulls out a piece of Trident gum for himself in reply, I ask, "Oh, can I have one?" trying to keep things casual.

When he hands me a piece, he doesn't even look at me. "Remington is already on top of that, so don't even fret about it."

"What?" He completely blanks out my thoughts with that statement. With a dazed expression, I stare down at the proffered gum, then fold the silver foil open and pop the gum into my mouth, the juice bursting in my mouth so completely that it makes me have to bite several times before speaking.

"What do you mean he's on top of that? The last thing I want is him involved with anything to do with that Scorpion fucker."

Pete grimaces as if the gum in his mouth tastes like bitter whole coffee beans. "Neither do I. But Rem's already made contact to open talks about her being returned to you. I warn you, it's not going to be easy. Apparently your sister didn't want out even when Rem offered *a lot* of money."

My stomach shudders. Okay, truth time. I find it extremely generous and so bloody hot Remington is doing this for me, but I can't allow it, especially now that I know the truth and certainly don't want him tripping any of his triggers. "Please, Pete, I want Remy to forget about it. I don't want to get him in trouble."

At one of the carousels, a little boy runs around, tripping with suitcases while his flustered father tries to catch up. We both watch with an amusement completely at odds with our conversation, which doesn't feel right.

"Don't worry, Brooke. We'll take care of Rem. I've him convinced to let *me* talk to that insect's goons now. There's no way *in hell* I'm letting Rem interact with Scorpion on his own. Too many things between them. He was adamant about going himself, but I reminded him if he got kicked out of *this* league, then he wouldn't be able to hire *you* anymore. He grumbled in protest but, in the end, calmed down and agreed to send me or Riley."

My smile hurts on my face. I find it incredibly amusing that Pete used *me* to bend Remy's iron will.

"Is there a reason they're so friendly, our little lamb Scorpy and Remington?" I ask Pete.

"*Scorpy*," he sarcastically answers, with an amused smile, "is the douche his competition hired to get Rem kicked out of pro. Rem loathes his fucking ass and can't wait to mop the floor with it."

"He's the one? Oh, I *hate* that asshole ever since the club!" I explode, then level a glare at Pete. "Well, then, now you must agree with me it's best if we leave Remy out of this mess? I don't want him to even be tempted to talk to Scorpion himself, and I *certainly* don't want him to pay for my sister. She's a free woman! She should leave on her own. Pete, I'm sure if I can only talk to my sister, I can reason with her."

The little boy trips and falls on someone's small black duffel. His laughter stops, and then his cries break through the bustling noises as Dad finally picks him up and carries him back to where Mother waits for their suitcases.

"Okay, Brooke," Pete says, his thoughtful brown eyes turning to me, "I'm all for keeping him stabilized and away from that motherfucker. So what do we do?"

I go throw my gum to the nearest trash can and Pete immediately tags along. "All I need is to talk to Nora, but I don't think he'd like me to, so you can't let Remington find out that I went to see her." Nervously, I survey Pete's reaction. I've never been sneaky, but I can't let Remy in on this; it goes against all my protective instincts toward *him*. "You understand this is something I have to do, don't you, Pete? From what I saw, Nora needs a serious reality check, and I need to talk some reason into her."

"I understand," he agrees, with a slight nod, as we prop ourselves against a pillar. "I just don't like what will happen when Rem finds out."

"He won't. Melanie will help me get a message to my sister during the next fight. I'll fix a meeting with her at a nearby restaurant, and you'll only have to cover me when I go."

"Brooke, he'll have my *head* if something goes wrong, and I'm a little bit attached to it, you understand."

"Nothing will go wrong. I've taken more self-defense classes than I know what to do with. The only guy I haven't been able to knock down is Remy."

Pete bursts out laughing. "You knocked that man flat off his feet, Brooke."

"You're funny, Pedro." I'm delightedly grinning now, which makes my puppy-dog eyes perhaps not very effective. "Come on. Help? Please?"

A thoughtful frown crosses his features, and he taps his chin twice as he goes deep in thought. "Only if Riley goes with you and your friend when you go to the meeting."

"Thanks, fine. Yes! Thank you, Pete." Yielding to the impulse, I give his hand a quick squeeze and realize I've grown attached to everyone in the team. I'm dreading the day my three-month stint ends.

I want to stay with them. There's no question about it. But I at least have to escort Nora safely home, if I'm lucky to convince her, and then, afterward, decide what I'm going to do, depending on how things with Remington are going. The thought of leaving unsettles me, even if it's only temporary. "Do you have any brothers, Pedro?"

"Rem."

My eyes widen and I can't believe this guy is going to surprise me again. "Wait, he's your actual brother?"

"Not by blood. Hell, we don't look anything alike! I'm like a book and Rem's a bull! I don't *have* genetic brothers—my soul brother is Rem."

I'm thinking how sweet Pete is to think of Rem as a soul brother, and if Rem is my soul mate, then Pete is my soul brother-in-law. . . .

So here I am thinking stupid things, when here comes my best friend in the world to thankfully save me from my thoughts. Right out of a *Legally Blonde* movie, there she is. My sweet Melanie, hauling a flashy pink suitcase behind her with her blonde hair loose and a pair of sunglasses atop her head. She's not a bimbo, but she sure likes dressing like one. As an eclectic interior designer, she brings a touch of the eccentric to her person too. As far as she's concerned, everything goes well together. And today she looks like a rainbow, lighting up my world.

"Mel!" Leaping forward, I wrap my arms around her and let her wrap me in her slim arms and her Balenciaga fragrance.

"You look like you just got a damn facial peel, you're absolutely glowing, you bitch," she says, pushing me back for a narrow-eyed inspection. "And wearing a little dress rather than exercise gear? Well, well, well now." She appears thoroughly impressed, and then immediately her female instincts hone in on Pete, and her voice goes to the do-me-lover tone. "Well, hello there."

"Hello again, Miss Melanie," Pete says.

"Oh, Pete, call her Melanie. Melanie, call him Pedro. Come on, let's get you in the car," I tell them.

"I brought you a little present," Melanie says once we're in the back of the Escalade we rented, and she produces a huge packet of condoms—extra-large and ribbed for her pleasure—from her big travel purse. "In case you want to wait a little longer to pop out those babies Remy wants?" she taunts, waving the string of foils in the air.

"I don't need these, girl, you can go right ahead and put those back in your bag. I've got a capsule in my arm that puts out hormone, remember?"

"Oh! So you can actually feel everything during—"

"*Everything*," I happily say, and my body clenches remembering every. Single. Inch.

"Brooke, you have a seriously horny look on your face. Tell me everything about you and that sex god!" Melanie demands.

My eyes widen, and then laughter takes me over so hard, my head falls back and I clutch my stomach. "You did not just call me horny."

Melanie grins wide and varies her tone. "Horny. Horrrny. Hornyyy. You can't even say his name without looking *hornaay*. Hell, I can even feel your horniness in your texts. Especially that drunken one, you closet alcoholic."

Belatedly I realize we're so excited, we're having a totally personal conversation in the backseat while Pete drives, and suddenly I can feel a hot red flush creeping up my cheeks. Grabbing Mel's hand, I twitch my eyes in Pete's direction so she knows we can't keep saying "horny" with him around, for the love of god. Not that I don't trust him, but he's a guy. This is personal, damn it.

"Ahhh," Mel says, and nods; then she squeals and hugs me again, and I just let her give me some love and give her some back, because I just missed my bubbly little Mel.

So she ends up talking to Pete about the weather in Chicago, which is windy but sunny and frightfully chilly in the evening, and then I take her to lunch at the hotel.

After some whoppingly large salads and panini, we get her stuff into her room and I take her to the presidential suite. For hours we're both barefoot on the queen bed in the spare room catching up, and eventually we order room service.

She tells me a bunch of stuff while we chow down again, including that Kyle is dating someone and that Pandora went back to chain-smoking ever since the battery on her e-cigarette stopped charging and the FedEx shipment with the replacement got delayed due to bad weather. Obviously it wasn't Pandora's day that day.

And then Melanie wants to know everything about me, so I tell her about *him*. The songs we share, the time I bashed Scorpion's goonies with those bottles. I also tell her about Nora.

"She was always too innocent for her own good, but what do you suppose she was doing sending those fake postcards?" Mel asks in complete puzzlement.

"I don't know, I just can't get over the fact that she ran away from me when I tried to see her."

We think about it some, both frowning hard in concentration; then she sighs. "Honestly, Nora was always an adorable little airhead. Maybe she just needs some redirecting?"

"Maybe so."

"Okay, okay, we'll figure out Nora—I promise—but stop with the wandering and tell me about your drool-worthy new romance."

Rolling onto my stomach, I swing my legs up behind me as a dreamy sigh works its way up my throat. Remy is working out and I think he planned to run today, and I miss not having a run with him. I miss stretching him, watching him. But it feels so good to talk, I'm fairly bursting with things to say that I'm having trouble vocalizing.

"It's so crazy, Mel." I'm whispering reverently even though

there's no one around to hear. But confessing this is so monumental for me, I can't even say it any louder than this. "I've just never felt like this. Every time Remy touches me, Mel, I feel *a thousand* good things rush through me. Better than endorphins. I think its oxytocin, you know how powerful they say it is? The cuddle hormone? But I'd *never* felt it before."

"You *love* him, stupid!"

I wince at that, then nod vigorously. "I just don't want to say it out loud," I admit, my heart already doing hopeful turns and twists in my chest at the thought of being loved back by him.

"Because?"

"Because he might not feel the same!" The mere thought makes me heartbroken.

How do emotions work with someone like Remington? Can you love and unlove someone through your different mood personalities?

It hurts to think about it.

The front door closes out in the living room, and Melanie and I both listen to footsteps sounding on the carpet until he appears at the door.

My heart accelerates at the sight of him. He wears a damp black T-shirt that reads CHICAGO BULLS in red letters, and today the sweatpants hanging low on his narrow hips are red. He looks so hot, so doable, and so manly and comfortable in his attire my breasts seem to swell up inside my bra.

"Hey, Melanie," he says when he spots her.

"Omigod." Her eyes are round as pizzas as she straightens on the bed, obviously awed by those delicious dimples, finger-tempting messed-up black hair, and heart-robbing blue eyes. Her hand flies up to her mouth. "Ohmyfuckinggod, Remington. I'm such a huge fan."

He doesn't answer back because his head has swiveled in my

direction, and now he looks straight at me, and I can't help the way the sight of him affects me. My entire body responds and I feel instantly tight inside, damp and achy.

"Hey." He uses an entirely different tone on me, and when I respond, my voice is also different. Huskier.

"Hey."

I'm unsettled to my core.

He does that to me.

He unsettles me in any way. In every way.

From his electric baby blues, to his muscled arms, to his dimples and the way he looks at me right now, studying me top to bottom, like he doesn't know what part of my body to lick and bite first when he peels my white linen dress off me . . .

"You have dinner yet?" he asks me in that roughened voice.

I nod.

He nods in return. Then asks me, his voice still in that pitch that seems sensual and deep and just for me, "You coming to bed later?"

I nod.

And he nods in return, his eyes glimmering in excitement. Then he lifts a lazy hand to Mel.

"Bye, Melanie."

"Bye, Remington."

He shuts the door behind him, and I still can't breathe.

"Brooke, that guy is in love with you. Even *I* felt butterflies for you, and they were so big they were like bats in my tummy."

The bats are in my stomach too, flying up to my chest. I swear nothing can calm them down. "It could be anything," I counter, while inside me, I can't help but hope like crazy. "It could be lust. Obsession?"

"It's *love,* you fool. Why else would he bring me here but to make you happy, you goose! Are you going to tell him?"

My stomach winds up at the mere thought. "I can't yet."

"You used to love to be the first, Miss Olympic Contender," Melanie reminds me.

"This is different. I don't even know if he can say it back to me."

I think back to what I've learned about his bipolar episodes, and all I can wonder is if in his different gene expressions, he could feel differently about me? If I told him I loved him, would he push me away, when all I want is to be closer to him?

"Brooke, he's so fucking into you, *of course* he'll say it back!" Mel's excited green eyes twinkle.

Hope and dread war in my chest, and I still don't think I have the courage to risk what we have.

"I'm not sure that he's . . . equipped to love me like this. He's different, Mel."

I wish I could tell Melanie the truth, but I will guard his secret for him if it kills me. I remember the "Iris" song so clearly now, and the words of wanting to be known. He wants me to know him. Not Melanie. And definitely not the world. So I don't elaborate any more.

"Brooke. He's Remington Tate, of course he's different. Tell him, Brookey! Tell me, what have you got to lose?" she taunts.

My stomach clenches in nervousness. "Him. He could push me away. He could . . . lose interest and go after something else. I don't know! All I know is he's too important and I don't want to ruin this."

I never fully recovered the last time I broke something—it's been the worst experience of my life—and that was only my knee. The thought of getting my heart broken makes me bury my face in my palms with a groan. At least if I keep my love a secret, he and I can still have this wonderful, odd, exciting relationship together where I love him in silence and pretend he's loving me in silence too.

"I want to wait for him to tell me first," I pleadingly tell her. She seems immediately disgusted.

"Argh, little chicken." She gets up and comes to mock-slap me on one check, then the other, and then she smacks me for real with a kiss on my forehead. "All right, so while you go bang your Prince Charming and begin your happily ever after, I might go use my condoms. Or I might go hound Riley and Pete and see if anyone can take me out somewhere. See you tomorrow? Details, details."

I squish her tight before I shove her out the door and slap her butt as she leaves.

Silky ribbons of excitement unfurl inside me as I pad barefoot into the master bedroom. I hear the shower water running and a bolt of excitement rushes through me at the thought of stealing into the shower with him.

When I close the bathroom door quietly behind me and see Remy soaping his head behind the glass, my whole being fills with wanting. Tingles of anticipation tickle the inside of my stomach as I strip down to my skin. I've never been so blatant with a man, but this is *my* man. My one and only man. And he's sexy and nude and I missed him like crazy.

I open the glass shower door and step inside with his beautiful slick skin and big hard muscles, pressing my naked breasts to his back as I wrap my arms around his waist. He groans and tugs my arms tighter around him, and the words *I love you* are there inside me, right near the surface. I've never loved anyone in my life and I never imagined it could be like this.

It is the most amazing, invigorating, frightening feeling I've ever had in my life. As addictive as endorphins and more. I lick up his spine to the side of his throat, sliding my hands downward to touch his erection. He's already fully erect, and my every sense becomes attuned to him. The contact of our bodies, my front to his magnificent back, the feel of his throbbing length pulsing under my fingers.

I get a rush thinking it's for me. Just me.

Through the pounding water, I hear his slow exhale. "Hmm. Touch me, Brooke," he murmurs, grabbing both my fists in a tight grip and guiding me over his cock.

A hot shudder courses through my body. I'm completely turned on by his huge fists guiding my hands over his slick, long hardness. Burning hot between my legs, I lick the drops of water from his back. Like a cat, I rub my aching breasts to his hard back muscles and twirl my tongue up his beautiful lean spine. "I get butterflies when you say my name."

He flips around and takes my hair in his hand and yanks my head back so our eyes meet. He stares at me, his look positively feral, and my sex clenches in needy anticipation as he speaks. "Brooke Dumas."

I shudder and lean my wet body into his. "Definitely butter-flies."

"Let's take care of them"—his smile is slow and wolf-ish—"Brooke Dumas."

I laugh, but he doesn't, and when his lips settle over mine, it isn't to give me a slow sampling of a kiss, but instead a burning, plundering kiss that wipes out any coherent thought from my mind. He takes my wrists and slowly pins my hands at my back, and a bolt of excitement shoots through me.

He shreds me to pieces with that unexpected restraint that lets me know he plans to do whatever he wants to me and I'll like it. I moan feebly as his teeth graze my neck, undulate helplessly as he tugs my flesh so firmly, I think he's going to give me my first hickey.

With both my wrists still manacled in his large hand, he draws back, panting, and his piercing blue eyes linger on my bare breasts. The savage need in his face makes my breath ripple unevenly past my lips. Desire arches my spine, and he sweeps down, his mouth covering my breast to suck me as fiercely as ever. He fondles the other tip with his free hand, his palm slick and urgent, and I love how his dark, tanned skin contrasts with the fairer color of my breasts. Expertly he squeezes the flesh and sucks the hardened point into the heat of his mouth, his other hand firm around my wrists.

My smaller body shudders against his bigger one, my pussy gripping with red-hot need. Mist coats both of our bodies as the shower water pounds on his back, and I become frantic, suddenly needing him now, fast, urgently. "Take me," I plead, straining up to him.

His eyes glimmer as he pinches one nipple and then the other. "That's the plan."

He lifts me easily by the waist and instead of lowering me onto his cock, he brings my breasts to his mouth. He sucks one, then the other, his arm muscles flexed as he keeps me in the air, feeding himself my nipples. Sensations hit me like lightning; his every movement zaps down to my toes. And when I can't stop whimpering and grimacing from the mind-boggling pleasure, he drops me down on his erection with such force that the instant he rams into me, I'm so jolted a breathless cry tears free from me.

"Too hard?" Voice craggy in desire and concern, he yanks me back up, his biceps bulging like rocks as he waits for me to speak.

Breathless, I shake my head and grab his shoulders. "I want you," I whisper. "Please let me have you."

His face clenches with need.

He lowers me more slowly this time, but he's still massively big and drags thickly through every inch of my inner muscles. A haggard whimper tears from my throat as I hang onto his hard shoulders, and when he starts moving, fucking me for real, I lose it and run my tongue along the slightly scratchy whiskers on his jaw and suck his ear, gasping and moaning as I ride him as fast as I can. As fast as he's riding me.

Electricity splinters down my spine when he slides his tongue into my ear, gently fucking me with it. "I love," he rasps, the unexpectedly sexy way he utters the word catapulting me to within a breath of my orgasm, "how you fit me. . . ."

"I love it too," I say, part moan, part gasp.

He tugs my earlobe with his teeth, his ragged breaths straining his chest muscles as he holds me in the vises of his arms and speaks in my ear as he continues thrusting. *"You're so tight. So wet. Feel so good. Smell so fucking good. I knew you would be mine the instant I saw you. Aren't you? Aren't you all mine?"*

"Yes," I gasp, mewing because I love every word, trembling at each and every one he utters, letting them turn me into something wild and free until I'm whispering back to him, *"Give me more, I want all of you, Remy, harder, please, harder, faster,"* until I explode in his arms, the spasms in my pussy clenching rhythmically around his cock, milking his release out of him.

When I sag all around him, he grabs the back of my head in his open hand and holds me so tightly buried against his neck, I don't even try to get my feet on the floor. He turns off the shower and carries me out, rubbing a towel over me before quickly dragging it over himself, and I get all gooey because he's so strong he never even has to put me down before he heads across the room and we hit the bed naked.

This is only our seventh night together, but I'm already anxiously awaiting the way we snuggle in bed.

Tonight he tucks me in and covers us up, and when he notices I'm limp and languid, he adjusts me so that he's spooning me. I sigh in contentment as we settle down.

He scents the back of my ear. Then I feel his hand, scraping down my hair, softly petting me. His tongue follows, lightly lapping the place on my neck he bit in the shower. He drags it along the curve of my shoulders, my ear, awakening every inch of my skin.

I feel like he's a lazy lion, bathing me with his tongue, licking and nuzzling me.

He's done this other nights too. The unexpectedness of his raw petting drives me crazy with lust and love, and I'm getting addicted to this moment after the orgasm, where I'm so relaxed and he still has the energy to position me in a way where he can spoon me or hold me, and do all his manly, possessive, lion-like OCD things with me.

Sometimes he washes his semen off my skin, but other times he gives me a series of slow, drugging kisses as he reaches between my thighs and fingers his semen back into my pussy like he wants to always be there.

Sometimes he asks me, with cocky blue eyes and in that sexy, lust-filled murmur he uses after making love, "Do you like it when I smear your skin with me?"

God, I love how he calls his semen "him."

I love everything this guy does!

It's still a novelty to me, to be sleeping with him. I've never spent the night with anyone before.

Every time we reach a new city, I wonder which side of the bed he'll want, but Remington seems to always go for the one closest to the door, which is good since I like the one farthest, which tends to be closest to the bathroom. Although, now that I think of it, even on the first night we slept together, the arrangement seemed to happen automatically.

He lies down on the side of the bed where he can put his right arm around me, and I can roll to my right side and drape myself all over him like a warm gummy worm.

The first nights we were together, I wore his plain black T-shirt to bed but I don't even bother anymore since he always takes it off me at some point. He sleeps butt-naked and I can never even *see* him without wanting to jump his sexy bones. Remy is made to advertise everything that is manly, muscular, and sexy. I think that's where a lot of his millions came from when he was in the pro league. Advertising boxing gloves, some whip-fast jump rope, a sports drink, and a brand of sexy, tight white boxer briefs.

He looks positively delish in those.

Tonight we're both naked and deliciously entangled, and my sexy blue-eyed lion now seems content to have petted me for a long while, until I feel groomed down to my bones.

He's pinned me to him while his head rests on the bed headboard, and I notice one of his long, thick legs restlessly moving under the sheets. He doesn't seem even the least bit tired.

"Are you getting . . . speedy?" I ask groggily, turning in his arms, hating that I'm now also using the term.

"I'm just thinking." Smiling to comfort me, he plants a soft kiss on my lips. "But if I ever get out of hand with you . . ." He reaches into his laptop carry case, which is on the nightstand, and retrieves a syringe with a clear liquid. He hands it to me with the cap on.

Wincing, I ease away from it like he's going to use it on my butt. "No, Remy, don't ask this of me."

"It's just to make sure I don't hurt you."

"You'd never hurt me."

He groans and rakes his free hand through his damp hair, pulling in frustration. "I *can*. I can very well get crazy over you."

"You won't."

"You don't know how you make me feel! I—" He snaps his mouth shut and a muscle jumps restlessly in his jaw as he clenches it. "I get jealous, Brooke, when I'm normal," he says, his expression fiercely bleak. "I don't want to know what I'm going to do when I'm black. I get jealous of Pete, of Riley, of your friend, of anyone who gets to spend time with you. I'm even jealous of me."

"What?"

"I'm jealous of being with you and not remembering what I did to you. What you said to me."

My insides diffuse with tenderness. "I'll tell you, Remy." Reaching out to turn his sexy dark head to me, I kiss his jaw.

He's still restless.

"Come here, Rem." Taking the syringe, I set it carefully on the nightstand on his side; then I pull his head down to my chest and kiss his forehead as I massage the back of his neck with strong, nimble fingers. He groans and plops his face down on my breasts, instantly relaxed.

"Thanks for bringing Melanie up," I whisper, into his hair.

"I can bring up your parents too. Do you want me to?" He sounds sober when he asks, nuzzling my bare puckered nipple.

"No." I laugh.

He's so protective and so unexpectedly giving that I just want to crawl into his big, lean body and curl myself in a ball and live inside his big gentle heart, because that's the only place I'm interested in living in.

"Your sister." He seems entranced with my nipple, looking at it and rubbing a thumb over it as I keep working on his nape. "I'm going to get her back to you, Brooke."

My stomach tangles. I definitely, definitely want him to forget I even mentioned Nora. "No, Remy, I think she's going to be all right and we should just leave her alone, please. Just fight for me and you. All right?"

He stays in my arms for a bit, but when my hands start slacking and I begin to doze off, he gets up.

"Come sleep with me," I thickly whimper. "Don't get up."

He comes back with an apple and his iPad and I snuggle to his side as though magnetized. He uses my hip to prop up the screen and turns off the lamp for me.

"You're going to hurt your eyes," I complain.

"Shhh, Mother, I've just lowered the glare."

He licks me, and I lick him back, and we laugh together.

"Did Pete tell you your parents went looking for you?" I ask.

"Yeah. I sent them some money. That's what they want."

My eyebrows come down. "They said they wanted to see you."

"That's what they say. They never wanted to see me until my face was public."

"Shame on them." I feel instantly protective and don't want him to feel bad, so I tenderly cup his jaw. "It's such a handsome face."

He chuckles, the soft vibrations reaching me. Delighting at his closeness, his warmth, the scent of his body, I turn in his arm and bury my face into his neck so the light doesn't bother me, and as I'm dozing off, I hear crunching sounds and a fresh liquid drop of something splatters on my cheek.

I frown. "Remy."

"Sorry." He kisses the spot where the drop fell and licks it up, and I groan in unbidden desire.

He playfully nips my mouth and his lips taste of apple. I love it, and suddenly I'm wide awake, feeling hungry, and it's not for apple. I love his smell, the feel of him, his eyes, his touch, I love sleeping with him, showering with him, running with him. I feel crazy. Crazy about him. Okay, I'm going to go to sleep before I break out in song. Instead I hear myself speak.

"Remington . . . ?" I murmur in a question, my voice groggy but already thickened with arousal.

He puts the iPad aside and his hand coasts up my curves. He clamps his fingers around my waist and draws me to his length, where I can feel he's hard and ready. I'm so ready for him, I was born ready.

He ducks to kiss me, murmuring, *"Hmm, that's what I was hoping for."*

❤ ❤ ❤

"THIS IS SO exciting, top-of-the-line seats. Either you give one hell of a BJ, or the guy's definitely in love with you," Melanie decrees as we sit in the first-row center seats of the Chicago Underground.

"Well, I haven't gotten to the BJ part since the actual penetration is so exciting, you know?" I tell Mel, but suddenly all I have on my mind is getting my lips around his cock. Giving the man I love a delicious, whopping BJ that will make him love me forever.

Mel's eyebrows sweep up. "Are you actually bragging to me?"

"No! I'm actually honestly—no sarcasm here—admitting to my best friend that I'm eager to give my guy my first ever BJ as soon as I can manage to take my mouth off his delicious lips."

The unbelievable has happened. I think I just managed to make Melanie blush. She's red-faced as she stares at me like I just confessed to an orgy. "My god. What did you do to my friend? Where the hell is she, you alien? Brooke, you are madly in love with this dude. Since when do you talk BJs to me?"

My smile suddenly fades, and so does my voice. "Please stop saying the 'L' word—it only makes my stomach clench."

"Love. You love Remington. Remington loves you," Mel taunts.

"Here, girl." With a playful glare, I hand her a piece of bubble gum I stole from Pete. "Put that in your mouth, will you? It's made of glue and it will seal your trap together. Now tell me if you spot Nora anywhere."

"I see her at three o'clock."

Surprise siphons the blood from my face. "You do?"

My frame tenses when I see her. It's Nora. In a deep, innermost part of me, I'd hoped it had been a nightmare, and that the chick with the bloodred hair, the pale face, and the black scorpion tattoo had been someone else. But no.

It is. Nora.

This sad-looking waif of a girl.

And I have to save her from herself.

As Nora takes her seat across the ring from us, I clench Melanie's arm and shove a little paper I'd been clutching into her palm. "Okay, you need to take her this very discreetly, so those big types near her don't really notice the exchange."

"Gotcha." Melanie gets up, flicks her ponytail, and goes around to the other side of the ring. Nora hasn't seen me, I don't think, but she tenses when she spots Melanie. Mel walks by, all flirty and bimbo-like. She stumbles over the feet of one of the men with her, then bends to apologize to Nora, patting her hands as if saying, "There, there, no harm done," and then she's heading back to her seat beside me.

My insides tighten with tension as my eyes stay trained to Nora. She glances down at her lap and sees the note. Looking around for a moment, she opens it furtively, and while she's reading hope and excitement twirl inside me. She seems to read it a second time.

So she's interested?

"Done," Melanie says, and when Nora lifts her head, she sees me, her hazel eyes flaring slightly, and I exhale a long breath of gratitude that at least she isn't running away. When our stares lock for several seconds, I smile at her, just so she knows that I want to see her in "friendly" mode. She smiles back, barely, almost shakily, and then tears her eyes free as the presenter begins.

My chest swells with even more determination to save my

baby sister, and suddenly I can't wait for it to be tomorrow. I just pray she'll come.

"And nooow, ladies and gentlemen . . ."

"He's coming out." Melanie squeezes me.

Just knowing he's going to come out puts me in hyper-excitement mode, and when his name rings across the crowd, my heart has already kicked into overdrive and I'm quaking in my skin. ". . . Remington Tate, your one and only, RIPTIDE!! RIPTIDE!! Say hello to RIPTIIIIIIDE!"

He comes out like a sun after months of night, and the world can't stop shouting in gratitude. He swings up to the ring and whips off his red robe in a motion that somehow transports him to the center of the ring. And there he is, doing his signature turn as the crowd roars his name, his muscular arms outstretched, corded with veins, and the screams get louder and louder—for the people love the way he turns, his boyish face and manly body, the wicked glint in his eyes that promises them a good show. He stops right where he always does, and his dancing blue eyes tell me that he knows he's the bomb and that I want him, and his dimples come out to kill me. *Kill. Me.*

The fact that I know that man is mine at night won't even let me breathe.

But I thankfully manage a smile even through the little earthquakes that I'm feeling. I'm so bursting with excitement, my smile feels like its being torn out of me.

The fight begins, and I sit drooling next to Melanie watching those arms, with their sexy vine tattoos where his shoulders and biceps meet, as they flex out to strike his opponents. His strength, his footwork, his speed mesmerize me.

Melanie shouts to him all the things I want to tell him and more, delighting me. "Kill him, Remington! Yes! Yes! Omigod, you're a god!"

Laughing with pure joy, I hug her. "Oh, Mel," I sigh. Then I whisper in pure mischief, "Tell him he's hot."

"Why don't *you,* little chicken?" She narrows her eyes and shoulders me. "You little nugget, *tell him!*"

"I can't. I can never seem to shout in a crowd. I was the one usually shouted *at,*" I admit, shouldering her back. "And I feel like my voice will distract him. Come on! Tell him from me. Tell him he's so hot."

Up on her feet, Melanie cups her mouth and yells. "Brooke thinks you're the hottest thing ever, Remy! Remy, Brooke loves you, Remy! Every inch and centimeter of you!"

"Melanie!" Shocked, I pop up and slap a hand over her mouth, shoving her back down to her seat. Fortunately, the crowd is so noisy today, I'm almost sure he didn't hear. "Have another piece of gum, Mel," I say, glaring darkly at her. "And I'll have your word you're not saying that again."

"Oh, all right, I'll just tell him he's so hot and all that."

Laughing when I stiffly nod, she comes back to her feet and nudges my ribs, calling me a little Chick-fil-A sandwich, because I'm so chicken, and then she keeps on shouting all the things I think and don't have the courage to scream. That he's so hot, that he's a god, that he's a sexy beast and is so fucking sexy nobody can stand it . . .

I swear if I could even shout, I'd also shout that he's *mine,* that *I love you,* that he's *my* sexy beast . . . but I can't even cheer his name alone among the crowd.

And I realize maybe I do feel a little fear, after all. Because I've never given my heart to anyone until Remington. And he has the strength to pound it down as hard as he's pounding his opponents.

ELEVEN

SECRET MEETING

We're supposed to meet Nora at a small Japanese restaurant situated only blocks from our hotel, but I feel completely awful about lying to Remington about this evening.

"I'll make up a business meeting for him," Pete assured me when we met at the gym this morning. "I'll say you and Melanie are out sightseeing and that Riley will pick you up after dinner so that Remy can go through his monthly finances with me."

I nod in satisfaction, but I confess that I'm still not thrilled about it. At *all*. I'm queasy and nervous in the afternoon, but even then, I allow a deep, secret part of me to enjoy the way Remy watches me from the boxing ring. I wave at him from the gym door and signal to Melanie—who stands next to me in all her miniskirted and spaghetti-strap-topped glory—while I mouth to Remy, "Going out with Mel."

He yanks off his sparring headgear to shoot me a smile and a quick nod, his eyes shining like they do when he spots me, and only Mel's hand on my elbow seems to keep me from leaping up to the ring and kissing each of his devastatingly beautiful dimples.

Upstairs, I dress sensibly and comfortably in a button-down blouse and formal black slacks.

"I still don't understand why you don't want Remy to know about this," Melanie says as Riley drives us to the restaurant.

"Because Remington's got some alpha tendencies."

"Which is sexy, last I checked."

"Mel, this isn't a movie. I don't want him to be unable to concentrate or get in trouble because of me."

Mel huffs. "You take away all the romance of your relationship, Brooke."

I groan and then bang my forehead on the window in total exasperation. "Mel, I feel bad as it is. Please. People who do what he does for a living are considered lethal weapons. They can't legally fight outside of the ring, do you understand?"

"Yes. Although why one man can't fight with his fists in the street while others run around legally with guns is beyond me. I really should complain to Senator . . . Whoever."

"All right, ladies, if we leave the letter to Congress until later, here we are."

Melanie glares at Riley as he opens one of the hotel's back doors for us, and he glares back as she passes. I have no idea what is up with them. Melanie is usually sweet to everyone, and Riley is usually easy-breezy. But all righty then.

"Thanks, Riley, I'll be right back," I tell him.

"The hell you will. I'm coming with you."

"We don't need you to," Melanie says, shooting him a superior look with the tip of her nose high in the air. "Brookey and I have done excellently for twenty-four years without your assistance."

"I'm doing it for Remington, not for you," Riley says stiffly.

Thankfully, they stop bickering when we enter the restaurant. I soak up the quiet atmosphere with one sweep of my gaze,

taking in the peeling green painted walls, which hold an assort-
ment of framed pictures of raw fish plates, and then my eyes slide
along dozens of black wooden tables to notice that all of them are
empty except one.

To my astonishment, the only people here, aside from the
three of us who stand by the door, are a concerned-looking Japanese man doing nothing but watching us from behind the sushi
bar; Nora, who sits stiffly at a small round table at a corner, and
it breaks my heart that all I can see of my sister's expression is the
disgusting scorpion marking on her face; three tall, beefy men
who I recognize as the same goonies whose skulls I had the pleasure of bashing in back at the club; and, of course, the big mean
Scorpion, who now strides toward us like he's the goddamned
host of the evening.

I don't know if he pulled some strings with the restaurant
managers, or if he vacated the premises by intimidation or Benja-
min Franklins, but then, who in their right mind would want to
have dinner with dudes like these?

Well. Apparently my sister.

Nora was always the starry-eyed one of us, always wanting to
"rescue" some cat, dog, rat, or guy. I never bought the romance
stew she seemed so intent on tasting, until I met Remington, of
course.

I'll drink anything that guy feeds me—I won't deny *that*.

Now I see Scorpion come forward , bulky and muscular, and I
feel an instant moment's regret that Remy doesn't know I'm here.

A kernel of fear blooms deep inside my center.

Fear not only of these men, but of what Remy will do if he
finds out I was ever here with them. This is so new to me, being
in a relationship. I don't know what he would do for me. But I do
know that I would do *anything* for *him*. Including making sure
that he remains oblivious of my meeting with Nora.

I just hope that I won't regret dragging Pete and Riley into this alongside me.

My breathing hitches nervously when Scorpion halts a foot away from us, his eyes green and mean. His presence, coupled with the fish smell coming from the bar, makes me a little nauseous. It feels like the black tattoo is all you see on his sickening face. I don't see why anyone would want that animal on his skin. It's a 3-D tattoo, and the scorpion appears to be crawling up into his eye.

"Well, if it isn't the little whore." He flings the words like stones at me and glances derisively past my shoulder. "Where's Riptide? Hiding under your skirt again?"

Impotent anger rages through me, making my throat curl tightly around my words. "He had better things to do."

He narrowly eyes me, then Melanie and Riley. "Only you," he says, jabbing a finger in my direction, "can pass."

I start passing, but he blocks me with an arm, and a red flush slowly creeps up his face: eager anticipation. "You have to kiss the scorpion first." Eyes glimmering meanly, he taps the icky black scorpion on his cheek, and his teeth flash, his entire mouth covered with a grill of diamonds.

My organs halt in pure shock and horror at his request, and I clench my lips in response as my gaze jumps past his shoulders, across the little restaurant, to the corner table where Nora sits. I meet my sister's honeyed gaze and despair runs through me at the blank look in her eyes.

How can I let her do this to herself? I can't.

I just.

Can't.

Scorpion wants his fun and wants to demean me. He wants to show me he has the power today. But he can't demean me if I don't allow him to see how much his request *revolts* me.

Wildly trying to convince myself that it means nothing, I take a deceptively steady step forward. But my entire body begins to tense at what I'm about to do, and an awful flush of embarrassment burns fast across my skin.

"Brooke," Riley says in a warning that also sounds like a plea.

But it's either kiss a stupid tattoo, or sacrifice Nora to this man, or risk involving Remington to tangle with these losers, and I just can't do any of those things.

The awful man's gaze feels like a snake slithering upon me as he watches me approach, and I remind myself to concentrate on is my sister and freeing her. I draw a deep breath, forbidding myself to tremble.

As I take the last step, suddenly his request seems as impossible as asking me to climb Mount Everest and dig a hole to the bottom. My stomach roils in protest, and I'm dangerously close to vomiting at the sight of the black crawling insect up close.

He smells of fish and pure mean asshole.

And I wish I had the guts to try to kick the shit out of him.

Suddenly a vivid reminder of a show my dad used to watch called *Fear Factor* strikes me, where people do all kinds of gross things, getting in boxes with live snakes and scorpions and the like. If people can do that for money, I can *certainly* do this for my sister.

Shoving my pride aside and seizing my determination, I force my lips to pucker so hard they feel like rocks as I press up on my tiptoes. Nausea roils up my chest before I even make contact.

"Look at this, Remy's fucking whore is kissing the Scorpion." His goonies spit the words out contemptuously, and the humiliation the words bring makes me want to run and hide with a force I haven't felt in years. Revolted at myself, I quickly smack the air and drop back on my heels.

"There. All done now," I say, loathing that my voice shakes.

His laughter is deep, dark, and awful as he turns to his goons. "Did she kiss me? Did Riptide's bitch actually kiss the Scorpion? I don't think so." His beady green-yellow eyes slither back to me, and, coupled with that glare, I'm not feeling very powerful at the moment. "I didn't *feel* your kiss. Now you're going to have to *lick it.*" He beams his diamond grill at me again.

My eyes widen in horror, and my determination to see my sister falters woefully at the thought of licking any part of this man. Omigod, I want to run so bad from here, my veins already feel dilated as the blood pumps into my muscles, priming me to flee. Flee to the car, back to my Remy.

Riley grabs me, his face a mask of concern.

"Brooke," he says in warning, which snaps me back to what I'm here for. I quickly squirm free and once again face Scorpion.

How can I leave? How will I otherwise get to talk to Nora about this shit she's in? Just the thought of her in this human worm's grasp disgusts me. How can I see her with this type of pervert and not do something to help her? Swallowing back the painful dryness in my throat, I tip my face back with false bravado, desperate to do anything except lick that grossness on that man's disgusting cheek. "I'll kiss it, you have my word."

Fear Factor.

You can do this for Nora.

If you could do the hundred meters in 10.52 seconds, then you can kiss this sucker's stupid skin mascot!

Evil lurks in his eyes as he studies me thoughtfully, then speaks mockingly down at me. "If you're not going to lick it, then you'll hold it for five seconds, hmm, Remy's bitch? Go on now. Kiss the scorpion." He taps his mark, and my stomach again seizes spasmodically. I struggle very hard to keep my expression blank and show the human insect how unconcerned I am with his revolting request.

Drawing a deep breath, I forbid my knees to quiver as I go up on tiptoes, pucker my lips, and squeeze my eyes shut, loathing and rage seizing my insides as my lips hit his dry painted skin. Holding the contact, I feel poisoned as I count toward five, my heart black inside me. Hurting and coiling in complete and utter embarrassment. My legs waver as another second passes, and my systems feel paralyzed in this purgatory, where every ounce of my body is repelled by this embodiment of Rotten and only sheer willpower holds me up.

These are the longest five seconds of my life. Where I am humiliated beyond humiliated, angry beyond explanation, and feel as low as when I saw the video of my broken self on YouTube.

"All right then." With a smile nothing short of disgustingly wide, I drop back down, surprised there is even ground under my feet. He extends his thick arm out to Nora, and I reel with self-loathing as I hold my spine straight and head for Nora, resisting the urge to go into the kitchens and scrub my mouth raw. It feels dirty and cheap. No, not it. I. *I* feel dirty and cheap, and the thought of kissing my beautiful Remy with this same mouth makes my eyes tear up and my throat constrict.

I already feel drained by the time I reach my sister's table. There are empty tables with upside-down chairs littered throughout the place, but our small table is set with one electric tea light at the center and chopsticks for four.

"Nora." My voice is deceptively soft, but inside I'm a mess of conflicting emotions, including resentment toward my sister for sitting here, watching me have to kiss her filthy boyfriend's tattoo. But seeing the lifeless expression on her face, I just know the girl across the table from me, willowy and frail, pale and not really happy, isn't really my sister.

Reaching for her hand on the table, I'm saddened when she doesn't let me hold it and instead shoves it under the table with a little sniffle. We stare at each other for a moment in silence, and it strikes me that the sight of that black scorpion almost crawling into my sister's eye is the most disturbing thing I've ever seen in my life.

"You shouldn't be here, Brooke," she says, her eyes on the men and Riley and Melanie, who wait in stunned silence by the door. When our eyes meet again, I'm shocked by the animosity in her eyes and the way they openly lash out at me.

A sudden anger seizes me too, and I narrow my eyes. "Mom wants to know if you liked the Australian crocodiles, Nora. She loved the postcard you sent and can't wait to see where else you're heading to. So? How *were* the crocodiles, sister?"

There's a world of bitterness in her voice when she answers. "Obviously I wouldn't know." She wipes the back of her hand across her nose and looks away, scowling at the mention of Mom.

"Nora . . ." Lowering my voice, I gesture at the empty Japanese restaurant containing the Scorpion and the three goons, who watch us from the sushi bar. "Is this honestly what you want for yourself? You have your whole life ahead of you."

"And I want to live it my own way, Brooke."

There's a bunch of defensiveness in her tone, so I try to keep from sounding aggressive. "But why here, Nora? Why? Mom and Dad would be heartbroken if they knew the things you've gotten yourself involved in."

"At least I keep them from knowing the truth!" she snaps out, and this is the first spark of life I actually see in her gold eyes.

"But why would you do this to them? Why would you drop out of college for *this*?"

"Because I'm sick and tired of them comparing me to you." She glares, then starts making a mocking voice that resembles our mother when she whines. "'Why don't you do this like Brooke?' 'Why don't you find something meaningful to do with your life like Brooke?' They just want me to be like you! And I don't *want* to. What's the point? You missed all the fun growing up so you could be this hotshot gold medalist and now you're not only *not* an Olympic medalist, you can't even sprint anymore."

"I may not sprint anymore but I can still kick your ass right," I reply angrily, hurt beyond words at what she's saying to me.

"So what?" she continues. "You were the best track athlete in college. Everyone couldn't stop talking about how talented you were and how you were going to make it. That's all you did and talked about, and now look at you! You can't even do what you loved and will probably end up like Mom and Dad, living in the past, with your stupid high school medals still hanging in your bedroom!"

"For your information, I am *happier* right now than I have *ever* been, Nora! If you'd only paid a little attention, you'd realize that my life went on, and to places I didn't even imagine I'd ever be. You want to be independent? We get it. Go for it! Just be independent on your own, not tied to some man who makes me lick his gross tattoo before I can see my sister!"

"I like it that he's protective of me," she shoots back. "He *fights* for me."

"Fight for *yourself*, Nora. I promise it will give you tons more satisfaction."

Nora sniffles angrily and wipes her hand across her nose, glaring down at the tea light as a silence falls between us. I drop my voice once more.

"Are you doing coke, Nora?"

My sister seems to take to the Fifth and doesn't respond, which only serves to double my concern and frustration.

"Come home, Nora. Please," I plead, my voice a whisper so only she can hear.

She touches her nose with the back of one finger, then brings her glare up to me as she continues brushing that finger across her nostrils. Sniffling. "What do I want to go home for? So I can be a has-been at twenty-two like you?"

"I'd rather be a has-been than nothing at all. What are *you* accomplishing now? Don't you want to finish college?"

"No, that's what *you* wanted to do, Brooke. I want to have fun."

"Really? And are you having loads of it? Because I don't even see that your smile has any place on your face anymore. You might not like the fact that I failed to reach my dream as much as I do, but I am *over* that. I happen to like where I am now, Nora. It's not where I planned to be, true, but I have so many other things. Better things. I have a great job, am working with amazing people, and I'm in the first relationship I've ever had in my life."

"With *Riptide*?" she sneers. "Riptide doesn't do relationships, sister. Women fling themselves at him everywhere he goes. He goes through them like his opponents, and fucks them all and barely asks for their names. I watched him before you got here. Don't forget, I've been in this scene longer. One day he's going to look at someone else, and you will even be his has-been girlfriend too!"

"And your precious Scorpion will want you for all eternity? Nora, the man you're with doesn't look right," I hiss, stealing a glance at him past my shoulder. He smiles a satanic smile as if he's hearing every word, and suddenly I am consumed with the urge for my man to get up in the ring with this asshole and *kill* him. And I have no doubt that Remy will. Knock him within an inch of his life. Maybe *then* Nora will want to leave this sucker.

"Benny's good to me," Nora explains with a little shrug. "He takes care of me. He gives me what I need."

"You mean *drugs*?" I lash out in pure fury.

Her eyebrows furrow, and I instantly regret that I made her go into defense mode again.

A tense silence lengthens between us, and I clench my hands on my lap until my nails bite my palms as I try to calm down and reason with her gently.

"Please, Nora. You deserve so much more."

"Time's up!" A hard clap from the bar alerts us, and Nora flinches, which just confirms what I've suspected: she doesn't want to be home, but she doesn't want to be here either. She feels like she has nowhere to go, and she can't leave because she's got more coke up her nose than I even want to think of. Shit.

"Unless you want to kiss the scorpion again, say goodbye to her now." Scorpion stands threateningly at my side, his eyes glimmering that snaky yellow-green color that tells me how much he would love to humiliate me again.

Nora stands, and a sliver of panic runs through me at the possibility of never seeing her again. I push to my feet, experiencing a gamut of perplexing emotions. I want to hug my sister in my arms and tell her it's going to be all right, and at the same time I want to freaking punch her for being so stubborn and stupid.

Instead, I go around the table to hug her, ignoring the way she stiffens when I turn my lips to her ear and speak soft as cotton to her. "Please let me take you to Seattle. At the end of the New York fight, meet me at the ladies' restroom and I will have two tickets home. You don't have to stay there, but you need a time-out to think this through. Please." Pulling away, I look down meaningfully at her face.

A shadow of alarm touches her expression; then she nods, sniffles, and swings to leave, the sight of her retreating back heading toward the back exit making me feel like I've just lost something very dear to me.

With a sinking in my gut, I feel Scorpion's beady green eyes on me as I head to Riley and Melanie and leave, and I can't shake off a feeling of complete and utter dirtiness in myself.

"Does anyone have any mouthwash with them? I feel like I'm getting a rash," I say as Riley drives us back in the Escalade.

Mel frowns thoughtfully. "I can't determine why what you just did felt so sickeningly wrong, when it wasn't a big deal. I mean, I've kissed grosser men in grosser parts of their anatomies, you know? What you did was *no big* deal."

"It's a fucking big deal!" Riley rants from behind the wheel. "Brooke, I hate to break it to you, but Remington is going to find out about it and he's going to get majorly, MAJORLY BLACK!"

My stomach clenches, and I shake my head as I struggle for calm. Me kissing that filthy tattoo is something I sincerely never again want to remember. Never. Again. "He's not going to know if you don't tell him, Riley. Let's all relax, why don't we?"

"What's he talking about?" Mel asks, genuinely perplexed. "Black what?"

"These men will make sure he knows, B. And they'll make it *painful*," Riley insists.

A frown pinches into my face as I wonder if that's what they'd intended to do when I arrived. Was this all planned out to get at Remy really? Shaking my head, I look at Riley's accusing light eyes through the rearview mirror from where I'm riding with Mel.

"What did you expect me to do, Riley? I don't have fists like that bastard does, and I have to use other means to get what I want, and what *I want* is for my poor sister out of that living turd's grip!"

"Jesus, I hope to god she's worth it."

"She's my *sister*, Riley—so she is, she is. She's going to show up after the New York final match. I'd kiss the sidewalk and lick a toilet to make sure she's all right, you have to understand!"

"That's so gross, Brooke," Mel squeals, laughing.

"Rem is like a brother to me, B. This is going to . . ." Riley shakes his head and seems to get out all of his anger on his hair, raking it with his fingers. "Let's just hope he doesn't find out that you . . ." He shakes his head again, fisting another handful of hair. "He's done tons of shit for me. For my family, when my parents got ill. Remy is a good. Fucking. Man. He doesn't deserve—"

"Riley, I *love* him." The words just tear out of me out of my pain and frustration of having kissed his enemy. "Do you believe I'd ever deliberately hurt him? I don't want him to get involved in this, *because* I *love* him. Can't you see? I don't want him to go *black* because of me. God!"

Riley breaks at a stoplight, then seeks my eyes in the rearview mirror again, his lips pursing as he nods. "I get it, B."

I feel instantly vulnerable and revealed, and squirm in my seat. "Please don't tell him. Not just about tonight's debacle. About the other part."

He nods in silence, and we're quiet the rest of the drive. But by the time we're all walking to our rooms, I've calmed down a bit and add, "Riley, thank you for taking us." He nods again, and when he walks off, ignoring Melanie, she shoots tons of invisible knives in his direction with her eyes.

"That guy gets on my nerves."

"I think you get on his too."

"You do?" She scowls at me, then her eyes widen in pure disbelief. "You mean he doesn't *like* me?"

Groaning at her obtuseness, I push her in his direction. "Mel, just go do him."

"But I don't like *him*," she argues, but I've already swung around to board the elevator up to the P, and when I slip my key into the lock of our room I'm wild with anticipation.

Remy sits at the desk with his laptop open and with his music in his ears. He lifts his head when I approach, and when those heartbreaking eyes look at me from that boldly handsome face, my insides shudder uncontrollably.

His spiky black hair gleams in the soft hotel room lighting, and in his comfortable sweatpants and tight T-shirt, he exudes pure raw masculinity. The sight of his full mouth opens up a ravenous hunger inside me, and I just hurt with the physical pain of wanting that mouth on me. His arms on me. His voice telling me it's all going to be all right. Because with every second that passes, I loathe myself more and more for what I did.

But Remy has protected me from his fans, and I will protect him from this too. From anything. Especially from Scorpion. I will protect him so that the only time Remy has to face him will be in that ring, where I will gladly watch him make that bastard wish he were dead.

Close to exploding with all my emotions, I jump onto his lap, then take off his earphones and slip them briefly over my head so I can listen to what he was hearing. A crazy wild rock song bashes into my ears and I frown in confusion.

He watches me with darkened blue eyes that go half-mast as he leans to kiss my nose, cradling my jaw as his thumb runs sensually across my mouth. My stomach cramps, and I worry that Remy can actually see the fear and self-loathing that I am tamping down inside me.

Slipping his headphones back on him, I ease to my feet and hurry to the bathroom, feeling so violated I wash my teeth and add Scope until my mouth feels swollen. I barely take a step out of the bath when I suddenly need to return and thoroughly do it all again. For the awful sensation across my skin, I swear I could have a live scorpion crawling up my cheek, and the sensation is eating at me.

Finally I come back out. My mouth is minty fresh and even my lips feel numb with cleanness.

Remy has set his music aside. His full attention is on me, his dark eyebrows furrowing as he tracks my return. He seems confused and slightly distrustful.

The sight of him makes me emotional, and I'm afraid I'm going to break down at any second. I hate that I feel like I don't deserve him anymore, even when all I wanted was to keep him safe and uninvolved.

I've never wanted to take care of someone in my life like I want to love and take care of him.

A painful lump builds inside my throat.

"Remy," I say thickly, my heart pounding because I don't know how I'll cope if he questions me about tonight. "Would you hold me for a bit?"

I desperately want my special place in his arms, the place I fit in like nowhere else. He makes the perfect nook for me, engulfing me like a nest and warmer than anything. I want it so bad, my heart aches in my chest.

I wait, shaking a little, and I think he notices and relents.

"Come here," he says softly, shoving his chair back as he extends his arm. I eagerly snuggle into his engulfing male hug. He chuckles when I squirm to get closer, which seems to delight him, for I'm acting so needy that his dimples peek out at me.

"You missed me?" His eyes dance as he cups my face and I feel his calluses on my jaw and cheeks, and that comforting feeling that only Remy can arouse sweeps through me.

"Yes," I gasp.

He gathers me close and holds me snug to his chest as he lowers his lips to mine. Our mouths graze softly, then connect, and he opens up with a soft breath that claims my mouth, his tongue sending shivers of desire racing through me.

His fingers outline the curves of my breasts as he drags his mouth along my jaw and sinks his nose into the back of my ear, inhaling me, groaning softly in pleasure, and blood pounds in my brain, leaping excitedly from my heart. "Remy . . ." I plead, grabbing his T-shirt and shoving it up to his shoulders.

He grabs the cotton in his fist and with a muscular yank tosses it over his head. I quickly slide my hands over his chest, kissing every part I can get.

"I missed you so much," I choke out emotionally, kissing his collarbone, his jaw, grabbing his hair as I press my face into his neck—anything to get close to this man.

He engulfs me in a big hug and strokes my back, then holds my face as he whispers, "I missed you too," setting a kiss on my lips, then on the tip of my nose, my forehead.

I tremble with his admission. "But I missed your voice. Your hands. Your mouth . . . being with you . . . watching you . . . touching you . . . smelling you . . ." I trail off. He smells so good, like he always does, clean and manly. I take his lips more desperately.

He returns my kiss, slowly at first, then with more compulsion as he unbuttons my shirt and strips me bare with fast, anxious hands.

I know he's not as verbally expressive as I, but I can feel his burning urgency when he grabs my hips and pulls me back to his lap, as though he needs to be inside me as fiercely as I need him to fill me. I'm naked and he's still wearing his sweatpants, but I'm dying with love and the need to physically express myself to him.

My whole body clenches when his erection settles hot and pulsing between my thighs, and there's an overwhelming need in me to give him something I've never given any man before.

Shivering uncontrollably, I slide between his powerful thighs at the same time he yanks down his drawstring pants and shoves them partly down his hips. I catch a glimpse of his star tattoo and then his erection pops free, and the instant my knees hit the carpet, my fingers and hands are all over his heat, his hardness, his heavy testicles, all full and primed for me.

"I want to kiss you here. . . ." My voice shakes with desire as I look into his lust-tightened face through eyes that I can barely keep open from the want. "I want to drown in you, Remington. I want your taste . . . in me. . . ."

The sound of a hungry male being thoroughly pleasured rumbles up his throat when I take him in my mouth, and he skims my hair with all his fingers as he rocks his hips, slowly, up to my mouth, gently giving me what I asked for and taking what I desperately want to give.

My sex burns wet with every drop of escaped semen that I taste, and I'm so intoxicated with this man, I can't stop enjoying the raw look on his face as I work my tongue along his enormous hard length.

He's as undone as I am when I add my teeth, suck his tip, then take his length down to my throat until I have to suppress my gag reflex. I'm still dying for more, I will never get enough of this man, and when he's pumping out of control into my mouth, and his fingers are fisting into my hair, and his muscles are tightening for orgasm, I suddenly notice his eyes are a little less blue as he watches me.

♥ ♥ ♥

HE'S DEFINITELY SPEEDY.

Super. Completely. Speedy.

Medically, Pete says it is called *manic*.

And he suspects that this episode might have been triggered the night I went out with Melanie and Riley, for during their financial meeting, Rem apparently asked only three questions of Pete, and none of them had anything to do with the finances he'd been explaining.

At what time did she say she'd be back?

You sure Riley's getting her?

Why the fuck are they taking so long?

Pete says he closed the money topic and dispatched Remington to his room as soon as Riley texted we were on our way back, and that's when I found him listening to the loudest rock song I'd ever heard and wearing that somber, thoughtful expression on his face. Did he think I would never come back?

And is that what he does when his insides begin to spin in turmoil? Listen to hard rock?

I don't know. All I know now is that he fucked me four times that night, like he needed to claim me all over again, and now Remy has totally gone rogue and appears to run on Red Bull 24/7.

He's like fully charged.

His usual cocky self to the tenth power.

He attacks me in bed like a lion this morning. "You look especially good, Brooke Dumas. Good, and warm, and wet, and I wouldn't mind having you on my breakfast platter." His tongue paints a wet line between my breasts with his tongue, then goes all out and licks my collarbone like my lion always does. "All that's missing is a cherry on top, but I'm sure we have some."

The mischief in his eyes melts me as he produces a cherry from within his hand, which makes me realize he'd probably fetched it from the kitchen during the night and had been waiting to pounce on me the instant I woke up.

Lord, he is a predator indeed.

Groaning groggily, I roll to my back and look into his heart-stoppingly handsome face. Scruffy jaw. Dark eyes twinkling. Dimpled smile.

God, I'm done for.

"Who's your man?" he asks gruffly, and he kisses me, rubbing that cherry against my clit. "Who's your man, baby?"

"You," I moan.

"Who do you love?"

Tremors run across my limbs as he tortures my clit with the cherry and at the same time penetrates my sex with one long finger, and I stare dazedly into his eyes. I can see miniature flecks of blue in their mysterious depths, and oh, I desperately want to tell him, *You, I've only ever loved you,* but I can't. Not like this, not when he may not even remember.

"You drive me crazy, Remy," I whisper, and brazenly grab his cock and drag him anxiously to me, so that he can fill me up and rub my swollen sex with his hard cock and make me smell of him again.

The entire week, he's on high-maintenance mode, and I can barely keep up with him, but I really love it. I'm riding the high with him. His smiles blaze. He needs to take sex breaks now from training. He can't see me without needing to fuck me. When I go stretch him he wants me as soon as I touch him.

I now notice that when he's black, his eyes aren't really black, but a really dark navy, flecked with gray and blue. But his mood is . . . somehow black. Not always, but sometimes. It's either supremely elevated, or super pissy. Sometimes nothing makes him happy. Diane is feeding him shit. Coach is not training him hard. And I'm looking at Pete too much, for god's sake.

But even as ridiculous as it sounds, these things seem like a very big deal to Remy, and now it seems like my entire day is absorbed by his energy and stamina, and I'm just scrambling to keep up.

"Who are all these people here for?" I ask when we land in New York to find a crowd of spectators have lined up to see his jet land, and they're barely being held back by yellow cords and airport security.

"For me, who else?" he declares.

He sounds so cocky even Pete cackles and says, "Get off it, Remy."

He grabs me seductively to him. "Come here, baby. I want these good folks to know you're with me." Large, sure hands grab my butt cheeks as flashes go off.

"Remington!"

He laughs and ushers me into the Hummer limo before all the others get in, pinning me down to his side as he fits his mouth to mine and kisses me like it's our last night alive, his hunger wild and unleashed. "I want to take you somewhere tonight," he rasps into my mouth. "Let's go to Paris."

"Why Paris?"

"Why the fuck not?"

"Because you have a fight in three days!" He makes me laugh when he's like this. I grab him and kiss him back, deep and fast, before anyone else boards, and I whisper, "Let's go anywhere with a bed."

"Let's do it on a swing."

"Remington!"

"Let's do it in an elevator," he insists.

Laughing, I shake an index finger at my big, bad, naughty boy. "I'm never, ever, doing it in an elevator, so you're going to have to find someone else."

"I want *you*. In an elevator."

"And I want you. In a bed. Like normal people."

His gaze dips below my waist, and his expression morphs from one of a playful, smiling sex-god to one of a dark, sex-starved sex-god. "I want you in those pants you're wearing."

Feeling warm and wanted, I nod, grin, and lace my fingers through his, kissing each one of his bruised knuckles.

His head tilts in curiosity, and his dimples slowly vanish. He looks like he's never been given these kinds of attentions until me. Suddenly, it makes me want to give him more.

So I do.

Crawling closer to him, I cup his jaw and kiss his hard cheek and run my hands through his hair, watching his gaze go heavy with desire along with something else. Something that makes his eyes look mysteriously dark and liquid.

Car doors open.

It appears the others will be sharing the limo with us, Coach up front and Pete, Riley, and Diane on the bench across from us. Remy squeezes my fingers as I try to ease away—that action alone telling me not to—then he slides down the edge of his seat and slumps his big shoulders as if he's trying to make himself less bulky. When that proves impossible due to his size and muscles, he grabs me closer and ducks to settle his head on the soft part of my chest, grunting softly and then sighing.

I'm so surprised I don't move.

Pete lifts one eyebrow as he watches Remington wrap his arms even tighter around my hips and draws me closer until the side of his head is perfectly cushioned on my breast. He grunts and sighs again. Riley lifts two eyebrows. Diane smiles tenderly, like she just melted.

I am not only melted. I'm liquid beneath him.

My parents, a coach and a teacher, are wonderful people but not big on hugs and kisses like, for example, my friend Melanie is; she was showered with affection and spreads it around the world like it's her duty to. But the way Remington looks at me, the way he doesn't hide his attraction to me even to his public during his fights, and the way he just cuddled me like a big hibernating bear that just found a cave makes me ache in inexplicably deep places.

Quietly, and with all the tenderness in the world, I run my nails through his spiky dark hair, then trace one fingernail along his ear. He holds both arms securely around my waist, somehow trapping me to him like he'd trap a pillow.

"You guys want a time-out when we get to the hotel?" Pete asks us, and his timbre vibrates as if some deep emotion has touched him.

I'm engrossed in sifting his hair through my fingers when I feel Remington nod against my chest, not even bothering to lift his heavy head.

I've never seen him so quiet when he's manic.

Or sit so utterly still.

Pete's and Riley's stunned expressions completely confirm that they haven't either.

When we hit the rooms, we receive our suitcases in our suite, and then I do what I always do. I unzip mine and tuck my small cosmetics bag hidden under the sink and pull out my toothbrush, to begin with.

Remy watches me from the door with such fierce longing I stop brushing, my mouth full of foam when I notice his stare. He looks hungry. Feral. Almost desperate. I quickly rinse as he approaches and towel off my hands. He's not smiling. His black eyes swallow me in their depths. He lifts me easily in his arms and carries me back to the room.

I can't help the way my insides flutter as I cuddle into his neck and breathe him in while he lowers us to the bed. I think I know what he wants, but I'm not sure. So I wait and watch him for a moment.

He pulls off my shoes and tosses them aside, then comes the big *thunk* of his own crashing to the floor. "I want your hands on my head."

I nod and edge back to make room for him. "Does it calm your racing thoughts?"

He shakes his head, then takes my hand and spreads it open over his wide chest, his voice textured as he traps my gaze with his. "It calms me here."

A tangle of emotion hits me as I feel his heart beating, slow and powerful like only great athletes' hearts can beat. I stare into his eyes, seeing that same fierce longing in them I just saw, and I love him to such a degree I swear that my heart just picked up the rhythm of his.

He slides next to me, both of us dressed as we settle on the bed's comforter. He drops his head to my chest and snuggles every bit of his huge muscles into me, inhaling my neck. I lower my face and kiss the top of his head as I start running my fingertips over his scalp.

He hasn't slept in long, endless, restless, crazy days.

Days where I've felt him stroking my hair and my back at night. Where I've heard the low muted noise of him listening to his music. I've heard him eating in the kitchen at midnight, taking cold showers, and when those showers don't seem like enough, I've woken up to find him well on his way to making love to me.

But I haven't heard him sleep for so long. . . ,

So when his breathing evens out, and I realize that he's fallen asleep in my arms, in the middle of the day, in the middle of a manic episode, I don't know how I can contain the emotions swelling in my chest.

Quietly, I wipe a tear from my cheek, and then another. I never imagined this kind of man existed. Or that I could ever have something like this for myself. These moments. This . . . connection. I never thought that the desperate, almost painful longing I feel for him could ever be reciprocated.

Crying in happiness for the first time in my life, I stroke his hair, his jaw, his neck, down his arms, looking down at his perfect, full lips, his hard, strong jaw and forehead, his perfect nose, quietly loving every inch of him.

Sunlight steals through the room and illuminates him completely, allowing me to drink his perfection in like a junkie. Our shoes are discarded on the floor, our suitcases still bursting full near the door. We're in yet another beautiful suite of another luxurious hotel, and I swear that in my life I've never felt so complete as I do this moment, with this man sleeping in my arms, his thick arms around me, his nose in my cleavage, his breath warm on my skin. In a strange place, in a new room, far away from everything I've known . . .

I touch my lips to his ear. "It's because of you," I whisper, closing my eyes. "I'm deliriously happy. Completely at home anywhere you are."

I'm so determined to guard his sleep, I skip dinner even when my stomach rumbles. Soon it calms down, and all the time, I keep giving his big, beautiful body little touches that quietly say, *I love you, Remington.*

He stirs in the middle of the night, and by this time, I'm exhausted but as determined as ever, my arms heavy as I caress him and pet him.

Coming awake with a soft groan, he easily grabs me and tucks my body into his so that now I'm the one cuddled into his deep chest as he languorously kisses the hollow of my ear. "Brooke," he says.

Just one word.

Thick with sleep, and so low and intimate, it could have been a proposal, any proposal, to which my reply would be and always will be *yes.*

"Yes, Remy," I whisper, my voice just as groggy as his as I nuzzle his collarbone.

He growls and slowly inhales me. "My Brooke." Voice still thick and raspy, he fingers the top button of my skinny jeans and lovingly kisses my neck as he pats my butt with one big hand. "Why are you still wearing these?"

Before I can remind him why, I hear him flick open the button and slide the zipper purposely downward. My every muscle clenches. I groan softly and press my nose to his neck, pressing closer like a kitten aching for his petting.

"I was waiting for the sexiest man in the world to take them off me."

♥ ♥ ♥

AROUND 3 A.M., Remington grumbles "hungry" in my ear and gets up to assault the kitchen, and as I lie in bed and stretch, my stomach instantly agrees.

I turn on a lamp and slide into the first thing that pops out of his suitcase, which ends up being one of his RIPTIDE red satin robes.

I tie the sash tightly around my waist, and the fabric feels delicious and cool against my skin. The robe is huge on me, reaching all the way to the bottom of my calves, but I grin because I just love wearing his things. I pad out after him to inspect whatever Diane left for us in the kitchen.

Inside the hot drawer are two warm plates of parmesan-crusted chicken and a spinach and beet salad with a side of red potatoes. I pull them out and am getting our utensils when I spot Remington already lounging at the dining table, gloriously bare-chested and in a pair of low-slung sweatpants.

He's scooping up peanut butter on a celery stick and munching, but he stops eating when he spots me and immediately swallows whatever he had in his mouth.

His eyes widen, and he drops the remaining celery stick and leans back in his chair, crossing his muscled arms so the ink vines at the top of his biceps look dark and sexy. "Look at you," he says, the words a growl of pure male pleasure.

The word RIPTIDE burns deliciously into my back as I head

over with the plates, grinning. "I'll return it when we get back to bed."

He shakes his head and pats his lap. "If it's mine, it's yours."

I set the food on the table, and he cups my hips through the satin and draws me to sit on his lap. "I'm so fucking starved."

He grabs a slice of red potato with his fingers and pops it into his mouth, licking his fingertips.

"You would love my mom's red potatoes. She adds cayenne pepper and gives them just a little kick," I tell him as I fork one up and munch, the taste of rosemary and the perfectly cooked potato melting on my tongue.

"Do you miss home?"

The question makes me look at him as he finishes another potato, and I realize he hasn't ever really had a home. Has he?

His home has been a fighting ring and hotels. His family has been his team and his fans.

My chest swells to near bursting for him.

The time he locked me with him in his hotel suite, just after I saw Pete sedate him that first time, Remy had been in a depression and I hadn't even *known*. He'd been holding on to me to stay sane, but I hadn't known this either.

All I'd known was that he didn't want me to leave that room and he didn't want anyone in. He wanted me there. He wanted my touch as if it grounded him, and my mouth was the only warmth in his cold, the only light in his dark.

Remington is not a man of words. He is a man of gut and actions.

This big, strong man sometimes needs to be taken care of, and I swear I'm dying to be the girl who takes care of him more than I've wanted to be anything else.

He, who's never had a home, wants to know if I miss home?

When I sleep like a queen, in a soft bed, in his arms, and eat the best food there is, and do my job, and spend time with him when he is sometimes cocky, sometimes grumpy, and always adorable?

Setting my fork down, I turn to face him and stroke the scruff of his jaw with my fingertips. "When I'm not with you, I do miss home. But when I'm with you, I don't miss anything."

His dimples briefly appear, and I bend to brush my lips over the closest one. He growls softly and rubs his nose against mine. "I'll tuck you close so you don't miss it," he rasps.

"Please do. In fact I'm sure there's enough space right here." I wiggle meaningfully on his lap, and he nips my earlobe and hugs me tight, saying, "That's right!"

We laugh, and we end up eating from the same plate, the same fork, taking turns feeding each other.

When I sense his restlessness, the one that comes with his mania, I realize he seems to want something to do. So I yield while he completely overpowers me and teases my lips with a brush of the fork, and I obediently open up and let him feed me.

I love the way his eyes darken every time he looks at my mouth as it opens for food.

He slides his free hand under the robe's satin sleeve and lovingly caresses my triceps as he turns back to his plate and forks up a bit of everything for himself.

I watch him take a big bite, and then I wait for him to cut up more chicken and bring it, and a little bit of everything else, to my mouth.

He watches as I bite, savor, and finally, swallow, his lips curved in a tender smile. "Who do you belong to?" he asks softly, stroking up and down my spine. My heart melts as he sets the fork down and slides that hand into the robe through the parted fabric, curving it around my waist. He bends his head and brushes a kiss over my ear, rasping, "Me."

"Entirely yours." I maneuver so I'm straddling him, and I

bury my nose in his thick, warm neck, sliding my arms around his lean waist. "I'm getting so nervous about the big fight. Are you?"

His chuckle rumbles in his deep chest as he edges back to peer down at me. He looks thoroughly amused. "Why would I be?" He tips my head back by the chin so that his laughing dark eyes capture mine. "Brooke, I'm going to break him."

The certainty in his voice carries such depth and power, I almost feel pity for Scorpion. Remy is not only going to break him, he's going to have fun doing it. "Remy, I love the way you fight, but you have no idea how nerve-wracking it is for me."

"Why, Brooke?"

"Because. You're . . . important to me. I wish nothing touched you, and every few nights, you're just . . . out there. Even knowing that you will win, it still does a number on me."

"But you're happy, Brooke? With me?"

His face tenses on that question, and suddenly he looks super intent, very much like the times he asks me "Did you like the fight?"

I see the fierce need in his eyes, and I know my answer matters to him just like what he thinks about me matters to *me.*

"Deliriously," I admit, and I hug him and smell his neck, loving how his scent relaxes me. "You make me happy. You make me deliriously happy and delirious, period. I don't want to be without you for a second. I don't even want all those women to look at you and shout at you the things they do."

His voice changes like it does when he talks intimately to me during sex. "I'm yours. You're the one I bring home with me." He smells my neck, then nuzzles the back of my ear, and whispers into me, "You're my mate, and I've claimed you."

With that, he adjusts me to the side and resumes feeding me. He seems to delight watching my lips open and close over what he brings to my mouth. He likes feeding me, and I think the obsessive male delight he's deriving from it dates back to his ancestor, the Neanderthal man.

We gobble up all the food, pet and kiss each other, and I tell him about Melanie, how she and Riley slept together one night and now seem to have become great texting friends, and he laughs and encourages me, "Tell me more," as he keeps eating.

So I tell him about my parents, how Nora used to fall in love with anything that walked, and he smiles and I just love making him smile.

"Do you remember anything nice about your parents?" I ask when we head back to the master bedroom and I climb into bed.

"My mother used to make the sign of the cross over me every night." He locks the door, and I know it's to keep Riley from bursting in the next morning and seeing us naked. "She crossed me on my forehead, over my mouth, and over my heart."

"She was religious?"

Remington shrugs his big shoulders, and I see that he stops by his carry-on to pull out his iPod and headphones.

Honestly, the thought of Remington's parents is torture to me. How could someone so religious abandon the best, most complex and beautiful human being I have ever known? How *could* they?

Remy carries his stuff to the nightstand, and I realize he's setting up all his items close by. He's preparing to hold me the rest of the night because he's fully aware he won't sleep.

"Do you miss your family?" I ask as he joins me.

The bed squeaks as Remy settles into it and he immediately reaches for me. "You can't miss anything you've never had." I don't expect that reply, and I want to both cry and nurture and protect him from everyone who's hurt him.

He pulls loose the drawstring of his "Riptide" robe and eases the satin off my shoulders. He likes me naked so he can do all his licking, lion-like things, and I like pleasing him. So I pull my arms out and toss it aside, loving when he cuddles me up against him, skin to skin.

Suddenly, with all my might, I want to give him all I have. My body, my soul, my heart, my family.

"If I told you something," I whisper as we find our favorite spot, facing each other, my leg between his thighs, our bodies entwined and touching as much as possible, "would you remember tomorrow?"

He pulls the covers up over us and tucks my face into his neck, his hands wandering up and down my spine. "I hope I do."

I feel his feet moving restlessly against mine, and I smile and reach up with my arms to stroke his hair to help him relax, and then I get an idea. A brilliant one. One where he will understand what I want to say, and in this way I won't pressure him into anything he might not feel comfortable with. In fact, he won't really need to respond to it at all.

I reach over him to the nightstand and grab the headphones and his iPod, praying that I will find the song in there. I am crazy about this song and I have never, ever, identified with it until this second, when I want to shout each of these lyrics to Remington Tate right now.

"Put these on," I say excitedly. He grins because I know he loves it when I play him music. He straightens up against the headboard and puts on his headphones and then drags me toward his lap, and I crawl there.

I find it. It is the perfect song to tell him I am crazy about every special part of him.

So I select Avril Lavigne's "I Love You" and play it.

I hear the music start, and excitement courses through my

veins as he raises the volume and I can hear the lyrics start speaking to him even from where I sit on his lap.

I know he might not remember this tomorrow. I know his eyes are black, and that playing him a song won't count as having said the words, but we've spent so many nights together. We train with each other, bathe together, run together, eat and feed each other, caress and talk, and I don't think Remington has ever opened up to anyone like he has to me. I've had my walls up all my life, and I've never let anyone inside until I suddenly realized he was . . . *in*.

I breathe him and live him every day, even dream about him while lying next to him in bed.

Even if this man doesn't recognize the emotions in his raw and untamed heart, I at least hope he will know by my song that he's become my . . . everything.

Excited beyond words, I hear the song continue playing and watch his face, gnawing my lip as I study his expression. Every lyric is so perfect, the entire song is meant from me to him, including the chorus, which I swear I can hear right now:

You're so beautiful
But that's not why I love you
I'm not sure you know
That the reason I love you is you
Being you
Just you
Yeah the reason I love you is all that we've been through
And that's why I love you

He listens while assessing my face, his expression intent as he scans my features. My full lips. My amber eyes. My high cheekbones.

"Play it again." His voice sounds so asperous, I almost have to read his lips to understand what he's saying.

I click the button to replay, but instead of listening to the song again like I expected him to, he rolls me over and lays me on my back, then sets the headphones on my head and adjusts them to my smaller frame as the song starts.

And in the next second, I'm listening to the "I Love You" song that I just played for him.

And which Remington Tate now plays for me.

I close my eyes, my heart shuddering in my chest, what I feel for him swelling inside me until I feel full and helplessly consumed on the inside. I feel his lips on mine, the song playing in my ears as he starts kissing me in a way that is not sexual, but infinitely tender.

This is the way Remy opens up to me, and I'm tingling from the top of my head to the soles of my feet as I soak up every single thing he's trying to tell me, with this song, with his lips, with his whisper touch. Even knowing he might not remember any of this doesn't make it any less real to me.

TWELVE

PICTURES OF YOU

My afternoon starts off perfectly fine.

Remington has a day off from training and is now completely carb loading and piling up his muscles with energy— and his plate too. He refused to eat Diane's meals and brought us all down to the hotel restaurant buffet instead. The men are eating separately, discussing "fight" stuff, and I'm having a lovely time with Diane trying to determine the ingredients of what we're eating. A taste of . . . orange? Hint of cardamom?

And then my phone bleeps. I'm thrilled to see it's a message from Mel. She flew back to Seattle before we left Chicago, and we've texted only briefly since.

> Melanie: I hate to give that ahole Riley any credit, but he was right. There's a picture on the Internet of you kissing that embodiment of Gross that night!! And it's going viral!

My world stops.

I'm flashed back to that night, where I'm up on tiptoe kissing the embodiment of Gross, and suddenly it makes perfect sense that someone—his goonies?—would capture it on camera. *Of course.*

If someone spent four minutes taping me at my Olympic trials, in the most humiliating moment of my life, of course there would also be someone ready to tape me at the second-most humiliating moment of my life. Of course they captured it on camera. Maybe not the first time I failed to hit the spot. But how about the second time I had to hold it for five seconds?

The floor drops from underneath me, and I feel like I'm drowning before the storm even comes, just at the mere sight of the incoming cloud.

With frozen lungs, I lower my phone back into my purse, somehow feeling as though everything I do is in slow motion. I glance at the table where the men are discussing their strategy for tomorrow night, and I notice Remy is easily listening to them. One second he's normal, relaxed and lounging back, with his legs splayed open on a pink dining chair of the hotel restaurant, and the next I see him looking intently at his phone as it vibrates.

My heart sinks to my toes, but seconds pass, and nothing happens.

I can't read his profile, but he has gone utterly still. Then it all happens in a blink of an eye. He turns the entire table over with a gigantic crash, and Coach ends up on the floor, with a thousand plates and food all over him.

In the same movement, Remington catapults to his feet and shoots his cell phone across the room, where it crashes into pieces against the wall. Then he starts for me.

Pete scrambles to his feet and reaches into his back pocket.

"No, Pete, no!" I burst out, loathing the idea of Remy being tranquilized.

I try to stay calm but my heart is pounding a thousand beats a minute. I've never dealt with Remington angry at me since we've been together, and suddenly I'm a little afraid of him, but I don't want him to know that.

Trembling in my seat, I stay utterly still as he comes to stand before me, breathing like a bull, his nostrils flaring, his eyes burning black in his face, his fists trembling at his sides. But it's the hard desperation in his gaze that sends awful chills down my arms.

It takes me about ten times the normal effort to speak. "Do you want to talk to me, Remington?" I ask, my voice raw.

I brace myself for his shout, but somehow, the cold sliver of a whisper he answers with is infinitely more threatening.

"I want to do more than talk to you."

The hairs at the back of my neck rise in alarm. "All right, let's talk. Excuse me, Diane," I say with deceptive calm, pushing my chair back so I can stand up, my legs wobbling.

He looks bigger than ever, and the entire restaurant is looking at him.

Diane scrambles away to the toppled table to help Coach clean up.

Remington's hands flex and fist at his sides as he glares down at me. His jaw works as he breathes, fast and choppy, and I notice Riley has just come up behind him, next to Pete.

There's a fierce battle inside Rem's eyes. He's struggling like he knows he has to control himself but can't. As if the anger is beyond him.

I try to calm my pulse while I burn with the need to calm *him*. I know that when I set my hands on any part of his body, he relaxes under my touch. I know he needs to receive my touch sometimes as fiercely as I need to give it to him. Except he's never been like this, and I'm afraid that for the first time in my life, he won't welcome my touch.

The thought of the only man I have ever loved feeling betrayed by me is almost crippling.

He still hasn't let go and told me what kind of terrible person he thinks I am now, but I can feel his turmoil so completely surrounding me that whatever he has to tell me already hurts somewhere deep and profound inside my body. I hurt him. I hurt him, and I instantly hate myself for it. My windpipe swells in pain.

"I only went to see my sister," I painfully breathe, a well of regret and anxiety roiling inside of me.

He reaches out with a fiercely trembling index finger and touches my mouth—the one I kissed Scorpion's filthy cheek with—and then he leans forward to nip me with his teeth. I gasp in mingled shock and desire at the prick of his teeth on my skin. "You go negotiate with scum like him? Without me knowing?" he asks in a low, turbulent voice as his thumb scrapes unsteadily over my lips.

"I went to see my sister, Remy. I couldn't care less about the scum."

He touches my hair, and the touch is so very unexpectedly gentle, I want to die with the way it contrasts with the lighted frenzy in his eyes and the way his thumb starts desperately scraping over my lips. "Yet you kiss that fucking *asshole* with the same mouth you kiss me."

"Please just count to ten." Helpless, I touch his sleeve.

He narrows his eyes, then rushes on to say, "One-two-three-four-five-six-seven-eight-nine-TEN."

He leans over and seizes part of my shirt collar in his fist, drawing me closer to him, the distressed look in his eyes cutting me like talons. "You kiss that *motherfucker* with the same mouth I would kill for?"

His eyes are wild as he touches my lips again, this time with the tips of two fiercely trembling fingers, and suddenly all I can see is torment. His eyes are black. Dark and haunted. And I can't stand that I put that darkness there, and I feel his pain—with every bone in my body I feel it.

"My lips hardly touched the tattoo." My voice is whisper-quiet as my windpipe begins closing down. "I did just what you do when you let them get a hit on you and give them false confidence, so I could see my sis."

He slams his chest with a loud noise. "You're *my* fucking girl! You don't get to give anyone false confidence!"

"Sir, we need you to leave the premises now."

Remy's head swings around as the manager comes forward, and suddenly Pete and Riley stop the poor man from getting closer, Pete swiftly extracting a checkbook as the term "cost of damages" echoes in the room. Remy's narrowed eyes slide back to me, and he's so angry and gorgeous, and such a damn handful, I just don't know what to do with him.

He comes closer and slides a finger down my jaw, and I respond to it, my scared body primed for sex with the barrage of hormones his temper has shot through me. "I'm going to go break that fucker's face," he whispers, the velvet promise laced with threat as he leans and slips his tongue into my mouth, "and then I'm going to break *you* into submission."

"Remy, calm down," Riley says.

"That's all right, Riley, I don't break that easy, and he's sure welcome to try," I snap, finally giving Remington the big black scowl he seems to be begging for.

He scowls back and ducks his dark head, breathing hard into my face as he grabs my hair in his fists and crushes my mouth with brutal possession, swiping my lips with punishing flicks of his tongue. "When I get you in bed, I'm going to scrub you raw with my fucking tongue until there's nothing anywhere on you from him. Only me. Only *me*."

His erection bites into my stomach, and I realize he's gone

completely territorial, claim-my-mate, prove-to-her-my-own-ership crazy on me. My thighs go liquid, and I gasp and strain closer. "All right, take me there," I plead, weak with the urge to ease the both of us.

He jerks back and narrows his eyes. "I don't have fucking time to take care of you," he snaps as when he starts for the door, I cry out in breathless panic, "Remy, come back. Don't get in trouble!"

He spins around, and my stomach knots as I see the look of determined murder on his face, his fists shaking at his sides as he jabs a finger in the air and points at me. "Protecting you is my *privilege*. I will protect you and anything that *you* value as if it were *mine*."

My breath catches at the way he stares at me.

"That sick asshole has just begged me to end his miserable life, and I'm happy to oblige," he snarls, his eyes raking me angrily from the door. "He's just taken something sacred to me and pissed on it!" He storms back, pushing his finger in between my breasts as he points. "Understand me. You. Are. *Mine!*"

"Remington, she's my sister."

"And the Scorpion will never let go of her. He keeps his women drugged and dependent, their minds in pieces so tiny they can't even think. He'll never give her up unless he wants something even more than her. Is it you? Does he want you, Brooke? He could have drugged you. Stripped you. Fucked you—goddamn my life, he could have *fucked you!*"

"No, he could *not* have."

"Did he touch you?"

"He didn't! They're doing this to provoke you! Don't let them! Save it for the ring tomorrow. Please. I want to be with you to-night."

"I was with her the whole time, buddy, nothing happened,"

Riley intercedes, patting Remy's arm and trying to back him off a bit.

But when he hears Riley speak, a look of betrayal settles into his eyes, and before I can stop him, he swings around to grab Riley's shirt in his fist. "You let my girl get in that scumbag's face, you little shit?"

Panic seizes me when he lifts Riley off the ground. "Remy, no!" I come to his side, tugging futilely at his arm.

He shakes him in the air, and Riley is getting purple. "You let her kiss that fucker's ink?"

Pete looks at me. "I'm sorry," he mouths, and then to Remy, "All right, buddy, let's put Destroyer to bed now, huh?" and he rams a syringe into his neck, and Remington drops Riley to the floor and yanks the syringe out of his skin, tossing it aside, empty.

I hold my breath when he comes and grabs me. He stares at me, his eyes blazing, and opens his mouth, hesitates, then makes a low, pained noise as he crushes my mouth and delivers a kiss that both claims and punishes me; then he lets go of my arm and stomps to the door, leaving me licking my raw, swollen lips and staring after him.

Riley coughs as he pushes himself to his feet, rubbing his throat as we all realize Remington is gone.

"What the hell?" Pete blinks in complete disbelief at the open doorway through which Remy just exited.

"It's supposed to put down an elephant, no?" Riley glumly asks Pete.

"'Supposed' being the operative word."

Shaking his head, Riley dusts the glass from his jeans. "Must be all the adrenaline in him. Shit."

"Pete, get your shit straight, both of you! You just shot him up with a sedative! He could drop down in an alley for all we know, be robbed and . . . oh god." I cover my face as I think of all the things he can do wrong, or that can happen to him.

"Calm down, Brooke, we've got it. Riley, you get another two of these tranquilizers—I'll meet you in the car," Pete says. Then he turns to the manager and signals at the check he still holds. "So if you could send the bill to the presidential suite? I guarantee we'll be moving out by morning."

"I want to help!" I yell at them.

"Damn, you've helped enough, Brooke," Riley answers, looking at me like I just unleashed the apocalypse. "Just go upstairs and wait for him. You've got your work cut out for you when he gets back."

❤ ❤ ❤

I'M PACING LIKE crazy as I wait to hear something. Anything.

I see all of his things across our suite—his iPad, iPod, laptop, his toothbrush in the sink, his clothes still in his suitcase, some hanging in the closet—and a horrible anxiety works its way down my nerve endings.

Remington just went out there ready to throw everything away for me. My lips are sore from the torture of my teeth as I go back to the past and wonder what would have happened if I'd said I wouldn't kiss that stupid tattoo. I might never have talked to Nora. She'd never have a chance to break free like I offered her.

At the moment, it seemed relatively harmless, considering, and also it had felt like I had no choice, but how I sorely wish Remington had never found out about it. Even angry, I could feel his hurt, and now I'm worried sick about him. If he has his fists on Scorpion's jaw right now, an Underground championship will be shot to hell—and I can't even wonder what that awful reptilian sick-dick might do to Nora as retribution if Remy hurts him tonight.

Oh god.

The thought of me ruining not only my own career but Remy's as well positively shatters me.

My stomach is so unsettled I feel like I'm going to toss out my intestines. I want Nora to be safe, but I desperately need Rem back in the hotel, where I'm sure I can appease him with sex. If he wants to break me into submission, then by god I'll let the man believe anything he wants, just to get him calm and easy again. I'm not afraid of him. I won't be. He's still *my* Remy, only in a bad fucking mood.

But at 5 a.m. he's still not back. I'm checking the Internet like crazy and have the local news playing on TV, fearing the worst. I hear a door and raise my head, my heart pulsing in my throat when I see Riley. Instantly I jump from the couch to my feet. "Remy? Where *is* he? What did he do?"

Riley won't look at my face, just walks directly into the master bedroom and searches the closet. "He's at the ER."

An awful tension stretches from one end of my spine to the other, and suddenly I feel whipped in the tail and charge determinedly after him. "What did he do? Let me go get my things. I need to see him."

Riley grabs Remy's toothbrush and razor and tosses everything into a small leather bag. "It's better if you wait here. It's just some stitches." He then gets some boxing shoes and an outfit for the match. "They're not disqualified. Neither one of them is telling. The fight goes on tonight, or shall we say, continues. Tonight."

The acids in my stomach start to bubble uncomfortably. I really lack the testosterone for all this. It used to be sexy in movies when a guy fights for a girl but this is *my* guy, fighting because of me, and I feel about as awful as possible and more than a little desperate to go and nurture and protect him.

"What ER is he in?" Following him through the bedroom, I snatch up a pair of jeans and slide them under Remy's black T-shirt—the one I sometimes sleep with.

Pivoting on his heel when he reaches the door, he stays me back with both hands. "Please *don't*, for the love of god, show up, B. Neither Pete nor I want him to see you. Please, Brooke. Just listen to me."

"But how is he . . ." I blink at him, my eyes blurring as my voice breaks. "Just tell me how he is."

"He's pissed off. They sedated him at the hospital. Honestly, I don't know how we can expect him to fight tonight. But at least he's *angry*."

I scowl at the slamming door and am left staring after him. I feel angry too, but I also feel eaten inside. The urge to see him is acute, but I don't know if I would help or hinder him, I just don't know anything about this. Using his laptop, I Google "bipolarism" and come upon tons of articles describing manic episodes. People suffering them tend to be either in an extremely happy or an extremely irritable mood; engage in an excess of pleasurable activities like sex, gambling, alcohol, and sometimes experience hallucinations; feel rested after zero or no sleep; act recklessly or violently; and often, after such episodes, enter a depressive state in which they can barely get out of bed. I'm sure Remy is manic right now, and I'd already seen he was speedy all these nights of hard sex. I remember him telling me the night he told me about being bipolar how I'm going to leave if it gets steep, and I'm doubly resolved not to be chickenshit and stick it out with him.

But I wonder how he's coping right now, after he tussled with that damned reptile freak.

God, please, please, don't let me ruin his fight tonight.

That's all I think of as I grab my sneakers and my knee brace and head into the hotel gym, grab a treadmill, and pound it for two hours. I focus on planning what to do when I see him. I want to say I'm sorry that I felt it necessary not to tell him about me visiting my sister, but I had to talk to her and didn't want to worry him. I want to kiss him and forget all this ever went down, but unfortunately, the morning goes by, and I don't see him at noon, or even at one, or at two, or at three.

I don't see him until the fight.

And by then, I'm absolutely, positively a mass of quaking nerves. I haven't seen Pete in all this time either, only Coach and Riley, who both ushered me to my seat when I tried wending my way backstage to see him.

"Please just let him get into the zone," Riley says.

All I can do is nod, and I'm assaulted by a sick yearning as I take my seat and wait and wait endlessly. There's only one fight tonight. Only Remington and Scorpion. And this one match will last for hours. It's already felt like an eternity by the time I hear his name tear through the speakers, and my heart rises in my chest at the same time the spectators fly to their feet to cheer for him.

"And nowwww, ladies and gentlemen, the moment we've all been waiting for. Our reigning champion, the defender, the one and only, Remington RIPTIDE Tate!"

The crowd goes wild, and I'm suddenly buoyant as my eyes see a flash of red at the beginning of the tunnel.

He comes out trotting to the ring, and the butterflies explode inside me. My eyes burn with the urge to see him up close. He hops into the ring and stretches out his arms, and when Riley pulls down his red hood and sets the robe easily aside, my eyes rake down Remington's body—and a cold, hard shock holds me immobile for several long, disbelieving heartbeats. Bruises color purple all the way up his torso. There are gashes on his lips, and several stitches run across his right eyebrow.

Forcing myself to sit down, I anxiously wait for Remington's usual turn. But he doesn't make it. The crowd screams his name in a chant, and I notice the Underground is packed with more fans of his than Scorpion's. But tonight Remington isn't his cocky self, and he doesn't turn and smile at them. He doesn't turn and smile at *me*.

My spirits sink, and suddenly I realize I have never, ever, ached for someone's smile as badly as his.

I've never felt so painfully invisible until I feel the lack of his eyes on me tonight.

When the presenter calls out, "And nooow, ladies and gentlemen, the nightmare you've all been dreading to come alive is here. Watch out for Benny the Blaaaaaack Scorpion!"

A nauseating sinking sense of despair hits me when Remy still won't bring his blue/black eyes to mine as he watches Scorpion come slowly down the tunnel with both his middle fingers stretched out high in a bold, obvious "Yeah, fuck you, Remington Tate, and fuck the public too!"

Icy dread spreads through my stomach as I study Remy's proud, hard profile as he waits by his corner, and the lack of his cocky response to Scorpion's outward bravado becomes painfully obvious to me. Suddenly I wonder if he's too proud to forgive me. Will he never kiss me? Make love to me? Love me back like I love him? Because I kissed his enemy? I'm twisting inside with the need to talk to him, to explain, to say good luck and *smile* at him.

But he doesn't glance in my direction and I'm filled with the suspicion he's doing his damnedest to glance anywhere *but* at me as Scorpion hops on the ring.

I watch as Scorpion's black robe is removed and notice he looks bad too. His face is pounded purple, and now a scarred area with at least a dozen stitches lies where his black insect used to crawl. Scorpion's yellow eyes land instantly on Remington, and a familiar, satanic smile spreads across his thin lips, a smile that already seems victorious compared to the somber, quiet intensity in Remington's face.

Heart twisting in anxious fear, I look for Nora among the crowd and try to locate her among Scorpion's thugs, but she's nowhere in sight. My dread doubles when I wonder if all this I caused, all this . . . was for nothing?

Ting-ting.

The bell rings, and all the atoms in my body hone in on Remington as both fighters go to center and toe to toe. Scorpion lands a punch in Remy's ribs, then quickly slams his jaw back in an awful one-two punch that I can hear striking flesh and bone. Remington holds his ground, but shudders as he recovers and continues going at Scorpion, his arms folded low at his sides.

My eyebrows draw together in confusion. In every fight I've seen him participate in, including the time I tussled in the ring with him and learned some boxing moves, Remy has never kept his guard this low. An awful premonition sinks its awful claws into my stomach, and I glance up to try to read the dark frowns on Riley's and Coach's faces. The grim lines etched on both their features only confirm my suspicions.

Remington's guard is completely *down*. His thick, muscled arms hang relaxed and idle at his sides, and now he's just bouncing on the balls of his feet as if waiting for the next hit to come. His eyebrows are drawn, his eyes narrowed fiercely, but he looks almost . . . hungry for it, in a raging, reckless way.

Scorpion rams a punch into his gut, then follows it with an uppercut to the jaw that Remington takes too easily, straightening almost right away and glaring back at Scorpion as though begging for another one.

He almost seems . . . *suicidal.*

The next three punches, Remington takes in the body again, two in the chest, one in the rib cage, and he still hasn't landed a single punch on Scorpion. His guard won't come up, but all you can see of Remington's spirit is in his eyes. Which blaze fire into Scorpion as he quickly recovers from each blow and steps back up as though daring the monster to hit him again.

I'm speechless.

There's no way to still my erratic pulse, or stop my mind from spinning. I can't stop fretting over whether his ribs can take any more blows, and I'm wildly trying to determine what other injuries he sustained during the night they fought privately. What if he's not punching because he's *unable* to stretch his arms out to punch?

He is. Not. Punching. *At all.*

My heartbeat won't calm, and that alarming premonition of something awful happening has seized me in its grip. I want to go up there and hug my guy and pull him out of there!

Scorpion swings out with his left hand and lands one in the jaw, then lands a straight punch in the face that knocks Remington to his knees. My throat goes raw with unuttered shouts and protests as the public begins booing.

"Boooo! Booo!!"

"Kill the bastard, Riptide! KILL HIM!"

When he stands again, the fight continues, endless, gray as night.

In all of Remington's fights, I used to feel all kinds of twisting nerves as well as excitement, but now it is only anguish and pain roiling inside me as, blow after blow, Remington takes it.

Every punch breaks me inside. I can feel the ache in my bones as if his bones were mine. I'm so wounded by the sixth round, I need to take him away in my head, where he will play me a song.

I need to take him for a run, where he will look at me and smile with shining blue eyes. I need to take him to our bed, where we're warm and happy and peaceful. I need to take him somewhere, anywhere, where he can tell me what . . . the fuck . . . is *wrong*!

I sit here and watch the man I love getting beaten to death, and when he falls to his knees after taking an awful set of punches to his abs, he still won't give up. Panting for breath and with his forehead and mouth dripping blood, he delights the public by jumping back to his feet and angrily spitting blood on Scorpion's face, rebellious as he takes a stance once more.

"Remy, fight him!" I suddenly hear myself scream, and I'm screaming at the top of my lungs in a way I have never in my life screamed before. "REMY, FIGHT HIM! FOR ME! FOR *ME*!"

He still doesn't look at me. And the next punches that come in a fast series of jabs, Remy once again takes. *Ooof, ooff*, I hear, as his breath is knocked out of him.

Fight or flight rushes all over my body, and it mercilessly eats at my blood vessels, my nerve endings, my lungs. For the first time in my life, the adrenal response is so overpowering that I want to take flight like never before. Run for him, grab him to me, and take him away, away from Scorpion, from himself, away from self-destruct button the man I love has pressed.

Scorpion pounds him several straight punches in the head, and then *crack!*

Remington falls facedown on the floor.

Blood oozes from his body, leaking to the canvas floor. Raw, primitive grief overwhelms me, and a black snake of fear starts gnawing painfully into the thickest arteries of my heart. Remy's face is swollen, and he's panting for breath and shuddering with each breath as he plants one hand on the ground, then the other. A chill black silence surrounds the room as the counting begins, and Remy tries pushing up.

His image becomes a big blur through the tears in my eyes, and I have to swallow back the plea building in my throat where I want to beg him to, *for the love of god*, stop with this bullshit and just stay down now!

I broke my knee by accident, but the thought of willingly breaking yourself again and again and getting up for more makes my eyes well up in horrified despair.

But Remy pushes up and spits more blood at the ground, using his arms to get back on his feet only to catch a powerful left hook right to his temple that swings his head around.

Riley and Coach yell loudly at him. "Your fucking guard! What the fuck is wrong with you?" they're saying, over and over, their shouts loud and painfully distressed.

People yell across the room, every one of them unwilling to give up on him as long as Remy keeps standing.

"KILL HIM, RIPTIDE!!! KILL HIM!" they scream.

And as I watch him take another hit that splatters more blood across the ring mat, I want to scream back at the public to please just *shut the hell up!* To please, for heaven's sake, just let him *fucking stay down* and *stop this fucking nightmare!* I can't control the spasmodic trembling within me.

But the people continue: *"REM-MING-TON! RE-MING-TON!"*

But I can see Remy's hurting. One of his arms is dangling at his side, hanging limply. He's hurting and he's still going, and he's going to keep going, and going and going, until he *can't* get up. When that realization finally sinks into my stunned head, I'm shattered to a million pieces. A hot tear streams down my cheek as sounds rip through the room when another series of hits lands on Remington's flesh, the awful impacts backing him up toward the ropes.

"*Remy, Remy,* Remy!" some people nearby begin yelling. And when the sharp chant takes over with equal force across the room, Scorpion's face scrunches in rage. Remy spits right into the place where his tattoo should be, whispering something taunting that seems to anger the other man so much, he swings his arm back with a deafening roar and lands an uppercut that knocks Remy like lead down onto the floor. My heart stops.

Silence falls.

I blink in mute horror at Remy's motionless form, fallen on his side, and I take in those perfect shoulders I know by memory, his beautiful bones probably broken, his beautifully trained and beautifully made body bruised purple and bleeding on that ring floor. His eyes are frightfully closed.

And I want to die.

There are gasps of outrage when the ring doctors appear up on the platform, and people start booing out loud as the announcer speaks.

"Our victor of the night, Benny, the Black Scooooorpion! The new Underground champion, ladies and gentlemen! Scooor-pioooon!"

The words somehow make it into my brain, but I don't even register them as I sit motionless in my seat, trying very hard to keep it together as I watch the medics—the medics!—surround Remy.

I never thought anything in my life would ever hurt me as much as tearing my ACL and wobbling off the field at the Olympic tryouts, my spirit broken.

But no. Now the worst day of my entire life has been this one. When I watched the man I love break his own body to uncon-sciousness, and every millimeter of every quadrant of my heart is broken.

Through burning eyes, I watch the medics haul his body onto a stretcher, and the reality of the situation hits me like a cannon blast. I jump to my feet and run like crazy through a throng of people as the doctors start carrying him away. I fling myself between a pair of them and reach for one bloodied hand and squeeze two bloodied fingers. "Remy!"

Strong arms wrench me away, and a familiar voice speaks close to me. "Let them look at him, B," Riley pleads in a craggy voice, hauling me back as I struggle to be set free.

Spinning around to hit him so that he releases me, I notice his eyes are red as he tries to keep hold of my struggling form, and suddenly, I break. Deep compulsive sobs wrack through my body as I grab his shirt, and instead of hitting him, I just cling. I need something to hang onto, and my big, strong tree is broken on a stretcher, beaten to a pulp.

"I'm sorry," I cry, every inch of me jerking and shaking as the tears flow out of me, just as they did six years ago. "Oh, god, I'm sorry, *I'm so sorry!*"

He sniffles too, then pulls away and wipes his own cheeks. "I know, B, I don't know what the fuck . . . It's just . . . I don't know what the hell went on down here. *Jesus!*"

Coach comes to us, his face grim, his eyes also brimming with tears and disappointment. "They suspect a concussion. His pupils aren't responding correctly."

A new burning wetness pops up in my eyes, and the knot in my throat tightens as Riley starts after Coach.

Nora. Oh, fuck meeeee, I still need to wait for Nora!

I grab Riley back, more tears threatening to spill out when I realize I won't be able to go with him.

"Riley, my sister! I told her to meet me here."

He nods in understanding. "I'll text you the name of the hospital where we end up."

Nodding miserably, I watch him leave, wiping away more tears and not even knowing what to do with the whirlwind of emotions inside me. I desperately want to go with Remington, but I can't ask Riley to trade places with me. Nora doesn't know him, might change her mind if she sees him instead of me. I swear it's the hardest thing I've ever done, to watch him be taken away, all bloodied, without running after him.

I lean on the door of the women's restroom and wait, and wait, restless with worry and haunted by what I just saw.

My mind keeps spinning and I feel I will wake up soon and realize this was just a bad dream, and Remy did not just commit the most painful almost-suicide up in that ring.

But he did.

He *had*.

My Remy.

The man who played me "Iris."

The man who laughs with me, runs with me, and says I'm a little firecracker.

The strongest man I've ever known, and the one who's been most gentle to me.

The one who's a little bit bad, a little bit crazy, a little bit too hard for me to handle.

When three hours pass, I've run out of tears, and my hope is gone too.

And as I go get a taxi, I'm the one who feels like whatever just got broken inside me will never, ever, heal.

❤ ❤ ❤

I SIT IN a hospital chair for the first week and stare at his beautiful face with the tube that helps him breathe, and I cry from anger and frustration and helplessness. Sometimes I put his headphones on his beautiful head and play him every single song of the ones we shared, waiting to see if his eyes twitch or if there's some indication of thought in there. Other times, I walk out in the hall just to wake up my legs and arms that have fallen asleep. I haven't seen Pete, and nobody will tell me where he is. Today Riley peers into the waiting room, where I'm staring down lifelessly at my bag of peanuts. I just didn't know what to get that would be moderately healthy, and I already finished all the granolas. I think I've lost some weight, for my jeans are hanging loose from my hips, but my stomach is about as closed as a fist and the few times it seems to relax enough to let me eat something, my throat is to blame for not letting it past.

"He's awake," Riley says.

Blinking, I'm suddenly, immediately, on my feet. I toss the uneaten bag of peanuts into the empty chair next to mine and then run down the hall only to stop and stare at the door to his room. Afraid to see him. Afraid of what I'm going to say.

I've been thinking a lot these few days. That's all I've done, actually. But out of all my thoughts, my mind goes blank as I step inside. A deep, dark anguish overwhelms me as I head for the bed. I thought I was getting numb already, but I realize I'm not. I step slowly forward and fix my eyes on the very spot around which my world seems to revolve.

And I see him. His eyes are open. I don't care what color they are. He's still Remington Tate, the man I love.

He's going to be okay, and I am not. I don't think I ever will be.

The tears burst out, and all of a sudden, all my thoughts come rushing back. I have so many things to say I just stand in the middle of the room and tear my guts open. My words are angry, but they're barely understandable through my sobs. "How d-dare you make m-me watch t-that . . . ? How could you stand there and make me watch h-him destroy you! Your bones! Your face!

Y-you . . . were . . . mine! Mine . . . to . . . to . . . hold . . . How d-dare you break you! How dare you break me!"

His eyes go red too, and I know I should stop because with the tube in he can't even respond, but this dam has opened and I can't stop it, I just can't. He made me watch and now I have to make him listen to me, to what his stupid fucked-up shit has done to me!

"A-all I wanted was to help my sister and not g-g-get you in trouble. I also wanted to protect *you,* to take care of you, to be with you. I wanted to *ss-stay* with you until you were sick of me and didn't need me. I wanted you to *love me* because I . . . I . . . Oh, god, but you . . . I . . . can't. I can't anymore. It's hard to watch you fight, but to watch you murder yourself is . . . I won't do it, Remington!"

He makes a pained sound in the bed and tries shifting even with one arm in a cast, and his eyes are burning red and tearing me open.

I can't stand the way he's looking at me. The way his eyes claw into me. Destroy me.

Hot tears continue trickling down my cheeks as I yield to a reckless impulse and go to him. I touch his free hand and bend my head to his chest as I lift his fingers and kiss his knuckles feverishly, aware that I'm getting them wet with my tears, but I can't stop because it's the last time I'm going to kiss this hand and it hurts.

He groans as he awkwardly places the hand of his casted arm on the back of my head and heavily strokes my hair. His throat is tubed, but when I wipe my tears and look up at him, his eyes are screaming things at me that I can't bear to listen to. I stand, acting as cowardly as Mel says I am, and he grabs my hand and won't let go. I don't want him to, but I need him to. I pull my hand free with force and grab his forehead and set a kiss at its very center, a kiss that I hope he will feel all the way down to his soul, because that's from where it's coming from inside me. He makes a rough sound and starts pulling at his tube, and the machine makes a beeping noise when he starts succeeding in yanking off all the wires attached to him.

"Remy, don't, don't!" I plead, and when his efforts only intensify and he growls in anger, I open the door and yell for a nurse. "Nurse! Please!"

A nurse rushes into the room, and I feel such pain as she shoots some sort of tranquilizer into his thigh that it's like there is nothing else for me except to become this knot of pain. I can't believe I'm going to do this to him, that I'm as cowardly, as worthless, as everyone else. But when the nurse settles him down and adjusts his respirator, I stare at him from the door, his appearance calmer now as he gazes back at me, and I smile, a smile that is fake and that trembles horribly on my face, and I leave.

I hate that he will wake up again with his beautiful blue eyes and might not remember what I said, or where I am, or what happened to me. But I just can't stay.

I find Riley at the cafeteria and show him an envelope I acquired from one of the nurses several days ago. "I'm leaving, Riley. My contract was over several days ago. Just . . . say goodbye to Pete and please . . ." I hand him the envelope with Remington's name, watching it tremble violently in the air. "Give this to him when his eyes are blue again."

That night, I'm flying to Seattle, slumped in my seat, feeling as heavy and empty as an abandoned building, and I wonder as I stare unseeingly out the window if he's already back to blue, and if he's already reading my letter. I've read it a thousand times in my head, and read it a thousand times when I wrote it the third night at the hospital, when I knew I was not going to stay.

Dear Remington,

The very first moment I laid eyes on you, I think you had me. And I think you knew. How could you possibly not know? That the floor was shaking under my feet. It was. You made it move. You colored my life again. And when you came after me and kissed me, I just knew somewhere deep inside me, my life would forever be touched and changed by you. It has been. I have had the most amazing, incredible, beautiful moments of my life with you. You and your team became my new family, and never for one second did I really plan to leave. Not them, but most of all, not you. Every day I spent with you only makes me crave more of you. All I wanted for days was to be closer. It hurts to be close and not to touch you, and I wanted to spend every waking moment with you and every sleeping moment in your arms. So many times now, I wanted to tell you all the ways you make me feel, but I wanted to hear you say it first. My pride is gone now. I have no room for it, and I don't want to regret not telling you: I love you, Remy. With all my heart. You are the most beautifully complicated, gentle fighter I've ever known. You have made me deliriously happy. You challenge and delight me, and make me feel like a kid inside, with all the amazing things to look forward to, just because I was looking at the future and thinking of sharing it all with you. I've never felt so safe as when I am with you, and I want you to know I am completely in love with every part of you, even the one that just broke my heart.

But I can't stay anymore, Remy. I can't watch you hurt yourself, because when you do, you're hurting me in ways I never thought anybody ever could, and I'm afraid of breaking and never being right again. Please never, ever,

*let anyone hurt you like this. You are the fighter everyone
wants to be, and this is why everyone in the world loves
you. Even when you screw up, you get back up fighting
again. Thank you, Remy, for opening your world to me. For
sharing yourself with me. For my job. And for every time
you smiled at me. I want to tell you to get well soon, but I
know that you will. I know you will be blue-eyed and cocky
and fighting again, and I'll be in your past, like all the
things you've overcome before me. Just please know that I
will never hear "Iris" again, without thinking of you.*

Yours always,
Brooke

THIRTEEN

SEATTLE IS RAINIER THAN EVER

Not even Mel can cheer me up.

I talked to my parents and told them things are great, especially because I don't want to worry them about Nora until I figure out how I'm going to bring her home again. I've already researched, and Scorpion, according to his fan site, he's reportedly celebrating his win in an undisclosed island location until the Underground's next season begins—which isn't until February of next year, in Washington, D.C. I *hate* there's no trace of my sister.

I'm probably going to accept the job offer from the Military Academy of Seattle with my middle graders to begin in August. But if I do, I might not be able to travel in February in search of Nora. Which I don't like. But when I go after Nora, I don't know if I'll be strong enough to see Remington in the Underground again.

Melanie, who's been stalking Twitter, says all his fans are speculating on whether or not he will return to the fights next year.

"Please," I tell her when we're running and she brings the topic up again. "Please don't talk to me about him anymore."

"Why not? Come on, little nugget. You've never had a love interest before and it's fun to finally talk about drama that isn't mine."

"Just don't talk to me about him, please! I love him, Melanie. I *love* him. He's not just a star; he's the whole fucking sky to me. He's the sun and every planet in this galaxy. It hurts me to think of him, don't you understand?"

On the verge of tears that finally shut up Melanie, I grab my iPod and stick the buds in my ears, but as I turn it on, even listening to music affects me, because every song I hear makes me want to find a meaning in it that will make me want to play it for *him*.

Completely distressed over how volatile I've become, I switch my music off and focus on running, tap-tap-tap, on the ground. Now the sun is getting higher, and as we round the corner to my building, we see a black Escalade parked right in front of it.

We keep trotting toward it, and as we approach, the doors open and a man in black that looks remarkably like Pete steps out. Followed by another who could be Riley.

And suddenly, standing across from me, every inch of him beautiful, healthy, and vital, is Remington Tate. I see his gleaming dark hair, his sexy boyish face, his slightly scruffy jaw, and all of his manly tan skin and perfect muscles, and my heart stops.

I stop running.

Stop breathing. Stop *existing*.

My brain goes blank, my lungs close up, my ears shut off.

I look at him. And he looks at me.

And as we stare, my eyes on his, his eyes on mine, my heart resumes with one burst of emotion.

It leaps and runs to him, slams into him, explodes in him,

and although it hurts like an open wound to look at this man, all my senses have sizzled to life and I couldn't take my eyes off him even if my life depended on it. A private Fourth of July is happening in my stomach as I feel Melanie's nudge at my back, and we begin walking toward them at a slower pace.

A nerve-wracking pace.

It feels as though the entire world is in slow motion. Every step of mine takes ages.

Remington looks so . . . *large* as we approach. Larger than life itself, and I can't even believe this striking creature was once a little bit mine.

The bad part is, my body cannot distinguish that he's no longer mine, and every pore of me seems magnetized by him, like they all still think that *he* belongs to *me*.

"Holy shit, that man is hot," Melanie gasps at my side.

I nod helplessly and drink him in several times, head to toe. Something rushes through me, as if this is the first sip of water I've had in long, dehydrated weeks, and every atom in my body is thirsty. A tremor wraps itself around my heart. I know there's no doubt that I'm every bit in love with him as I was before. And this is nothing, nothing, compared to the instant, the very second, he briefly, almost boredly, smiles at me.

"Miss Dumas?" Pete says with a grin, as we approach. "We believe this belongs to you?"

He signals in the direction of Remington, who watches me with that bored smile slowly vanishing as he studies me. My pulse goes so wild I can hear it in my ears, and then I realize another figure is stepping out of the car. A female figure. That looks like . . . Nora.

I blink, and my heart stops. "Nora?"

"Nora?" Melanie repeats, sounding even more stupid than I'm sure I do.

"We just wanted to make sure she got home safe," Pete says.

"Nora?" I repeat. And now I really sound more stupid than Melanie.

"It's me!" my little sister says, and she looks lively and like her old self as she comes to hug me, shaking in excitement as she does so. "It's me, big sis! I'm back! I've done work in rehab. Pete helped me," she rushes to explain. "And I got the tattoo off." She points to her rosy cheekbone. "I felt so little when you looked at me that day, Brooke. I felt so little and so . . . dirty."

"No! No, never!" Reeling in surprise, I drag her in for another hug, still stunned and disbelieving that my little sister is in my arms, and then Melanie grabs her and gives her some Mel-love.

"Nora!! Nora Camora Lalora Crazyora!" She hugs and swings her around and squeezes her, and I turn to stare at the three men before me, and since I can't make myself speak to the one I really want to speak to, I speak to the least intimidating one instead. "Pete, what's going on?"

"Surprise," he says, wiggling his eyebrows and signaling to Nora. "She's done great. She's such a sweet girl."

I keep staring impatiently, and he nods at Remington, who's just rammed his hands into his jean pockets. His eyes are raking me top to bottom, nonstop, making me aware of my athletic gear and the way it hugs my butt, my breasts, and my waistline, which has expanded a little from mood-boosting dark chocolate meant to help with my completely frustrating heartbreak blues.

"The night Remy went to fight with Scorpion, Scorpion offered your sister to him in exchange for the championship," Pete tells us. "And Remy agreed."

I stand motionless for a moment, blank, wavering, and very baffled. When my eyes confusedly seek out Remington's, I feel a shock run through me at the intensity in his stare.

Then I'm bowled over.

"You mean he agreed to . . . lose?"

First, there's disbelief.

Then . . .

A powerful emotion zip-lines through my body, settling like a burning bolt of light in my brain, illuminating me with the magnitude of something that sounds impossible.

Briefly tossing my head from side to side, I cling helplessly to those dark-lashed, achingly familiar blue eyes. My pulse spins with confused disbelief. A war of emotions rages within me as strange and disquieting thoughts race through my mind, clenching around my heart.

"You did this for . . . Nora?" I breathlessly ask Remington.

His face is so beautiful, I just want to grab his spiky hair and kiss him senseless, but at this point, I don't think I even deserve to have him standing here. Looking at me, not even telling me what a jerk I am for leaving him the way I did.

Feeling painfully hammered inside, which is not the optimal feeling to experience when you're told your baby sister is, thankfully, happily, back home, I sit down on the stairs to my building, knocked out by my attempts to blink back a well of tears threatening to fall.

Pete grabs a green duffel bag from the back of the Escalade and heads inside with Nora. "Let me take this in for you, Nora."

I'm left with Riley, whose gaze shifts from Melanie to me like a Ping-Pong ball, and I'm also left with Remy. My Remy. The Remy I abandoned in the hospital. The one I adore. The one I am mad over. The one who got his guts torn apart and humiliated for the sake of my sister. For me.

A ball of pain gathers at my throat and I can barely stand it.

He's so handsome, so familiar, I feel like a prisoner in my own body, screaming to touch what I had, for weeks, viewed as *mine*.

His big hands are still deeply buried in his jeans, and I wonder if he may be struggling with the same issues too? But there's a somberness in his expression that is rarely there when his eyes are blue. And they are so blue I'm drowning in them.

I wrap my arms around myself and drop my head as the shame continues building inside me. "Why didn't you tell me? That you threw the fight for . . . her?"

I can't even say "me"—I feel awful.

But Remington says softly, "You mean for *you*."

Riley interrupts. "I didn't know either, Brooke. Or Coach. Only Pete knew. He's the one who found him that night, and he helped secure your sister while Remington delivered the win."

My eyes shift to the face of my dreams, and my voice drops as the pain of what he did for me seeps through my pores. "How are you? Are you all right?" I look at him, and his eyes are blue and on fire with emotion as he nods.

He's angry at me. I think. I don't know. I feel punched in the gut when I look at him, but at the same time, it's all I want to do.

"What does this loss mean for you now?" I ask. Oh, god, I missed my Remington so much that when I look at him, all perfect blue eyes, beautiful face, I feel water in my eyes.

I think he's having trouble talking too, because there's a silence.

A violent and unexpected despair surges wildly through me as I stare at this surprising, unpredictable man, the ever-changing mystery of Remington Tate, and suddenly, nothing in the world has hurt me more than having had him and lost him.

"The loss? Other than we're poor?" Riley finally answers when it seems neither Remington nor I is going to speak. He chuckles a bit too loudly and rakes his hair back. "He has a couple million to get him through the year. We're making a comeback when the new season starts. Remy's fans demand retribution."

"You do have loyal fans, don't you?" I quietly ask, directing my question to Remington as I remember all the flowers he made them bring me and I feel queasy and excited again.

This second it feels like my entire life I've been waiting to talk to him again. My running partner and friend. My lover. My love.

"Well, time to go." Riley slaps Remington's back, and my insides feel pain. "Actually, Brooke, we're also here because we're looking for a sports rehab specialist for the upcoming new season. Good to get a head start on training," Riley says, producing something from his back pocket. "In case you're interested, Mr. Tate's number is on the back. There's the hotel where we're staying too. We leave in three days."

I watch Riley climb into the car, and then Pete strides out of my apartment and says goodbye.

I look at Remington, and he looks directly back at me, and through all the emotions I see in his eyes, I can't decide which one reels me in the most. My skin breaks out in goose bumps in a silent plea for his touch—tingling in remembrance of his rough hands, the way he drags his tongue over me. My dark-haired lion. Licking and claiming me.

My heart hurts me as we both stare, but neither of us is talking, even when there are a thousand things weighing on us both.

"You're looking good, Remy," Melanie says with a sunny smile.

He graces her with those dimples that kill me, and then his eyes flick back to me and the dimples are gone. "You know where to find me."

He climbs in the car and leaves, leaving a trail of goose bumps in his wake, all along my skin.

Melanie goes inside first, but I stay outside under the sun, just . . . processing.

When I eventually stride into my place, my heart swells at the sound of Nora's excited voice, reminding me she's here. Suddenly my apartment sounds like a college dorm with laughing friends, and all because of *Remy*.

"I really think he likes me!" Nora is saying on a little squeal.

"Nora!" I come into the eclectic living room—courtesy of Melanie's free decoration skills—and squeeze my sister in a big bear hug again, where *I* get to be the bear. "Let me look at you. You okay?"

I inspect her head to toe, and admit she looks good. Rosy cheeks, brilliant grin. She's cut that soft brown mane into a cute bob to her elfin ears, and there's color back in her sweet, curled lips. She looks slender and wholesome, and the animation in her eyes enchants me. This is the Nora I remember. My baby sister.

She squeezes my hands and nods emphatically, lacing her cool fingers happily through mine.

"Nora was telling me how Remington fought Scorpion for her." Melanie widens her eyes at me and nods meaningfully. "She thinks Remington is way *hot* because of the way he fought."

A sneaky hint of jealousy curls around my tummy. "Oh. Of course."

Nora has seen him for the past four weeks, maybe, and the thought of any woman enjoying his smiles and his voice, while I've been denying myself of it, makes me a little sick.

"Brooke, you should have seen him," Nora bursts out, oblivious to my inner torture chamber called a "heart."

"He just barged into our rental rooms and knocked out two of the men, and then he went straight to pound Benny's face, nonstop. He rammed a pencil into his tattoo so deep he completely deformed it."

"Wait! Who the hell is Benny?" Melanie asks.

"Scorpion!" Nora explains, her smile eager with delight. Seriously, I'm still staring at her in awe because she looks like another person compared to the drugged, fiery-haired girl with a facial tattoo I saw at the Japanese restaurant. The wonders a month of rehab can do. *And my dark-haired fighter . . .*

"Oh! Benny is the he-beast Scorpion—got it!" Mel says, rolling her eyes.

"Remington was like a devil unleashed from hell, nonstop hitting. Benny couldn't stop him as he kept shouting about staying away from his girl, that he wasn't leaving without what his girl wanted—and tons of bad words—and then Benny scrambled to stop him and offered me. He said if he stopped that he would set me free in exchange for the championship. Then Remy looked at me and asked me if I was your sister. And I didn't know what to say, because I knew that if I said yes, he'd take me to you. I could see it in his eyes. But then I remembered . . ." she trails off. "I remembered the way you looked at me, Brooke. And I was so mad at Benny offering me to save himself like I was worth nothing! I decided to leave and so, I nodded. And so Remington agreed. He didn't even hesitate. He demanded I get out of there that same night, but Benny said I was to be on lockdown until Remington delivered the championship, so Remy called Pete to get me. Pete took me to a rehab place in Connecticut and Remy paid for my entire stay."

I fall into a chair and just can't hold myself upright, my eyes a mess. After all the tears I've cried, I feel like I could still cry another great lake. For Remington Tate. And for myself. For underestimating someone who I believed did something wrong and who instead did the best and most incredible thing possible for me. Remy, when he goes black, has done a lot of bad things, or so they say. But boy, oh boy, did he make it right with Nora. For me.

I know, despite Nora's romantic side, it is for *me* he fought. For me he threw the fight. For me, and for who I love.

I remember how proud he was during the fight, taking every blow. How it must have hurt him not to fight back! That's all Remy *knows* to do. He's a fighter at heart. Even in his eyes I could see his fierceness. He can barely control himself when provoked, and to think of him holding back when he was being hurt this way, only for me. For my sister.

Something clicks in my mind, and my heart swells until I think I'm going to pop with pain and emotion. I'm bombarded with thoughts of the first night I ever saw this man. All glinting blue eyes, golden tan, spiky black hair, playful face, and hard male body.

"Your name," he growls, panting, his eyes wild on mine.

"Uh, Brooke."

"Brooke what?" he snaps out, his nostrils flaring.

With trembling effort, I pry my hand free and glance fearfully at Mel, who comes up behind him, wide-eyed. "It's Brooke Dumas," she says, and then happily shoots out my cell phone number to my chagrin. His lips curl, and he meets my gaze once more.

"Brooke Dumas." He just fucked my name right in front of me, and right in front of Mel. He steps forward, and his damp hand slides to the nape of my neck. "Brooke," he growls softly, meaningfully, against my lips, as he draws back with a smile. "I'm Remington."

Oh, god, I knew my life would change. I just never knew how much.

I. Love. This. Man.

Yes, he is a man who will be difficult, and bipolar to boot.

He's strong, and he's proud, and I don't expect him to beg me.

But even though he probably won't beg me to come back, he's at least not asking me to beg his forgiveness for being a chicken-shit and dumping him while he was stuck in the hospital either.

Feeling the first real sense of joy I've felt in weeks unfurl in my tummy, I glance down at the hotel address written on the card, and my insides move in anticipation.

He wants to be my real, not my adventure. Even when he will be the realest thing in my life, I know it's still going to be an adventure. Because that's him. An exhilarating bungee jump . . . a free fall . . . Olympics all year round for me . . . that's what being in love with him is going to be like for me. What wondering when he gets black . . . and all the pushing and pulling and reasoning with him . . . will be like.

And suddenly, this is all I can think of.

Suddenly, my bad knee is all that's stopping me from running after him.

I want the job.

I want to be with my big, crazy, sexy beast of a man, and I won't apologize to anyone for it. He's bipolar, and I'm crazy about him.

He never said he loved me. But he came back for me. He gave me my sister. He lost his wealth, his fight, and lay unconscious in a hospital bed. Because of me.

"Nora, I'm going to call Mom and Dad so you can spend some time with them, would you like that?"

"Yes, Brooke, I thought about what you said, and I *do* want to finish college."

Mel chimes in. "Oh, yay! Nora, college is the place for hot guys, girl! It's something you definitely *do not* want to miss," she adds in total excitement, still all sweaty and red-faced from our run.

Plopping down next to Nora, I tell her, "The thing is, I may not be around for a while. My new job will require I travel."

"New job?" Melanie perks up, then her tawny sleek eyebrows lower over her eyes. "Dish out, Brookey!" she says threateningly.

"Mel. I'm going to get the job I want with the man I need," I confess.

"You mean you're getting back the man you need with the job you want."

"Same difference!" I laugh, flinging the card at her. "I'm getting my job back."

"With Remington?" Nora asks.

"Nora, your sister is, despite her not being the type to fall so hard, head-over-heels, crazy in love with this guy. And he's been after her for months," Mel tells her, handing me back the card.

We both gauge her reaction, and her mouth parts in surprise as she points at herself. "Oh. You thought I . . . ? I wasn't talking about Remington wanting *me*. I said Remington is super hot, but I was talking about Pete."

"Pete!" I laugh in delight and relief and squish her between my arms again. "Oh, Pedro is such a great guy. If I go back to work, I have a feeling you'll be seeing him."

"Brooke, I realize I've always been a bit too . . . romantic, but what he did," she tells me, her eyes serious. "Remington, I mean . . . Brooke, I've never, ever, seen a man fight like that for anyone."

Closing my eyes, I nod and hold one arm around her shoulders until Melanie squeals, "Sandwich!" and comes to hug me from the other side until they're both almost killing me with love.

"You're going to fly me up often?" Mel murmurs in my ear when she moves back.

"Both of you," I promise.

❤ ❤ ❤

THIRTY-SIX HOURS LATER, I've settled Nora with Mom and Dad, who keep asking her about those crocodiles. Poor Nora is going to have to pay for all her lies now that she's being asked about the Indian culture and the Eiffel Tower and the works.

Melanie helped me pack and was a little tearful when she waved me off in the taxi, but I kept telling her, "It's not forever! It's seasonal, you little wimp. And I'll be flying you up like crazy."

My voice was confident, but honestly, I don't even know how my meeting or interview or whatever it's going to be called will go this evening. I just know that I'm heading for Remy, and my body already feels like a battlefield of desire, fear, longing, love, need, and regret.

I'm not sure which Remy I'm going to get tonight. All I know is that Remington Tate is not a man people plan long-term relationships with. He's a magnet to women and trouble, and he has a dark side that's not easily controlled.

He's my beast. My dark and my light. Mine.

There's just no other option for me except ending up with him.

"We're so damned glad to see you! I'd hug you if I wasn't afraid of losing my neck later in the day," Riley says when he opens the door to the hotel's presidential suite. He's grinning so hard, his sad surfer eyes seem to light up in real glee.

"Hey, I thought you guys were poor. Poor people don't rent such lavish suites," I say as I come in and drop my bags.

"Poor by Remy's former standards." Pete comes over and totes my bags into one of the rooms. "He spends several million a year, so naturally, he has to keep producing as much, but he sold the Austin house, and we're working on getting some new endorsements as we speak."

Nodding, I steal a longing glance down the hall at the bedrooms, wondering if he's here. When the guys usher me to the living room, I finally break down and say, "All right, so I need to know if Mr. Tate is still interested in my services? As a rehab specialist?"

"Of course," Pete assures, plopping down on a couch and playing with his tie like he always does. "He wants to focus on what's important. He wants *you*. He's been very specific about accepting no one else."

I laugh, then go sober when they both stare at me like I'm a falling star and they've just caught me. "Guys," I say, rolling my eyes. "Don't be obtuse. Is *he* here? Did he tell you to torture me endlessly?"

"Never!" They both laugh, and Pete recovers first, his expression sobering. "He's paced the length of the room a thousand times these past days. He just went out for a run." He holds my gaze in a haunted way, his voice dropping considerably as he sits up and leans on his knees. "Your letter, Brooke. He's read it about a thousand times; he's fixated."

The sound of a closing door reaches me, and when I leap to my feet and look toward the entryway, my breath goes.

Standing across the room, covered in sweat, is the reason I'm ready to go all out and gamble everything on love. My heart stays still for a moment, and then it jumps to full speed, because this man does that to me. I sprint for him even when I'm standing still.

His hair is perfectly messy, and he stands there, the sex god of my dreams, my blue-turned-black-eyed devil of my dreams. He looks at me, then at Pete, then at Riley, then he starts for me, his kick-ass running shoes muffled in the carpet. I can see the emotions evolve in his eyes, starting with surprise, with a hint of anger, and then morphing to pure red-hot need.

I don't know how long I stare at him, but it's a long time. Chemistry crackles in the air like something unreal and electric leaping between us. His chest rises and falls, and a wild, desperate need to close the emotional distance between us makes my chest ache.

"I'd like to talk to you, Remington, if you have a moment."

"Yes, Brooke, I want to talk to you as well."

His flat tone does nothing to help my rapidly fleeing confidence, but when he heads toward the master bedroom, I follow closely at his heels. The slight autumn smell mingled with a scent of ocean clinging to his skin gets me awfully hot, and I'm almost cross-eyed with desire.

He closes the door behind him and turns to me, and a bolt of heat shoots through me as he curls a hot, big hand around my neck and bends to scent me. Undone by the possessive gesture of him burying his nose in my hair, as he drags in a long, deep inhale, I grab his T-shirt in my fingers and hide my face in it, aching for him. "Don't let me go please," I beg. He wrenches free of my grip and releases me, almost as if he's annoyed to have grabbed me in the first place.

"If you want me so much, then why'd you leave?" He unnerves me as he watches me sit down on the bench at the foot of the bed and crosses his powerful arms, his eyebrows drawn together as he widens his stance almost threateningly. "Did I say anything when I was manic?"

With a sudden vivid recollection, I remember every amazing memory, and I seize on one. "You wanted to take me to Paris."

"That's a bad thing?"

"And make love to me in an elevator."

"Did I?"

"And to have me in my pink pants," I thickly admit, and an unexpected warmth climbs up my cheeks.

He keeps staring at me, his face taut in an unreadable mask.

His arms are crossed tight as if he's holding his raging emotions in. I'm shaking because I can't determine if the look in his eyes is love or hate. It is simply consuming. Consuming *me*.

"You forgot the part where we played each other a song," he tells me in a quiet murmur, and the realization that he probably remembers the tender way he made love to me after that causes a burning emotion in my chest to quickly spread up my throat.

I hold my breath in silent shock when he reaches for my hand and takes it in his dry, firm grasp, lifting my fingers to his lips.

My heart speeds up as I stay seated and watch in delicious agony as he turns my hand in his grip. He stares down at the center of my palm before he bends to flatten his tongue over my skin and gently lick me. Need explodes in my tummy.

"That picture made me very angry, Brooke," he rasps into my skin, as he drags his tongue wetly across the sensitive nerves at the center of my palm. "When you belong to someone . . . you don't kiss anyone else. You don't kiss his enemy. You don't lie to him. Betray him."

My systems roar back to life as his teeth graze the heel of my palm.

My voice shudders out of me. "I'm sorry. I wanted to protect you, like you protect me. I won't ever go behind your back again, Remy. I didn't leave because you were manic, I just didn't want you to get manic or low because of me."

He gives me a dark nod as he rakes a quick, thirsty look over me, and he lowers my hand back to my lap. "There's something I might have missed then. Because I still can't understand why the fuck you would leave me when I fucking *needed* you!"

The pain in his voice strikes a chord within me, and instantly my eyes sting.

"Remy, I'm sorry!" I cry wretchedly.

He groans, agitated, then he pulls out the letter I wrote from the pocket of the jeans draped haphazardly on a chair by the corner. The paper is crumpled and broken in the middle from so many reads. "Did you mean what you wrote to me?" Hearing his dense, distressed voice causes the little hairs on my body to jump.

"Which part?"

He grabs the paper, and yanks it open, ramming a thick finger to the words:

I love you, Remy.

Then he crumples it in his fist again, watching me in anger and despair. My heart constricts as I realize he can't even say the word out loud to me.

Who has ever told him that they love him?

I have.

In a letter.

In a thousand songs.

But not out loud.

Even his parents only wanted money. They never accepted him or gave him the love he deserved. And me? Oh, god, I left him. Just like everyone else.

Throat thick, I nod up and down really fast, and his jaw clamps as hard as rock, as if he's holding some wild feeling back.

"Say it," he coarsely whispers.

"Why?"

"I need to hear it."

"Why do you need to hear it?"

"Is that the reason you left after the fight?"

Burning tears fill my eyes.

There's desperation in his question, and I think he wants to know so badly because it might be the only reason he'll be able to get over my leaving.

Raw pain opens anew in my chest as I imagine him waking up in that hospital bed, after what he did for me, to realize that I left. When I'd said I'd never get enough of him . . .

"Is it, Brooke? Why you left? Or because you're ready to quit on me? I thought you had more mettle, little firecracker, I really did."

He's wildly searching my face, and I feel just as wild looking back at his breathtakingly handsome features, noting the slight scar remaining above his eyebrows.

I touch it on impulse, and the instant my finger connects with his healing skin, the words burst out of me.

"I love you. I *love* you." His breath seizes in his chest, and I continue in a rush. "More than I've ever thought it possible to love any other human being. I left because you broke my heart, again and again that night, with every one of your bones. I left because I couldn't take it anymore!"

He closes his eyes, and his torment reaches me so deep, my own confession opening me, making me vulnerable. I hear his ragged exhale of breath, and I'm hurting all over at the memory of what he did for me, to rescue Nora. I drop my hand, and my voice trembles fiercely. "I don't want you to ever let anyone hurt you deliberately again. Ever. Not even for me, Remy. Never. You are worth too much! Do you *hear* me?"

He lifts fiercely trembling hands and cups my face, drawing me up against him, and I shudder as I absorb the feeling of his arms again. My heart pounds because I know this is the first night of the rest of my life, and I want it to be.

"I'd do it a thousand times for you." He scents me. And I scent him. "A thousand. A million. I don't care if I'm humiliated. I don't care about anything. All I knew was you were willing to kiss that motherfucker's ink for your sister, and so I had to give her back to you."

"Oh, Remy, you didn't have to do anything."

"I did. And I will. And I'd do it all over again. I'm sorry only Pete could know. He stayed in a hotel room with her and one of Benny's thugs, transferring her when I delivered the championship. I just couldn't let you stop me, Brooke."

"But you wouldn't even look at me . . ." I say, squeezing my eyes shut. "That was as painful as the rest of what happened."

"If I'd looked at you, I wouldn't have been able to go through with it." His voice is rough with conviction, and I cover my face and try not to think of the way Scorpion delighted in humiliating my proud fighter. It makes me want to fight and cry at the same time, and I shake my head.

He's quiet.

Then he releases me with a pained noise coming from deep within him.

He stands and paces, pushing his fingers like angry claws through his hair. "I knew this would happen." Dark clouds darken his blue eyes from underneath drawn eyebrows. "That's why I didn't want to touch you. I knew I'd go crazy if I touched you, and now it tears me open to ask you to *be* with me when I know I'm just going to do something to fucking hurt you again!"

"Yes! Yes you probably are, you idiot! And it's going to be a damned skydive for me, and I'm going to hang on tight and just jump with you because that's what you do to me. I'm crazy about you. My life now *sucks* without you. I'm not here for the job, although I love it. But it's *you* I want. It's you I came for that first night. It's always been about you. I want to be with you, but I won't do it only on my side. I want you to love me back, Remy. You've never told me how you feel about me!"

His eyes are brilliant blue, and they ignite with a fire that heats my entire being.

"Brooke, you honestly don't know?"

I stare, and he kneels on the bed and holds my face.

"Jesus, when I saw you that first night in Seattle, I felt like I'd just gotten plugged into a socket. I got high just with the way you smiled at me, Brooke. The way you looked at me with an expression of pain and awe drove me crazy. You turned away to leave, and you wore these really nice pants. Your butt was just up there as you walked away, all perky and round. And I just wanted to finish the damn fight so I could go after you. I swear I fought the previous fight just so you would watch me. So you'd see me. See that I'm strong and could fight for you, *protect you.* I day-dreamed of kissing you, of making love to you. I was planning it in my head even when I jumped out of that ring to go after you. When your friend gave me your number, I got to the hotel to find a roomful of girls, the kind Pete always has for me, and I couldn't look at any of them. I wanted to look into your eyes and make you smile at me.

"I Googled you, saved your number in my phone, and spent all night wondering about all the ways I would fuck you when I finally had my hands on you. I sent you those tickets, knowing for sure I'd have you that night. But then I saw a video of you when I Googled you again. It was your first Olympic trials, and you were hopping away with your torn ACL and crying so damned hard, and I just wanted . . . you. I wanted to burn the keyboards of the idiots commenting about your life being over, about the depression that hit you. You were *me,* Brooke. Me. And I wanted you to go out there and show them they were idiots, and at the same time, *I* wanted to fucking go out there and carry you across that damned finish line. We were leaving town soon, and I just knew I had to see you more. So I hired you."

When he confirms seeing my video, I almost break, a weakness seizing me in the knees. Instantly, I remember our first flight and how Remy was engrossed by inspecting my knee. He'd touched it almost lovingly, stroking the scar with his thumb. And how can I forget it when he toweled me off and was extra diligent with my knee, the day his fans threw eggs at me?

"I tried taking it easy with you. I wanted to know you, and for you to know me, and every day I wanted you more, Brooke. So much. I couldn't touch you and risk messing it up until you knew about me. I wanted you to care for me. I wanted to see if you could understand me. . . . I tortured myself every night, thinking of you in your room, while I was in mine.

"The night we went to the club, and you danced with me, I just couldn't stop myself. I'd been so wound up. And when you knocked down two guys for me, I went crazy protective. I wanted to tuck you into bed and go back and do some serious damage to all four of them. But you stayed with me, and I forgot about fighting, and all I wanted was to have my mouth all over you. I tried to control myself, but on the plane, you killed me with those songs about making love to me. I just had to have you. The thought of having you had me so damned high, I was already drugged with it, and by the end of that flight, I was manic and high on you before I could even get you into my bed.

"And then you woke up with me, and I saw that you'd cuddled with me, Brooke. Soft and sweet. The next time I was lying alone in bed, I wanted to cut open my fucking veins wanting you next to me, so I went back for you. That was all that got me through the day, those days. Thinking of getting you in my bed and kissing you breathless. I kept looking through my tunes just trying to find one that could tell you how you made me feel. Inside. I'm not good at saying this, but I wanted you to know you were special to me—you're unlike any other woman in my life.

"You wanted me to make love to you and you don't know

how many times I almost broke down. When I showered with you, I swear to god, I was breaking inside. But I couldn't do it, not without telling you there's something deeply wrong with me, and I'm such a coward, Brooke. I couldn't even find the courage to say the word 'bipolar' to you. So I prolonged my time with you. Because I'm selfish, and I wanted you to care before you knew. Thinking it would make a difference and you'd stay. Not even my own folks could do me long-term. But something about you made me think you'd *know* me, *understand me* on a level no one else does."

"Remy," I breathe out.

"I was right, Brooke," he adds in a deep, raspy whisper, holding me entranced with his words, his liquid gaze. "When I told you about me, you still wanted me. And I've been in love with you for I don't know how long. Ever since you tried to knock me down in the ring, and I ended up putting your little feet against my stomach to warm them. Jesus, when I saw that photograph of you and Scorpion I wanted to *kill him*. I wanted to give you whatever it was that had made you go to that fucking asshole and kiss his fucking face! I wanted to give that to you, so you would kiss mine instead.

"I went to him, and he was waiting. Of course he was. He knew I'd come. He saw me at the club. I've never been protective of a woman before. He saw me get out of the ring for you and get disqualified. He knows you're my weak spot. We had a go at it, and he was crying like a goddamned weenie. He wanted me to stop. I wasn't planning to until I'd knocked out his fucking teeth. But he offered me your sister if I gave away the championship. He was done with her. She was restless since she'd seen you, and he wanted no trouble. She was watching us fight, crying. I asked her if she was your Nora, and she said yes. So I said yes. I called Pete over, and he'd stand by while I delivered the championship and they released her to us." He drags in a breath, then scrapes a hand down his face as he sighs. "It's the first time I did something right when I was . . . not at optimal."

Leaning to me, he drags his nose along my temple, and a tremor of heat slips down my spine as he whispers close to my ear.

"I'm sorry I couldn't tell you, but it had to happen like this. When I told you I wouldn't let you leave me the night I made love to you, I meant it. I want you, Brooke, for me. I can hurt you, I can do stupid shit, but I . . ." His stare galvanizes me. "I'm so fucking in love with you I don't even know what to do with myself anymore."

The knot is at massive proportions in my throat, and I'm nodding as I wipe my tears, unable to tell him how much and how crazily I have fallen in love with him.

He makes me feel so good. He puts on my music. Runs with me. Kisses and touches me. Licks me deliciously. Gets all sexy jealous over me. He's grumpy one day and cocky the next, and I love all sides of him. He looks at me with his blue eyes or black eyes, and every time he does, I just know I'm right where I want to be.

"You're going to want to leave me again," he whispers, tenderly, as he cups my jaw. "You can't, Brooke, you can't leave. You're mine."

He strokes his other hand down my hair and I turn into his hand like a kitten again, seeking more of his petting.

"You've claimed me, little firecracker. You kicked a pair of two-hundred-pound men's asses. I will never get over that. You kicked my whores out, Pete told me. You staked your claim on me, even before you realized I'd staked mine already." He fists my hair and pulls me close to his lips. "I'm yours now, and you can't ditch me like you just did. Even if I screw this up, I'll still be *your* screwup."

I need him close, so I press my body to his as I drape my arms around his neck, his sweat slicking deliciously into me. "Not my screwup. My real."

He groans a male sound as he turns his head and licks my cheek. The heart-melting realization that my lion is back unravels me, and I feel myself sinking into his arms as he drags his lips down lower. He slowly, wetly, licks my jaw. My chin. And then . . . my lips. I think he feels me shudder against him, for he slips his hands around my lower back and draws me protectively against his frame. He licks his way into my warm mouth, with soft, probing strokes until I'm open and gasping, letting him have his delicious way with me.

"Don't fucking leave me ever again," he murmurs, his tongue retreating to trace my top lip, my bottom, then pushing deeply inside me as he spreads his hands along my ass and squeezes me possessively.

I'm drunk. The sensations his kiss and licks bring me are deep, and they tremble in my core like consecutive earthquakes, each one bigger than the last.

I rub my nipples against his massive chest, and my sex throbs to feel him inside me. He looks so delicious in his exercise clothes, drives me so wild with the way he smells when he works out, I want to strip him. Take him.

"I've got about a thousand songs in a new playlist that says 'Brooke,' all about me missing you, loving you, hating, and adoring you," he rasps as I feel him reach under my dress for my panties.

This is exactly why I wore a dress. In record time, I've pulled it off as Remy pulls my panties off both legs.

"I've got some too, I want to spend all day playing them to you," I whisper and remove my bra.

He hauls me back, naked on his lap, taking my mouth again.

He has me so wound up with his kisses, I'm afraid I'm going to climax the instant he thrusts inside me.

Oh, god, I need it so bad, I don't even realize I'm curling my legs to straddle him, rubbing myself over his hard-on. I want it. Inside me. I want him so fiercely I can't stop trembling. "I love you," I breathe.

It's incredible. I lived my entire life without him, but we made this crazy connection, and I just feel empty without him.

He drugs me with another kiss as I undulate my body against his, teasing me with his hardness, his hot mouth, his groans. He's making me want him in the wildest, most intense ways. He pulls free, reaching into his running shorts.

"I want to play you Avril Lavigne's 'I Love You' again," I say as he tries pushing them off without sacrificing my spot on his lap.

"I'll get my headphones when we finish," he murmurs, successfully shoving them off one leg, his arms bulging as he works to get them off the other.

I moan in gratitude at the thought of being able to hear music again with joy, especially when all I had been able to think of was listening to "Iris" and fearing how deeply it would cut me. Every single song, without Remy to play it to, cut me open.

I'm inundated with emotion as I nuzzle his hair, sliding my fingers in it. "And also 'That's When I Knew' by Alicia Keys." I start to sing this heartbreakingly romantic song in his ear and he makes an odd sound between a chuckle and a groan.

"You don't sing for shit, baby," he murmurs.

We stop laughing when he enters me. I gasp. He groans.

His mouth crushes mine, and our thirst is unquenchable. He rocks his hips powerfully, his muscles clenching, his thighs underneath me, his abs against mine, his biceps around me. I love feeling his strength when he makes love to me, in his rocking motions, in his arms, in his powerful erection. I love . . .

Here I go again.

I love everything about him.

"Brooke Dumas," he murmurs, licking into my ear, his eyes sparkling. "I'm Remington."

I laugh, then moan and dissolve into him.

Seriously, he's so fucking sexy I can't stand it.

FOURTEEN

EPILOGUE

Remington

I still sometimes can't believe Brooke loves me.

I get crazy when she talks to Pete and Riley, and sometimes I can't sleep for fear of waking up and finding she's not next to me. I start getting jealous and fear I'm going to lose my shit, but when she touches me, I find anchor.

I fight for her tonight, and I want her eyes only on me. I want her hands on me later. And the way she tells me she loves me. She shows it too, but I have never in my life heard it before. She puts love songs to me, and I cling to the lyrics like she wrote them for me. Sometimes I have trouble putting to words how I feel. Sometimes I feel a thousand things at once and can't find a single word to tell her what I want to say. That's why I look for songs, and as soon as it hits a chord in me, I can't wait to play it to her. I played "Iris" for her because I wanted her to know that I'd do all kinds of crazy shit just to be with her, and more than that, I wanted her to know me.

She does.

She may know parts of me even I don't.

Every time I wake up, I check her out. "Did I hurt you?" I ask.

Sometimes I remember when I'm black, but other times I don't. All my life falls apart when I'm black.

I'm afraid to hurt her.

I'm afraid she's gonna go again.

But then she tells me she promises to let me know the shit I did or said, and that appeases me. Honestly, I don't think I have it in me to hurt her. It's grounded in me to protect her, even from myself. I think even black Remington would kill himself before he hurts her.

But I still dream I wake up and hear that I did something stupid and she's gone.

She tells me every night I'm her real.

She's my real. She's my only.

But I want it on paper.

I want to win this year, and when I do, I'm going to ask her for it.

Because she's mine.

Tonight, I hear the crowd as I come up to the ring, and I suck their energy into me, let it feed me, but I'm already turning to stop at the point where she's sitting. Every detail of what she is wearing tonight is in my head. I see a face that has eyes so gold and I feel richer than a country. Her cheeks rosy. Her smile wide.

And the sight of her hits me like adrenaline.

A rise in dopamine.

Testosterone.

Endorphins.

I'm jacked with it. She jacks me with it, and I smile and point at her, as I plan to do from now on so she knows, "This one's for you."

It's all.

For you.

Brooke Dumas.

She blows me a kiss and I catch it in my palm.

Crowd loves it like I love her.

And then I put it in my mouth, and they roar.

And I point at her, laughing, seeing the lights in her eyes, and I can't wait to be inside her, hear her sigh for me, come for me.

I'm high already. The surge of adrenaline pumps through me. I'm going to beat anything they put in my way just to show this female that I—me, Remington Fucking Tate—am the male she wants.

"The one and only, Remington RIIIIIIIIPTIDE Tate!"

I hear my name once more, and I'm high with the crowd, high with her smile.

High on her.

DEAR READERS

If you're like me and love Remington and Brooke with a passion, then please be sure to keep an eye out for the sequels, Mine *and* Remy—*both stories in the Real series that are coming in 2013!*

I can't wait to share more of Brooke and Remington with you!

Xoxo,
Katy

ACKNOWLEDGMENTS

I am so excited to be releasing *Real* and the wonderful Real series through Gallery Books!

I am eternally grateful to my wonderful agent, Amy Tannenbaum, for her support and encouragement, to my amazing new editor, Adam Wilson, who is the best I could have ever hoped for, and to the talented people at Gallery Books who are making it all happen and bringing more of Remington, Brooke, and the cast to you. Thank you all for believing in this series like I do!

And, of course . . .

Thank you to my beautiful husband, my beautiful children, and my beautiful parents; you are the light of my life!

To the loveliest daughter in the world, for reading before everyone else did and giving it a thousand thumbs-up.

To Stacey Suarez, the best fitness expert and dearest friend I could have ever hoped for, who was with me every step of Brooke and Remington's wonderful journey.

To Monica Murphy, for the beta read, the hours e-mailing, the laughs, and the friendship.

To Alicia G., Paula G., Gaby G., Paula W., and Marcela B.; for being amazing friends and supporters.

To Erinn and Georgia for helping me prep this baby and "beautify"—you ladies are amazing! I admit, any lingering grammar mistakes are fully mine. ☺

To Julia from JT Formatting and Georgia Woods for the great formatting, and to Sarah Hansen for the amazing cover art.

To Anita S. for the excellent proofread and extra-gentle touch with my manuscript. I love the raw realness of the narrative in *Real*, and she helped me "keep" it while trying to make it readable for you all.

To bloggers extraordinaires Jenny and Gitte from *Totally Booked*, Momo from *Books over Boys*, Aseel Naji from *My Crazy Book Obsession*, Anna from *Anna's Romantic Reads*, Michelle from *The Blushing Reader*, Malory from *Loverly's Book Blog*, Julienne from *Bookaholix Club*, Hillz from *Love N Books*, Triin, Trini Contreras, and Becky N from *Reality Bites*, Autumn from *Martini Times*, Ellen from *The Book Bellas*, Miss Ava, the passionate and amazing Dana, Erin, and Kelly, and all of you advance readers for your fabulous taste in books and becoming instant Remington Tate fans. Thank you so much for the support, I have you each on a *pedestal*!

To the Universe, for giving me the health and joy of sitting down and sharing this story, and to the Angels out there who let it happen (you know who you are)!

And to all you amazing, beautiful, supportive readers, who have opened your hearts to *Real* like I did, thank you for soaking up my words and loving these amazing characters like I do!

XOXO!

ABOUT

Hey! I'm Katy Evans and I love family, books, life, and love. I'm married with two children and three dogs and spend my time baking, walking, writing, reading, and taking care of my family. Thank you for spending your time with me and picking up my story. I hope you had an amazing time with it, like I did. If you'd like to know more about my books in progress, look me up on the Internet —I'd love to hear from you!

X0, Katy

Website: www.katyevans.net

Facebook: www.facebook.com/pages/Katy-Evans

Twitter: twitter.com/authorkatyevans

E-mail: authorkatyevans@gmail.com